CONNIE MONK

Fortune's Daughter

This edition published 1995 for
Parrallel Books
Units 13–17 Avonbridge Industrial Estate
Atlantic Road
Avonmouth, Bristol BS11 9QD
by Diamond Books
77–85 Fulham Palace Road
Hammersmith, London W6 8JB

Published by Diamond Books 1994
Published by Fontana 1988
First published in Great Britain by
Piatkus Books 1985

ISBN 0 261 66695 9

Set in Garamond
Printed in Great Britain

FORTUNE'S DAUGHTER

Connie Monk is the author of several novels published in Fontana, this being her first. Her third novel, *Jessica*, was runner-up in the Romantic Novel of the Year Award.

She comes from a family of generations of musicians, is married and lives in Devon.

CHAPTER ONE

'I'd like it well enough, Bethie, you know that, but 'tisn't for me to tell you you can live here, not without a word with the Master. And what do they say at home?' Syd was concerned for his young sister; the thought of her having to go with the rest of the family to make a new life up in Oldbury worried him; he couldn't picture her in some smokey town.

'Whatever they may say I'm not going.' Young Beth raised her chin defiantly. 'Alice and Cecily seem to be looking forward to it, actually wanting to go and take work in that smelly factory. I won't! If you won't have me here I'll find somewhere else, but I'll not go to some beastly factory.'

''Tis you I al'ays thought would be the adventurer – not that I don't want you here along with me but I never thought the countryside round these parts would hold you. Is it Bill Baines? I know he's been sweet on you for – '

'Ach! Bill Baines indeed!' Apparently she had little regard for the young wheelwright who worked with his father in their comfortably successful business in Tilmarsh. 'I've never given him any reason to think I'd have him, honestly I haven't Syd.'

No wonder Bill had cast longing looks her way, her brother thought. She wasn't a bit like the rest of them and, twelve years her senior, Syd had always fallen under her spell, ever since she'd first learnt to trot round after him.

'Look, Bethie, I'll see the Master, and tell him you earn your keep stitching for Mrs Dickson; would only be a bed in the coach-house wi' me; you'd see to your own food.'

'Tomorrow, Syd – promise you'll ask him tomorrow.'

5

'Well – if I see him. Don't al'ays though. More times than most 'tis Mr James comes for the trap.'

'You go to the house for prayers. Tell him you need to talk to him.'

Syd frowned. It wasn't that he didn't want to do what he could for her but she had no idea what she was asking. There, in the hall at the big house, the Master reading from the good book in the voice of authority. It wasn't that Henry Copeland intimidated his staff, at least not intentionally, but Syd couldn't imagine any of them stopping him in his tracks as he turned away from their prayers. His tone never varied; come what may, nothing altered the pattern of that seven o'clock gathering in the hall. Even the morning after Mrs Copeland had died he'd read from the book just the same, led their prayers and dismissed them with: 'God be with you', just as he did every morning. And Beth thought one could step out in front of him and ask him to listen!

They were interrupted by the sound of wheels in the stable yard.

'Hark!' Syd rested a hand on her shoulder. 'That'll be Mr Harknell's party arrived. Now don't you fret, Bethie, we'll get something sorted out. Tell the truth I can't see you in the factory. Pity Mrs Dickson hadn't room for you.'

'Poppycock! You think I want to be a seamstress for twenty-four hours of every day? We'll make a cosy home for ourselves Syd . . .' She turned to him, her lovely green eyes enough to melt the hardest of hearts, and his was never that.

The guests had been taken to the front door and now the arrival of their coachman put an end to the conversation, so Beth had to be content. As Syd went down the wooden stairs she turned to watch out of the window. She couldn't see beyond the corner of the house but it was easy to imagine – lights blazing from all the windows, the bustle and excitement.

'Evening Syd. A fair night for their party. Mrs Murphy'll be expecting us over at the house I don't doubt?'

'Ah, you'll take your supper along with us, you're expected.'

It wasn't the first time he'd been entertained in the servants' hall at Merton Court; the two families visited each other often enough. Tonight marked a special occasion though, for they all knew the cause of the air of festivity that had hung over both their houses; the betrothal of Hal Copeland and Edith Harknell was on the tip of all their tongues. Even in the kitchen supper tonight would be something above the ordinary.

Beth moved away from the window. By now they'd all be gathered in the big drawing-room she'd never seen but in her mind she could picture it all; the bright glow of the gaslight, the fire piled high blazing up the chimney and shining on the polished furniture, the richly coloured walls and carpets. There was no self-pity in her; her own surroundings might be a far cry from all that – bare wooden floorboards, a wooden table holding the single oil lamp, rush-seated chairs – none of it had any power to depress her. She never doubted that life with a capital 'L' waited just around the corner; where and how was still to be discovered. So with no resentment she let herself imagine the scene in the big house, some of it of her own creation. Sitting in Mrs Dickson's cottage, hadn't she stitched the trimmings on the dresses made for this special evening, tacked the long seams of Amelia's wide layered skirt, set the sleeves of pale lilac silk in Naomi's first grown-up supper gown? Her clear green eyes might look on the sparse furnishings of her brother's room but her vision was in another world. How handsome James must be; his dark hair and sideburns, his brown eyes, his slim hands well shaped and, as she'd heard people say, able to make beautiful music on the piano that stood in the drawing-room where they must all be gathered.

She'd listened to odd snippets of conversation at home

7

where life in the Court was always of interest, but she asked no questions and gave no hint that she cared. Oh no, not she. She'd not gossip with the servants nor even with her family; in truth she shared her thoughts with no one.

'Beth, me and Arthur'll be to house to get our supper. You staying up there, or are you off home?'

'I'll go home soon.' Soon, but not yet. She'd rather turn up the lamp and read her book. The upheaval of packing up left nowhere untouched at the cottage. Her parents and Alice and Cecily, her two older sisters, seemed caught up in it, yet surely they couldn't want to go? The previous year had seen plenty of folk having to tear up their roots and start afresh and 1861 was no better. Not just here but all over the country it had been happening, for now that it was cheaper to bring the corn from across the sea what chance had the farmers at home? They had to cut their losses, their labourers had to go and, like so many more, George and Jane Machin had no choice. Beth wasn't going to spend the evening arguing; there was nothing they could say that would make her go with them. Not that she clung to the life she knew, far from it; she longed for adventure and change, but what adventure was there in moving in with relatives, finding work in one of the factories? Let them go their own way. She was sure Syd would have her here – at any rate until she could think of something different. 'It's funny not knowing – something's going to happen, I can feel it is, something good . . .' All her life the real pattern had been unchanged; only in her mind had thrilling things beckoned to her. Her mother, a hard-working woman, had never understood her and as for her father – well, many a whisper had been passed from lip to lip, for it was strange that this one child should be so different from the others, her hair vivid copper, her eyes clear and green. No wonder the less kindly disposed nudged each other knowingly; not often did one see such colouring. It's unlikely that anyone (except her father, that

8

is) gave a thought to Albert Hargreaves, why should they? He'd been in Wilhampton for but a few weeks, weeks of mid-summer when some strange madness had taken hold of Jane Machin, already married for fourteen years to her plodding George. Sanity had returned; Albert moved away, his wild oats sown, not knowing of the bright spirit he'd left behind in this backwater. If George saw more than most he chose not to acknowledge it and Beth had been brought up as if she were no different from the others, and who was to know for sure that she was? But in her own mind she knew herself to be apart from them. It was just a question of time. So far she had waited in the wings of life.

This evening a book couldn't hold her. Alone in the coach-house, she lifted her skirt, then, toes pointed, humming her accompaniment in a clear musical voice, she stepped and pivoted and twirled. The splendour at the big house was nothing in comparison with the grand ball she dreamt herself into, the fiddlers, the jewellery, the huge skirts, the gentlemen in their tail coats, the white gloves. She fluttered an imaginary fan as she curtsied to her partner's bow.

Standing alone in his room Henry Copeland took the pair of silver-backed brushes, one in each hand, and drew them over his hair. The occasion of this evening's supper party would see a change in his own life as well as in Hal's. He fitted the brushes together and put them back on the dressing-table neatly in their appointed place, then turned to the bed where he'd laid his tailed evening jacket. As he reached for it his glance fell on the miniature of Isabella, that little oval picture which had stood for so long in its silver frame on his tallboy. Instinctively he picked it up, but the sweet face of the nineteen-year-old bride she'd been seemed like a ghost from a life long gone. It had been painted nearly thirty years ago, thirty years that had seen such changes. What a slow, gracious world they'd known

9

then; to remember the atmosphere of the early thirties was to look back to a different life. How the pace had quickened! If they could have had a glimpse of today they wouldn't have recognized the modern world their family took for granted. Progress! And so it was, no one could dispute that. They all lived more comfortably, their houses well lit, a postal service that led the world, railways making it possible to travel with speed and comfort (even here, now that the line had been brought to Wilhampton), his own firm turning out machinery not contemplated thirty years ago – always improving, always striving for something more. They were all caught up in speed and change, growth and development, he as much as any.

He slumped on the edge of the bed only half aware of the turn of his thoughts, an unanswered cry in his heart as that child-like face looked back at him. For the twenty-two years they'd been together had taken away her girlish loveliness, her confidence in life's kindness – and so much of it must have been his fault.

At fifty, how many years had he still ahead of him? Empty years, the children gradually going their own ways. Little Phoebe, he'd have her with him for a long time yet; but, dear though she was, how could she ever share his thoughts, his interests, his memories?

'Oh, Bella,' he mouthed the words silently, 'Bella.' He found no answering spirit. Now it was Hal's turn. Soon they'd all be gone. When she'd been taken from him young Hal had been hardly out of school. How could she know the closeness of the bond that had grown between father and son with Hal's manhood?

His lonely reverie was broken by the sound of the girls, Naomi and Esme, in their room. A door was slammed, feet running along the landing, high-pitched giggles. They were excited at the prospect of joining the grown-ups for the supper party.

Amelia must have heard the skirmish, for her 'Hush! Remember Phoebe' brought a smile to her father's face. If anything woke Phoebe it would more likely be her calling up the stairs to her young sisters.

'Ah, well . . .' He put the miniature back in its place, stood up and took his tail coat from the bed. Of course he was happy for Hal in his coming marriage, of course he was thankful too that the union would cement his future in the business, and yet he viewed the years ahead with foreboding. The evenings so often spent in the boy's company, their shared interest in the foundry spilling into their home life, all this must soon be gone. In its place – what? He knew the family would welcome him to share their pleasures in the drawing-room, take part in their readings, listen while James played the piano, which seemed to fill his thoughts. No companionship there, not with James. 'Mooney, that's his trouble.'

He threaded the chain of his gold watch through his buttonhole, opened the case to check the time was correct, wound it and slipped it into his waistcoat pocket, then turned for a last inspection in the pierglass. The reflection showed a good-looking man, at fifty his hair as thick and the same brown as it always had been, his slim build no different from the husband Isabella had known. His appearance was important to him for he hated any form of sloppiness. He was satisfied. Adjusting the chain on the gas bracket to lower the light he left the room and went down to join the family.

The large marble-floored hall was brightly lit and the drawing-room radiated warmth and cheer. From the volume of voices it seemed he was the last to assemble, all determined the evening would be a good one.

'Aren't we all beautiful?' fourteen-year-old Esme was quite unable to contain herself, for this was the first time she'd taken her place at such a grown-up gathering, and here she was wearing an elegant pale pink dress with trimmings of ivory lace and ivory slippers, such as she'd never possessed, with their pearl studded buckles.

'Esme, you disgrace me! Have I taught you no better

11

social graces than that?' Margaret, the eldest, tall and austere, looked at her young sister in genuine amazement. The child was over-excited, it had been a mistake to allow her to stay up. Beautiful indeed! As if by any standards Esme could ever hope to be that – and to say so herself too! Margaret was ashamed for her.

'Nonsense,' James laughed. 'She could disgrace no one. And she's right, you all look charming. You agree, sir?'

'Indeed, our ladies do us great credit.' Henry had every right to be proud. A fine set of children, two sons and six daughters (for this evening he wouldn't let himself think of those other three who shared a grave with their mother who'd died giving birth to little Phoebe, asleep upstairs). The future was secure. There was no doubt that one day the business would be safe in the hands of young Hal, and now that he was to wed Edith, it must surely put the seal of success on generations to come, for Percy Harknell's engineering works had long been one of the foundry's most important clients. Hal's glance met his, only momentarily, but enough for him to be aware of the empathy always between them.

The guests arrived and, supper served, Amelia took Mr Harknell's arm and led the way to the panelled dining-room. In pairs they followed, Henry with Elizabeth Harknell, Hal with Edith, Margaret with William, Lucy with Edward, the two girls Naomi and Esme together, then finally James.

It was a splendid meal, formal in the toasts to the health of the young couple, the speeches of good wishes and, on Hal's part, in his assurance of the pride he had in gaining Edith's hand; informal in the undercurrent of friendship between the two families, the common interests.

'Perhaps we should leave the gentlemen. Are you ready to move to the drawing-room, Mrs Harknell?' This was the first important function at which Amelia had had to play hostess, for until Lucy had married she'd been of no special importance, no more than the third daughter and fifth child, a nothing in the social scale. Now that Lucy, like Margaret, had an establishment of her own it fell to Amelia to assume a dignity that had never been part of her nature. A nod from her father reassured her, she was doing well. A little too eagerly she pushed back her chair and jumped up, then as if forcibly to put a brake on her movements, she gripped the back of it waiting for her guests to follow.

A smile tugged at James's mouth. Only eleven months her senior, this was the one who understood her best. The party tonight was for Hal but it was to James she looked. Had she acted well, talked enough without showing how nervous she'd been? His right eye half closed; yes, came his silent answer. He rose to his feet to pull Mrs Harknell's chair back for her, his manners were always natural and charming. Henry looked on them all benignly, not one of them failed him, or so he thought at that moment. By tomorrow things might look different; James might show his usual lack of interest in what his father considered the realities of life, Amelia might shirk her duties and seem even more of a child that little Phoebe upstairs in her bed hours ago – but that was tomorrow. The men moved nearer to him, filling the seats vacated by their ladies, the glasses were filled, the cigars lit.

There was Margaret's husband, William, kindly but ineffectual, or so his father-in-law considered. Certainly his appearance did little for him; tall with a stoop, thin and pale, his long nose giving the only rosy hue to his countenance, his left eye with a tendency to wander outwards, and his sandy hair receding; yet there was a gentleness in his manner which made the family secretly pity him living with the domineering Margaret. He moved to the seat next to Edward, Lucy's husband, vicar of St Agnes in Wilhampton, their nearest town. By contrast, he resembled a rosy-faced cherub, making it hard to realize he was approaching thirty and three years William's senior. With his fair, curly hair and fluffy sideboards, his

13

unlined brow gave him the look of a child in fancy dress. But then life with Lucy must be a pleasant affair.

'You've seen our new hopper of course, Percy. Are you ordering?'

'I'm sending for two. Clever idea and simple too.'

'It'll sell.'

Percy took a sip of his port. 'Ah, no doubt it'll sell. Cut the labour, that's where it'll come in.'

They'd known each other for years, Copeland & Sons producing so much of the machinery supplied and kept in repair by Harknell & Company, farm machinery, now when work on the land was fast being mechanized. The day of the small tenant-farmer and his wife ekeing a living from his plot by the graft of their own hands was passing. Farms were bigger, more and more of those who had worked on them had left the country to try their fortunes in the factories. Many who'd gone to the towns had regretted it; they worked hours just as long in conditions often worse, but if at the end of a week they could bring home a sovereign that was more than could be said for 'the old days', as they nostalgically thought of them. As the farms became larger, the foundries and workshops turned out more machinery, the suppliers profited – and the numbers needed to till the soil grew less.

The air was heavy with cigar smoke. James alone wasn't adding to the haze, but then James wasn't adding to the conversation either. Hal, on the other hand, had pushed his glass to one side and on the back of a concert programme he found in his pocket he was drawing a sketch, while his future father-in-law lent across the table to watch.

'Surely, sir, if we can drive a pulley to turn the drum, the design could be relatively unchanged, simply quicker, more efficient, and a big saving on time and labour. The same engine, if we devise a pulley attachment . . .'

'And you, young sir, have you no suggestions?' Henry turned to James.

14

'I'm sorry Papa. I was thinking of something else. Saving labour, Hal says. Did you hear that Syd Machin's father has lost his job on Mr Ghrimes's farm?'

'Don't know the man,' Henry frowned. Typical of James; never could show any interest in the business, always thinking of something else.

'Syd looks after our horses, but I wouldn't know his family.' He spoke to Percy, dismissing James from the conversation. 'I've a lot of thoughts on the dairy. Now you know the churn we make, good enough as far as it goes, but time-consuming.'

'Woman's job to make the butter though Henry. Not the cost there; time's not so important. A fine port this, my friend.'

'Fill up. James, the port for Mr Harknell.'

They'd happily stay with their decanter for the rest of the evening but Hal was getting restless to join Edith and, as for James, to be honest he found the whole party irksome. Had it not been for Amelia's need of his support he wouldn't have made the effort he had.

Now it was he, with an intuition that could make one forget his failings, who said: 'Papa, Edith will believe Hal has forsaken her. I suggest we others join the ladies and leave you and Mr Harknell to follow when you're ready. Perhaps they'd like some music — not to your taste, I think?'

'Splendid idea. No, I can well do without the music. I notice, William, that you brought your songs with you, that's good, that's good. We'll stay here for a while, eh Percy, business before pleasure for us, eh? You young people go off and enjoy yourselves. We'll listen from in here.' Well, young James had used his wits then, his father had to grant that. An evening of singing around the piano or, even worse, listening as William sang in his weak tenor voice, was the last thing he wanted. Purposely he bracketed them all together with their amateur efforts, for that James's ability was in another category he wouldn't admit.

15

The boy's future must be in the business, just as surely as was Hal's. If he wanted to play the piano in the evenings it was a harmless accomplishment – but not a man's way of earning his bread.

Within minutes, from the drawing-room came the sound of the piano. Certainly not James. With raised brows Henry turned a silent enquiry to his friend.

'That'll be Edith; that's the piece she always plays.'

Her repertoire must be small and, listening, Henry privately decided it should be restricted further. He wouldn't offend her father though so simply nodded and murmured: 'Charming'.

Next came William accompanied by James:

> 'O Mistress mine
> Where art thou roaming?
> O Stay and hear
> You true love's coming.'

The older men said nothing but their glances met; four eyes twinkled, two glasses were re-filled. They were well out of it.

James played his brother-in-law's accompaniment with his mind elsewhere. Syd Machin had told him the news only that tea-time when he'd returned the trap to the stable. They were country people, they always had been. How could they hope to fare in town? Yet that was what was to happen to them; they were going to relatives in Oldbury where at least they'd have a roof over their heads and, according to Syd, his mother and grown-up sisters would be sure of work.

'Like as not he'll be taken too, but it's women's wanted, so they say. My cousin Prudence, she works at this sauce-making factory, Mis'er James, nine-and-tenpence she's paid each week, her being a woman, see. Now if it were a man, t'would be more, much more, more'n twice the sum. Likely they won't want m'father.'

'It's all wrong, Syd. They've never been town folk – and your sister Beth (isn't that what you call her?) will she go with them?' Surely that lovely girl couldn't be imprisoned in a factory. Nine-and-tenpence – good money they said! And what of all those hours shut away from the sunshine, what of the smells, the grease, the hopelessness? With the memory of his conversation came the same feeling of sick shame he'd felt listening to Syd.

'It's the living place y'see, Mis'er James. She's good with the needle, could go on with her sewing but she needs a roof. Doubt Mrs Dickson would have her live in.'

James hardly knew Beth except by sight, had only spoken to her a couple of times but there was something about her he couldn't bear to think of being shut in some grim factory. In her eyes he'd seen hope, sure anticipation of what life would bring her. He remembered one particular day about five years ago when the ground had been covered with snow. He'd been to the river, taken food to the swans who were walking and half slipping across the icy surface, when, instead of coming straight home, he'd decided to climb Chazey Hill the better to survey the wintry scene. Almost to the top, his footsteps silenced by the snow, he'd realized that someone was at the summit ahead of him. She'd thought herself alone so he'd hung back in the shelter of the trees, fascinated as he'd watched her, letting his own mind marvel, as hers must, at the beauty all around. Slowly she turned full circle feasting her eyes, then her arms flung wide she'd raised her head to the winter sun. Like some pagan goddess, how beautiful she'd been! To him she hadn't looked a child but a woman already, almost as old as he was himself. Suddenly she'd sunk to her knees, seemingly oblivious of the icy carpet, taking the snow in her hands and rubbing it into her face. Then laughing from sheer delight she'd jumped to her feet and picking up her skirts twirled round and round until she'd fallen still laughing to the ground.

The memory of that bright morning came back to him tonight, the urge he'd felt to join her, to warm himself in

17

the joy she'd radiated. Seeing her alone and yet complete in what the world around gave had only added to his own desolate misery, for his mother's death so recently had left him numb. There had been an empathy between him and his mother. With her going he was left with an emptiness and need for something that he hardly understood.

Henry and Percy joined the party, the music stopped and vaguely James was aware of the talk of the forthcoming wedding, of the choice of a house for Hal and Edith, the eagerness of both fathers to help their young; for surely in the fruit of this alliance was the future of all they'd strived for.

A factory . . . shut in for twelve hours a day, twelve hours or even longer . . . nine-and-tenpence.

The party was coming to an end. He found himself shaking Mr Harknell's hand and bowing over Mrs Harknell's. Hal saw them to their carriage, only lightly touching Edith's cheek with his lips and watched by her parents. James wondered what thoughts were in her head, so calm and serene, her hair smooth, her cheek turned briefly to her betrothed to receive his salute. Again he thought of Beth Machin, those red curls tumbling to her shoulders with no regard for fashion, her green eyes so large and luminous, the way her lips parted slightly as if she knew she was on the verge of something exciting.

'Time we retired I think. No more piano tonight if you please.' Henry could see the direction his younger son was taking as they came back to the warmth of the drawing-room. James said nothing as he closed the lid of the piano. 'I have something to attend to in the library, then I shall go to my room. Rake the fire if you please, James, and extinguish all the lights safely.'

'Yes, sir. Goodnight.'

'You did well, Millie my dear, and looked as pretty as a picture.' In truth, how could she fail when of all his family she was the one so like her mother?

'She did indeed,' James agreed. 'Sleep well, sir.'

18

'God rest you both.'

Hal had gone straight to his room after seeing the last departing carriage on its way, Naomi and Esme had been allowed to stay only for supper and the music, so with Henry's going just the two were left.

'Wasn't it all gorgeous, Jamie?' Amelia knelt before the fire. 'Don't go to bed yet or it will all be over.'

'I didn't imagine it was your sort of party. Our Willie never fails, does he?'

They both giggled.

'It was fun though, all of it, Naomi and Esme staying up, even Willie's song. Edith looked so beautiful – Hal is quite enthralled.' She sat back on her heels gazing into the fire, dreaming of what? How little any of them knew each other. Upstairs there was Hal – enthralled, she'd said – yet all he talked about was engines or pulleys!

'Did you know the Machins were going away, looking for factory work?'

'Oh, how horrid of me, Jamie. I've been so full of the party I'd forgotten all about them. Syd told me this morning.'

'I keep thinking – oh, dammit, life's unjust. Here are we warm and comfortable while just down the lane they must be so wretched. Can't we do something, Mill?'

They sat silently and after a while she said what they both knew was the truth.

'Even if we could, Jamie, they'd not want charity. They're proud folk.'

Warm and comfortable, he'd said, and with no effort of their own. The gas light was turned low, the fire still piled with glowing coals glinting on the highly polished brass of the fender; even to see it gave a sense of wellbeing. Over the fireplace hung a portrait of their mother painted not long after that miniature upstairs, her dark hair worn in the fashion of the day, parted in the centre with ringlets clustered each side of her gently smiling face. She still had the innocent look of a child and to James and Amelia the

19

picture bore little resemblance to the mother they remembered. In the twenty-two years of her marriage she had borne eleven children, suffering greatly with each pregnancy until her final confinement had proved too much for her worn-out body. That lovely face smiling so sweetly down on them was no more than part of the background of furnishings, too familiar to be noticed. Tonight, though, it was the thought of Beth that made James see the girl Isabella Copeland had been, for didn't they both bear the stamp of confidence in what lay before them? His mother had had so much, all that money could buy, a husband who'd loved her even though that love had been the cause of her suffering. What hope had poor Beth with circumstances so against her?

The coals slipped and in the light of the sudden flames the pleated silk front of the high-backed piano shone. Instinctively he raised his hand to it, letting it touch the fabric almost in a caress, the smooth material familiar on his hand. In front of the instrument the revolving stool tempted him and sitting on it he raised the lid.

'Papa said you musn't play, it's too late.'

'I'm not playing.' He told himself he should be grateful for the comforts that surrounded him, yet he was aware only of a deep longing, a lack, a need. Even Millie who was nearer to him than anyone didn't know the emptiness he felt, nor could she have helped him fill it, for he didn't know how to begin to satisfy himself or what it was he sought.

'It's late, Millie. We'd better rake the fire and fix the sparkguard.'

'Umph.' She got to her feet letting her hands fall on the pale-blue silk of her flounced skirt. Each layer, and there must have been ten of them, was edged with lace of the same hue, yards and yards neatly stitched to add the final touch of elegance. 'It's the prettiest dress I've ever had. Isn't it strange, Jamie, that I'm wearing it tonight while we talk of the Machins. Beth Machin sews for Mrs Dickson; I

20

saw her there when I called one day to ask Mrs Dickson to come to collect some work. She was sitting bent over her sewing; she didn't look up but I'm sure it was her. She's got the brightest hair I've ever seen.'

As she chattered James's mind was busy.

'Millie, you speak to father. He'll never refuse if you ask him. Tell him of the sewing that always needs to be done, the dresses that you have to get Mrs Dickson to make. If Beth were to come here she could do it all, the mending and the making.'

'But Mrs Dickson has done our work for so long, even for Mama.'

'Mrs Dickson has other people to work for, and she has a home. Please Millie – it would be like shutting a wild bird in a cage to send Beth to a factory.'

'I didn't know you knew her so well. Why are you so interested, Jamie? Why can't you speak to Papa?'

'I don't know her, I've hardly spoken to her. But Papa would think as you're thinking. She's only about as old as us. How would you feel this night if your home was lost and you had that ahead of you?'

'Jamie, I'll speak to Papa, but promise me, it's not for yourself you want it. Promise me that.'

'Of course it's not for myself. Did I not just say I hardly know her?'

'Well enough. I'll ask Papa tomorrow.'

She was so like his dear Isabella, there was little Henry could refuse Amelia. If the child found sewing irksome then let her have help. There would be parties ahead. She was of an age to have a place in the social life in the county and ''pon my soul, there's not a maid among them to compare with little Millie'. They'd find room in the house for another girl. Mrs Murphy would make up somewhere for her to sleep. For twelve pounds a year and her keep it was surely a wise move. With four daughters still at home there must be stitching enough for the wench to earn her wage.

21

In the event Beth didn't share the back attic with Jenny, the parlourmaid; she persuaded Syd to let her have a bed over the coach-house with him. The servants' quarters were repressive and in any case she had no intention of living under the rule of Mrs Murphy. Over the stable block she reigned supreme, only going to the kitchen at dinner time.

Syd misunderstood her aversion for those basement rooms in the big house. 'Don't see what you're feared of Bethie. She's a good enough soul as long as you know your place.'

Beth didn't answer, for what chance was there of Syd following her reasoning when she could hardly explain it even to herself? 'Know your place,' he'd said. There in the kitchen she would be seated between old Ben, the gardener, and Dolly, the kitchenmaid. As if that could ever be her place!

James seldom saw her; perhaps he caught a glimpse when he came to the stables to collect the trap on their way out in the morning. Knowing she was there, safe from the life in a factory he imagined, he was content to forget her. Perhaps his interest would have gone no further had it not been for a chance meeting as he drove the pony and trap towards Wilhampton. Rounding a bend in the lane somewhere about halfway between Merton Court and St Agnes Vicarage, he recognized the figure ahead of him, trudging along, a woven rush basket on her arm, head down against the blustering April wind.

'Ahoy, there,' he called as he neared her, to be rewarded by a broad smile of recognition as she wheeled round. A sudden gust sent her free hand to hold down her pancake-shaped hat which was tied down by a muslin scarf knotted under her chin, but which even so she'd come near to losing, while her cloak blew shoulder high.

She laughed, enjoying the wildness of the day. 'How glad I am to see you – you are offering me a seat?' She

22

knew he was, of course, for already he'd drawn in the reins and was starting to climb out of the trap.

'Indeed I am, and glad of your company. I'm on my way to the Vicarage at Wilhampton – and you? Where are you bound for with this great load? Wherever it is I declare I shall take you, for this is too heavy for you to be carrying.'

'I am strong, as strong as any lad,' she assured him proudly, 'but since I'm bound for the Vicarage too I'll come with you with pleasure.'

How prettily she spoke. Strong as any lad she may be but her voice had the gentleness of a lady. She would have been delighted if she'd been able to read his thoughts for not without care she had cultivated the tones of those born to a higher station than her own. She spoke as they spoke, she knew better than most how a lady should dress even though her own wardrobe was made up of other people's cast-offs carefully altered to suit her, and she never missed an opportunity to learn how a lady should conduct herself. It was only a matter of time, that she never doubted. For the moment she was well enough at Merton Court. Fate had stepped in and rescue her once and so it would again when the right time came. She still had things to learn before the next stage presented itself. In her imagination was a hazy picture of a laughing young giant of a man, fair curly hair and twinkling eyes, broad shoulders and strong arms. He'd wear his tall silk hat at a rakish angle, use a cane with a silver top . . . one day, when the time was right.

'I am to fit a gown for your sister, Mrs Wentworth' (for I'll not call her Miss Lucy like a serving maid, Beth thought). 'She is expecting me at half past the hour. I had thought to take much longer. Do you know what time it is now?'

'It is but two o'clock, we have no need to hurry. Let us walk through Hampton Woods to the pond. If I tether the pony on the brow we can cut across the high track. It's ten minutes' walk.'

She musn't let him see she was concerned about her slippers, worn especially as she was going to his sister's home. Usually she only used them on Sunday with her best gown for church but something had prompted her to look as well dressed as her meagre wardrobe would allow, some stirring of excitement had warned her that today was no ordinary day. Perhaps it was no more than the feeling of spring in the air.

'Yes, there are primroses in Hampton Woods, near the brow. I collect them each year.'

'Then so you shall today.'

As he climbed down and tied the reins to a low branch she momentarily forgot her refinement and jumped from the trap.

'I'll not need that!' She threw her hat on to the seat, shaking her red curls free. 'Oh, just feel the wind, this is the very best kind of day, a warm wind from the west. It will rain by dusk, you can smell it, can't you?'

He didn't answer – there was no need – and she didn't guess how tongue-tied he suddenly was, faced with such eager beauty. Not for a moment did either of them think of themselves as master and maid, for surely any man must happily be her slave, or so he was sure.

Ten minutes' walk would take them to the pond but they spent longer than that gathering the primroses. At the back of her mind was the nagging thought that at half past two Mrs Wentworth would send down to the servants' hall expecting her to be waiting.

'It is so beautiful, I wish we could walk right across there as far as the eye can see, over the meadows and into Matslock Woods. But your sister will be vexed, the minutes go so fast.'

He took his watch from his pocket and glanced at it as he answered: 'I'll tell Lucy it was my fault. No one should be tied to time on a day such as this.'

'No, indeed they shouldn't. But then how many can be truly free, free like the birds that fly overhead? I am tied to

24

the work of making pretty things for your sisters, mending and stitching the buttons to your shirts – but you, are you not tied too? To your father's bidding, spending your days amongst things which I suspect mean little to you?' She turned and met his gaze squarely. 'Little to the real person you are?'

'Ay, you're right, Beth, but I'm not proud to admit it. I ought to care as Hal does and play a proper part. But I come and go, care nothing for their iron and steel, their new-fangled machines.'

'And I care nothing for your sisters' finery or for the buttons on your nightshirts! Are we not of a same mind? But it's of no matter. This is what counts, the wind in our hair, the primroses, and the moss underfoot. We have our lives before us. Why, just think of all the wonderful things that may be waiting, that we can't know. But one thing we can be certain of, whatever else fails – this time next year the primroses will be in flower again and the birds mating.'

They walked on towards the edge of the wood where the pony and trap waited.

'Are your family settling well in town, Beth?'

She shrugged. 'Oh, I dare say. They aren't great letter writers.' She sounded disinterested, uncaring and he was aware of a sense of disappointment.

Perhaps he'd misunderstood her meaning. He went on: 'I'm so glad you didn't go with them.'

'Me!' She laughed. 'But I wouldn't have gone.'

'But if you hadn't come to Merton what could you have done?' She seemed unaware that he'd been responsible for her change of plans.

'If . . . if,' she laughed. 'Who's to say what "if" might bring. Your father wanted a seamstress. I knew something would happen. Don't you see you only have to wait and when you're ready something always happens. What's the matter? You look put out. Have I said something to offend you?'

25

His manner had changed, she was sure she didn't imagine it.

'How could you have? Come, Lucy will be waiting.' He took her arm and helped her into the trap, his mouth set in a hint of a pout.

Strange boy, something's made him cross. And he was so easy to talk to, she silently pondered the change glancing sideways at him. He flicked the reins and the pony started forward at a brisk trot. It was already nearly ten minutes to three.

If Lucy was surprised to see them arrive together she didn't show it but simply raised her round face to kiss James's cheek, saying: 'This is a rare treat, Jamie. Edward is in the library; go and surprise him while Beth does my fitting. I'll be with you in just a few minutes.' She led the way indoors, James ushering Beth through while he followed carrying her basket. No servants' entrance for her today. With head high she followed Lucy into the square, stone-floored hall. 'Bring the gown, Beth, and we'll go to my room.'

The fitting didn't take long and once it was over Beth helped Lucy back into her dark-red afternoon gown with its nipped-in waist and wide crinoline skirt. Instinctively she stood straight, grateful for her own trim waist. These fashions did nothing to help Lucy with her stocky build. This new creation could look so much better on someone else (if the someone she had in mind was herself perhaps she may be forgiven) for it was indeed beautiful in mauve brocatelle with black leaf design on the enormous skirt; carefully she folded it into a sheet before packing it in the large woven basket.

No mention had been made of the journey home or even of how long James intended to stay. Their drive together, her temporary elevation, only added to her wretchedness as she followed Lucy from her room. On the landing Lucy dismissed her.

'If you like to go down those stairs, Beth, you'll find Mrs

26

Plumley in the kitchen. Tell her I said you were to ask for a cup of tea before you start back to Merton. The dress is coming along beautifully, thank you.'

Beth bit her lip, tears of mortification misting her vision as she turned to go down the steep wooden flight of backstairs. Halfway down she stopped, listening as Lucy opened the drawing-room door, hearing male voices, laughter; then the door closed. The stairway was dim, carrying her heavy basket she groped her way on down the unfamiliar steps. She didn't want their tea. Not for anything would she go to the kitchen, begging Mrs Plumley indeed! At the bottom she turned to the side door and let herself out. Better go straight home. It was nearly four miles and she'd be lucky to get back before the rain came. The afternoon bus that went from Wilhampton to the surrounding villages, pulled by its four grey horses, must already have left. If James hadn't chosen the same time as her visit to the Vicarage she would have walked both ways, even enjoyed the glimpse of Lucy's home. In that hour with him, though, she'd been able to forget her lowly state, talking to him as naturally as any two young people with much in common. And if she were honest she'd allowed herself to indulge in the fancy that he found her attractive and saw her as his equal. Fancy?

The wind had dropped in the last half hour. Now the rain started, heavy drops falling straight down. She hurried on. The sight of her thin slippers again reminded her of her place in life. A fine sight she'd look in church on Sunday if these were ruined and she had to wear her old button-side boots.

Half walking, half running, the bag getting all the time heavier and still two miles to go, she heard the sound of the pony and without looking round instinct told her who it was. She'd not let him see her running. That same instinct slowed her pace and tilted her chin a little higher. A moment later as he helped her to the seat at his side she handed him her basket and stepped up with all the assurance of a lady born.

27

CHAPTER TWO

Between Esme and young Phoebe was the family's largest gap, brought about by one miscarriage and the death of two of the three who'd lived but a short time. Phoebe was only five, yet perhaps having had no children to play with, she had a maturity in advance of her years. Like a wise old lady, Henry sometimes thought; so different from any of the others.

The rearing of babies had never concerned him so when Phoebe had been born and he'd lost Isabella it had fallen to twenty-year-old Margaret to take control. Babies may not have appealed to Margaret at that time but taking control did and until she married William Ponsonby two years later she surrounded the infant with kindly order and certain discipline. At her going Lucy, plump, good natured and baby-loving, had taken over, mixing discipline with a show of affection that had never been allowed when Margaret held sway. Two more years and the Reverend Edward Wentworth had whisked her away leaving Phoebe to the mercies of eighteen-year-old Amelia who proved much better at playing games than the others but less consistent in her care and training. Hal and James had been there of course but to the young Phoebe they'd seemed remote and grown up, whereas Naomi and Esme, ten and nine years her senior, were too old to want her with them and too young to be entrusted with her care. So she built a world of her own, imagined playmates happily enough, not knowing as she chattered to them and formed their replies that folk would call this loneliness.

'Is someone out there with Phoebe?' Henry asked, raising his head from *The Times* as he heard her laughter.

28

'No Papa, just her hoop.' Amelia didn't need to look out of the window. 'She often chatters.'

'Humph. It's not healthy. Why do Naomi and Esme not play with her more?'

'Oh, Papa, they're too old for her games.' She peered out into the garden. 'But I'm wrong, she does have someone with her. It's Beth Machin, you know her, the sewing girl. She's bowling the hoop with Phoebe's whip. Oh, do come and look Papa. Right round the lawn she's running. Did you ever see! Really it's not seemly – but how pretty she is.'

The hoop was gathering speed as, her skirts held nearly to her knees (really Millie regretted calling her father to the window, she hadn't expected such a display of frilly knickerbockers!) the sharp quick lashes of the whip driving it on. Beth ran by its side. They were both laughing uproariously, the little girl jumping up and down in an excitement rare to be seen.

'Is the girl always such a hoodlum? I'm inclined to think it's not wise to encourage Phoebe to spend her time with her.'

'She's not a hoodlum, Papa, truly she's gently spoken and neat,' then she too joined in the laughter, 'but aren't they enjoying it! I could never make a hoop run like that. It looks so jolly – don't stop them Papa.'

'Certainly it's a treat to hear the child so happy. But watch her Millie, she's young and impressionable. She needs a woman's training and I'm afraid my dear it has to be your job.'

'Truly I do, Papa. You mustn't worry about Beth though, she can do Phoebe no harm. While she sews she reads to her quite often and she is teaching her her stitches. Already Phoebe can do a better cross stitch than I can, I swear, and Beth has already started her on a sampler.'

He half listened, glad he needn't concern himself with the red-headed tomboy outside. He was conscious now as he seemed to be more and more frequently as time went

29

on, of the void in his own life. Millie was a dear child, yet he heard her youthful chatter and knew a profound loneliness, for some reason made the more acute by the sound of the laughter from the garden. Turning away he went back to his armchair, once more opening the newspaper.

'I'm going to cut some flowers, the first of the roses. Beth is supposed to be pinning our bridesmaids' gowns but Phoebe is having such a happy game I hate to remind her.'

He didn't answer, so supposing him to be engrossed in his reading she went through the conservatory to the garden.

Another summer, roses in bloom again. They were all so young, so sure. And he? What future had he? Oh, time enough, he didn't doubt that, but what of the quality of those years before him? To all his family he was the rock they depended on, yet they held him in awe, only Hal looking on him as a companion. He had their respect — no doubt he had their love — yet he was alone.

Folding the paper he put it aside and went back to the window. Now Phoebe had the whip and Beth was running by her side keeping the pace right. Amelia joined them and he smiled, reading her thoughts, knowing she too would have liked to take part in the fun. The hoop bowled on; the girls, age and station forgotten, delighted in Phoebe's prowess. How could he give way to self-pity, let himself be isolated in these moods of depression, when he had so much? That little hoodlum (for so she must be, gentler than her background might suggest perhaps but a tomboy for all that) what had she? Yet her spirit radiated a joy of living. What a life though, sharing the stable rooms with Syd — a good enough fellow but so different — taking her meals in the kitchen and spending her days making pretty things for other people to wear. My, but she was a beauty, but even so how could she hope life would use her? Had he known better he might instead have asked how she would use life.

30

She must have remembered her duties for, leaving a pouting Phoebe behind, the two older girls turned towards the house. As they disappeared from his view the day was suddenly duller; the little girl left on the lawn with her hoop must have felt the same for taking her whip she bowled it, running by its side as she tried to keep it going with the leather thong. It wobbled and fell. She tried again; again it toppled. The light, lifting tap Beth had shown her was lost; she slashed at it, it rolled away and fell. Once more she tried but somehow with Beth's departure the fun had gone out of the game.

From an upstairs window they'd been watched too by Naomi and Esme.

'Amelia ought not to allow it!' Esme frowned. 'Phoebe is becoming entirely uncontrolled. Mama never permitted us to play with the servants.' She was nearly a year younger than her sister but already taller. In an age when small feet were a sign of beauty Esme's would have been more comfortable in James's boots than in her own pointed-toed slippers, and her hands hinted at a strength to be envied by many a worker in the fields. In another era she might have worn her tweeds and brogues well but at that time to be 5ft 10ins tall, to have feet that proved difficult to shoe, to have teeth that overcrowded her mouth and crossed in front — small wonder her view on life was jaundiced. As if by contrast her fifteen-year-old sister was undoubtedly the beauty of the family. Naomi's hair was pure gold, falling into waves and curls that glistened, her eyes were the blue of a summer sky and her teeth even and white. No blemish ever marred her fair skin; everything about her was lovely, face and figure too. Each night Esme twisted her lank locks around the strips of rag she knotted on her head, each morning she hoped for a miracle, but none ever came. If the two girls hadn't spent so much time together perhaps Esme would have been less conscious of her failings. Was it jealousy that so often made her bite at her fingers when she watched her older sister, or was it unhapppiness? Either way the large hands weren't improved by the nibbled nails. Today, as happened so regularly to announce to the world that this was her time, her chin was disfigured by three angry spots.

'But how good it is to hear Phoebe laugh like that! We always played together, Esme. We can't know what it's like to be alone as she is.' Easy to smile on a world that treated one as well as it did Naomi. She never lost patience with Esme no matter how carping her tongue.

Amelia and Beth came towards the house and Phoebe disconsolately bowled her hoop alone, but as the girls upstairs turned away from the window, she let it run into the bushes and wandered off towards the orchard. No doubt some of her 'playmates' would be waiting for her.

As the weeks of summer passed, the thoughts of the young Copeland girls were centred on Hal's wedding and Beth figured in them only as the creator of their lovely clothes. The long hours she spent turning the handle of her sewing machine (and thankful she was to have it when she looked back to the days when every long seam took hours of patient work with her needle), the evenings that stretched past what should have been bedtime while she sat close to the oil lamp, for even now so much still had to be stitched by hand. No, they gave no thought to her, neither for that matter did she to them, dreaming as she worked; for all that, she loved clothes, particularly she loved pretty clothes, so the hours she spent brought her a certain satisfaction.

A three-storey house built towards the end of the previous century and fronting the High Street in Wilhampton was purchased. It was Henry's wedding present to his eldest son and the main furnishings were provided by Edith's parents. So on the 21st of August in the year of our Lord 1861 Henry Copeland, Junior, took himself a wife, both families rejoicing in a union that must bring continuity of their lines and of the friendship between their houses. The best man was the brother of the groom, four of the six bridesmaids were his sisters and the ceremony was performed by his brother-in-law.

A grand affair indeed, the church crowded, for not only relatives, friends and business acquaintances came to see the knot tied, but many locals as well, employees of Harknell's or Copeland's, or parishioners of Edward who were interested in his wife's family. At the back of the church sat Beth. Her work could make her justly proud but it wasn't just the dresses she'd come to see. That she was there at all they appeared not to notice which was surprising for she was lovely enough to catch any eye. Today, though, was Hal's day as far as the family were concerned.

Sitting in the second pew from the front Henry heard his son's strong voice as he made his vows. He tried to think back down the years, to feel again as he had when it had been his turn and he'd said those same words, his hand holding Bella's. They'd been so young. The years had moulded them – the Bella he'd lost had been different indeed from that young bride. Lost? Sometimes he struggled to find her and knew himself utterly alone – then at other times it was as if she was with him still, a part of him as surely as she'd become with those years. It was like that as he watched Hal step into his new life. In Bella he found the courage to face the gap the boy's going would bring.

The bridal party were driven in their coaches to the house on the High Street where, in the happy couple's own dining-room, they ate the wedding breakfast. By tea-time it was all over, Henry, James and the bridesmaids had been driven home. James saw his father retreat to the library, his conscience telling him he should follow. So often Hal had shared the early evening hours, the talk no doubt of the business. Now he was the only son, he ought to make an effort. Just a few minutes at the piano first (he'd leave it a while, later on would do).

Even as he silently resolved that once he'd had a few minutes music he'd try and make the effort, he heard the sound of a tread crossing the hall to the library. Someone was ahead of him; his father needn't be on his conscience. In relief he struck the opening chords of Beethoven's *Moonlight Sonata*.

'Papa, please Papa, can I be with you till Amelia finds me?'

'Please Papa may I ...,' he automatically corrected. 'Yes, Phoebe, I think we might very well keep each other company. What have you in your hand?'

'It's a drawing. I did it for you Papa, it's – look who it is – it's Hal and Edith. See how high his hat is and how wide her dress is too.'

'My word, yes, and you drew that for me? Well, Phoebe I'll treasure it. See, I'll write on it "Hal and Edith on their Wedding Day, 21.8.61. Drawn by Phoebe." There!'

'Are you really and truly going to keep it, Papa?'

'But to be sure. I promise you I shall treasure it.'

She sighed contentedly and climbed on to his knee. None of the others had ever shown their affection as naturally as did Phoebe, but then none of the others had been without a mother. He rubbed the side of his face on her head as she leant against him.

'Your whiskers tickle. Do it again,' she giggled moving her cheek up and down against his sideburns. Then sitting straight her round little face took on its grown-up look, or so she hoped. 'Shall we talk about the wedding, Papa? Would you like to talk about that?'

'You talk, I'm listening.'

'It was beautiful, everyone singing. I like to listen to Jamie singing. I stood right up close to him. Why did Mrs Harknell cry? Didn't she want Edith and Hal to be married?'

34

'Ladies sometimes cry at weddings. Happy things, beautiful things, sometimes make people cry.'

'Oh. Make you all screwed up in your tummy, don't they? Were you all screwed up, Papa?'

'Perhaps I was. Yes, that's about it Phoebe, all screwed up inside. Don't tell the others that though, that's our secret.'

She leant against him again putting her arms around his neck. 'We have lots of secrets, Papa.' Again she sat up straight and this time her face was puzzled as she turned to him. 'We all went to church in carriages but Beth walked all that way.'

'Beth? Beth Machin? Why didn't she go with the other servants? Ben was driving them in the brougham.'

'She made all our dresses and then she walked on her own. We had some room, Papa. I wanted to stop and offer her a ride; she was nearly running when we passed her. Esme said I was being ridic'lous. Was I, Papa? Why is it ridic'lous? It's such a long way and she was almost running.'

Henry was puzzled. Why should the girl have elected to walk? She could have driven with the others and sat with them in church. Certainly he'd noticed her sitting away from them at the back. He thought she must have come in late, yet if she'd walked she must have left long before them.

'Is it wrong for me to play with her, Papa? Esme says I'll be no better than a gypsy and she tells me I shouldn't go to her room while she sews. But, Papa, James isn't like a gypsy and she doesn't tell him he shouldn't play with her.'

'James? Oh come, Phoebe.' What was the child saying? 'He's friendly with all the servants, it's just his way.'

'But Beth is different, Papa. She's not like any of the others and knows all about so many things. I expect when they walk together she teaches him too, all about the birds and the wild plants growing in the hedgerows. She knows

35

how to cook nettles and she says you can use violets for flavouring. Did you know that Papa?'

He only half listened as she chattered, wondering about James and what he was learning at the hands of the lovely Beth. It might be many years since he'd been nineteen but he was sure he'd not have walked with her and learnt of nothing but wild flowers and birds.

Later when they all sat at supper – all except Phoebe who was already in bed – he noticed how often James looked at the clock. But for the child's remark he would have thought nothing of it, yet now he found himself watching to see where the lad would go once the meal was over. One thing was certain, wherever he went it wouldn't be to the library with his father. How empty the evenings would be now that Hal had gone.

He heard the side door close behind James, and he heard him come back nearly two hours later when dusk had already long given way to the moonlit summer night.

'What can take you abroad at this hour, James?' His voice surprised James as he came back through the hall.

'I've been walking, sir. To be indoors on such an evening is a sin. You should at least go to the garden and breathe the scented night air.'

It told Henry nothing and later when he heard the soft notes of the piano he couldn't start to guess at the thoughts in his son's head. Perhaps it was no more than the magic of a summer night stirring his own memories.

In fact, on this particular evening James hadn't been with Beth. He'd walked, as he usually did, down the lane and across the meadow but tonight she'd not been sitting on the gate at the far side, as she was so often. Their meetings were always by 'chance', never by arrangement, chance that guided them in that same direction. Certainly he'd been later than usual, the wedding had altered their regular routine, but he'd expected that she would have waited, she must have known he'd come. How was he to

36

guess that she'd been on the far side of the next meadow where it edged the river?

She had intended to wait for James, but how could she on such a night, warm, clear and utterly perfect? The pull of the water had proved too strong. The tight lacing of her corset, her layers of petticoats, all were a prison to a body that longed to be free. There, in the evening dusk, sheltering under the old willow tree that overhung the towpath she'd shed them all then gently lowered her naked body into the cool river. It was nothing new to her; ever since she was a child she'd come to this old tree to undress and then, alone, learnt to keep herself afloat and even to kick her legs like a frog and move through the water. Solitude was her friend, the river clear and cold on her sticky skin. James sitting disconsolately on the gate only a quarter of a mile away, was forgotten.

The hot spell lasted and for the next two evenings James saw nothing of her. It was on the Friday that, again, finding no figure waiting for him on the gate he walked on across the second meadow. Not for a moment did he expect to find her by the water. More likely she'd been given extra household sewing to do, for with Hal gone Amelia had ideas for new curtains and chair-covers in his old room. Fancy in this heat sitting by her lamp sewing – he could just picture her, head bent, the moths fluttering round the light. Reaching the river there in the dusk he took off his jacket and put it on the ground, then pulled the bow of his tie undone and removed the front stud from the wing collar that was sticking to his neck on this sultry night. There would be a storm before morning. Not a breath of breeze, just stillness in the fast fading dust. A fish jumped, or so he supposed hearing the splash, then again. Peering through the gloom he saw her, floating on her back, just at the moment when she realized she was no longer alone.

'Beth, it is Beth isn't it?' for although it was too dark to

37

recognize her he knew it was her even before he heard her voice.

'I didn't expect you, not here.' She swam towards the bank, then stood, the water almost to her naked shoulders. 'Why don't you swim too? You've no idea how wonderful it is after such a day.'

'I have no bathing suit, nor a towel.' Even as he said it his eyes were riveted on the whiteness of her bare shoulders.

'Nor I. God gave us bodies, did he not. Why should we cover them when the water is so clear and pure. Go under the willow and leave your clothes. I will stay here while you get in.'

'But Beth I have no towel.'

Her irrepressible chuckle sent a tingle of excitement through him. Never had she called him by his first name, always she'd avoided calling him anything.

'But James,' she mimicked his tone, 'I have petticoats. Come, do come.'

How could he resist? By the time he slid off the bank into the water, night had fallen and it was only because they'd been out so long and their eyes were attuned to the dusk that they could see at all. He wished he could swim too. Watching her as he stood chest high in the water, moving his arms but careful to keep at least one foot on the riverbed, his respect for her grew.

To dress they had to move from the shelter of the overhanging willow to the open meadow and even then to grope for their clothes.

'Here, James, you may dry yourself with this.' She passed him a cotton garment. 'Wasn't it fun!' Instinctively she whispered.

He didn't seem to be drying very fast. She was almost ready for her dress (for here in the dark she'd no intention of lacing herself into that beastly corset, nor yet wearing petticoats or stockings). He could see the whiteness of her skin; the petticoat she'd given him still seemed to hold the smell of her body, and he buried his face in it.

'You'll get cold,' she whispered and he felt her hand, already warm again after her swim and an invigorating rub in her underslip, as it touched his shoulder. 'You're shivering.'

'No, I'm not cold.' Yet she was right, he was shaking. He rubbed her petticoat over his body which was already half dry from the warm night.

What was she doing? Instead of pulling her dress over her head she was laying it on the grass. 'Put your shirt on the ground. Let's just sit here. As soon as we dress we'll forget that glorious cool water on our bodies.'

His face was hot. It wasn't the way he was used to hearing his sisters talk. Bodies were private things. He was grateful now for the darkness that hid from her what was happening to his, so quickly recovered from the cold water and already hardened and erect. It seemed he had no power to argue even if he'd wanted, not even to hold back when she moved her full skirt to make room for him too and raised her arm to pull him to her side.

He sat very straight, his arms clasped around his pulled up knees, almost frightened to breathe as her warm fingers touched the base of his spine and started to walk upwards.

'You're warm again now; so am I.' Still she whispered.

'I'm on fire. Beth, Beth, we must dress, you don't know what you're doing to me.'

For answer she moved to kneel by his side, turning his head to her so that the whiteness of her flesh was clear in the dark. She took his hand and in a shock of excitement for the first time he felt the firm heaviness of a woman's breast, the nipple hard against his fingers.

'Beth, you don't know . . .,' he said again, then he knew the secret of his own body was hers too as her hand closed round him.

'Love me, James. The night is so beautiful, make it

39

perfect. You want to, you know you want to, come, come . . .'

He'd never touched a woman before. All he knew he'd learned from dreams that had disturbed his adolescence, and the rare masturbation with its attendant guilt and shame. Only in the privacy of his own bed had he ever done the thing he knew to be sinful, always expecting that the morning would give some sign to set him apart, fixing his father's steely glare on him and telling everyone what he'd done.

And Beth? Hadn't she known that something was waiting just around the corner for her? She must be in love. These weeks of summer when she and James had been together they'd talked so freely, they must have been leading all the time just to this. Only if she were in love could her body ache with this longing. Until this night she'd not been sure where her future lay. Now suddenly everything was crystal clear, made plain to her by the need they had of each other. She was lying on her back her arms reaching out to him.

Afterwards, remembering, he marvelled that she could have known so well how to use her body, hers and his too, her passion mounting with his own. That was later though. All he knew on this night was that whatever it was he'd been lacking, in her arms he found it.

Wordlessly they dressed, then his arm around her shoulder they turned back towards Merton. At the gateway to the stable yard he held her close.

'Tomorrow, come tomorrow,' he whispered into her still damp hair. 'My darling love, how can I wait?'

For answer she raised her face to his and under his lips he felt her mouth open.

Later lying between his cool sheets he remembered it all, not with shame or guilt, for this surely was love. This was what man and woman were made for.

August was nearly at an end. Soon summer evenings would give way to the damp mists of autumn. He looked no further, although he couldn't contemplate a future without her. To marry Beth would create trouble in his home, that much he knew; but if only they'd come to know her they must see she was no ordinary servant. For a week or two he let himself ride along on the bubble of love. Two more evenings of joy by the willow tree, then Beth telling him with all the honesty of a child: 'Just hold me, James. We can't love tonight, it's my time.' He'd never loved her more. All the ecstasy he'd found in her hadn't moved him to the tenderness he felt as she leant against him.

'One day, Beth, we'll be together always.'

Hadn't she known? 'You mean . . .?'

'You must let them know you first. Already Phoebe loves you – and I love you. Whatever Papa says, Beth, it's right for us to be together. First they must know you and you them. It'll take a little time.'

She didn't answer and in the dark of the evening he couldn't see her clearly enough to read her expression.

Those days of the heatwave soon took on a dream-like quality to the impatient Beth, but more than that they cut her past off from her future. Until then she'd been content to wait, sure that something good was ahead. And now? She'd fallen in love, nothing less could have given that wonderful week such a aura of magic. Each morning she'd woken to thoughts of James, his dark handsome face, his soft voice, his beautiful hands, the words he'd whispered in the warm summer night. Hadn't he told her he wanted them always to be together? She didn't want to acknowledge any disappointment in him. If all that he had said were true, though, surely he ought to be man enough to say so, or was she being unfair? She wouldn't listen to the voice of doubt. Never had Beth been frightened of anyone, yet it was soon obvious that fear was James's foremost feeling for his father – and perhaps he was ashamed of her, whispered that sneaking voice again. The thought that

41

this might be the truth didn't so much hurt her as tarnish the image she'd built of him.

One evening in October Syd had to take Henry Copeland to Wilhampton where he was having supper with Hal and Edith, and as soon as Beth could she escaped from Mrs Murphy's kitchen back to the coach-house.

'Miss High and Mighty! Too good to sit at our fireside, I suppose!' The housekeeper watched her go with tight lips, but Beth didn't give a thought to her. This evening she'd be alone and James knew it. She turned up the lamp in their living-room and, putting a looking glass on the table, peered closely at her reflection. How soon the 'roses' of summer disappeared when she was shut away, hour after hour with her sewing. Not that being out of doors would have made much difference these last few weeks. She pinched her cheeks hard to bring some colour to them. In a jar she had the raw beetroot she'd peeled and mashed that morning, so now she drained off the juice and dipped her finger in, then carefully dabbed her lips. That was better; she was honest enough to be pleased with the result. Now a shake of rosewater, and she'd be ready. More than anything else what she wanted was to re-create the magic of those summer evenings.

'Who is it?' she called when his tap came on the door.

'Who were you expecting?' he laughed.

'James. I hoped you'd come.'

'You knew I'd come.'

She'd been making a pretence of reading while she waited, and now he took the book and closed it pulling her into his arms.

'Its been so long. I thought he'd never go out for an evening.'

The cold finger of disappointment jabbed at her. 'Do we have to be so secretive?'

'Just give it time, sweetheart. When they've come to know you they'll understand.'

He sat on the horsehair sofa and pulled her to his knee,

reaching to dim the light. It seemed he didn't want to waste time; his lips were teasing hers as she felt him start to unbutton the bodice of her dress.

'No James, not yet . . .' This wasn't how she'd dreamed. She wanted to make love to him, but not like this, as something separate from his life at home, something to be kept secret and hidden. As his warm hand touched her flesh she pulled away and stood up.

'Let's wait. We've not even talked for ages. Tell me what you've been doing. Don't you see, James, I want to feel part of your whole life, not just a woman you make love to?'

'You're not being fair, Beth. I love you, truly I swear I do.'

'Of course, I know, dear James, and I love you. But I can't feel right in watching for your father and Syd to go off so that I can have you here.'

'I'll tell them about us, Beth. As soon as I have a chance to talk to Papa I'll tell him,' and at that moment in his desire he was strong enough to believe that he spoke the truth. Nonetheless she buttoned her bodice and he had the sense to talk of other things.

It was much later, the evening had flown even though he'd come no nearer to his goal.

'James, you should go. Do you know the hour?'

'They'll not be back yet, Papa said he'd be late. Edith's parents are there too and when he and Mr Harknell get together it's always late.'

'Still I think you should go.'

'Beth, please don't send me away like this. You're mine, you know you are. I'll talk to him, I'll ask him – tell him. Just let me hold you.' Already he was doing that and, close in his arms, she remembered those evenings by the water's edge. It could be like that again, he wanted it, she wanted it, no one would disturb her. Why then did she hold back? That finger of disappointment must have made quite a dent when it had stabbed her.

43

'Not like this, James. Can't you see?'

'No I can't. Dammit, Beth, you want it too. You can't say you don't.'

'Not furtively. I want us to be proud of loving – not ashamed.'

'Of course I'm proud you love me . . .'

'Ah-ha,' whispered a silent voice in her ear. 'Not quite the same . . .'

'Hark.' His head was raised as he listened, thoughts of making love dampened. 'Wheels on the drive. They're earlier than I thought.' Even as he spoke he was reaching for his coat. 'Syd's taking Papa to the front. I'll slip in through the kitchen and up the back stairs or he'll want to know where I've been.'

He apparently crept in without meeting his father for Beth heard no more, and no more either of his promise to tell his family about them. During the winter he still came to the coach-house if he knew Syd and his father were safely out of the way, but under the pretext of being busy she sewed as they talked, finding it easier than she'd expected to keep him at arm's length. She felt let down, disappointed, at him and even more at herself. Perhaps it was her surroundings that made his presence so often irritate her. He didn't fit in here in this bare room, sitting uncomfortably on the rush-seated chair. When spring came and they could meet outside the old magic would come alive again, or so she hoped.

So in the meantime she kept her hands busy at her needle and certainly the household kept her occupied: new lace to be stitched to pillowcovers, buttons to be replaced, dresses for fast-growing Phoebe and Esme, to say nothing of Naomi who had reached an age when the clothes of last year didn't match up to the new image of herself. Add to that a layette for Lucy's first baby expected in April and little wonder that the handle of the noisy sewing machine turned hour after hour, and even on James's visits Beth's needle still flew.

In January they struck an exceptionally cold spell, too cold even for snow. The earlier rain had given way to sleet and then frost, making roads and paths into sheets of ice and so they remained for days.

It was a Tuesday, Beth's regular day for going to Wilhampton and this time she went on the bus, glad of the speed with which the four horses covered the distance. Her basket was heavy with work to be returned, some to the Vicarage and some to the house on the High Street. Edith employed no sewing maid and most of the household stitching she did happily enough herself. Last week when Beth had arrived at the Vicarage she'd found Edith waiting by the fireside with Lucy, a pile of neatly folded garments on the stool.

'I told Mrs Hal to bring these petticoats over. I said you could do them for her, Beth. Take them with my things and if it's easier you may leave them with me on Tuesday.' Perhaps it was her condition that made her sound irritable – certainly the woman she was becoming was very different from the sweet girl of a few months ago.

'There's no advantage in her doing that, Lucy,' Edith said. 'She has to pass my door; she can hand them to Mrs Herbert.'

Beth's cheeks flamed. They spoke of her as if she weren't there! No 'Do you mind?', no 'Please' and next week probably no 'Thank you' either. She didn't trust her voice – and if she had she felt that neither of them would have heard her. 'One would think me invisible.'

That had been last Tuesday, before the rain turned to sleet and froze underfoot. She'd trudged home, for the bus had already left on its return trip to Tilmarsh where Merton Court was, then on to the outlying villages of Tamworth and Micklefield. Today she'd been glad of her old button boots; it was impossible to avoid all the puddles on the muddy road. Petticoats fit to grace any lady, yet Edith had found a lace edging she preferred so Beth must unpick all the neat stitching that some poor soul had put into the making of her trousseau and sit sewing on new lace, her hands often blue with cold as she worked. At the back of her mind was the thought of James. One day he'd alter her position, she'd be as fine as any of them and then they'd have to treat her differently.

She came no nearer to knowing any of them except little Pheobe who took every chance of being with her, but then Phoebe was no more than a lonely child glad of anyone's attention. As for his father, how could she hope to overcome a hurdle such as she was sure he would present. Except for the few minutes each morning when family and staff gathered in the hall she hardly saw him – and she doubted if he saw her at all! Promptly at seven o'clock he would join the assembled group waiting in the cold marble-floored hall, his Bible in his hand. He acknowledged their 'Good day, sir' with a slight nod of his head, then opened the book at the page he'd already held ready with the silk marker.

'Today we shall read from the Book of Isaiah, chapter two, starting at verse one . . .' or whatever had been his choice for the day's thoughts. She seldom listened to the words; she did mean to, but her thoughts had a nasty habit of wandering. He has a fine voice, she'd think without heeding what it said, and such good hands. James has beautiful hands too – not so strong as his father's though. I wonder whether the ice ever cracks, whether he ever loses his temper or even laughs. You wouldn't expect that James could have a father so cold, but his mother was warm and beautiful. He must take after his mother . . . Then she'd wake up to find the reading was over and the Collect for the day too, both missed entirely despite all her good intentions, and the mumbling voices around her were added to his clear lead of 'Our Father . . .' bringing the morning prayers to a close.

And that was as much as she knew of the man who could make or mar her future for, dream as she might, in her heart she knew that James would never stand up

46

against the wrath of 'Himself' as his father was called below stairs.

On this icy Tuesday she went first to the Vicarage for there was always a chance that Mrs Hal might go there. From the kitchen she was summoned to the drawing-room where she found Lucy lying on the chesterfield in front of the fire. Overweight at any time, six months pregnant she was already uncomfortably large, and the full skirts did little to hide her condition. Her face was red from the heat of the fire, not a healthy colour, and the deep shadows under her eyes spoke for themselves. In the kitchen at Merton Court it was said she was having a difficult time.

'Are you still feeling poorly? Oh I am sorry.' Beth's resentment was forgotten.

Lucy ignored her solicitude. 'I suppose I must look at what you've made.' She put her feet to the ground and heaved herself off the chesterfield. Only for a second did she stand then, eyes closed, she sat down heavily. 'Oh dear,' each breath was more like a sigh, 'oh dear, dear, dear. It was making me stand. You should see I'm not well. Dear, dear, oh dear ...' As she muttered to herself Beth seemed to be forgotten.

'Will you take some refreshment, Mrs Wentworth, would that help? Let me pull the bellcord to save you moving.'

Really the girl forgot her place! If food or drink (oh, the very thought) were needed she'd instruct her. 'I want nothing. Leave your work on the table, and thank you for your trouble.' Then with an unexpected flash of the pre-pregnant Lucy she said: 'Today I cannot even look at his clothes, he's making me too wretched. But thank you, Beth. Tell Mrs Hal I am giving you no work. Perhaps she can use you.'

'I have work a'plenty at the Court,' Beth flashed. 'Are you sure you should be alone? Would you prefer that I stay until this spasm passes?'

'Just leave me. Dear, dear, oh dear, dear ...'

Beth left her. Was she really as ill as she made believe or was she one of those dreadful women who liked a fuss? Never would she have expected it – Ludy'd always looked such a jolly girl. One thing was certain, the petticoats would be left at the servants' door with no request for work; with an empty basket to carry she could keep her cold hands tucked under her cloak.

She delivered the bundle, rolled up her basket and put it under her arm wrapping her long cloak about her, basket and all. Through the town she walked, head high, her usual cheerful nature soon asserting itself. When, Wilhampton not far behind her, she heard the clip-clop of a pony and when a moment later a trap drew alongside her, she looked round with pleasure; it must surely be James. Who else would stop for her?

'What brings you so far from home and on such a day?'

'The day is beautiful. Where better than under the open sky when it is such a blue,' her smile was friendly, giving no hint of the nervousness she felt when she found herself face to face with Mr Copeland. Even as she spoke she remembered how important this meeting was, for James's sake as well as her now. 'I have been to the Vicarage to take the clothes I have made for the coming baby.'

'Ah.' He climbed down from the trap and walked round to help her to the high seat. 'I called there too but Lucy had retired to her room. You had no chance to see her?'

'Oh yes sir, I found her in the drawing-room.' She settled herself comfortably on the bench seat as he climbed back to take his place at her side. This was the trap she'd first ridden in with James. She wished it had been he who'd met her today. They would have driven up the track into the woods, probably walked to the frozen pond. With an effort she called her wandering mind back. What was he saying?

'. . . never had any sickness. It appears that Lucy is to be like her mother. To me it seems unjust.'

'To be like her mother in any way could never be that.'

48

She had his full attention now. 'You remember her?'

'How could one forget her? She was a person of such warmth and gentleness. I remember when I was a child she used to call at our cottage, often carrying a basket of exciting things. Sometimes jam if Mrs Murphy had been making, or a bottle of wine. Father always said that one glass of Mrs Murphy's wine did more for him than a whole jug of ale from "The Owl and Crescent",' she chuckled. 'But it wasn't for the things she brought, simply for herself. Indeed I'll never forget her. If I close my eyes I can remember the scent of her, the smell of the fur cape around her shoulders and the softness of it. Once when I had been poorly she held me on her knee with my head against her shoulder – I buried my face against her, lovely, like violets. I've never known anyone like her.'

They drove on in silence. Beth's words had brought Isabella so close. Strange that this girl he'd thought to be a hoodlum should bring her nearer to him than any of their own children could. To bury his face in that soft fur, the warmth of her skin, the smell of her, the child had said, her soft voice . . .

Glancing sideways Beth tried to read his expression. Had she been too familiar? She couldn't guess his thoughts but there was something about him that made her speak impulsively, forgetting her position. That a chit of a girl should speak like that to 'Himself' hadn't entered her head, nor did it as she went on: 'Of course I remember her. Why everyone around you does and loves her too. That's the way we hold her with us still. If she's in your heart she'll be with you forever.'

He drew rein and turned to her, his penetrating look moving her so that her throat felt dry and closed. 'She's in my heart, but – I can't seem to – to draw on her. It's almost as if she'd been a figment of my imagination sometimes. You've brought her near and yet I hardly know you.'

'She was there all the time.' Beth forgot the cold – and

49

forgot her place too – and laid a hand on his arm. 'You just weren't looking in the right place.'

'When I came home each tea-time whatever she was doing she'd turn her head, always hold out a hand . . .' Silence, once unleashed the memories were crowding in. 'It's so empty, Beth. They're all so good – and I'm grateful – but no one knows . . .'

Beth's tell-tale green eyes were swimming. When she'd climbed into the trap she'd been full of determination to impress him with her bright chatter, she'd dig into her mind for intelligent conversation. Now all that was forgotten, she wanted just to help him. 'Do you talk about her to them? They must miss her too,' then as an afterthought, 'sir.'

'They talk about her. Mama did this, Mama taught me that – but I'm outside it. That's not my Bella. Child, forgive me, I've never talked like this to a soul.'

'We know each other so little don't we, families I mean? From somewhere we have to find strength to face what has to be faced – our own Queen even, she must feel just as you do. The Prince we all mourn must be so different from the Albert she alone would recognize; perhaps because we do mourn him publicly it might be making it harder for her to find comfort in her own Albert.'

Where did the child get her understanding, for she was surely little older than Millie? Yet she looked as though she'd seen visions. Too young to have been spoiled by living and yet as wise as time. The hand was still resting on his sleeve and as he became aware of it a concerned frown puckered his brow.

'You look frozen, child. Have you no muff?'

'I carried a basket, I needed my hands.'

'They're purple from cold. Here, take my gloves, they'll warm you.'

'Really? Oh thank you.' Wearing his gloves, sizes too large, she held out her hands and laughed delightedly.

50

'You must tell me if you want them, don't let yourself be cold.'

'My hands are usually warm.' He'd been strangely moved at the sight of hers. So small and pretty they could have been, but the knuckles were raw and chapped and deep cuts disfigured the fingers at each joint. Poor child, with hands like that to sit and sew in this weather.

It troubled him then and the memory returned time and again perhaps from the comfort of his own hearth or at the sight of his daughters' smooth skin. He pictured her as he'd handed her down from the trap, her unaffected laugh as she'd returned his gloves with: 'They were beautiful, I'm like toast now. Feel!' Then her hand against his. With her head held high there was something about her that defied pity yet made him want to protect her. The memory was to haunt him.

She had no idea whether she'd made any impression on him but in her own mind she lived the minutes of that homeward drive time and again. Remote? Proud? There was something beyond all that, something that disturbed her and she couldn't forget.

Perhaps other things would have put her out of Henry's mind in the normal course of events. His life was busy, his business thriving and filling his days, there was the anxiety over Lucy, mingled with the pleasure that Edith was to bear Hal a child. With the easing of winter's grip he must surely have forgotten Beth.

It was the end of February, and the family had been to morning service at St James's, the parish church of Tilmarsh. It was the family's custom to attend there, although nowadays they did join Lucy and Edward at St Agnes's on special occasions. Today was not such a one. The Reverend Gilstone, Esme and Naomi's tutor, excelled even himself during Lent and the services went from solemn to miserable. The harmonium had wheezed its way mournfully through the hymns and the sermon, which James had timed to have taken thirty-five minutes, had been rendered

51

in a voice so dreary that it was small wonder Mrs Crisp (the village's oldest inhabitant) had given up the battle and slept. Only her occasional and violent snores had relieved the monotony, those and Naomi's giggles which were made worse by her father's warning glare.

Coming home he spoke sharply to her. 'I was ashamed. Did you hear even the servants act so disgracefully, or Phoebe at half your age and less? You'll not behave like it in future, is that fully understood?'

'Papa, I am sorry, truly I am.' Then with an irrepressible twinkle. 'Twenty-nine snorts, I counted and I swear each one grew louder.'

'Hush,' Amelia whispered, for with more perception than her younger sister she could read the signs that her father was in no mood for jests.

From his seat where he held the reins of the pair of horses James sat silent. Where had she been this morning? Never before had Beth missed Sunday morning service, always sitting on her own away from the rest of the staff from the Court. He would have been surprised to know that his father's thoughts had followed the same channel, and were responsible for the scowl he turned on Naomi.

'Drive us straight to the stables, James. It's not cold. It will do us no harm to walk to the house.'

'It's no trouble to take you to the front, sir,. It'll save the mud of the yard.'

'Do as I say, if you please. A little mud can hardly harm one.'

James would have preferred to take the carriage to the front steps and then go on to the stables alone. How could he hope to see Beth with the family in tow? To their surprise it was she who came to help unharness the horses, her face always a mirror of her mind, now making no secret of her anxiety.

'What is it, Beth?' James forgot the family at the sight of her. 'Where's Syd?'

'He is back in his bed,' she answered briefly, then turned

52

to Mr Copeland. 'What should I do? For days he has had the gripes. He has struggled to keep going but seemed only to get worse. All night he's been ill but this morning he insisted he could manage – he couldn't though, I helped him harness the horses. Please,' those hands he'd thought of so often pulled at him, 'please will you come and see him. He's not like himself a bit.'

'You children, see to the horses, then go on to the house. I'll follow.'

'But Papa . . .' James floundered. To be pushed aside when Beth needed help wasn't right. It was to him she should have turned or so half of him said; the other half accepted his father's bidding, as he always had.

'I'll help you, James,' Amelia offered, already unbridling the horses. 'Papa and Beth must go to Syd.'

Syd had never been a man to make a fuss and in any case, as he'd told himself more than once over the past week, 'no man ever died of the gripes'. But by that Sunday he'd given up the struggle and gratefully returned to bed.

'. . . sorry 'bout this, sir, be up later . . .' He tried to sit up as the Master came in. The pain had momentarily eased and he spoke more rationally than he had earlier.

'You stay where you are, Syd. I'm sending young James straight off to fetch Doctor Bailey to have a look at you. I shall wait until he's been.'

Beth was conscious of a weight being lifted. All night she'd hardly shut her eyes and this morning had had to help Syd out of his clothes to get him back to bed. Gripes, colic, whatever they chose to call it, in his worst moments he'd been helpless without her. His involuntary moans as he'd been bent double in pain had made her aware of her uselessness; she'd not know what to do to comfort him. If anything happened to Syd – oh, but what nonsense, as if anything could. He'd never been ill in his life – but if it did? As long as she could remember he'd been behind her, dear kind, solid Syd.

With Henry Copeland's coming the responsibility was

lifted, her fears disappeared. She'd nurse him, she'd fetch and carry, and do whatever was needed; but the doctor was coming. Henry had known what to do and had acted straightaway. For all her anxiety she felt safe again.

James was sent to bring Doctor Bailey, the patient was examined, pummelled and poked until he cried out in agony. Medicine was given.

'I'm grateful, thank you, sir.' She stood at the head of the wooden stairs with the Master, the doctor having already gone.

'I'll come over this evening. I dare say he'll start to feel better soon now that he's taken something, but for a while James will take care of the horses. You're not to attempt to. You have enough on your hands.' As he said it he looked at those little hands, less chapped now the days were warmer but rougher than he cared to see all the same.

The next day Doctor Bailey returned, shook his head, pushed, probed, gave more medicine. That was Monday and Monday night was the third to find Beth sleepless. From the start it was obvious it would be useless even to take off her clothes, Syd needed her constantly. His colic continued and by now he was too weak to move from his bed.

'. . . Bethie . . . sorry . . .' He clenched his teeth in pain.

'Silly,' she took a cool sponge and wiped the sweat from his face. 'Doctor Bailey said he'd try some different medicine if you weren't easier by tomorrow. Syd – Syd – ' She bent close to him. 'Can you hear me? Is it getting easier?'

Something about him was different. After that last wrenching pain he'd changed. His eyes were open, his breathing fast, but he seemed not to see her.

'Syd! Syd!' If only he'd give some sign, just try to answer. The clock ticked loudly, the only sound except for his shallow panting breath as the hours of the night passed.

The next morning Mr Copeland too saw the change and sent James straight off again to fetch Doctor Bailey. The doctor had no faith in the knife; it was something to be avoided until the very last resort.

'If he shows no improvement by tomorrow I'm afraid there's no alternative.'

CHAPTER THREE

From that cold day in January her sore roughened hands had haunted Henry, and seeing her vain attempts to help her brother he'd discovered a spirit to match them in determination. What was to become of her if she were left without Syd? From the look of him and from what Doctor Bailey had said away from Beth's hearing he knew his passing was something to be considered. Mrs Murphy would make a bed for her in the house, he supposed, or she'd go away to join her family. Somehow neither alternative satisfied him. She wasn't like any of the other servants, nor yet like her family either. There was something in her spirit that set her apart; he'd known no one like her. He came frequently to the coach-house where Syd tossed and groaned. He watched her as she tended him and he marvelled at her courage, the tasks she undertook without flinching. It wasn't just for her care that he admired her, it was some indefinable quality in her, her acceptance of life as if she didn't question anything that came yet kept faith in the future. It was the trust in her clear green eyes that tugged at his heart. A way to help her had to be found.

Phoebe put the idea into his mind quite unconsciously.

'I shall call at the coach-house of course before we go, James,' he said during breakfast on the Thursday, the morning that turned out to be Syd's last. 'While I see Syd you'll attend to the trap if you please.'

'Yes, sir.' It should be he who called on Beth. How tired she must be getting; they ought to have Syd taken away to the infirmary.

'Papa, when can I see Beth? She reads to me and, Papa, she is teaching me how to read too.'

The child's interruption at the table went unrebuked: 'Beth is? Surely this is your responsibility, Amelia.' He turned towards her frowning, 'Were you aware of this?'

'Yes, Papa. I have tried but Beth does it so much better. She teaches her to stitch too and – '

'And to sing, Papa,' Phoebe chimed in, spurred on by the lack of correction that she should be joining in the talk at the table. 'Beth has such a pretty voice. She teaches me about flowers and the birds. She has taught me to add up and to take away, we do it with buttons – '

'How is it you aren't attending to your duties, Amelia? Surely such things aren't beyond you?'

'No, Papa, of course I can add up and take away and read and teach Phoebe her letters, but she never learnt from me as well as she does from Beth. 'Tis a pity her station isn't higher. She would make a truly excellent tutor.'

'The trap, James, when you've eaten. I shall be in the coach-house. Amelia be sure you keep Phoebe from worrying Beth for the time being – we shall have to consider this.' He seemed keen to be gone, leaving James still not halfway through his plate of cold meat.

That morning he looked at Beth with new eyes, seeing more than her bright trusting gaze, her willing but roughened hands, her neat dress and shining curls. He listened to her voice with a critical ear. Was she fit to instruct Phoebe? In honesty he could find no fault with her soft tone. Everything about her belied her background. Perhaps Bella has seen it too when she'd held her on her knee all those years ago. Beth had told him she would never forget; he believed there had been an empathy between them for hadn't she recognized in Bella the spirit he'd known himself? All that day Bella seemed very close and when the next morning Beth told him Syd's battle was over he knew exactly what must be done and just as surely he knew it was what Bella would have wanted.

He ended that day satisfied that the girl was safely taken

care of. Now that she was to be settled in the house he'd be able to forget the whole issue. Phoebe's instruction would be ensured for a few years until she was old enough to go to Reverend Gilstone, the household sewing would still be attended to, the wheels would turn smoothly and a worry be lifted. It may not have been a conscious thought on his part but at the back of his mind was a feeling of relief that Beth would be there to support Amelia. All he told himself was: 'Well, the girl will be cared for and no doubt earn her keep and I need worry my head no longer on her account.'

Yet as the months of spring came he was to watch Phoebe's progress with interest, taking every opportunity to go to the nursery where she was having her lessons. Of course it was the child he cared about; strange though, he'd taken no interest when Millie had been her tutor.

Beth surveyed her new surroundings, surroundings that seemed to share the dream-like quality of these last few days. A week ago Syd had been struggling to carry out his work, believing his pains were due to something he'd eaten. Now he'd been carried away in the undertaker's cart and she'd been brought to the house and given this room adjoining the nursery. Her hand stretched out to the heavy curtains, deep red, warm and rich compared with any that had covered her windows before. The room had at one time belonged to a former governess, that was until Naomi and Esme had started to go each day to Reverend Gilstone. Not as well furnished as the household bedrooms but so much prettier than Beth had ever had before. The wooden floor had on it three good-sized rush mats, the wall paper was dark red with a pattern in brown, the washstand had a marble top with a pink and white basin and jug (the jug full of water for her needs) and on the platform under it stood a matching chamber pot and enamel pail. There was even a wicker chair at the bedside

58

and a walnut wardrobe so large that her few clothes looked lost and two of the four drawers remained empty.

No wicks to trim and light here; the chain that hung from the gas bracket adjusted the glow from the flame. Gently she pulled it to the right, the room flooded with light and the gas hissed. Perhaps it shouldn't be as fierce as that but how exciting to control it herself, soft rich shadows or clear brilliance at a touch. She hadn't liked the hiss it made though so she pulled the chain again to the left cutting down the brightness. When she sewed she'd be able to see her stitches without having to sit huddled to the lamp, partly for warmth and partly for light. Here in the nursery next to her room a fire burned in the grate in the wall.

The days had passed like a dream, for all the certainty she'd always had that destiny was shaping her future.

A warning tap announced Amelia's arrival and it struck Beth just as it so often did Henry how like her mother this dark-eyed gentle girl was.

'I expect it all seems strange, Beth, but you'll soon settle and Phoebe is looking forward to her lessons. Has everything been brought over from the coach-house? Matthews looked after your boxes.'

'I had nothing except my clothes and a few books. Thank you, it's all here.' James had helped her but she didn't tell his sister that. Time was on her side now. She smiled, with just enough gratitude in her manner, or so she hoped, enough but not too much. Somehow she had to make Amelia her ally, somehow she had to bridge that impossibly wide social gap. She must show respect without servitude, she must win confidence – while ever increasingly, unknown to the rest of the family, she would become more necessary to James. If that warning voice whispered to her she didn't listen. Always she'd put her trust in fate, and what other reason could fate have had in bringing her here to his home? Her path was clear.

Only later lying in her new bed (the feather mattress so

59

deep and warm, making her straw palliasse of the coach-house worlds away) did she remember Syd. She was ashamed; all her thoughts had been centred on herself, when only last night, less than twenty-four hours back, he'd still struggled for breath. Now he'd been taken away and her own life uprooted, the excitement of what had happpened to her overriding everything.

With the habit of childhood training she climbed out of her bed and knelt on the floor. Purposely she moved off the mat, the wood hard on her knees a penance for her wandering and selfish thoughts. Hands together, eyes tight-closed, she remembered her brother, a good many years older and so, through her early years, a protector more than a friend. They'd never been very close, never quite understood each other's thoughts, but they'd loved each other nonetheless. She asked that his soul would be given rest and peace, his pains forgotten. Then her prayer took on a familiar note: 'Take care of him, please, God. He didn't have much fun while he was here, let it be better for him now. And thank You for bringing me here. Please don't let me make mistakes; You know the sort of thing I mean.' She sat back on her heels, settling for a companion-able chat with her Maker. 'There's so much I'm not sure about. Should I say Miss Amelia, Miss Naomi? I know I should but You see I'm to be their sister – with Your help of course,' she remembered to add. 'It would be better if they could start to think of me as a person right away, if You could please put those sort of thoughts in their minds. Oh dear, there I go again. Please forgive me, it was Syd I was praying about. Please, Lord, bless his spirit and take him to live in your heavenly kingdom. I know You have. He must be there now.'

For a second or two she knelt up extra straight, head bowed as if to put the seal of respect on her plea, then assured that Syd was in good hands she climbed back into the glorious depths of the soft mattress. She'd stay awake and think of all that was waiting for her: James who said he loved her, his father — fancy being frightened of him, how blue his eyes were, how safe he made her feel — she'd think of Phoebe — she wasn't frightened of him, you could tell from the comfortable way she'd slip her hand into his — his hands, beautiful, strong, 'My hands are usually warm . . .'

So soon she slept.

Lucy gave birth to a son, a birth so difficult that they feared they'd lose her and in her final hours of agony she'd almost wished to die. Little Edwin was more than a month old before she was allowed to leave her bed. He was cared for by Mrs Edgewick, the same lying-in nurse who had attended Isabella on the last three occasions. The child was small and wrinkled, not a bit what one would have expected with stalwart Edward for a father and plump Lucy for a mother. Who would think one so tiny could have made her life so difficult all these months or caused so much trouble coming into the world? Lucy lay flat with the foot of her bed raised on wooden blocks, only sitting to take food or try and feed the child. Margaret, tall, long-backed and angular, had already borne three children with apparent ease, yet there was nothing maternal in her make-up. Lucy had always been the motherly one, the sister Hal and James had taken their troubles to, the one who'd showered love on Naomi and Esme and the baby Phoebe when their mother had been taken.

'Come now, Miss Lucy' (for to Mrs Edgewick so she still was even if she was married to the vicar) 'just harken to him. Sit yourself up now. 'Tis time to suckle our young man. You're ready for it aren't you, my hinney?' she cooed at the screaming bundle in her arms.

Lucy struggled to sit, she unbuttoned her nightgown and took the heavy breast in her hand. Why should they imagine she was full of milk to nourish the baby? She'd always been large. For ten days he'd been brought to her

61

every three hours, day and night, but he was never satisfied.

'I'll ring when I need you.' She wanted to scream, 'Just go away, leave me alone.'

The door closed behind the black-clad figure and, shutting her eyes, Lucy let her body respond to the wild and indefinable love that surged through her, a love that united her with this tiny child, his blue eyes fixed unblinkingly on her. This was culmination of all the miserable months, the final agonizing hours; this was the very reason for her existence. She was revolted by the unclean state of her torn body, sickened and frightened to look ahead to years of marriage and her duty to Edward. There was love in her only for this perfect little creature. For him she'd suffered – and only she knew how she'd suffered – now he was hers, hers alone, her trusting, perfect love ... The little head turned away and with his face red and mouth wide open yelled. Her moment of joy was over, the battle to find enough to satisfy him, and invariably have it thrown back at her, followed its usual miserable pattern. Twenty minutes later she gave up the struggle and rang the bell by her bedside.

'Put him in the nursery,' she greeted Mrs Edgewick. 'Then come back to me before you see to him. I need cleaning. It's been just a waste of time and I should be lying down. I shall need a fresh gown and I think bedding too. Oh, how he screams! If he felt as wretched as I do he'd have cause to scream.' Her eyes were swimming in tears, frustration at her inadequacy, distaste for her body. 'Take him away, then hurry back to see to me.'

The only way she resembles her dear mother is the trouble she had in giving birth, was Mrs Edgewick's silent comment, but her face was expressionless as Edwin was passed back to her still yelling.

Lying against her pillows Lucy heard the nurse's footsteps retreat and the cries grow fainter. The warm trickle of blood, the warm trickle of tears ... That life had been a happy thing only months ago seemed impossible; now she'd sunk into a slough of misery that saw no hope. Was this marriage? To recover from one birth (if indeed she ever did recover) for her duty to lead her to another? Wasn't that what her mother's life must have been? Strange to think of her. Now she felt she could have understood her so much better. The tears rolled unheeded down her cheeks and were salty on her lips. If she had a mother to talk to it might help her.

Footsteps were coming along the corridor. She ignored the discomfort of moving her tightly swathed body and wriggled to lie down, pulling the covers to her chin and shutting her eyes. Edward would only peep in quietly and, seeing her asleep, she knew he'd creep away.

The door was flung wide and in surprise she turned her head to see who could disturb her with so little ceremony.

'Well, my girl, feeling better now?' In his brown-and-white checked sackcoat and vest her father looked out of place, vigorously healthy; nothing of the sick-visitor about him. He threw his brown bowler hat on to the armchair and came to the bedside, seeming to bring a breath of the outdoors with him.

'Why, child, crying?' The bed creaked as he sat heavily on it. 'Nothing to cry about now surely. You've a fine son, a good start to a family to have a son first, you and Edward have got it the right way round. Now what you need is a blow of God's fresh air.' His expression told her that the bedroom smelt stale and unpleasant, lying here day after day she hadn't realized it, as the air became putrid.

He flung the bottom window up, pulled the top one open and then shut the bottom. 'Let some of this out. No wonder you look pasty.'

'Oh Papa . . .' She turned her face away. 'You've no idea . . .'

'There now, it wasn't that bad, Lucy. Your mother used to take it hard too, but afterwards she always said once it

63

was over it was gone from the mind. And each time she
. . . ah well, you'll see for yourself, child.'

'Each time! Each time!'

'You'll feel differently when you're on your feet. It's
nature. You're a good wife and you'll be a good mother.'

'You say it wasn't so bad! What do you know about it?'

Even her voice was different, full of venom unknown to
the chubby girl she'd been. Henry conjured up a picture of
Bella, gentle and uncomplaining, thankful when each
battle was won and the baby safe in her arms. He tried
once more: 'He's a fine boy, Lucy, a good set of lungs.'

'He's hungry, he's always hungry. That's why he
screams. I told nurse to come and see to me. Papa, on your
way out send her through. She knows I need her.' The
reddened eyelids closed and her whining tone made it clear
that her lot was one of misery and neglect.

He got up from the bed, crossing to the chair for his hat.
'I'll leave you then.' He came back to kiss her forehead.
'Perhaps by my next visit you'll feel better. Just you
remember to thank your God for a safe delivery and a
healthy son – the harder the birth the more reason for our
gratitude that all's well. But with Edward for a husband
you won't need your father to remind you of your duty.'

Had she even heard him? Her round face gave no sign,
her lips still drooped petulantly and when she spoke all she
said was: 'I feel a draught from that window. Push it up,
Papa, before you go.'

He ignored the request and left her, passing Mrs Edgewick waiting outside the nursery door, a jug of warm
water and a pile of clean linen on the landing table ready
for her use.

The visit left him depressed and disappointed, worried
about Edwin too. Such a wizened little fellow and with a
mother seemingly unable to provide for him. Instead of
going to the foundry, early though it was, he went home.
If only Bella were here she'd be able to understand and
help Lucy and to lift his own spirits. Yet it was ridiculous

of him to let himself be so cast down by young Lucy. Women often went through a moody patch after child-birth, or so he'd heard. It was surely no more than that.

Amelia was in the orchard gathering a bunch of wild daffodils. She waved and started towards him as he slowed the trap.

'No need to come in,' he called. 'Get along with what you're doing.'

'Are you sure, Papa? I'll come if you wish, truly.'

'No, no. I have a good deal to do. You enjoy the sunshine.' He drove on. Why should he feel guilty? Millie was happy with her flowers.

He'd lied though. Once in the library he had no intention of working; it was no more than an escape. They tried so hard, these children of his, watching him, fitting their mood to his, talking as if to protect him from himself, but what he needed was the companionship of a shared silence, what he needed was — what? Amelia's smiling obedience, Lucy's resentment, James's ill-disguised indifference to the working hours they shared, the girls with their giggling dreams of adolescence, Hal with his mind so full of Edith and their coming child, little Phoebe and her warmth; all of them dear to him. Wasn't he then surrounded by the ones he loved?

Leaving his hat on the hall stand he climbed the stairs two at a time and turned along the corridor to the nursery. He needed the unspoken understanding he knew she was capable of giving. Age had nothing to to with it. So young that Isabella had taken her on her knee yet with wisdom even then to recognize that dear spirit. Old enough to earn her living by the skill of those sore, chapped hands he'd never forgotten, yet innocent as a babe as she'd rejoiced in the clear blue of the sky.

His step quickened as he neared the nursery, but when he flung the door open on the empty room he was unprepared for the shock of disappointment. Only then

65

did he realize how like a homing pigeon he'd hurried to find her – and the realization didn't please him.

Lucy gave herself up to Mrs Edgewick's efficient hands. Soon she was in a fresh gown and lying between cool, clean sheets. Her father's obvious distaste for the sickroom had shamed her even though she hadn't admitted it and as well as clean clothes she'd insisted on being washed and toilet water sprinkled on the bed. At last she was alone and feeling almost wholesome again.

The next time a tap came at the door it opened quietly on Edward. 'I came along just now but Mrs Edgewick said she was on her way to make you pretty' (not her exact words!) 'You look better, more like Lucy again.'

'I'm tired – Papa came – I think I'd like to sleep for a while. You don't mind do you, Edward?'

'There's no need for you to lie here alone you know, Lucy. I could bring my books in here. I've some writing to see to.'

'Go to your study, Edward, I'll rest better on my own.'

'Then do that, my dear. The sooner you're yourself again the better I shall be pleased.'

Didn't he know how she felt? She heard the door close after him but as soon as he'd gone sleep was miles away. He'd want to start it all again, everything he expected of her. She'd have no more children; she'd not go through that again! If they were wanting more family she'd accept, after all that was the way it was ordained. She bit her lip and turned her head into the pillow. It wasn't the act of love-making that repelled her, not when one wanted to create from it a new life, but she was haunted by her revulsion of all that went with it – and no child would come of that. If she'd have no more family, is that what he'd demand of her? She was sick at the thought, her body no longer her own.

Above all else she loved Edwin and she longed to escape to be just with him.

On that same afternoon Beth had been tempted out by the spring sunshine and she and Phoebe had carried their book to the riverside. There, with complete disregard for decorum, she'd taken off her slippers and stockings then, holding up her skirts, had clambered down the bank to pick rushes. Much too lovely a day for concentration on their reader, or so they both thought.

When James caught sight of them as he crossed the bridge on his way home, they were on the far side of the meadow and too busy plaiting their rushes to notice, so it wasn't until he was nearly on them that Phoebe called: 'James, look, Jamie, Beth's teaching me to plait rushes. She can make lots of things, baskets, mats . . . she's going to teach me.'

He joined them. 'Beth is clever indeed, and you, young Phoebe, are the luckiest little girl for all the hours you have with her.'

'Oh yes, I know. And do you know what else . . .' on she prattled.

But James wasn't listening. Sitting close to the barefoot Beth he went on speaking softly, just for her ears: 'Had I but half the hours with her my life would find the purpose it lacks.'

'No life should lack a purpose, it is a sin.'

'I seem to get no nearer, Beth. The weeks go on – '

'We need a few more rushes, Phoebe. Take off your shoes and stockings and see if you can get them but carefully, just along there where the cattle come to drink and the water is shallow.' Without a second bidding Phoebe busied herself with her buckles, her elders forgotten. This was even better! 'Hush James, wait a while.'

Once Phoebe was out of earshot he tried again: 'Since you've been at the house I have no chance to see you.

Before, at least I could come to the coach-house, but now there is always someone . . . even in the evenings now that you eat supper with us I can never really be with you.'

'Why, that's nonsense. Often I sew by your fireside, I am there when you play the piano, I am there when we sing our hymns on Sundays.'

'You know very well what I mean, Beth. Have you forgotten those evenings, here on this very spot?'

'Dear, James, of course I've not forgotten.' Perhaps not, but how far away it seemed. 'Did you not say yourself that it must take time for me to know your family and they me? Surely that is happening.'

'Oh, what's the use! They know you as they knew Miss Hepworth who lived with us before the girls went to Reverend Gilstone, or that Mrs Dickson where you used to sew. What use is that?'

What use indeed!

'And how can I make them see me differently? I am as I am, James, the same now as I'll be if one day I'm your wife – or anyone else's.'

'You'll be no one else's! How can you even say that? Have you not already given yourself to me? Oh Beth, listen to me, let me come to your room. Tonight – hey? What do you say? No one would ever know, I'd come late, after my father's abed. Just you and me again, Beth, please, I beg . . .'

'No, James, it could never be right like that, there in your father's house. How can you suggest it? Have you no respect for any of us, your sisters, me, him?' And what if someone heard him, how long would she be kept at the Court? She'd believed herself to be in love with James (well, of course she must be) but that was no part of her plans. Life away from the Court was unthinkable. 'James, what we did last summer was natural; it was all part of the wonder of what happened to us. But now we must wait. It would be degrading. I wish I could explain better what I feel. Perhaps to a woman these things are not the same, but, James, I'd feel like a harlot if you were to creep into my room while your family slept. I could not look them in the eyes. Very well for you, if you think it right to use me like that – '

'Use you? Oh, Beth, how can you say it like that?'

'And how else would it be, to come stealthily to my bed, you the master, me the maid? That's the way it would seem to everyone, and to me too. But it wasn't like that last summer.'

'Nor ever will be, Beth, I swear it.'

Glancing sideways at him she saw a new resolution on his face, and she turned away. Well played, Beth – perhaps that might stir him to action!

'Turn your back, James. I'm going to put my stockings on.' The time had come to change the conversation. 'Phoebe,' she called, 'bring what you have and let me dry your feet. Have you a large handkerchief, James?'

Suddenly the atmosphere was light. Phoebe's feet dried, the rushes gathered into a bunch and tied with the damp handkerchief, the three of them set out for home. Holding hands, with Phoebe in the middle and Beth carrying the 'bouquet', the sang as they part walked and part skipped and part marched, suiting their steps to their songs. Phoebe laughed delightedly. Life had never been so good before Beth took control.

For all James's determination the pattern remained unchanged and with summer, if only she had wanted, there could have been opportunities enough for those hours he craved with Beth. Each evening as dusk fell he wandered outside, for surely one day she'd follow; but she knew better and no matter how tempted she might be by the warm night-scented air or the need in her to be told again that she was loved, she knew that to follow James now would be wrong. There was something in her, something she couldn't fathom, that told her she could no longer lie with James by the riverside. In truth, many an evening as she went back to the solitary nursery and sniffed the summer air through the open window, she'd remember her days of 'freedom' with longing. At the cottage with her family no one had bothered where she went or what she did; they were busy and she had always been one on her own. If she wanted to walk up the hill in a thunderstorm or bathe in the cold river or lie under the stars, then more fool her. All her life she'd been the wayward one; they'd long since ceased to concern themselves. She worked and brought home her few shillings each week, she'd always been healthy and even-tempered, and what went on in her mind had been her own affair.

When a letter from her mother told her of the family's change of plans, what then held her back from accepting what surely was an adventure? This was a very different proposition from a factory in Oldbury. This was a new life, a New World. For they were sailing at the end of July to Canada, that colony in North America. There would be work there for her father on the railroad – a speaker had come to the Town Hall in Oldbury trying to recruit people to emigrate from all they knew, to leave their disappointments and make a fresh start. Her mother stated the facts – letter writing didn't come easily to her – but behind the few stark sentences Beth could recognize the pent-up longings that had once burnt bright in Jane Machin. Did she want to come with them? Her mother had written never doubting Beth's reply. A year ago she would have gone without a backward glance. Strange, for a year ago wasn't she spending her hours and her summer evenings with James? The realization disturbed her.

In August was the Festival of St James, and the village prepared for the usual Wake. The foundry was closed for this annual event, so were the shops, even the offices, for no man could be expected to work and miss it. In the kitchen at the Court food had been prepared in advance and Jenny, the parlourmaid, had saved up for a more splendid hat than she'd ever worn before.

'And very handsome you look, dearie,' Mrs Murphy boosted her flagging confidence as she came down the backstairs with the flower-trimmed 'pancake' topping her straw-coloured hair. An exaggeration, for by no standards was fat Jenny handsome, but with the eagerness left over from a childhood not far behind she was ready for the big day.

'Algy is getting the carriage ready for them for church,' Mrs Murphy said, casually enough, but she missed nothing and she watched the girl's expression.

'Aw! Gotter take them, 'as 'e? Can't 'e be comin' wi' us?' In her disappointment Jenny's aitches went down like ninepins.

'Taking themselves they are, then on to Miss Lucy's for their meal. So we'll walk together to the church and after that you can have the day.'

'All day? Oh Mrs Murphy, you sure? Cor, thank you, Mrs Murphy. Me and Algy'll be at the fair right after parson's finished wi' us. The mummers are comin' from Wilhampton and you mind that teller from last year? Wonder if she'll come again. Makes you go 'ot and cold Mrs Murphy — our Syd went to see her, crossed her palm an' all and she wouldn't tell 'im nothing. Makes you cold with fright.'

'Don't waste your money on her, child. You get what the Lord sends you in this world. No good trying to dodge it and a waste of silver to know beforehand. Ah, there goes Mr James for the Victoria; they'll be off in a minute. Time we were all of us ready too. Wonder if young Milady expects to ride with them.'

'Likely she'll walk with us do you think?'

Mrs Murphy sniffed: 'Likely she'll not! She never has. Lady High and Mighty.'

Jenny went to the window to crane her neck so that

71

from the area kitchen she could just see the gravel in front of the main steps.

'They're coming out now – yes, she's going too. Oh but isn't she a picture though, Mrs Murphy, ma'am? Look they're all outside waiting for Mr James, you can see from just here. Here 'e is now. Cor, there's Himself handing her up like she was a duchess. Look, ma'am! Wonder what she's saying to 'im, 'e's laughing ever so friendly. Cor I'd be scared 'alf to death, such an 'aughty one 'e seems.'

'Naughty – oh come, Jenny! The Master?'

''aughty, proud like . . .'

'Ah, I see. Time was when he was different, easier you understand me, when his poor dear wife was alive. Lonely for him now, just the children. Needs a good woman to care for him and run things.'

'Aw, you run the house lovely, Mrs Murphy. And we all does our best to keep things going nice.'

'Yes you do, all of you, and I do my best too. It's not what I mean though. It's someone to sit at his hearth with him he needs, a bit of company as he gets older, take him out of that library where he shuts himself away.'

'Misses Mr Hal, that's the trouble,' kind-hearted Jenny was no fool. 'Well now, you look nice too, Mrs Murphy ma'am. You put a new ribbon on yer hat, haven't yer? Don't mean to be pushy; you don't mind me saying?'

No one else would dare compliment Mrs Murphy on her dress, and certainly not comment on her efforts to up-date her hat, but in her clumsy way the honest Jenny had found a soft spot unknown to the rest of them.

Young Cyril Matthews joined them, looking sheepish in his best suit, its straight-legged checked trousers and dark short jacket and waistcoat never failing to make him self-conscious by its elegance. That it had belonged to someone else before him no one would have guessed for luckily the son of his previous 'family' had been just his size. His flat bowler had known no head but his own and the spotted cravat, new for today, added the final touch of glory.

72

Kathie the kitchenmaid was heard running down the back stairs, then a step in the passage from the yard announced Algy and old Ben. The staff were ready to celebrate St James and if they looked on the hour in church as the pill to be swallowed before making for the village green, who could blame them? There was nothing new in attending a service (they sat in the same hard pew each week), but days of holiday were rare. A fortune teller (if Mrs Murphy weren't looking Jenny was tempted to give her piece of silver), Morris men, mummers, sideshows, booths where one could buy cakes or ale, ribbons or trinkets; there'd be a pig to be bowled for and this year even a second chance to win one by the first person to climb the greasy pole erected in the middle of the green. Not that any of the staff from Merton Court would be able to compete for that. That was all very well for the rag, tag and bobtail in their working clothes. Perhaps Korinski and his dancing bear would be there; it must be three years ago he came and was remembered for months after. No wonder they all hurried towards the church, keen to get the service over and be on their way.

The afternoon's activities were well under way when the carriage skirted the green on its way home. The village band was having difficulty making itself heard above the cries of the sellers shouting their wares, the hurdy-gurdy, the cheers as some stalwart slid down the few feet he'd managed to scale the pole, the screams of a child, and the barking of a dog rushing wildly through the crowd. Certainly none of the staff noticed it, but why should they? 'We'll be home for late supper,' Amelia had said, making it clear that everyone was free for the whole day.

Henry had the reins and on Beth's knee sat Phoebe, a shawl wrapped round her and only an occasional hic-coughing snort telling of the tears that had gone before.

'Soon be home, sweetling,' Beth whispered, to be answered with a convulsive sniff.

This would be the first year that Beth hadn't been out

there heart and soul in the fun, but today she hardly spared a glance as they drove past. Esme looked on it warily; it wasn't the noise and bustle she shied away from so much as the ability these folk had to forget themselves in their brief patch of wholehearted pleasure. Come rain or shine today was their big day. There would be nothing to equal it for a whole year, for the Mop Fair that came to Wilhampton in the autumn had its serious side as well as its jollification. Fine for the lucky ones who came just for the sport of it, but underlying it would be the line of jobless who waited to be hired for the coming twelve months; only when their future was settled would they be able to abandon themselves to the celebrations. Today though there was nothing but pleasure, and looking at the sea of happy faces Esme's set in a frown of disapproval, determined to hid any hint of envy at their ability to forget themselves in the fun. Well enough for Naomi. Didn't they all know that if Papa were to stop the carriage and let them step down and join the merrymaking, in a flash Naomi would be one with it all? While she? Her chin went up, then her baleful glare fell on Phoebe.

'For mercy's sake, stop your snivelling. I really wonder Papa allowed her to come at all. It would have been far better without her. She's been whining all day. She and Beth could have stayed at home.'

Another snort from the little girl. Beth held her close. It was so unlike Phoebe to behave as she had today, tears at the slightest word, no appetite for her dinner – and no graciousness in refusing it either, Beth thought as she recalled the scene at the table. Indeed Esme might well be right; it would have been a happier day for all of them if she and Phoebe had stayed at home. To sit at Lucy's table, yet know herself not accepted as one of them, had been the most humiliating hour in her memory. The men had talked together, only James giving an ear to the ladies, and he'd been no support. At the start Beth had entered into the feminine conversation, for surely she knew every bit as

74

much as any of them as they spoke of fashion, menus, babies. Heavens above, but their minds are narrow! Have they no learning of anything beyond their own little lives, no interest in a world bursting with new ideas, new thinking? She would rather have added her voice to those of the men but instinct told her that that would diminish her even further in the eyes of the women. She'd never before experienced that feeling of wanting to creep away unnoticed, for it soon became obvious that any comments from her were to be ignored. That she should try to take part in their conversation appeared to embarrass them. The atmosphere must surely be noticeable to everyone at the table. Phoebe felt it, not understanding but sensing the animosity towards her dear Beth, the resentment, and probably jealousy too if any of them had been honest enough to acknowledge it. The effect on her had been tears, tummy ache she'd said, and a fit of behaviour so out of character with her placid nature that soon after the meal Henry had ordered James to get the carriage. That the cause of her scene had been anything other than physical hadn't entered his head for he'd paid no attention to the women's chatter. Only James had been aware of it, he'd been embarrassed on Beth's account and had let her glimpse his feet of clay.

'See to the carriage, James, if you please.' Henry climbed down as he reined in the horses at the steps to the front door. 'I'll take her, Beth. Pass her to me.'

Beth stood Phoebe on the floor of the carriage. 'Down you go, hinney.'

'Stay on hand, James. I may want you to go for Doctor Bailey.' Perhaps the memory of Syd lingered. 'Does it still hurt you, dear? Tell me where the pain is.' Gently he lifted the chubby little girl from the carriage and carried her up the steps.

'You take her to the nursery and I'll make her some warm bread and milk. She's had nothing,' Beth spoke with

75

authority. Gone now was her humiliation, her only concern was for Phoebe.

'Bring it to the library, Beth, will you, she likes to be in there with me.'

It took Beth a little while to warm the milk, the great kitchen range had been banked up to last the day and was smouldering in a cheerless way. 'Come on, you black devil.' She jabbed the poker into the lifeless coals; 'burn, can't you, burn.' Even lifting the lid off the range and putting the iron pan directly on to the fuel, it was ten minutes before the milk was warm enough to be poured on the crumbled bread and in that ten minutes Henry had been allowed to share a secret with Phoebe that might have accounted for the penetrating look he gave Beth as she came into the library.

'You'll like this, Phoebe. Doesn't it smell good?' Her anxiety for the little girl was hidden behind her encouraging smile.

'I'll put this big cushion on my chair and you sit at my desk, there's a good girl. We'll both stay with you while you eat it all up.'

'Thank you. Smells nice, Beth. I'm going to eat every bit because, do you know, I'm enormously hungry?' Phoebe was herself again and over her head they looked at each other in relief.

'Too much excitement I dare say,' was Henry's comment, that same feeling he'd had once before that Beth should be protected making it vital to him to keep from her his knowledge of the truth.

A light tap on the door – for none of the family ever came unannounced into the library, it was a rule instilled in them from early childhood – and James appeared.

'Is she better? Will you need me to fetch the doctor, sir?'

'No, she's eating. It seems to have passed. Thank you James, there'll be no need.'

'In that case I thought I'd go to the village – win the pig perhaps, eh?' Today was his golden opportunity. In front

76

of his father, taking his courage in both hands, he turned to Beth: 'And you, Beth? Surely today is a holiday for you too. Why do you not join me? They're having great games. I'd have you home by Phoebe's bedtime.'

'Go if you wish, Beth. As he says, today is a holiday.'

Somehow she couldn't quite look at James as she refused. This should have been an important step yet something held her back.

With a pout James went, mumbling something about taking the girls. What had stopped her? The Wake alone was an attraction but to be there with James and with his family's knowledge, what more could she want?

'I'm glad you're staying with us aren't you, Papa?'

Henry was looking out of the window, his back to them.

'Papa – aren't you glad?'

'Yes, of course, as long as you really don't want to go Beth?'

'No, really I don't want to go.'

Strange how keen she suddenly became when only half an hour or so later, James and the girls having gone off together, she changed her mind. When Phoebe said she'd never been to the Wake one thing followed another. Her own reminiscences seemed to awaken Henry's memories of the times, so long ago, when he'd taken Isabella. Phoebe looked from one to the other as they talked.

'Do you remember the huge man, I never did know his name, he had a block of wood with nails in and you had to swing a huge mallet? Every year he came, you surely remember . . .?'

'Indeed yes, I can see him now. If you hammered a nail right home you won a rabbit – I never did.' He chuckled, seeing it again in his mind, remembering how as a young bridegroom he'd wanted to acquit himself well in front of Isabella.

'I doubt he ever parted with a rabbit. It would have taken a giant to swing that mallet.'

'And the tumblers, they used to come from Rushbury . . .'

'So they did. I'd forgotten the tumblers. Last year, do you know, I almost won the pig? I was the second highest score, wasn't that splendid?' Her green eyes were sparkling, she was as excited as a child and as natural as few women know how. His throat was dry and that awareness he'd recognized before held him.

'Let us go, Papa, you and Beth and me. Let us go and see the fun. Please may we? I'm better now, truly my tummy ache has quite gone. May we? Please . . .?'

Those eyes were on him. She said nothing but they spoke for her. She'd not wanted to go she'd assured him – but those eyes belied what she had said.

'Get your bonnets on! We'll see if the old magic's still there, eh Beth?'

'Oh, it is, I promise it is. Come Phoebe,' then laughing delightedly, 'before he changes his mind.'

The magic was there indeed. He bought them garlands of flowers to wear around their necks. They bowled unsuccessfully for the pig. They watched the Morris men. They laughed to see the hopefuls attempting to climb the greasy pole. They put their money in the hurdy-gurdy man's bowl and watched the antics of his monkey.

It was years since Henry had had such an afternoon, indeed perhaps he had never had one like it, for he'd never before had Beth for a companion. She wasn't rowdy; outwardly there was nothing in her behaviour to set her apart from any of his family even, and yet to be with her was like drawing near to a burning brazier on a winter's day. Did the magic come from the Wake or did it come from her?

When Esme and Naomi saw them, by unspoken consent they mingled with the crowd and remained unnoticed. James glowered his disapproval from a distance and wished Amelia had come home instead of accepting Lucy's suggestion that she stayed at the Vicarage.

Beth gave a thought to none of them; she wanted just to store these precious hours for ever. She didn't want to analyse her thoughts. For the first time in her life things were getting out of hand and she was frightened to take stock. Tomorrow she'd think – but today she'd just live every moment.

The day wore on. Home once more, Phoebe was given a supper of cold meat and bread, an apple and a mug of warm milk, then seen off to bed. Much later, cold supper was served for the adults with Mrs Murphy back at the helm, the range poked and prodded into life as the kettles steamed and the kitchen clock ticked with loud monotony in the almost empty room. Tonight she hammered the gong, then carried the food to the table at the foot of the stairs herself. After all they were only young once and she couldn't drag them away when the dancing was just beginning. Old Ben, well, his dancing days were over long ago, the same as hers, but the last she'd seen of him he was competing for the fastest to down a yard of ale; no hope of any help from him this evening. She'd get M'lady High and Mighty to carry the things up and do the serving.

They were all at the table when she knocked and opened the dining-room door; five heads turned expectantly.

'I'm on my own downstairs, sir. Could you spare Beth to do some carrying?'

'Still out are they Mrs Murphy? Why yes of course you must have help. James, go down to the kitchen and help, there's a good fellow. No Beth, sit down my dear, James will see to it.'

The room was full of silence. Then James followed Mrs Murphy.

One wouldn't expect that an afternoon so happy could lead to a mood of low spirits such as Henry hadn't known since the early days without Isabella. Except at mealtimes the family hardly saw him, at least the girls hardly saw him. James was less fortunate for at the works it was he who bore the brunt of his father's wretched state of mind. There was nothing new in this. James's almost total lack of interest in the business that fed them had always been an irritation to Henry. Even as a child he'd been a dreamer. Bella had understood him and for her there'd been nothing the boy wouldn't try – but then she'd encouraged him in the hours he'd moon at the piano, liking nothing better than to sit by the keyboard. Never would he get his books out, do his sums, concentrate on the chemistry he'd need to be some use in the works that supplied their bread and butter. Thank God for Hal, Henry had thought often enough. Now in those weeks of late summer he seemed prepared to leave Hal alone. It was James he watched, his sharp tongue ever critical. The evenings were long and lonely shut away in the library. The sound of the girls' voices, or that everlasting piano, would disturb his silence, but to hear their enjoyment seemed only to drive him further into himself.

One Thursday evening in September, as he sat at his desk, a design drawing in front of him, he became conscious of an unfamiliar silence. Not just a momentary silence, but now that he thought about it, he realized that since supper the evening had brought no sound from the drawing-room, no chattering or laughing from the girls, no piano. Curiosity got the better of him and he crossed the hall to see what they were all doing. The room was empty, the lid of the piano closed and no books or embroidery frames were left out.

Frowning, he mounted the stairs and turned towards the nursery. He'd ask Beth where everybody was. That was his only conscious reason for seeking her out; not for a second would he acknowledge that he was clutching at any excuse to give him a genuine need to speak with her.

Without knocking he opened the door. From where she knelt on the window seat gazing out on to the garden, she was caught in the last rays of the red sunset. Lost in her own thoughts, she didn't hear him and he stood silently looking at her, forgetting his reason for coming, forgetting his misery and self-hate for the way his mind was turning; forgetting everything as for those few silent seconds he let the picture she made imprint itself on his mind. Then she realized someone was there and turned. With her back to the light he didn't read the expression in those tell-tale eyes and if he had perhaps he wouldn't have understood.

'Ah,' he blustered, too loudly. 'You're here.'

In contrast she spoke softly: 'But of course I am. Is something the matter?'

'No, no, I was looking for the others, James and the girls. Do you know where they are?'

'Why, yes. Don't you recall, at supper they told you? Mr Hinton is ill and can't play the harmonium at church. James has said he'll do it on Sunday and this evening they all went with him while he practised – it's such a beautiful night.' Automatically she'd used the name 'James' and if his father noticed he gave no sign. Beth, with the naturalness so much a part of her character, held out a hand. 'From this window you can smell the stocks. Come and sniff the air. It's still full of the scent of summer now the rain's over.'

He stood by her side and she pushed the bottom window wide from where she knelt. Only a few inches from him, with every beating pulse she was aware of him, him and the beauty of the evening. She clenched her teeth together and kept her hands firmly on the window sill, for they seemed to have a will of their own and wanted to move towards his.

He breathed in the heavily scented air. 'Summer, and almost over. Spring, full of hope, summer and fulfilment – it's gone so soon.' Spring, she was like the spring, the hope, the promise, the light . . .

'What is it, sir?' Gently she touched his hand, the spell of the dusk banishing all her resolutions. 'You are sad, and dear God knows I would give all I have to help you.' She

81

hadn't meant to say it. If the sun had been high in the sky, or the sounds of the house intruding on them, she would have been silent. But they were isolated from everything in the fast-fading light, only the last blackbird squawking his goodnight call.

'Beth, Beth child, I believe you mean it. How can I be sad when you can say that to me?'

'Don't shut yourself away. Let her into your heart. She would comfort you.'

'I can't reach her, it's – oh dammit, Beth, I try to think of her, to find her, but it's as if the past and the future have no connection.'

'This is the connection, the now. It always must be, to carry the past with you to the future.'

'Our lives alter so, already she seems to belong to another age – only seven years and God knows how many ahead. If she were to walk in now she'd see so much she wouldn't understand. We're all so altered, even the way we expect to live. She'd be a stranger in this modern world we take for granted, we're moving so fast. I can't talk to her, can't find her understanding. To start with there was the agony of the loss – but this I sometimes think is worse.'

Beth's voice was gentle. 'The sounds of dusk don't change. Shut your eyes and listen – think of her laugh, her soft voice. Remember the feel of her, the way her hair grew in the nape of her neck. See her stepping down from the carriage – I always watched for her on Sunday mornings at St James's. "Poor Mrs Copeland," my mother said sometimes (for she could drop her babies with no more trouble than an animal in the field), but I could never see how she could be "poor" for she had so much love around her, she radiated it.'

'Bella . . .'

They were silent for a while then she said: 'She can't alter with you as the years pass, but one day you'll be with her again, the you she knows and loves, the you who'll always love her and never change for her. That's surely the man you'll always be to her, just as time can't age her.'

'And the future, Beth?'

'Forget the future, it's but the now of tomorrow. Let your heart rejoice in the present, in your family who love you, in the satisfaction of each new implement your brain devises, in God's wonders all around.'

'What would I do without you, Beth? Never have I talked to a living soul as I can to you.'

'Nor I you.' He could no longer see her distinctly. It was instinct more than reason that made him raise her to her feet and turn her towards him. He had to read what was in her thoughts, he had to see into her soul, he had to . . . her parted lips were only inches from his, closer, closer . . . As she clung to him for the first time in her life she had no control over her own destiny; it was not simply a happy hour running away with her, but so much more. Reason, ambition, all these things had been her guide but now none of them mattered; at that moment nothing had any meaning to her except him. This was far removed from the thrill of falling in love with James. That seemed as nothing now for, if he'd been anything less than the son of Merton Court, would she have allowed herself to be swept off her feet? But Henry, if he were to tell her now that he'd lost all he'd had it would but make her love him more. With passion, desire and with a tenderness that shook her as she held him.

A minute later they sat side by side on the windowseat, she waiting in confidence for the words she was sure he must say. He cared, nothing else counted but that he loved her.

His words put her feet firmly on the ground again: 'Dear God forgive me – you are younger than my own children and I talk of loneliness without Bella! Dear God forgive me.'

'Please,' she knelt at his feet, 'don't hold me away. Please, I beg. It's not wrong or wicked to care. She knows

I love you. Love can never be wrong. Are we not here to care for one another?'

'Ay, to care, yes. But that's only a part of it. I love you, before God I swear I do, but there's another side of what I want. You're but a child yet I'm haunted by the need I have of you – love, lust, desire – I have no right.'

'Only you have the right. I don't expect to take her place; she was your wife. All I beg is, let me be truly yours, don't hold me away. Let me comfort you when you're sad or lonely, let me love you with my body as I do with my heart. Use me how you like only let me be with you.' He knew she was crying; in her emotion she couldn't stay calm.

'Get up, my dear sweet love, don't kneel.' He gathered her on his knee. 'Beth, I'm more than twice your age, I should be ashamed. But marry me, put a meaning to the years ahead.'

As she raised her face and his lips covered hers again the devils that had haunted him were quiet. 'She knows I love you,' Beth had said. Bella had come close again, not in jealousy or anger but in understanding. In that brief second of her nearness he knew that in love he could never lose her, their past was secure, a rock to build on until one day the spirit of the man he'd been would be joined with hers. Wasn't that what Beth had said?

As he held her closer Beth too had a flash of memory; she recalled James's young arms, his boyishly slim naked body on hers. It had been but a step on her journey to Henry. Old, he said; certainly boyhood was far behind, but he was a man, confident, strong, wise, ageless. If she failed to add 'prosperous, successful, able and powerful' it was because to her what he had done with his life bringing him to this point was proof of the man he was. Had she not said that if he had nothing she'd love him still? And so she would, but then if he had nothing the man that he was would never sit down under failure. Her heart banged so loudly she thought he must feel it as he held her.

* * *

At breakfast the next morning, not quite looking at anyone in particular, Henry made his announcement to the family: 'Now that we're all here together I have something to say to you.'

Five pairs of eyes were fixed on him. Guessing from the mood he'd been in the last few weeks, they expected that what he had to say wasn't likely to be pleasant! Only Beth kept her glance lowered.

'I have asked Beth to become my wife and I'm proud to tell you she has consented.'

It fell like a thunderbolt. Whatever they'd expected it certainly wasn't this. Marriage, for him, and with Beth, their own age and a servant!

'No . . .,' James breathed, 'no . . . I don't believe it.'

'I hardly believe it myself, James, it –' then with a smile that he could repress no longer: 'She's agreed though, eh Beth, it's true?'

'Yes,' she felt all eyes on her now, theirs and Henry's too and it was to him she looked.

Only James found his voice. 'You can't do this, Beth, you don't know what you're saying.'

Then her courage returned and from somewhere she cluched at the dignity she knew she must find. Not for a second must she let his family guess how her heart was racing, how hard it was to meet the condemnation in James's eyes. 'I love your father. I pray I can always make him happy.'

Silence. Henry's smile had gone and his throat was dry. Then: 'Well? Has no one any word of congratulation?'

Phoebe had watched them, peering at each one who spoke, and now she pushed back her chair and ran to Beth. 'You'll be with us for ever. It shows that God really does listen. Each night I've asked him never to take her away.'

James got up from the table and went from the room, his food untouched on his plate.

'My dear, don't take any notice.' The wretched boy had

no right to treat her like it. 'You girls, in future you'll look on Beth as your friend and mentor and – rejoice with me that it is so.'

Surprisingly it was Esme who, although she said nothing, looked at Beth with something approaching acceptance.

'Now Beth, my dear, would you care to come with me this morning?' He was loath to leave her at home until the girls had had time to digest the news. 'I shall make our news known to the men and perhaps a tour of the works might interest you.'

'Oh, it would,' and in her pleasure she forgot the girls' silence. 'May Phoebe come? I usually spend my mornings with her and a lesson from the workshops will be better for her than anything from her books.'

'We shall have to re-consider her tuition now. You'll not want to spend your mornings in the nursery teaching her her sums.'

'Indeed I shall, I detest being idle. Phoebe and I enjoy our lessons, don't we sweetling?'

Phoebe nodded, still standing by Beth's chair.

'Eat your meat if you're to come with us. Sit to the table now.'

'I'll tell James we'll leave in fifteen minutes.' Henry rose, something of the old tight-lipped expression coming back at the memory of his son's disgraceful behaviour.

'Let me tell him Papa,' Amelia said; 'he'll be ready I promise.'

So he left her to follow James to his room and what passed between them no one knew, but fifteen minutes later the young man drove the carriage to the front steps. His face was pale, his bloodshot eyes speaking for themselves. He'd been so close to Bella, Henry thought, he was too young to understand. With Beth and Phoebe already seated, he climbed to the bench at James's side, for a second touching the boy's shoulder with his hand. If James noticed he gave no sign.

One thing Henry had done while he waited for Beth and Phoebe; he'd gone down the basement stairs to the kitchen and there told his news to the servants. If Jenny thought it was like a fairy story she had the wisdom not to say so in front of Mrs Murphy.

'I know I can rely on all of you to show the same loyalty to her as you always have to me,' Henry had said.

'Young minx.' Mrs Murphy poked at the kitchen range after he'd left them. 'Lady Muck she always did think herself, too good to mix with the likes of us. Can you stay here and work with her as mistress, Ben, or you, Cyril? 'Tis a pill to swallow and no mistake.'

'Give the lass a chance, Mrs M.' Old Ben hated upheaval. 'Likely she'll keep out of our hair. She'll know not to come it with us; we'd soon see her for what she is.'

'He needed a wife, you said so yourself Mrs Murphy,' Jenny reminded her.

'A companion, I said, not a chit of a girl with no learning.'

'Learning don't keep you warm o'nights,' Ben nodded his head knowingly. 'Comely young piece she is.'

'Achh, men! Well she'd best not come meddling in my kitchen or I'll be slinging m'hook and that's for sure.'

At the works the news was greeted with the pleasure Henry craved. Perhaps it was the sight of Beth, perhaps the smile on Henry's face so seldom seen over recent years, or perhaps the day's holiday they were to be given for the wedding had something to do with it. And, too, of all his children (and he didn't count Phoebe for she'd never known her mother) Hal took the news with a better grace than any. If he could understand then later the others surely would, once they too knew the meaning of a shared life. There were still two more visits to be made but instinct told him to go alone to Margaret and Lucy after he'd taken Beth home.

So, the announcement made, a tour of the works followed where Beth showed yet another side of her

87

character. Who would expect a woman to take such a genuine interest, ask intelligent questions, even make a suggestion about the new reaper that was on his drawing board? His cup runneth over, never was a man so blessed.

Margaret received the news with tight-lipped congratulations, but William's hand-shake was warm enough. Of them all Lucy was the bitterest.

'I can't believe it, Papa! If you want her company she's there in the house without your marrying her, but heaven knows there must be far more suitable companions.'

'Lucy, let us not say things we shall regret. She alone is the companion I want.'

Her expression wasn't pretty. Her voice was silent but her contempt was clear. Strangely, he was sure that if he'd said he was marrying a woman of mature years she could have accepted. Poor Beth, she had a rough ride ahead.

Had he but known it, while he drove the trap the final mile home, James followed Beth to her room where, unannounced, he walked in on her just as she was putting her hat away in the wardrobe. She turned at the sound of the door opening.

'James! What is it?' How wild he looked.

'You ask that! How can you do it?' The tears she knew he'd shed earlier threatened again, his voice broke. 'You're mine, you promised, you said you loved me. We were only waiting.'

'Don't, James. It seems so long ago. Truly, James, I thought then that I was in love with you, but I didn't know –'

'No, you didn't know. There was a higher bidder. That was it wasn't it? But you couldn't have known. Who'd want a second son, and a useless one at that, if they could have the breadwinner? That's it isn't it? You'll give yourself to him, old and full of memories – or have you already? "No, James," he mimicked, "don't come to my room, it would make me feel like a harlot".' His voice croaked on a sob. 'Is that what you say to him? Has he touched you, lain with you here on this bed? Has he? His old man's body can't give you what – oh, Beth, Beth don't do it. You're mine, you know you're mine – '

'James, stop it. I love him. I never knew before. I thought I knew . . . but I see now it didn't mean anything.'

'You bitch, you cheap, rotten, lowdown, whoring bitch – '

'Stop it! You don't know anything about it. One day you'll understand, you'll see I'm right. You'll find someone – '

'Some old lady with a fortune perhaps, humph?' His sneer was ugly, he came nearer, his bloodshot eyes and trembling mouth only inches from her own as she backed against the open wardrobe.

'Enough!' Henry's voice from the doorway was as cold as steel. 'You'll apologize to Beth or you'll leave my house. Now, this second.' He came to Beth's side. 'Forget what he said, Beth. Don't listen to the young fool.'

'Go away, James, I want to talk to your father.' It wasn't because of the accusations James had hurled at her that she wanted to be alone with Henry, they weren't important; it was the fear she'd read in Henry's eyes. 'Some old lady with a fortune,' James had said. 'Go away. Leave us.'

'First you'll apologize,' Henry said again.

'You don't think I'd stay here, see Mama's place taken by that – '

'Enough, I said.'

They heard him go to his own room, doors and drawers opening and slamming. They heard Amelia's voice, her pleading tone even if not her words, then the bumping of a heavy case, the front door, Amelia again, this time crying. From Beth's bedroom they went through to the nursery. She was conscious of the sound of James's departure but all she cared was to take away that fear his words had brought to Henry. Downstairs in the kitchen Mrs Murphy, who missed little, nodded her head sagely. Only the first day and that young minx was destroying them.

At St James's the lid of the harmonium remained shut the following Sunday.

The wedding took place on the last Wednesday in October, soon enough for many an interested eye to be cast in Beth's direction with the thought that she should be watched with curiosity in the months ahead. Edward, to appease Lucy, had refused to perform the ceremony and, not wanting to make an issue of it in the family, Henry hadn't tried to persuade him to change his mind. So they were married in St James's with no trimmings and only the family back at the Court to the breakfast. The Harknells had been expected; Percy was probably Henry's oldest friend and he and Elizabeth had spent many a pleasant evening at Merton Court in the old days.

'Mrs Harknell found she didn't feel up to it today. She's not ill but not up to a party,' Hal explained when they arrived back at the house. Then turning to Beth he added: 'She told me to be sure to explain to you; she knew you'd understand.'

She did – so did they all.

'She'll call when you get back from Weymouth I'm sure,' Hal added trying to fill the silence. That Edith wasn't there was understandable; Henry Junior was but five weeks old and she hadn't yet been churched. Beth met Hal's glance squarely, she'd understood the unspoken message and so did he her unspoken reply.

'I shall be delighted to receive her,' was all she said. There was a dignity about her that must surely deserve their respect, and not an assumed dignity either, for if Henry considered her worthy to be his wife then she had every right to be proud.

Afterwards Algy drove the carriage to the railway station at Wilhampton, found a porter to take charge of the boxes, hat cases and all the paraphernalia necessary for a week away, and from there they went by train to Weymouth. A few months earlier the promenade would have thronged with holiday-makers for now that travel was so easy anyone with time and money liked to visit the seaside.

There were only a few guests in the large hotel so recently opened but even with the season over Beth was spellbound by it all. The huge gaslights, the sweep of the wide curved stairway, the gilt painted banisters, the gallery, the orchestra that delighted her at mealtimes making it impossible to keep her toes from tapping; and, above all, far above all, her pride in Henry. So tall and straight, so handsome and confident in his manner, such an air about him. As she walked on the promenade holding his arm the world was hers. Hadn't she always known that her future held something wonderful? She'd only had to live each day appreciating all life's gifts, treading the path faithfully even though she'd not known where it was leading. And it had brought her to this, to Henry, to an awareness that was with her every waking second. She hadn't known – but then how could she until he'd shown her? Each day she loved him more, each night she thrilled anew to him.

For twenty-two years he and Bella had had a good and close marriage. His dear Bella, always her arms holding him tenderly as his mounting passion had found its release. With the years, and his concern for the discomfort she suffered during pregnancy, followed by the period of recovery, his passion had lessened, their love-making becoming less ardent even on his part. Never had he found the joy he knew with Beth.

There was no false modesty, no affectation in her. She loved him and instinct was her guide. Their first night, seeing him in his nightshirt as he took off his dressing-gown, he seemed like a stranger, and she, her long, high-necked nightgown hanging loose, moved close to him knowing so well how important these next minutes must be.

With lips parted she raised her face. 'Hold me, hold me

close.' In his touch she'd feel near him again. He held her, her hand moved from the back of his head, her fingers following his spine. Leaning against him she could feel the warmth of his body, her own excitement grew just as she knew his did. Her gown buttoned almost to the waist and standing back from him she undid it, slipped her arms out and let it fall about her feet.

'Ah, oh, Beth.' Did she know what she was doing to him?

She unbuttoned his nightshirt and somehow they were naked before the flickering fire, held close in each other's arms. She wasn't ignorant. Being brought up in that cottage where two bedrooms had to be shared by all the family, how could she have been? Privacy was a luxury her parents had seldom enjoyed even though the family had closed their eyes and feigned sleep. But those few visits to the riverside meadow with James had been in summer darkness. That Henry was ready and wanting her she saw and thrilled at the knowledge, but she couldn't know what this meant to him after his celibate years of widowhood. She backed to the bed top pulling him towards her, unprepared for his uncontrolled cry as he entered her, his immediate convulsive thrusts that told her it was over before it had started. Should she feel deprived, resentful? She didn't. A child in so many ways, in others she had a wisdom beyond her years. So she held him, arms and legs caressing him.

'. . . shamed . . . so ashamed . . .' He hardly had breath to speak.

'No, Henry, don't be. I love you so much.' And so she did, she ached with tenderness. Tenderness? Or was it desire? Either way the night was but beginning.

Later as they made love again his shame was forgotten. She was like a young animal, nothing of a dutiful wife in her movements, and when finally he heard her shout and covered her lips with his own he knew a thrill of shock that any woman could be so moved to abandon. Bella, always loving and gentle, a willing receptacle for his passion. Never more. So they'd neither of them realized the lack. Beth travelled with him, uninhibited in her every expression.

In the week in Weymouth they saw nothing beyond themselves and each other. If James's taunt that he'd been married for his money had any power by now that power was lost. In fact even the thought of James didn't enter their heads. In the four weeks leading to the wedding both of them had worried, she partly on James's account and also lest out of spite he should write to any of the family about his relationship with her. They wouldn't understand, how could they? They'd believe – even Henry might believe – that because she'd lain with James she was all the things he'd called her. They wouldn't know that she'd done it believing that that was love – and what harm to anyone? It had taught her the difference between infatuation of a summer-time romance and this. As for Henry, the thought of the silly young fool going off to God-knows-where had been constantly on his mind. But in Weymouth they might have been on another planet. Whatever the future held they'd look back on this one week as flawless, a perfect interlude, for neither of them was fool enough to expect life could go on in uninterrupted bliss. This would be relegated to memory, to be taken out and drawn on when they needed it, like the afternoon at the Wake, Beth thought, or the feeling of his warm gloves on her sore hands that very first day, or the gentleness of his touch as he'd raised her from her knees in front of him – hardly more than a month ago yet already it seemed a world away and she another person.

The old life, or at least the ghosts of it, were waiting at Merton Court. Quiet hostility from Amelia; she couldn't risk her father's anger by voicing her hatred but how could she not hate the girl who'd come into their home and destroyed the unity of the family? James had gone and no one was as dear to Amelia as James. She wasn't blind and she'd thought for a long time that he'd been infatuated with the lovely Beth. She was scheming and cunning too; Amelia had suspected right from the start there was more behind James's wish to help her than he'd admitted, but it was something even more important that had sickened him so that he'd not stay in the house. Like him she remembered their mother, and into their memories they'd both built a perfection beyond reality; but then they'd lost her when they'd been too young to accept and too old to forget. This, Amelia believed, was why James had gone and if only he'd send for her she'd gladly go with him, no more to watch her father making a fool of himself fawning around his girl-bride. Hatred is a sickness, it sours the mind, so Amelia's sweet nature gave way to jealousy, spite and a misery she couldn't fight. Naomi and Esme were less hostile but even they were wary.

'Papa is sweet tempered. We should be thankful for that,' Naomi whispered as they lay side by side in the large bed.

'If only James hadn't rushed off, that's the thorn, Naomi. Do you think he'll come home soon? I heard Papa tell him once, months ago, before all this – I've never told you this because it made me feel too wretched. I didn't want to even think about it – but Papa had sent me to tell James to go to the library. I knew from his tone there was trouble so I listened at the closed door. It was something James had forgotten to do at the works and Papa said such cruel things: "Not fit to have a wage": "Gave no thought to anything but that damned tinkling piano"; "Thank God for Hal"; "If he weren't his own flesh and blood he wouldn't take him into the works" – such cruel things, Naomi, for James meant no wrong.'

'Do you suppose Papa doesn't care that he's gone?'

'I heard Mrs Murphy say only today "no fool like an old fool".'

'Oh Esme, you weren't listening again?'

'And what if I was? Is he that? Is she just using him like Mrs Murphy thinks?'

'Mrs Murphy has no right to voice her views. Who is she but a servant! To us Beth is pleasant enough. If we're not unfriendly she'll be grateful, you'll see. I've told her I want to order satin for a gown for Christmas and she has promised to make it, she seemed to want to. I dare say she was pleased to be asked. You get some as well, Esme. If we give her our work right from the start, just as we always have, she'll not like to refuse if she gets too sure of herself.'

A dusky pink she'd have, Naomi decided, with the huge layered skirt lifted into tiers at the back in the new fashion, and with deep red bows at each raised peak. She chuckled to herself, nestling deeper into the warm feathers. Papa could have married some old matron with no dress sense and skills for nothing but running an orderly house!

November came and went with no word from James. Sweet tempered Henry may have been but always at the back of his mind was the nagging worry of the boy.

'If Hal had gone – God forbid that he ever could – I'd know he'd fend for himself.' He and Beth were on their own in the library, their habit after supper, the house so quiet in the evening without that piano. All the girls had had lessons but none had any talent. At any time they were unlikely to try to play and now that James wasn't there none would be the first to break the silence. 'James has always been in a world of his own,' Henry went on; 'no sense of business, no idea how to buckle down and work.'

'Has he enough money, Henry? He must have some I suppose?'

'Oh yes. Bella inherited money when her father died, quite a sizeable sum, and she left it divided amongst the children. He hasn't a fortune but he'll survive. It's not that I think he'll starve but, dammit, if a man doesn't earn his way his self-respect must go. What's to become of him? Young fool! Why could he not see the right of what we did? And don't you see, Beth, it's more than that. How could he believe I'd forgotten Bella? Where was his understanding? You understood, Beth — why couldn't he have had your perception?'

And she had the perception to know enough had been said and to answer him simply by dropping to the rug at his feet, leaning against him as she held her hand towards the blaze — such a soft white hand now with no chaps and cuts to disfigure it.

CHAPTER FOUR

What made him decide on Newbridge James didn't know, for it was but chance. At Wilhampton station he'd wanted just to get away from them all, even Amelia. Not one of them cared about him; even she had begged him not to go because she'd needed his support. None of them knew what today had done to him. To sit there coolly at the family breakfast table and dismiss him as if none of it had mattered. A gold digger, Millie had said, but Millie had known only half of it. Who could say even if he'd been the first she'd given herself to? No, that was wrong too – she'd not given, she'd snatched. All the time she'd led the way, and how could he have been expected to resist? It hadn't been his fault. That first time he wouldn't have touched her if she hadn't led him on. A whore he'd called her and so she was. Did his father know what he was taking on? Damned old fool! Well he'd met his match in her, she'd not be another like Mama. He bit his lips together holding tight to the quivering muscles at the corners of his mouth, frightened to breathe for fear the sob in his throat would break. Not again, he'd not let it start again and make a fool of himself here.

Where to go? A train was nearly due, the few people on the platform were peering along the track expectantly trying to catch the first glimpse of the smoke. He'd catch that. Newbridge, that would do as well as anywhere. He'd never been there, no one would know him. He'd get a room somewhere and have time to think. No more would he have to go to that hateful foundry, watch the men sweating over the molten metal; no more would he have to inspect the implements that came off the benches in the workshops. Ploughs, diggers, harrows, plough shares, tines

97

– what did he know or care of any of it? And his father fixing those light blue eyes on him, eyes as cold as the metal he seemed to worship. He was free to find himself, do what he was best at and stop acting a lie, always aware of his uselessness.

A ticket bought, he joined the expectant group on the edge of the platform. No time for further thoughts. A puff of smoke told them the train was coming. He checked his boxes and as he stowed them away and settled into a seat he was surprised to find that, even after the emotion of his leave-taking, he was excited by what he was doing.

Let his father have her! She'd make circles round him and no mistake, but wasn't that what he deserved? Always so sure he was right, if you didn't agree with him he had no interest in your views. Well, he'd met his match now, she'd not dance to his tune if it didn't suit her – but he'd dance to hers, for look what she had to offer. Damned old fool, he thought again, serves you right if she wears you out. Beth . . . Beth . . . you promised. No, he mustn't think that way; he should be grateful he'd had a chance to see her for what she was. Love him, she'd said, even that morning she'd said it. It wasn't in her to know what the word meant.

Only one other person was in the compartment and no one got in with him at Wilhampton. Thank goodness there was no one he knew. The motion of the train had a soporific effect; in no time his plump little fellow traveller had his eyes closed, knocking his stove-pipe hat forward as his head jogged against the back of the seat. With each jolt it slipped a fraction more and, fascinated as he waited for it to topple, James heard the ghost of Millie's giggle. The hat lost its humour, it was just another reminder of his solitary state; no one to give a sly wink to, no foot to touch his under the table to share a silent joke, or to press his in sympathy when his father had been particularly cutting. He felt those muscles twitching again and his vision blurred. No, not here, not now. Then he was saved.

98

The lurch of the carriage disturbed the old man's slumbers and with a loud snort he woke, just in time to save his headgear.

"'pon my soul, must have dozed. 'pon my soul.'

'It's the motion, sir, it's difficult to stay awake.'

Pleasant young man. The elderly gentleman peered at him. Umph, something wrong perhaps. Dear, dear, he looked as though he'd been weeping. Going on a sad mission no doubt. 'Ah, must stay awake. Do you take snuff, young man?' He pulled his enamelled box from his waistcoat pocket.

'Thank you, no, sir, I've never got on with it.'

'Ah!' With a little on the back of his hand he sniffed, first one nostril and then the other. 'Bad habit, my wife says. Still, some have worse I tell her. Are you bound for Newbridge?'

'Yes, I am.'

'That's where I come from too. King Alfred's School don't you know.'

'I have heard of it, sir.'

'Not from Newbridge yourself?'

'No, I've not been there before.'

Another pinch of snuff gave Doctor Pilfrey a chance to size up his young acquaintance. Something was wrong, no mistake about it. None of his business of course but the poor fellow was keeping his face stiff as if he were frightened to relax. 'Pleasant town, not too much hurly-burly, you understand, but busy, not small. A deal of building over these last five years, good houses I dare say and a fine Town Hall. I live at the school myself.'

'Oh yes?' He wished the old man would go to sleep again.

'None of my business, tell me it's none of my business, but if it would help to talk I'm a good listener. No good at giving advice mind you, but I never tattle and you look as though you've had trouble. Tell me not to meddle . . .'

James wasn't ready for sympathy. He held his jaw stiff

as he answered and his voice sounded high and unnatural to his ears. 'No, you're very kind, and you're right. But I don't want to talk about it – I'm sorry.'

'No, no, I shouldn't ask. Forgive me my dear boy, clumsy old fool, just thought if I could help . . .'

They sat in silence for a while as the engine chuffed and the carriage swayed along the track. James had wanted his companion to go back to sleep yet surprisingly it was he who spoke.

'I don't know why I chose Newbridge. Anywhere would have done. I must find some work.'

'What do you do?'

He hadn't thought of saying it, yet wasn't it the truth?

'I play the piano.'

'Aha, do you indeed. Do you teach?'

'I never have, but it's what I shall try to do. That and perhaps in time get a church.'

'You play the organ?'

'Enough – hymns, chants, that sort of thing. I've not had a lot of experience but at . . .' He'd been going to say that at Wilhampton his brother-in-law was the vicar and he often practised on the organ there, but he stopped; that belonged to the past. 'The piano is my first love.' There, he'd said it and already he felt better. It was his first love, no woman would come before it either.

'You'll be looking for rooms I suppose, or have you somewhere in mind?'

'No, not yet. This train came first so I decided on Newbridge.'

They were nearly at their destination, the rest of the journey having passed with more general conversation, when Albert Pilfrey surprised him by saying: 'Kitty always keeps a warm brick in the spare bed. Now what do you say to coming home with me for the night? Daylight will be gone in half an hour, you'll not find rooms today. Come to us, eh? Why don't you? And give us some music this evening and the pleasure of your company?'

Why, thank you, sir. If you mean it I'd be delighted,' was what James said but his brown eyes smiled warmly into Albert's. 'You've not even asked my name or why I'm here.'

'No. When you're ready I've no doubt you'll tell me these things. By the by, I'm Albert Pilfrey.'

'And I'm James Copeland.' After an hour in each other's company they shook hands.

Kitty Pilfrey was delighted to have a visitor. A small woman, possibly even older than her husband, but with a brightness that made James think of a little bird. Her hair – because it had become so thin but he wasn't to know that – was taken in strands and pinned across her head with no regard for fashion, and the grey of her unwired rather old-fashioned dress was only relieved by a white lace collar, with a white cap on her head. She fussed round him like a mother hen and it was just what he needed. When she placed a dish of boiled salt beef and suet dumplings in front of him he realized how extremely hungry he was. Breakfast had been left uneaten, the mid-day meal had been missed. In fact this supper was his first food of the day. Willingly he accepted a second helping, followed by a large baked apple. She beamed her pleasure at his appreciation.

When the meal was over and she'd rung the bell for Maud to take the dishes to the kitchen she tapped a fireside chair invitingly. 'Now come and warm yourself, Mr Copeland, and tell me all about what you're doing in New-bridge.' She had no idea she trod on dangerous ground for by the time the couple had reached King Alfred's James had so far recovered his composure that he gave no hint of any trouble.

So sitting here in a strange room with these two he'd known but a few hours and old enough to be his grandparents he found the tale unfolding. Oh, out of respect for them he didn't tell them of those evenings by the river last year, only that she had promised herself to him. Once the

101

floodgates were open there was no stopping him. That he was bitter they could tell from his voice but as he talked he found that his future was taking shape.

Later when they suggested some music he looked through the books in the canterbury and selected Chopin. He'd said he played the piano, inferring it was his livelihood; now they knew his story they knew this wasn't the case. But it would be. For the first time in his life he was free. He'd never played better than he did on that unfamiliar instrument in the parlour at King Alfred's and, what's more, while he played he didn't give a single thought to his father or Beth either. Even Amelia, whose evening was the most lonely and unhappy she'd ever had and so largely on his account, was forgotten

It was when he was in bed that night that the idea of a shop came to him. Of course he wasn't yet of age but he was positive Henry wouldn't try and get him home. Not he – he'd be too frightened of the competition! He needn't worry, he didn't want her, wouldn't have her back if she begged him. He'd show them! Now that he didn't have to waste his time in that hateful foundry, he'd show them what he was made of.

By the time Henry and Beth came back from Weymouth James had found an empty shop. It had a room behind where he could give his lessons, and behind yet again and, looking as if they had been added to the original building, a kitchen and scullery. A far cry from Merton Court, the only thing the two had in common was their age. The shop had none of the Georgian grace of his old home – but it was to be his own. The rooms above were tiny, and, so narrow was the back yard, the window of the kitchen looked almost directly on to a high brick wall. Gas had been carried no further than the shop and kitchen, for the rest candles had to suffice – but it was to be his own. In pride he wrote to Millie, not telling her his address for he wasn't ready yet even for her to visit. On paper it sounded surprisingly grand, a musical warehouse, a teaching room,

102

living accommodation. That the closet was in a shed in the back yard and that once a week he was to leave the gate unlocked so that it could be emptied was no one's affair but his own. Reading what he'd written he was impressed by the description, and after all it would be cosy enough to sit in a tub in front of the kitchen fire, or so he fondly imagined. Carrying the water outside to empty down the drain in the yard – he'd not dwell on that. It was only over the last few years that they'd had proper bathrooms at the Court; he could remember well enough when bathing had been something one did in front of the fire in the nursery. That it had never fallen to him to carry the water didn't enter his head.

The arrival of his letter was a relief to all of them. It was apparent there was no need to worry, he'd fallen on his feet and was doing what he most wanted. Even at Christmas he was to have company, for he was to spend it with the headmaster of a local boys' school and his wife. So at home thoughts turned to their own festivities, the two girls went off collecting holly and ivy to bedeck the house, Phoebe plodding after them with Beth's old rush basket. Only Amelia dreaded Christmas, the silent piano, or perhaps worse, one of the others trying to hammer out the carols.

'Henry,' Beth was sitting in her favourite spot on the footstool at his feet by the library fire, 'do you think we could have a party – dancing – perhaps engage the mummers?'

'Who would you invite?'

'Oh, I don't know. You used to have parties. I remember seeing the carriages come. People from Bampton Hall, usen't they to come, and the Ridley family from Brimley Grange? There must be others – you must remember – who used you to invite?'

'Beth, sweetheart, until people make the first move, call

103

and introduce themselves to you, it's better to wait. It's because of the approach of Christmas, everyone has been too busy. You'll see. When it's over they'll visit here, you'll meet people and then we'll have your party.'

'I know that's the right way, but surely it wouldn't matter? Everyone knows you; it's not as though you'd be inviting strangers.'

'I agree it's ridiculous, but that's the way it works. If you broke the conventions you'd make it difficult for yourself.'

She was quiet, mulling over what he'd said. Then, turning to look him squarely in the eye and wanting an honest answer: 'It's me, isn't it? They think badly of me and perhaps of you too for marrying me. That's the truth isn't it? I'm not from the right background, I'm not talented, nor some kindly, middle-aged widow who'd be a guide to the girls. Was I dreadfully wrong, Henry, have I spoilt things for you? Even Mr and Mrs Harknell don't visit now.'

'She's not been well, my dear. He was at the foundry only yesterday.'

'I'm so sorry, Henry. Not for me, I don't give a fig for me, but you had such respect. What sort of a love is it that can destroy a man's respect?'

He tapped his knee and she moved from the stool and curled up against him. 'Beth, none of that matters. If I have you I want nothing more.'

She wriggled closer and seemed content with his answer. But was she? All her life she'd battled for what she wanted. 'I don't give a fig,' she'd said and neither did she as far as their company went. But how dared these people treat her like that, insult her and so insult him. She'd seen their carriages come and go from the Court all her life, the Ridleys from Brimley Grange, Mrs Ridley so straight backed and with never a flicker of her eyelid as Syd had led the horses away. She remembered the fat pasty son she'd heard called Hector and a daughter, equally solid,

104

about her own age. What did she want with them? Nothing – except the knowledge that they counted her worth visiting. At Wilton End lived the Hatchers; Richard Hatcher had made a fortune from the wool trade. Syd used to say he liked their visits, they always gave him sixpence for his trouble with the horses. What a slap in the eye for them all that she was mistress of the Court. Not matter a fig? Indeed it did. True, she'd not been actually hurt by their slight, but curled in Henry's arms she was consumed by rage. Who did they think they were to have the right to decide on her fitness to be Henry's wife?

He probably read more of her thoughts than she imagined. She felt his chin rub against the top of her head.

'Henry.' She sat up straight, her thoughts had jumped in another direction. 'That cutter you had on the drawing board last night – I was thinking about it this morning while Phoebe did her sums. Why do we have to have the cutting edges like that, both the same, both long and moving against each other? If one of the sections had lots of separate knives – say each one bolted to the arm – surely it would act like lots of pairs of scissors? If one of them broke all the farmer need do would be to unbolt the broken piece, and put on a new one. Or perhaps if both the rods were fitted with separate cutters like that. Why would that not work, Henry – or would it? I puzzled a long time over it, even tried to do some drawings but I'm not very good at it.'

'Show me, Bethie.' Perhaps he said it simply because he wanted to please her, to try and make up to her for the disappointment about the party.

Not like Beth to be timid, but she knew the sketches she'd made were poor, the scale wrong, the diagram looking so different from anything he would have produced.

'It's probably nonsense. It's just that I felt it would be more flexible, less rigid – and cheaper to replace.'

105

His attention was held. 'Get your sketch, Beth. Let's have a look at it together.'

Another minute or two and chairs had been pulled to the desk and, with heads together, they worked as under his guidance she learnt to draw the plan. The party was forgotten, the cutter — or mower as it was to be known — was far more exciting. By the end of the evening it still wasn't right, there was work to be done, but it was the beginning of something new in their relationship, something that had she but known it was to mould her life.

From Hal's expression Edith guessed where his thoughts were. She knew what she would hear.

'Just imagine you doing it — or Margaret! It's not right having a woman there, it's no place for her. Just imagine you driving in with me each morning, getting to know the men, chattering to them about their homes. I've seen her standing there in the middle of that workshop floor, looking all around her as if she draws some kind of strength from the fumes, the noise. Even when she doesn't come with Father she follows before the day is half over. Even if you hadn't Henry to care for, can you imagine yourself following me there? She's out of place I tell you . . .'

'I can't imagine I'd enjoy it. But perhaps he likes to take her, to show off his pretty young wife.'

'More likely make a laughing stock of himself. Petticoat government, that's what the men must think. Honestly, Edie, I never seem to have a chance to talk to him without she's there these days. It's not a bit like it used to be.'

'Poor darling.' She sensed that that was at the root of the trouble. Not like it used to be. He and his father had been so close. Instinct showed her the way to heal his hurt and she passed the baby Henry to him.

The little face broke into a smile of glee, mouth wide open, eyes fixed unblinkingly on Hal.

'See that, Edie? He knows me, I swear he does. Hello then, my fine fellow.'

'Of course he knows you.' She leant over Hal's shoulder, gently tickling the infant's chin. 'I suppose, darling, we should be glad she wants to be with him. Remember what we all said, or thought even if we didn't say, when he said he was marrying her. We thought it was only for position she wanted to be his wife, that once she had a ring on her finger she'd rule the roost and care about nothing. She may not be suitable as a wife for him, I'm not suggesting she is, but at least she is trying to share his interests.'

'I can't see why he couldn't have let well alone. He'd had one good wife. Surely his family could have been sufficient for him.'

'He may have thirty years or more ahead of him – he always seems so much more youthful than Papa although I know he isn't – that's a long time to be lonely, Hal.'

'I dare say. And in a strange way you know I have a liking for her.' He saw the way Edith's brows shot up and the teasing look in her eye. 'Oh not because she's comely, I'll grant you she's that, but, Edie, there's a quality in her you can trust.' It was easy to talk to Edie for all her teasing, for both of them jealousy was a word that would never exist. Almost as far as her memory went Hal had been her 'special friend' and she his. Their families had always expected that the friendship would develop into more and were beginning to give up hope when the realization had hit the two young people with sudden clarity. Still, that's another story. Enough that their love had roots too strong for doubts or jealousy. 'Thirty years you say, Edie, and I hope you're right. She'll have an old man on her hands for a long time. She'll need to be a very special kind of woman. Look, see how he watches you. His eyes followed you right across the room.' This child would grow up close to him, just as he'd been close to his father – before she'd spoilt it. 'Well, we have to make the best of it I suppose. At least she can't have any real effect

107

on the business. She's quick to learn but even so there's more to a foundry than she'll be able to glean. That's for me to take care of – and one day, my fine fellow, for you.'

'Of course, darling. One day little Henry is going to be very important, aren't you, my lovely?' for her mother had borne no child but her.

'He's that now. Here, quick Edie, he's horribly damp. That's no way to treat your Papa, my son.'

The boy grinned his toothless grin, pleased with his performance.

This would ruffle her feathers! 'Won't have her interfering in my kitchen,' hadn't she said? Jenny wished it hadn't fallen to her to carry the message summoning Mrs Murphy to the morning room. Still, it had so it was no use putting it off. Her step, always heavy, was more positive than usual as she plodded down the wooden stairs to the servants' hall.

'Mrs Murphy, m'um, I just come from dusting the morning room . . .'

'What've you broken now? Not one of Mrs Copeland's ornaments off the little table I hope. Been here as long as I have, wedding presents mostly. Don't stand there gawping, girl. What've you done?'

'No, nothing. It's the mistress, she says she wants you up there, for a word like.'

'She! Sending for me! Too fine to use her own legs is she!' She took off her white cooking overall and pulled her cap on firmly, then marched up the stairs.

'Wouldn't like to be in young Beth's shoes when Mrs M. gets to her, coming it like that.' Old Ben had just brought the day's greens from the garden but he'd not hurry back; this looked like being interesting.

'We shouldn't call her that, Ben, she's not Beth no longer, she's ma'am now, and always ever so nice too. Not fair to make it 'ard for her. S'posing it was one of us, we'd

want a bit of help not folk allus trying to catch us out.'
Perhaps Jenny had her dreams. Did she think that if Beth
could rise to such dizzy social heights why not she? Or
was she so besotted with Algy that she wanted to love the
world?

'How's that kettle, girl? Mrs Murphy reckons to give
me a cup o'tea when I bring the veg you know.'

'Right y'are Ben, I'll see to it. You have a warm while it
comes to the boil.'

Upstairs Beth must give no sign of how she dreaded this
interview. That Mrs Murphy had always disliked her the
older woman had never been at pains to hide; but she
wasn't going to accept warfare from the kitchen and
neither was she going to let that tyrant get the better of
her.

A tap and the door opened before she'd had time to call
'Come in'. From her seat at the writing table she met Mrs
Murphy's look squarely.

'Come in, Mrs Murphy,' she said firmly, disregarding
the fact that she already had. 'So far I haven't had a lot of
time and I knew things had been running smoothly enough
so I didn't rush. It's over a month now since we've been
home and time I remembered I have certain household
duties.'

'No need for you to worry yourself. You've never been
used to it.'

'Indeed I haven't, but then it's seldom a woman has
when first she marries.' Beth ignored the housekeeper's
implication. 'What I intend is to prepare menus for a full
week and give them to you each Saturday morning, then
there will be nothing to worry about. I realize it's too late
for today and no doubt you have tomorrow planned, so
I'll give you these – all quite clearly written out and dated
I think you'll find, and you can start with them on
Monday.'

'Have you not been satisfied then, is that it?'

'On the contrary. But we all have our jobs to do and
you must see that that is part of mine. If you'll bring your

housekeeping books to me when you come next time, that's tomorrow week, I'll attend to those and the paying of the grocery bills. There is no need to worry my husband, he prefers that I attend to that side of things.'

'I see.'

'Mrs Murphy, I asked you to come up here because I believe you like privacy in the kitchen. I shall respect that.'

'Will that be all . . . Madam?'

'Yes, unless you have anything you want to say?'

So much she'd like to say. 'No. I'll take m' menus.'

It was on the tip of Beth's tongue to say 'If you think anything should be altered, tell me', for in truth her experience was slim, but something stopped her. With an incline of the head the housekeeper was dismissed and, hearing her clump off towards the back stairs, Beth's face flooded with colour. She was back at the Vicarage at Wilhampton being sent on her way with permission to ask for a cup of tea in the kitchen. Was she taking her revenge now on those downstairs? It wasn't their fault that Lucy had filled her with humiliation.

'Beth, haven't you got my dress ready for a fitting yet? You never seem to be here to sew nowadays. Even in the evening I don't believe you do it.'

Beth had been so well and truly on those uncarpeted servants' stairs of Lucy's that she'd not noticed Naomi come in and her old instinct almost brought her to her feet at the imperious tone.

'I'll have it done by Christmas, I promised you. But I was talking to your father last evening and he agreed with me, we must ask Mrs Dickson to do something about your clothes. We'll see what you're going to need for the Academy.' For in the New Year Naomi was to follow her elder sisters and take her turn at Mrs Sherwin's Academy for Young Ladies. Two years to polish her mastery of the art of running a home, supervising staff, entertaining, gracing a ballroom. According to Amelia a part of each day was even spent with a book on one's head to improve

110

one's deportment. Margaret was as straight as a ram rod, perhaps it had done something for her, but plump Lucy bounced her way through life just as much after the Academy as before. Whereas Beth, well, she'd had no training! Lucky for Naomi that the thought didn't strike Henry that what nature doesn't endow can't be bought – and at high cost too. Esme's turn would come in another year; in the meantime she'd go alone to Reverend Gilstone.

'Perhaps Mrs Dickson will refuse. After all when we engaged you we told her we wouldn't need her.'

'Naomi, I have other things to do. Quite happily I'll make any of you the occasional dress, just as I'll attend to the household linen, for that I should do, but I am not here as a seamstress.'

The girl's face flushed; she knew she'd gone too far and if Beth chose to repeat this to Papa she'd be for trouble.

'I had thought we'd go over your clothes together, decide what was needed. But, Naomi, we have to do it as friends. Is that possible?'

'Yes. I'm sorry I was rude. My bossy streak, James always calls it. Really I didn't mean to be horrid.'

'Then we'll forget it. Now this morning I'm going upstairs to work with Phoebe, then this afternoon we'll attack your wardrobe.'

'What fun! Don't you just love pretty things, Beth?' Did she know what a picture she made as she smiled her excitement, her rude outburst over? One thing they had in common was a delight in clothes. Beth found herself genuinely looking forward to the task.

So Beth had taken the reins. It was early days and she was far more frightened than anyone could guess but determined to run Merton Court in a way to show Henry how right he was to put his trust in her.

The preparations for Christmas couldn't have been better timed as an icebreaker. Beth was able to show the girls so much. The holly had always been brought in, some decorating the many pictures, some hung in bunches

111

entwined with mistletoe; the ivy had always been twisted around the banisters and over the doorframes. But no one had thought of making bells, the gauze covered entirely with the delicate mistletoe to hang from the chandeliers, any more than anyone had shown them how to make a huge 'snowball' that could be rolled into the drawing-room where the two halves would fall apart and presents tumble to the floor. Last year, while Syd was downstairs in the servants' hall, Beth had stayed alone over at the coach-house, but before that it had always been a time of magic. Poor the Machins may have been, presents usually home-made and humble, but in the manner of their giving their skill had known no bounds.

Teaching Naomi and Esme to shape their twin halves of the 'snowball' using wires from a crinoline as a base, Beth tried to picture her family now in their new land. Just as easy to imagine Syd one of those 'citizens of heaven above' they'd be singing about. She believed it would be very cold in Canada, deep snow and thick ice. No mail had come to her yet. It was as if her past had melted away. She had no address even to tell them she was married.

The nursery was full of industry, Phoebe twisting ivy around a circle of wire for Beth to make a wreath for the heavy front door.

'My word, but such skills.' Amelia's voice from the doorway had a ring of sarcasm. 'I hardly see any point in dressing the house up, no one is coming.'

'They always come,' defended Naomi. 'Margaret, Hal and Lucy and the children – Edwin and Henry this year as well – and Mr and Mrs Harknell.'

'You mean they used to come . . . before. This year Lucy says she intends to stay at home. Edward will be in church in the morning and in any case it's not the season to bring Edwin out.'

'What nonsense!' Esme held out her bell for inspection. 'Is that good enough, Beth? I'll improve as I do more.'

'It's splendid, Esme. 'Tis a pity if they say it's unseasonal to bring the babies the first year your father has had these two new grandchildren. Cannot you persuade them Amelia?'

'No.' She seemed to turn her shoulder on Beth as she answered and addressed herself to her sisters. 'Hal and Edith are going to Mr and Mrs Harknell's. I just came from Lucy's and she told me. She's inviting Margaret's party there and I'm going too.'

Beth felt her cheeks grow hot with anger. How dare Amelia! Her bright hair seemed to bristle. 'If your Papa consents to your going, I believe you mean, Amelia. Then there will be but five of us, so we'll have to think of games for small parties. There are many who are quite alone for Christmas, I know because last year I was one of them, but the magic's something you find in your own soul or not at all. Crowds and parties don't bring the spirit of Christmas, it's – oh well, I don't have to tell you. Listen to the bells on Christmas Eve and you'll hear them better if you're not one of a noisy crowd. They bring their message straight to your heart. That's lovely, Naomi. Here's a base ready for another.' Christmas should be full of love, yet here she was turning her shoulder on Amelia in just the way the girl had to her.

'I wish Jamie was going to come home,' Phoebe said.

'Won't our carols be miserable without him. It was unjust of Papa. He did but speak his mind truthfully. Papa has always told us to do that.'

Esme scowled at her.

'Anyway,' Amelia turned away, 'I dare say you play the piano amongst all your other talents, Beth?'

Beth kept her voice cool but only with an effort. Such sarcasm in the girl's remark, it was asking for trouble. All she said was: 'Unfortunately we didn't have a piano.'

'Well now, fancy that!'

'Are you going to stay and help us, Amelia? Because if not, go away, don't come in here spoiling the afternoon for everyone.'

For reply Amelia went out of the room, but the excitement of preparing the wreaths and garlands had gone stale.

That night as Beth pulled on her nightgown and brushed her hair she was busy planning. Just as Henry joined her, his quilted silk dressing-gown over his night-shirt, she put down her brush and climbed into bed.

'No prayers, Bethie?'

'It's so cold, the fire seems to give no warmth. Do you know even the inside of the window is still frozen over.'

That quick frown of his showed his disapproval. He took off his dressing-grown and knelt as he did every night of his life at the bedside, hands folded and eyes closed. What went on in his mind, what sort of relationship he had with his Maker, she had no idea, but she was pretty sure it wasn't as intimate as hers. A slight movement of his lips but not a sound and no expression to give her a clue. 'Himself', she knew they called him downstairs, an awesome figure sternly reading from the Bible each morning, yet here in humility was the real man who'd never let an easy path tempt him, who'd be just and honest. Dear, dear Henry. For his sake, for she couldn't bear to disappoint him, she climbed out of bed and dropped to her knees.

Once there she found she had a surprising lot to talk to God about. All this business of the family not coming home had to be explained. She had to put in an ardent request that Henry wouldn't be upset by it. Then she had to ask for ideas on how she could see to it that the festival was fun for the girls – and, as an afterthought and with a feeling of righteousness for her generosity, ask that James would enjoy himself too. She took longer than she'd realized and when she opened her eyes he was already under the covers watching her, his blue eyes smiling. She was glad she'd suffered the cold.

It must have been the getting out of bed that did it. God must have appreciated how cold she'd been, for by the very next day it seemed her requests had been met.

114

Margaret actually called on that Saturday afternoon to say she and William and the children were looking forward to coming as usual for the whole week. She turned to Beth and said it too, not speaking into the middle distance and letting her pick up the fallen words. Then, as if that weren't enough, inspiration came. On Monday she'd go to the village – or if necessary to Wilhampton – she'd buy whistles, tambourines and a drum. They'd have carols such as they'd never had before.

That Saturday night Henry didn't need to remind her, despite the continuing chill. When they were in bed and she'd cuddled close, the dim flicker of the fire the only light, she said: 'Isn't it splendid, Henry, how you can ask God for something and get it? I'm sure if we explain properly why it's necessary He understands.'

'What makes you think we're the best judge of what we need, you funny child?'

'Sometimes we just know, don't we? If you think that how do you know what to ask Him for?' Silence. 'Henry, answer me – you're not asleep already are you?'

'No. I suppose I try not to ask, Beth, I try to trust.'

'Whatever do you find to talk about so long every night then? Oh no, you don't have to tell me. Darling Henry, I've no right to ask you. Just cuddle me and forget it.'

'I think I try to thank Him for what He's given, and when things haven't gone as I'd hoped I try to understand and to accept.'

'I say thank you too, every night I thank him for giving us to each other. Are my feet very cold, your legs are beautiful and warm.'

'Beth, I love you.'

She wound her arms around his neck. 'I hope you're grateful then for the way I'm warming my feet.'

He showed her just how grateful, this adorable woman who aroused such passion in him, matching him move by move even while she retained a childhood innocence.

Soon it would be Christmas, her first with him. He'd

noticed how she'd listened when the girls talked of the tree; for some years it had been part of the decoration of the Court, just as it had in most large houses. Beth had never had one, never known its pungent smell that seemed to fill the room, the warm glow of lighted candles that set the seal of wonder. This year he'd give her a Christmas to make up for all she'd missed; if Millie wanted to go to the the Vicarage, well, so be it. It grieved him that she couldn't fine her way to love Beth but as long as James took this stubborn attitude he saw no hope. Each night he thanked his Maker for the steadily growing friendship between 'the girls' and her. Even Margaret was unbending and if only young Lucy would give a thought to anyone other than herself she would too. That there might have been two sides he didn't consider for in Beth he'd found everything his life had lacked. For a young man to fall in love is natural; it had happened to him before and together he and Isabella had built their lives. But Beth, ah Beth, she was something apart from the ambitions and cravings of youth. To have found her now, her warmth and under-standing, her beauty, and her love, he had no doubt was a miracle. Those empty years of middle age were no more than a memory, in her he was young again. His family were dear to him but in Beth he lived again and everything else dimmed by comparison. He hoped Amelia would soon realize who wrong was her attitude, and James too; to behave in the way they did was childish. Even so, if they couldn't recognize the pure gold of Beth the fault must be theirs and the loss too.

With the confidence that seldom failed her Beth was determined the family party would be a good one. The candlelit tree cast its spell, the lid of the piano remained closed but never had there been a better evening of carols at the Court. Old and new, they played and sang them all with their whistles, tambourines and drum. What Beth couldn't know was the difference in Henry this year. In Bella's day he'd listened, perhaps at her persuasion added his voice to theirs; in the years that followed he'd left the carols to the children, more often than not isolating himself in the library. Not so this year! His enjoyment was apparent, it infected everyone. Never had the 'Noels' been sung so lustily nor the games played with such fervour. As always on Christmas Eve the wassailers came and, as always, they were invited in and the family joined in their singing, but it must have been to please Beth that Henry went down to the kitchen and bid the staff join them in the hall where they were gathered. Mince pies, mulled ale, the message of goodwill was almost tangible.

Upstairs the children slept, Phoebe who'd whispered confidentially to her father as she'd bid him goodnight: 'Papa, is your tummy screwed up? Mine is. You can really feel the angel is near tonight, can't you?' She'd climbed on his knee as she often did, although his seven-year-old daughter was becoming a solid weight.

'Yes, Phoebe, indeed you can.'

'Do you suppose it's Beth brings the angel?'

From the mouths of babes! He rubbed his cheek against her straight hair. 'I think it's Beth who helps us to recognize the angel. Time for bed and, Phoebe, when you say your prayers remember it is God who brought her to us. She helps us to hear the angel but it is to Him we owe our gratitude.'

'Yes, Papa.' Then hugging him: 'But Papa we are 'stremely lucky aren't we?'

'We are indeed, extremely. Sleep well, God bless you. Here's Beth to call you to bed.'

As she'd gone out of the library on her way to bed she'd turned and looked back at him, a silent message of understanding passing between them as it so often did. 'Indeed,' it had said, 'they were 'stremely lucky'.

No sound from the room next to Phoebe's; Penelope and Richard must be already asleep. Only from Margaret and William's room where a cot had been put for their youngest, two-year-old Archie, did his shouts proclaim that he didn't approve of his strange surroundings. Hearing Margaret come out of the drawing-room Phoebe disappared into her own room; she wanted to be by herself to feel the magic, and the wonder, or was it holiness? She must remember what Papa said. Yes, she'd hurry into her nightgown, say her prayers as fast as she could then get into bed and just listen. Later the bells would ring and from downstairs there'd be voices, everywhere people were happy. It was the angel. At seven she knew nothing of misery; everyone was happy, she believed, her well-fed little body full, her bed warm, her family loving her. She wanted to stay awake until Beth came back to tuck her in, and even longer. She knew the angel was near and she was determined not to miss his coming.

Ten minutes later Beth found her asleep and hardly an hour after that, when the sound of the wassailers filled the house, she heard none of it.

At the Vicarage the three of them ate their supper late that evening for Edward had a service at half past eleven and didn't expect to get to bed until well after two o'clock.

'Edwin should sleep and in any case Mrs Price is in the house,' he said to Lucy. 'There's no reason why both of you shouldn't come.'

'I've told you, Edward, I shall stay here. The idea of leaving him at the start of his very first Christmas! The two of you go. To be honest I'd rather get to bed earlier than that. You forget I have broken nights.'

'It's surely time he slept. He shouldn't need your attention during the night.'

She turned to Amelia, choosing to ignore his remark.

'Mind you wrap up well, Millie. You may wear my astrakhan if you like, the church will be freezing on such a night.'

More and more over the last few months Lucy had wanted Amelia at the Vicarage. First of all she'd been glad to have her while she got back on her feet after the birth, but before long it was more for the shelter she found behind a third person.

The important moments in her life had all come to her with such clarity. The day she'd been visiting Edith's family and had gone with them to morning service at St Agnes's – as if it had only just happened, she could recall the physical excitement she'd experienced when she'd first met Edward, then newly appointed as vicar. Yet to remember it wasn't to re-kindle it. Then there was that other moment, the hell she'd so recently come through forgotten as Edwin had fixed her with his first unblinking stare. That was something she'd never forget, nor ever want to; her feelings strengthened with each day.

There was another occasion, though, and one that frightened her still. It had been when Edwin was six weeks old and, before she could pick up the threads of living, she'd had to be churched. Never a deeply religious person, this was a custom and she'd accepted it without question. Perhaps if Edward hadn't been the one to speak the words she would have ridden through the service, making her responses and going out into the summer sunshine without giving any of it any thought. That first moment of meeting him had hit her, but it had been nothing compared with the emotion she'd felt as she'd knelt alone in the front pew while from the chancel step his voice called on her to give thanks that she'd been delivered in the great danger of childbirth.

Her heart had raced and her hands shaken, hatred had filled her. He'd spoken the words that he commanded should fill her heart: 'Lo, children and fruit of the womb are an heritage and gift that cometh from the Lord.' The shock of her emotion had frightened her. It was as if he and the Lord he extolled were one, or rather as if he wanted her to see them as one. To hate one's God is a terrifying thing but she hadn't been able to separate Him

119

from the man who had the power to use her as he would. If Edwin was a gift it was to her, only to her.

'Like arrows in the hand of a giant; even so are young children. Happy is the man whose quiver is full of them . . .'

Any voice but his and probably she'd not have heeded the words, but to hear Edward saying these things, standing before her as if he were a messenger from on high, he who no doubt was ready to bestow on her the favour of his lust . . . Happy and placid her family had always thought her, only temporarily cast down by the difficult business of bearing a child. They wouldn't have believed the state of her mind as she knelt there only feet from the man she'd married. Just as love had come in a flash (or at least the first awakening of it) so she'd felt physically shaken by hatred. Her hands had gripped the wooden rail in front as she'd tried to steady herself. She was trapped, like an animal in a cage, and where could she turn for help? How could she pray to that God, yet where else could she look? She'd heard Edward's clear ringing tones beseeching that God whose messenger he apparently was to make her live faithfully. Until that moment she'd never known what hating a person could do to one; hands clammy, mouth dry, while her heart had banged and a trickle of sweat had run down her side from under her arm. After that his words had been lost, she'd not even tried to follow what he said.

In this same church she'd made her vows – well, she'd keep them, she'd be faithful, she'd be a comfort but 'Oh dear God,' she'd begged either from habit or because she had no one else to call on, 'don't let him come to me for that. It's so beastly, yes that's just what it is, beastly, like animals. I've done it for him already, we've got Edwin now, so please make him see, keep him away . . .'

'Come Lucy, what is it? You're not well?' It had finished and she'd not even noticed. 'Sit a moment, push your head down.' If he'd known what had made her feel ill and faint, would he have treated her with such sympathy?

Churched and ready for the world, ready for her husband too — but not Lucy. That had been the night she'd moved into the nursery so that Edwin who still needed a feed during the first hours of each new day wouldn't disturb Edward, and so too that Edward wouldn't disturb her. From that time onwards Amelia's day-time visits were extended to nights as well and became more and more frequent.

Now on Christmas Eve they were glad to have her here, both wanting the buffer of a third person, Lucy because she grieved for the girl with James gone and that woman at the Court, and Edward because — no he wasn't prepared even to ask himself the reason that the house was only alive when she was in it.

Strange that it should have been on that same evening, the memory of so many Christmases haunting him, that James wrote as he did to Amelia. Not a letter of pride in the place he was determined to make for himself, for despite the kindness of his elderly friends tonight he was only aware of what he'd lost. His rightful place was at Merton Court, surrounded by the comforts he'd always known. His spite was partly for Beth and the way she'd used him, but even more it was directed at Henry. How dare he take away what was his birthright! There was no doubt in James's mind that his father had been hoodwinked by a scheming wanton but he felt no pity, only triumph that Henry, whose word was never questioned, could have let it happen. One day he'd wake up from his fool's paradise, then he'd realize how he'd wronged his own son. A last fling at youth, his vanity flattered that a girl could want him; but what conceit not to see it wasn't him she'd wanted but the status of being his wife.

As the bells rang proclaiming it was Christmas there

was no goodwill towards men in James's heart. Once started the words poured out. If he'd expected to feel cleansed at the end he was disappointed but at least the responsibility for keeping silent was no longer his. Now Millie would know Beth for what she was and what she did with the knowledge was up to her.

CHAPTER FIVE

For three months Amelia kept her letter hidden at the back of her handkerchief drawer, watching, wondering, building up ever more hatred of the trollop who dared to make herself mistress of their home. She'd always suspected her, for what else could she be to worm her way into their father's affections as she had? The letter had confirmed her worst fears and more. Her father was surely old enough to look out for himself, but she hadn't known herself capable of such loathing as she felt for Beth. Dear gentle James, he who'd been the one to worry over the plight of the sewing maid, he who could never hurt a soul or say a harsh word – she'd done this to him, filled him with bitterness and spite so alien to his nature. It wasn't just for itself that the story he told sickened Millie – nothing she could have heard about Beth would have surprised her – it was the hurt she recognized behind his words.

Often lying in bed in the quiet of night she'd imagine herself facing her father with what she knew; she'd picture his face, anger giving way to shock as he realized the truth. She built up a scene where Beth would be banished and James brought home, where Henry would be humbled and grateful for their saving him. All dreams, of course, for face to face with her father she could never bring herself to find the courage. For too many years she'd been in awe of him – loved him, yes, but his word was law, his pleasure what they'd all striven for. So like a festering sore her resentment built up.

It was an April morning when at breakfast she'd been surprised at his reaction to her announcement that she'd been invited to stay the night at the Vicarage again.

'Do you not consider you spend too much time in your sister's household?'

'But Papa, Lucy likes me being there.'

'And Edward?' In truth the family at the Vicarage worried Henry. One heard of post-natal depression (a lot of nonsense in his opinion – Bella had never suffered from it – some of these women today had too little to do, too much time to think about themselves) but Edwin was a year old and it was quite time Lucy looked to the future, had more children.

'I don't know what you mean. Why shouldn't Edward want me there? We're good friends. I even think he's glad of my help in the parish for Lucy enjoys spending all her time with Edwin. Papa, I promised to be there, the Bishop is staying the night after confirmation and Lucy will be glad to have me.'

'Then be sure you're there to free Lucy to perform her rightful duties. Her place is at Edward's side, not as a nursemaid to an only child.'

The implication was obvious. Amelia's face flamed. Could he read her mind so well? No, of course he couldn't; as far as he was concerned there was only one viewpoint on any subject and that was his own. It would never occur to him to wonder why she was as she was, or Lucy either. With her mouth set in a tight line she made no answer.

It was that conversation and the memory of it, which she probably allowed to grow out of all proportion as she packed her boxes to take to Lucy's, that finally decided her.

After supper that night while Beth was seeing that Phoebe was settled in bed Henry went into the library and there, on his desk, was an envelope addressed simply to 'Papa'. He slit it open only to find another inside in James's writing. He frowned. Silly child being so secretive about having a letter from James. Why not pass it to him openly?

December? He scanned the date at the head of the page. But why give it to him now, in April? The two sheets in

124

James's unmistakable sloping hand had obviously been read and re-read. But why now? She must have left an old letter by mistake, believing it to be one just received. For still his letters were only to her and even to her he'd still given no address. As Henry read the frown deepened.

Phoebe tucked in, Beth crossed the landing to the head of the stairs intending to join Henry, in the library as she supposed.

'Beth!' His voice surprised her from their bedroom doorway, sharp and unfamiliar. 'Come here please.'

'Why, Henry, what is it? What's the matter?' From his tone she knew something was.

'Shut the door behind you – now read this. I want the truth, the whole truth.'

As soon as he passed her the letter she knew what it must say. In a flash she saw again these last months, like a brilliant bubble of happiness ready to burst and be gone.

'Well? Is it true?' "Made a cuckold of the old man" I think is how he put it.'

'No, no, never that . . .'

'What he says – you and James – dammit, Beth, he's my son! Is it true, you've lain with my own son? And I thought – '

'Don't! Oh, Henry, believe me, please, please . . .'

'You're telling me this isn't so? You've never been his?' he clutched at the hope.

What did it matter now, it was all over. The fight drained out of her and she slumped on to the bed. She couldn't bring herself to raise her eyes.

'Yes, that part's true.'

'Dear God . . .'

'It was long ago, at the time of Hal's wedding, that hot summer spell. It all happened in a week or two – I believed I was in love with him, truly I didn't do it lightly, Henry.'

'Go on . . .'

'I didn't even know you then. Can't you see? We were children, hardly more than that, he was different from anyone I'd known, I thought it was love, I wanted it to be and I wanted to be loved – I didn't know, I didn't know.' Her voice that had started in such hopeless calm rose to a sob. 'Summer ended and it was like a dream gone – yet I tried to hang on to it. He used to come to the coach-house, but I never, never let him touch me. I knew I didn't want him to yet I still tried to believe I was in love with him and he with me. But I knew, deep down I knew, it was no more than a game I played. My sin was that I should have told him but I didn't; I tried to pretend even to myself. Then I found you.' She seemed to crumple. From where she'd sat on the edge of the bed she slipped to the floor on her knees, clinging to his legs. 'Henry,' all her control was gone, 'don't hate me. You're all there is – nothing – no one – ' the words poured out; she had no pride. To both of them it was like a living nightmare.

'Stop it! Get up! Stand up, Beth!'

She didn't move but gradually her wild sobbing gave way to a silence that was almost worse. Her hold on him had slackened and when at last she spoke her voice was flat. 'What do you want me to do? Have I got to go?'

He moved away from her without answering, keeping his back to her as she still crouched on the floor. He should have torn the letter up, hung on to what they had, tried to forget he'd ever read it. She and James, they'd been young together, discovered the miracle of love together. He shut his eyes as if to blot out the scene he conjured up, and the memory too of Beth grovelling and broken, fighting to hold on to what they had. Did she feel as he did, numb? Or could her fear be partly for losing the security of their marriage? James's words echoed, taunting him. He felt sick.

'If you say you loved me, why couldn't you have told me? You let me send James away believing a lie.'

'I couldn't. I was frightened. You might not have understood. I was frightened, I tell you. I was wrong, wicked, I should have known it couldn't last.'

'Beth – oh, I don't know, I can't think, can't believe . . .'

126

Where was his re-born youth now? Tonight he was old and drained.

Her spirit was returning quicker than his. On the table by the bed was the Bible he carried downstairs each morning and, kneeling up, she laid her right hand on it while she clutched at him with her left.

'I swear to you on the holy book I've never been disloyal to you. Henry, I didn't even know you then. Once I did, then there was no one else in my world. Ever since that cold day, remember, you lent me your gloves. Remember? Beat me, whip me, but don't look at me like that, don't . . . don't . . .' Her voice was lost as she started to cry again.

In truth he didn't know how he looked at her. He envied her the relief of tears. Even anger would be better than this empty misery.

'You'd better go to bed, Beth. You can't let the girls see you looking like this. I'll tell them you have a headache.' Then taking his sleeping things he added: 'I'll stay in the dressing-room tonight, so I shan't disturb you.'

'Tell me what you want of me.'

'I can't talk tonight – I can't. Perhaps by the morning things will be clearer.'

He left her and went down to the library. Much later she heard him come up the stairs but he didn't come into their room. A second door to his dressing-room led off the landing and she heard it open and close behind him. Well into the night the light showed under the communicating door. So he couldn't sleep either. She longed to go to him, to beg him to trust her, but she couldn't stand another scene, she knew that neither of them could. 'If things aren't as I'd hoped I try to accept' hadn't he said? Was that what he was doing, wrestling with his soul, looking for a sign? She sat up in bed, gazing at the strip of light, her own mind too confused to seek help where she knew he'd be looking. The movement of the handle riveted her eyes to the door as quietly it opened and she saw him.

He'd wanted just to look at her, he'd expected to find her asleep, not sitting watching him in the dim light from the dressing-room.

Wordlessly she held out her arms and then he was holding her.

'Forgive me, Bethie, my precious love, forgive me,' His face was buried against her neck and she felt the warmth of his tears.

'And you, forgive me. I should have told you. Henry, there's a past we didn't share but the present and the future are ours, just ours.'

'Always. Beth, it's finished, behind us – I know now and it doesn't matter. Suddenly I saw, it hadn't touched us.'

'Come to bed, Henry.'

That night their passion had been spent on emotion, yet they'd never been closer. Silently she nestled against him, words had no place for either of them. The evening and where it might have led was something neither wanted to contemplate, yet out of it had come a trust and a maturity of understanding that seemed almost tangible. No, words had no place, love-making had no place, just gratitude and a deep peace.

It was three months and more since James had written his letter to Amelia. Many a time during those months he must have wondered what sort of a hornets' nest he'd stirred up. Whatever he imagined, it was certainly far from the reality. But then, for all the brave venture he thought he'd taken to build a life of his own, how could he hope to have learnt understanding?

Beth didn't look back. The girl she'd been before Henry came into her life was but a shadowy figure. She didn't look back and, so complete was the present, she didn't look forward either. Each day was full and satisfying, always bringing her nearer to being the wife she meant to be. Now that she had no secret from him her confidence grew. The running of the house no longer frightened her and the further Beth Machin receded into the shadows the more easily Beth Copeland handled the reins. Mrs Murphy recognized the difference and surprisingly, at least on the surface, accepted it. Once Beth gained the assurance of mistress the battle was won. In fact, in a perverse way, the housekeeper felt a secret — and even to herself not openly admitted — pride that 'one of us can play the part like she does'.

Not just at the Court was Beth finding her way but at the works too. Hardly a day went by without her trap appearing in the yard. No longer did she go just when Henry took her and, once there, she didn't spend her time only with him for amongst the staff she'd made a place for herself.

'Not right for a woman,' a few of them said, but 'can always talk to her, she understands,' was the view of most. 'She's comely to be sure. You'd never guess at the sharpness of her mind,' one pattern-maker told his wife — to be answered by a sniff and: 'Sharp enough not to be having babies it seems.' But she was wrong and, as summer gave way to autumn, what was known in the family was being guessed at amongst the workers. Beth enjoyed the hours she spent there now in an office she'd made her own. Much that she did could have been done by any young clerk, as Hal had said, but the fact that she was Beth Copeland and not just any young clerk made her position different from any other. To her the men brought their problems, whether domestic, financial or to do with their working relationships. She was a link between Henry and the staff, but more than that — for the business mattered to her, what it produced mattered, the happiness of the staff mattered — the future of the works mattered. And that future must surely be the child she carried. With all her strength — and she was never short of it — she willed that child to care as she did, never doubting it was in her power to mould his mind.

But none of that happened overnight. It was something that built gradually in the months ahead.

Without Naomi's chatter the room Esme had shared with her seemed dead. How often she'd watched her pretty sister as she'd sat before the mirror, holding her golden curls piled high, letting them fall, turning her head first this way, then that, and always prattling or finding something to laugh about. Now her letters came regularly, full of the exciting things she was learning at the Academy, eager to prepare herself to be launched into the social world where she had no doubt men would fall at her feet.

On her own, Esme gave up the 'battle of the rags'. No, that's not quite the truth; it was Beth who suggested to her she should alter her hair. One morning just after Whitsun Beth thought at breakfast time how unfair life could be. Even though on her own Esme didn't have constantly to bear comparison with her sister, it really was time she was taken in hand. The rags had been done hurriedly last night for Esme had been anxious to get into bed and read her book. The outcome was ringlets that hung well enough on the left side, whilst on the right side two rags had fallen out, leaving her lank hair straight and another had been put in wrongly so that a clump stood out at a right-angle behind her ear. As if that weren't enough, a large red gathering on her chin was throbbing its way into being a spot of more magnitude even by her standards.

'Are you coming in today, Beth?' Henry seemed not to have noticed that the plainest of his children had an even more than normally 'off' day.

'Later. Perhaps not before the afternoon,' for this morning she resolved to spend some time with Esme. The two girls had been so inseparable that now she hated to intrude even though she knew Esme needed some sort of help.

'Good idea. You have a quiet morning,' Henry agreed – but at that time only he and Beth knew what was behind his words. She laughed, enjoying their secret. Her own state of wellbeing gave her that extra will to do something for Esme, so gawky and lacking in confidence.

After breakfast the girl disappeared to her room, a habit that was becoming more and more frequent since Naomi had gone, especially as she wasn't expected for lessons with Reverend Gilstone until the following week. She pulled a chair to the window and sat down, opening her book where the ribbon marker had kept her place. She heard her father ride out of the stable yard, from the basement came the clatter of dishes, outside on the lawn she could see Phoebe bouncing a ball and clapping her hands as she counted her way through some game. Her fingers gently touched the swelling on her chin, hard, red and sore. By tomorrow it would have gathered to a festering head and there, just by her mouth, a sharp pricking told her another was teasing her ready to rear if she touched it.

A tap on the door. 'Esme, are you busy?'

'Well, no, I suppose not. Do you want me to do something?'

'No,' Beth came in and shut the door behind her. 'I'll go away if you don't want me – but I thought we'd talk.'

'Oh.' Talk! Whatever could Beth have to talk to her about? Had she done something wrong? For no one, especially anyone who mattered, could want to talk to her. 'Is something the matter? What have I done?'

'No, nothing's the matter.' Beth sat on the edge of the bed. Somehow she had to get through to Esme; she'd plunge straight in and hope. 'In fact it's because I'm so excited I wanted to tell you. I'm going to have a baby. Isn't it absolutely wonderful? I can't believe it.'

. . . wanted to tell you first, she'd said! Esme forgot her gathering boil.

'Fancy you telling me! Doesn't Hal know, or Margaret?'

'No, just us. Well, we're in the house, it's us it'll be most important to. Amelia's away more than she's here,

Phoebe's too little to know about babies, but you're nearly grown up.'

Esme was almost pretty. Her hair stuck out where it should have hung down and hung down where it should have curled, her teeth crossed in front, and when she stood up she managed to knock her thigh against the corner of the table, yet for all her clumsiness she was pretty in the warmth of her smile. She bent and dropped a kiss on the top of Beth's head, conscious from the sour taste in her mouth today that her breath wasn't pleasant.

Beth slipped an arm around her waist. 'It'll be lovely won't it Esme? Another baby; it seems to keep the wheels turning. Do you understand what I mean?'

'Yes. I really am pleased – for you and for Papa too, Beth.'

It was her answer that awoke Beth to the reason for her mission. Her own news had broken the ice but it was Esme's future, not her own, she was worried about.

'It gives one a lovely "moving ahead" feeling,' her excitement was evident, 'for all of us. Naomi seems to enjoy the Academy, Phoebe will start proper school soon – isn't it lucky Hilton House opening just when she's ready? And you, Esme, are you looking forward to the Academy? I wish I could too, but you have a good brain. I hate waste.'

'No one has said a thing like that to me before. They've all been to the Academy. Yet you didn't, Beth, and you run a house as proficiently as any of them.'

'I lack the social graces, Esme. Oh, I don't mind. Once upon a time I thought it mattered but I've learnt it's more important to know oneself and be what one is.'

'Surely we should strive to be better than we are, to be aware of a perfection that is our goal even though we never reach it? That's what Margaret always taught us.'

'Indeed she's right. But to do that we must know what we're best fitted for. It can't be right all to follow the same pattern. Look at us here. Every one of us so different; it's

132

trying to put us all into one mould that makes for frustration.'

'Like me and my beastly rags,' Esme laughed, but Beth knew it was only to hide her true feelings. Her light blue eyes blinked back the sudden tears of self-pity, blinked them back but not before they'd brought little bloodshot lines to the whites. Poor Esme, never one of those to cry daintily, just one tear would give her burning eyes and a red nose!

'That's about the truth, Esme, like your hair and like the fact the county doesn't call on me. I expect there's something with everyone, don't you? But once we recognize it it doesn't matter any longer. Certainly that I'm not on the visiting lists doesn't matter a jot to me now – I thought it did until Henry showed me it doesn't – and why should your hair not wanting to curl worry you? Here, sit down, let me brush these silly corkscrews out and see if we can't find the right way for it, the way that's really you and not a copy of someone else.'

It was only the beginning. There were days ahead when Esme welcomed Beth's guidance, when she let herself be persuaded into dresses of dark plaid or of a puritanical line so much better suited to her large-boned, angular figure. Then there were others when she'd look at the reflection of this new self, her smooth hair, the more comfortable shoes that allowed her to walk with long strides, and she'd blame her lack of femininity on Beth. Then her tongue would be sharp, her words as cutting as they had ever been, but whereas Naomi had accepted her moods with patience that wasn't one of Beth's stronger suits. On those days they had the good sense to recognize that they were better apart.

So summer saw changes; in Esne with the awareness of her true self, in Beth as the months of her pregnancy went on. And in Phoebe too, for now each morning she was driven by Algy to Hinton House, there to learn a lesson that was new to her; how to be a child amongst others of

133

her own age. She was finding herself standing quite firmly on her own two broad feet.

The same morning that Beth resolved to 'take Esme in hand' Amelia was at the Vicarage. Since James had gone she'd taken every opportunity of escape and after the day, six weeks ago now, when she'd passed the letter to Henry she'd been away far more than she'd been at home. No longer did she ask permission but if she had Henry would have given it gladly. It never entered her head that he might be concerned at the change in her attitude. All she saw was his disapproval, never considering it hid a hurt as deep as her own, for Millie had always been very dear to him. Such a short time ago those soft brown eyes used to watch him, ready to smile if he was happy, anxious if he wasn't; now, though, she avoided meeting his glance, sat quietly through the meals they had to take together, her mouth set in a tight line. Occasionally if Beth spoke he'd notice Millie's brows raise and her eyes turn on her in wordless scorn. Her whole personality seemed changed and, to be honest, he was glad to have her out of the house.

'Lucy, shall I do the flowers for the hall? That white lilac is perfect now.'

'I wish you would. You arrange them better than I do and I'm going up to the nursery to fetch Edwin.'

'Isn't it funny how one alters? Different people come along and the person you used to be seems gone. You know, Lucy, I just can't picture you without Edwin now.'

'Nor I. You wait Millie, one day you'll be the same.'

Amelia shrugged her shoulders. 'I can't picture the "me" I used to be either. Everything at the Court is different. Suddenly there's nothing of the old place left and yet the old days are no time ago. I dare say Esme's the same, but that's about all.'

'Papa doesn't come here very often these days. You'd think he'd want to see Edwin, wouldn't you?'

'It seems he's not interested to see anyone but her. I dare say too it's because you make me welcome. I'm a real thorn in his flesh and in her's too.'

'Of course we make you welcome. Edward is more cheery when you're here and I'm glad to have you, you know that. Nonetheless this afternoon I'm going to take Edwin and call on Beth at the Court. Bad feeling is so uncomfortable and, right or wrong, he's married to her so we have to make what we will of it.' Lucy liked life to be comfortable and uncomplicated.

'You won't find she'll fall over herself fussing Edwin and more than likely she'll not be at home, she'll be in the workshops.'

'No place for her, not in her position. That's the real trouble of course, I really cannot think why Papa couldn't have wed someone like Mrs Kendall from Marwell House, a widow and his own age, or even Miss Turnbull. You know her, Millie? She moved into that large grey house at the end of the High Street. A most refined person.'

Amelia remembered her indeed and the memory brought a rare chuckle. Thin, straight-backed Miss Turnbull, so well suited to the tall grey house on the High Street, was a far cry from the comely Beth. The comparison soon took the smile off her face. It was revolting and, worse, it was humiliating that he could behave as he had. Fallen straight into her trap, beguiled, bewitched . . .

It seemed that Lucy had had enough of the topic; she was on her way to fetch Edwin. Her days – and nights – were centred around him. A marriage as empty as hers might be expected to make her unhappy, but not so. In the baby she had all she wanted; he filled her days with such joy that she was truly content. Edward was outside it all but then he had his work and she never neglected the running of his home so she didn't consider he might be any less satisfied than she was herself.

The conversation had disturbed Amelia and not simply on account of Henry and Beth. She took a small sharp knife and went out to cut the lilac, but what Lucy had said kept coming back to her. Couldn't imagine a time without Edwin – but she'd had two years with Edward before the baby had come. Those years seemed as far removed from her as the old life she'd left behind at the Court. Then there was her attitude to their father's marriage, her willingness to make the best of it; surely that could only be because it didn't matter terribly to her, her own world was secure with her home and her baby? Amelia's thoughts went round in circles but each time they were brought back to the same thing, a truth so glaring that she couldn't avoid it. What honestly made her spend so much of her time 'sheltering' at the Vicarage? Did her father's marriage bother her so much? If she had a life of her own (or did she mean a 'love of her own') couldn't she accept just as Lucy did? Was Lucy's whole being centred on Edwin or was she no different from other women with a young child to rear? She thought she knew the answer as far as Lucy was concerned, but what of Edward? He treated Lucy well, was courteous, kind, yet Millie knew she was no true wife to him. Didn't he mind? Didn't he want her? Didn't he need a woman to love him . . . ? She'd forgotten all about the lilac as she stood in front of the flower-covered tree, the knife in her hand and her brown eyes gazing blankly as her thoughts ran riot.

'Let me reach some of the high branches down for you,' his voice was startling only inches behind her. She felt the hot colour rush to her face, almost as if he'd been reading her thoughts.

'Lucy's gone up to fetch Edwin,' she blurted, trying to slot him back into place in his family.

'She's in the morning room with him, I just saw her. I'm going to walk across the fields to see old Mrs Dilley. On Wednesdays she has communion. Walk with me, Millie. I'll wait until you've finished the flowers. She can't get out these days and she loves a visitor.'

'Won't Lucy go?' She knew the answer but loyalty made

her suggest it, loyalty and a warning voice that told her she was making things harder for herself. Even so she hadn't the will-power to make an excuse.

'No. She wouldn't walk so far and she likes her mornings at home.' He didn't quite look at her as he added: 'It's a lovely morning – please come, Mill.'

The brown eyes smiled, her hands busy again with the flowers. As soon as the vase was done she was ready.

Lucy watched them go from the morning-room window, happy to be left at home. She and Edwin needed no one else and when she'd taken him upstairs for his sleep she'd go to the kitchen and run through the grocery order with Mrs Plumley. Apart from being with Edwin there was nothing she liked better than to go down there, watch cook at work at the huge scrubbed wooden table, smell the cakes in the oven, listen to the activity of running a house. Lucy prided herself that the Vicarage had a good mistress, even that Edward had a good wife to see the wheels kept turning smoothly. So she saw him hold the garden gate open for Amelia to go through and had no misgivings. 'It's time she thought of being wed herself. A baby would soon fill her mind, poor little Millie. She cared too well for Jamie I dare say. My word, but Edward will be warm in those tall gaiters with this sudden heat. Come on then, Edwin, my pretty, you'll be crawling in no time.' Then she scooped the little boy into her arms laughing delightedly as he buried his fists in her hair.

James was ready for visitors, or at any rate ready for Amelia, and he had no doubt that as soon as she knew where he was she'd come. All these months he'd pictured her at home at the Court, looking forward to his letters, her own life following the same comfortable pattern they'd always known – the same except for the blank his going would have left and the anxiety she must feel for him. Had he been a little less wrapped up in himself he would have realized that her days must be very different; perhaps he'd never recognized how her personality had been sunk in trying to keep the atmosphere pleasant in a way that would please Henry. To think of home was to think of Millie, her eyes always ready to meet his in understanding sympathy or silent laughter. So when early that summer he considered No 11 Chain Street, Newbridge, was ready for a guest he wrote to bid her welcome, certain that she'd be relieved to be invited but never for a moment even imagining the real reason for her acceptance, how gladly she'd clutch at the escape for her own sake – for hers and for Edward's too.

Shuddering to a halt, the engine hissed, clouds of steam and smoke blowing back on to the platform as the few passengers alighting at Newbridge climbed out. Just for a second, at the sight of her, James forgot everything but how pleased he was she'd come; he even forgot to be self-conscious about his newly grown moustache, bristling and bushy and, he confidently hoped, adding a dignity in keeping with the businessman he'd become.

'Why James,' she hugged him, 'I hardly recognized you! How handsome you look.'

'And you, Millie. Oh, but you've no idea how much I've looked forward to this!'

'Then you should have told me where you were long ago. I'm not a visitor, you know, someone who can see everything only when it's perfect. I could have helped you. Each letter I hoped you'd ask me and each letter I hoped you'd tell me where I could write. I've missed you so much, Jamie. It's been dreadful without you.'

'Let's not talk about it, Millie. I try not even to think of what it must be like. I'll get your boxes and find a cab to take us home. It's not grand, Mill – but it's truly home,' for in the summer it was easy enough to forget the cold discomfort of those winter months, the mornings when he hadn't been able to make the fire burn to heat a kettle, the mice droppings he'd found on the larder shelf, the latch stiff with frost on the outside closet. No, in midsummer the picture was rosier. He was even prepared to believe that by next winter things would be different.

If the little kitchen behind the shop seemed cramped she gave no sign that she thought so. The range threw out a heat she could have done without, but by the evening they'd need to cook their supper on it and the two huge black kettles showed that at least there was no shortage of hot water. The closet was a far cry from what she'd been used to, she made her visit there as quick as she could, covering the container with its heavy wooden lid and hurrying back indoors.

'That's the worst thing, Mill; they come on Wednesdays to empty it – I wish it wasn't like that.'

'Never mind, Jamie. It's not very nice, but at least being in town the cart comes to empty it and it's away from the house. In here everything is sweet and clean. Oh I'm going to love being here with you. Can I make us some tea? Tell me where everything is and let me be useful.'

Gladly he let her – after all housekeeping wasn't a man's work. A routine evolved, one in which Amelia found herself busier than she'd ever been. From the moment she woke in the morning there were things to be done, the ashes to be cleared, the cooking, the cleaning, once a week the copper to light so that their clothes might be washed, the ironing, the mending and the marketing. No wonder when she lay down in bed at night sleep overtook her even before she had time to let her mind indulge in the dreams she wouldn't permit during the day.

No word was said of how long she might stay; the arrangement obviously suited James and, for all the lack of comforts, in hard work she found an escape. Bit by bit he formed a picture of life at the Court, but it wasn't until her third week when she'd still said nothing of his letter that he asked her if she'd told anyone what she knew.

'Not for ages, I wanted to. He fawns around her so I wanted to make him see what she is. But I was too

139

cowardly — it seems silly now that I think of it from here. Sometimes I wanted to tell him just to hurt him, then I'd see him as he always was and I couldn't. In any case, in truth I hadn't the courage.'

'So? When did you?'

'I left him your letter when I was going to Lucy's to stay.'

'And?'

'I was away for a few days. I kept expecting to hear. He must surely send her away, I thought, or, oh, I don't know what I imagined would happen. When I got home I was almost frightened of what I'd find. All he said was: "That letter from James you left for Beth and me to read, we read it of course and I've burnt it. There was nothing in it to keep I believe." You know how he can look at you, as cold as steel. I felt like a criminal, yet it's she who should be laden with guilt and she just stood by his side and said not a word. It didn't touch them, James, and now as her belly gets larger I swear so does the opinion she has of herself. Phoebe dotes on her, Esme is becoming a different person, Margaret and Hal seem never to give a thought to Mama or what used to be . . .'

'And Lucy? And Naomi?'

'Naomi is quite taken up with the Academy, grooming herself for the handsome young knight who'll come riding. Lucy — I hardly know. She's content with her own affairs, doesn't really look outside. I spend more time there than I do at the Court but I hardly talk to her, not deep down talk. Yet she seems to want me to be there.'

'You should be having a life of your own, Millie, not dancing attendance on the others.' Then, holding her hand in his for a moment: 'I'm glad you're not though, for you'd have no time for me then.'

'Silly, James, have you ever been in love?'

'You read my letter.' He frowned at the question.

'Yes, but if that had been love, real love, surely you couldn't have wanted to hurt her?'

140

'Of course it was love.'

'Do you know why I don't want what you call a life of my own? I'll tell you. It's because the only person I could share it with is Edward.'

'No, Mill, don't say that. You'll fall in love properly one of these days. He's good looking, I suppose women would find him attractive, and you've seen too much of each other; you've been thrown together I dare say and Lucy hasn't been herself.'

She shook her head, 'No, it's none of those things. I'll never be his, I never can be. I know that, but I'll never be anyone else's either.'

'Does he know? How does he feel?'

'Yes of course he knows, yet we've never talked of it — and I shouldn't have told you. But James, I had to. Lucy is so uncaring. Yet I'd do anything to make him happy and can do nothing at all.'

'Stay here, Millie. Try not to think about them. Perhaps if you're not there Lucy will pull herself together.'

'Don't you say that too. It's what Papa said, or at least what he meant, as if it were my fault and I was trying to come between them. She doesn't want him, that's what's so cruel; I swear if she loved him, if she tried to be a real companion to him, I'd be pleased for him. Do you remember how he used to be, so jolly always?'

'And so did she.'

'Then what went wrong, James? She's pale and pasty, her mouth turns down when she talks to him, it's as if he's an intrusion on her happiness. And he, oh I hate to see him like it, he seems to have forgotten to be young.'

'Poor Millie. Life's used us both badly. Stay here with me, it could be so good. You don't belong at the Court any more than I do. That trollop will fill the house with ginger-headed children and the old man's too intent on chasing his youth ever to miss us.'

'She's very interested in the works you know, Jamie.'

141

'Ah, I dare say she is. It's where the brass comes from, isn't it?'

A vague stab of conscience told her they weren't being fair to Beth, but it was so good to feel wanted that she didn't heed it.

So the months passed and as summer gave way to autumn Millie was still at the shop in Chain Street trying to turn the room behind the 'teaching room' (as they termed the little ante-room leading off from behind the counter) into something of a home. The black-leaded range shone from her brushing, a jug of flowers put her mark on the table; determinedly she put the past behind her. Only an occasional brief letter to the Vicarage or an even briefer one to the Court told them that the pair at Newbridge were thriving. And at the Vicarage, sorry though Lucy had been to see her young sister go, life was much too pleasant to leave time for regrets. Each day Edwin learned to do some new thing; by the autumn he was standing and each day she waited and encouraged for his first step. As for Edward, if his life had suddenly become empty his wife certainly didn't notice it.

And all the while at the Court Beth grew ever more determined that Esme should be given the chance she deserved.

'You say yourself how the world has changed. Why Henry, all around we see it, we're caught up in it at the workshops, you more than anyone, always looking forward, trying to find more efficent methods.'

'That's a different matter. She's just at a loss without Naomi, Naomi always was the leader. Another few months and she'll go to the Academy too, feel herself to be in the swim of things again.'

'You're wrong, Henry. Try and know her — forget Naomi and think just of Esme. Hal and James both went

142

away to school; you considered an education important for them.'

'My dear,' he laughed fondly, 'what a fiery little radical you are!'

'I am no such thing! All I beg you is to see her for what she is. Of all your children she has the best brain. Why should she be forced into a mould where her greatest attribute means nought, where she'll forever be a poor second to her pretty sister?'

'She'll be nothing of the kind. She's a dear child, she'll marry perhaps all the more happily because her looks won't sweep some youth off his feet. A good wife and mother she'll make. Beth my dear, I'm not blind to her good points, she's steady and kind, she has strength of character, she — '

'Oh, Henry!' Beth had to make him see, 'Listen to me, do. If I can't make you understand go and talk to Reverend Gilstone and I swear he'll bear out my words.'

'I've no doubt of it. He always speaks extremely well of her work.'

'Then move with these changing times. We're not in the fifties now. She's growing up to a world where there will surely be opportunities for a woman besides running a house and bearing children.'

'Is that of so little matter?'

Beth looked down at her bulk and he saw the twinkle light up her green eyes, eyes that only a moment before had been so earnest in the cause she fought for Esme.

'Little?' Both her hands rested on the enormous hump that had at last put an end to her activities, 'Nothing little about the making of babies, here's a proof of that!' She lowered herself on to the sofa with a new awkwardness, but when she tapped the seat at her side invitingly the face she turned to him bore no sign of strain or even tiredness. Her cheeks were pink, the whites of her eyes clear, the column of her neck slender; yet in all her uncomfortable pregnancies Bella had never carried such a bulge. From the

143

back Beth looked the same girl who'd chased a hoop with Phoebe, yet to see her from the side or front one must wonder where she found the strength to carry her burden. It must surely have been a sign of her stamina that even now her mind was still full of other things.

'Is it not enough for you Beth? Surely you don't want to see her fighting for a place in a man's world?'

'A man's world indeed! The world is as we make it and if God hadn't wanted women to play a part – other than bedding and breeding – why did He give us brains to use?' Another thought struck her and with customary suddenness she changed the subject. 'You know Henry, this son of ours, I swear he turns somersaults. Never is he still for a moment, he has arms and legs every which way.'

'Poor Bethie – and I say it's a man's world. No work we do can compare with that.'

'Poppycock! Even this we couldn't manage without you. Another month and I'll not know myself, with my insides my own again.'

He took her hand in his, content in this November evening to let the seconds tick idly by, not worrying about Esme's education or lack of it, not anxious as he so often was about how Millie was coping with the onset of winter in that wretched little shop. This evening Beth was enough. He saw her eyes were shut, dear Beth, she was probably more tired than she'd admit.

'When I'm not so fat and clumsy, do you know what I want, Henry?'

So she wasn't asleep.

'I'm about to be told I dare say.'

'Indeed you are. You can give it to me as a reward for this new son.'

'Or daughter.'

'Son. Even in today's world no girl could hurl herself about like this one does.'

'And what do you want?'

'Oh yes, I was telling you. Henry I want one of these

144

new contraptions with two wheels.' Her eyes were wide open now as she turned to him. 'A bone-shaker on two wheels, just fancy! You drive it with pedals on the front wheel. I've thought a lot about it since I've been so slow and awkward – just imagine, by January I could be pedalling to see you at the works.' Even she knew that was an exaggeration. 'Just think of the freedom, Henry; I could go anywhere.' She chuckled at the picture in her mind. 'The bassinet tied to the back and I'd fairly rattle along.'

He smiled indulgently at her but didn't reply. What a child she was, even the baby seemed not to be part of her, she was like a girl with a pillow (or indeed a bolster!) tucked in her skirt. Once the baby arrived she'd have more to think about than finding her independence on one of these contraptions she spoke of. Whoever heard of such ideas, a married woman – indeed a woman careering around the countryside on two wheels! Still Henry tried to keep abreast of the times, even to think ahead in his own industry, and by the time he bought her her bone-shaker he almost believed the idea of it had been his own.

Never had there been such a woman, time and again he thought it. Later that same night in the warm depths of their feather mattress even now she aroused the same passion in him she always had and responded to it with an intensity that seemed heightened by her condition. Ungainly she might have become, but to him she'd never been more beautiful. Her body might be unwieldy but her need of him found expression in her lips and in her hands. A need not now for herself but for him. Minutes later they lay close and still her eyes were full of tears, tears of tenderness that misted her vision in the light of the flickering fire.

'Bethie,' he whispered as soon as he'd breath to speak, 'not crying, Bethie?'

'I think I love you too much, it frightens me. Silly isn't it – must be my condition!' Her voice broke on a sob.

'Beth, Beth, my sweetheart.'

145

She clung to him. 'Never leave me, Henry, just hold me. I couldn't live without you.'

He held her close, both of them knowing so well the day must come when he would indeed leave her. Silently he prayed that she'd find the courage her life would need, for he knew what it meant to be alone; but Beth, who'd never been a faint-heart, couldn't let herself look ahead to a day when he'd not be with her. Usually she lived her hours as they came, each one full of itself. Suddenly tonight the hand of fear gripped her.

He thought she was comforted, he even drifted into sleep, but for her it was only the start of the longest night she'd known.

She couldn't understand herself. Was it a premonition of something dreadful that kept her awake? Her body couldn't find a comfortable way to lie. Even her arms and legs wouldn't be still and to turn over without disturbing him was quite an operation. The warmth half lulled her until with a start she felt the first stabbing pain. Involuntarily she cried out, its violence took her breath. The baby was still, in fact she realized now that it hadn't moved since before she came to bed. There it was again, she'd never experienced pain like it; it filled her whole mind and seemed to tear right through her. Then it eased and she gulped at the air trying to regain her composure – and her reason. She must have sweated with the pain, her still naked body was sticking to the wet sheets and between her breasts she felt the wetness trickle. She wanted to wake him, but perhaps it was over now. The baby must have lain on a nerve. If she was still it might not happen again.

No, not again, not again! Her cry woke Henry so suddenly and violently did it hit her, but she allowed herself only that one startled cry for Beth was nothing if not a fighter. Her teeth cut into her lip as she kept back a moan, for soon she knew what was happening.

'It's coming early.' She managed to keep her voice

steady. 'He's not supposed to come for weeks.' Henry heard the fear in her voice for all her effort to hide it.

'It won't be yet, Bethie, but I'll send Algy for Mrs Sedgewick.' All those occasions with Bella crowded back on him and the last time that had proved too much haunted him. Where now was his faith that should make him try to accept rather than question? 'Dear God, not Beth, not Beth. Anything, but not Beth.'

It won't be yet, he'd tried to reassure her but she knew different.

'Get towels, Henry,' she panted. 'Water — and I'm bleeding fast . . . ,' her voice was lost. From somewhere there were people, voices, she didn't know, she didn't care. The endless night enveloped her. In one moment when her thoughts cleared she remembered the fear and premonition of disaster that she'd known earlier and as the pain dragged her down again she believed she understood the reason for it. This must be what it was like to die.

CHAPTER SIX

The year 1863 drew to a close, a year which like any other
had seen changes in many a home. As the bells rang out
their message that midnight had come, doors were flung
open, customs of faith and superstition honoured. At the
Court old Ben opened the back door and the others
followed him outside, listening.

'There they are, that's the bells. Another year out and
gone and here we all are . . .' He meant it as a sign of
success. At his age he counted each one notched up a
triumph; still able to work and earn a roof over his head,
what he did still mattering – ah, and young Flo Murphy
(as from habit he thought of the now stout, middle-aged
ruler of the lower regions), she couldn't be such a chicken,
not if he stopped to take stock. 'In the warm we go then
and let's ha'a drop o' that port the gov'nor sent us down.'

'Ah, 'tis opened and ready. Pour it out, Jenny, and let's
drink to this brave new year.'

'That we will, Mrs Murphy, m'um and to those wee
babes up there starting on their first one,' Jenny agreed.

'Dear little souls, here's to them, red hair and all.' Mrs
Murphy took her port, loyalty to the house she'd served
so long stopping her adding anything about the babies'
mother. Fancy though, not five weeks after being brought
to bed with twins and there she'd been only yesterday
racing around on what Algy said she called her 'iron steed',
knickerbockers showing as her skirts blew up. It wasn't
decent! Mrs Murphy had been with the family so long that
loyalty to them was second nature, so she raised her glass
to drink to the babies and permitted herself no more than
a hint of a sniff of disdain – whether for Beth, for Henry
that he'd allowed himself to be so swept off his feet when

he should have been old enough to have had more sense to be sure, for the rumour she'd heard that Esme was to be sent off to one of these new boarding schools (not the same sort of thing as the others had all attended as fitted their station, but some place where her head would be crammed with book learning). Or perhaps her sniff was out of sympathy for those two dear children, James and Amelia. Like their mother both of them, no wonder they chose to go away where they couldn't see their home so altered. The others didn't seem to mind – well Mr Hal always had been his father's son and Miss Margaret had never had the sweetness of her mother. Young Lucy though, since the babies had arrived, even she came over with Edwin from Wilhampton often enough; she'd always been the same over babies though. Ah well, here's to 1864. Bring what it may, there was nought to do but accept it. Time they were all in their beds; little enough of the night left now.

'Now then, young Algy, just you make that your last. Two's enough at this time of night. No way to start the first day of the year with a thick head – and I'll be bound you've had a few at the Owl and Crescent.'

Like her, he kept his thoughts to himself, which was perhaps as well for she wasn't the sort to have her word questioned.

Ten minutes later the darkened basement showed them all to be gone. As they crept up the attic stairs (all except Algy who went across the yard to the coach-house) they could hear sounds from the main bedroom. Nicholas and Victoria had no intention of missing the start of their first year.

Beth took twins in her stride. Lucy marvelled, even if jealously. She'd had trouble finding enough to sustain her little Edwin, although thank God here he was at twenty months, his progress at last giving no cause for worry. But

149

Beth, up and about three weeks after her confinement with a waist as trim as ever, had no such problems. Two hungry mouths to feed and always enough. To Lucy motherhood had been everything, it had filled her whole mind; she'd held Edwin in arms weak with love believing he was the reason for her existence. To Beth it was no more than part. She delighted in these two wriggly little people, their soft red-gold hair, their eyes that by New Year had already changed from blue to a green as clear as her own. She gazed at them in wonder, recognizing that alike though they were physically there the resemblance ended; she'd seen it right from the start.

'Victoria finds life a puzzle, don't you my pretty?' She held the baby over her shoulder, tapping her back, talking to Lucy. 'Come on now or you'll have tummy ache. Hurry up, your brother's hungry too you know.' A loud burp was Victoria's answer. 'That's a good lady, now it's his turn.' Without further ado she put one baby in her crib, took the other screaming from his, put her left breast back into the bodice of her dress and gently eased the right one towards his open mouth. As soon as she took him into her arms his crying stopped, his mouth opened wide and his head moved from side to side searching for what he wanted. Once his hold was on her nipple he grunted, he gulped, he kicked, again he grunted, then drew his head back, stopped sucking and gazed at her.

'You see, Lucy, he's quite different. He knows it's here so now he's in no hurry. He'll take as much as she does but nothing's a battle to Nicholas.'

If Lucy thought it was all in Beth's imagination she didn't say so; after all it was good to see how well she was coping. If Papa had to marry some girl so completely unsuitable she supposed they should be glad she was turning out as well as she seemed. And surprisingly she found herself seeking Beth's company more than she did Margaret's.

Beth was sure things at the Vicarage were what she'd

call very wrong; perhaps she even saw how it had come about, what it was that frightened Lucy, but understand it she couldn't. This family of Henry's was so reserved; if only she could talk to Lucy, perhaps tell her things she didn't know, for although there might be no sure way of avoiding pregnancies (except the one she suspected Lucy took!) there were things one could do to make it less likely. She'd never been close to her own family but her mother had made no secret of these things to her daughters. She'd had a frankness seldom found – perhaps never found – in the social set that even now didn't accept her. One day the opportunity would come and she and Lucy would talk, but until then it was enough that Lucy was aware in Beth she had a friend. To rush would frighten her off.

Much later Beth was to look back on those early months of their friendship and wonder if she should have acted differently. So wrapped up was she in her own affairs though that it was easier to let Lucy's problems stay comfortable at the back of her mind waiting for the right moment to present itself.

In those first weeks she was prepared to give a good deal of her time to the twins; in truth she had no choice, their appetites made sure that she never had long free of them. Still, she delighted in propelling herself along on her bone-shaker by her own physical effort on the occasional bright day (Henry had forbidden her to take it out if the ground was slippery), feeling free as the wind with Jenny left behind in charge of the nursery. As soon as she could, too, she took the trap and went back to the workshops. She loved it there, the smell of it, the noise of the hammers ringing on metal, the men's voices as they worked and their obvious pleasure in seeing her. The time passed so quickly there, that often when she got home and hurried up the stairs to the nursery not only her aching breasts but the screams of two lusty pairs of lungs told her she'd outstayed her time away.

On just such a January dusk she opened the nursery

door to find Jenny rocking the yelling Victoria in her arms while the child stuffed her little fists frantically in her mouth.

'Here she is, my lovely,' she cooed. 'You just tell 'er what you think! Orful empty you are, orful, i'n't it, my ducky.'

Beth laughed. The girl delighted her, her rich country voice that she tried often enough to correct, yet more often still forgot to notice.

'Stay and talk to me, Jenny.' She threw off her hat and jacket, unceremoniously pulling open the buttons of her bodice. 'How long has this one been screaming?'

''bout ten minutes, m'um, not so long as she thinks. Once she makes 'er mind up that's it though; she knows what she wants and nowt else does. Cor, hark at 'er – her – gulp, gulp . . .'

She knelt close at Beth's side watching the baby adoringly.

'And Nicholas?'

'Awake for a good hour he was, cooing away. Gone off now. Don't know how he can with the noise 'is sister makes. Cor, m'um, don't you think sometimes it's like a miracle all of it? These two little angels. Don't you wonder what you must've done to deserve them?'

'Yes, I do, Jenny, to deserve all that my life is.'

Jenny sat back on her heels gazing into the fire, a position that would never have been allowed in Mrs Murphy's kitchen. 'Should I make you a nice cup of tea? Kettle's singing, m'um.' Tea made from the kettle heated on the nursery fire was her idea of real comfort.

'I wish you would. Get two cups, Jenny. I want to talk to you.'

And that's how there came to be a change in the girl's life, a change that turned out to be far reaching. When Beth suggested to her that she should move to the nursery bedroom (that room which once had been her own) and have charge of the twins she felt heaven had been dropped into her lap. Only minutes before hadn't she talked of what had happened to Beth as being like a miracle, and now here she was with one of her own. What if she could have known then that the new parlourmaid, Rachel, would replace her in her work and more than replace her in Algy's affections? For so long he'd 'courted' Jenny, it's doubtful if he'd intended anything more permanent. Before summer was out though, the wedding bells of St James's were to ring out for Rachel and Algy, leaving her to take comfort in the honest love of her charges.

'Bring what it may there's nought to do but accept it' had been Mrs Murphy's attitude and, as far as she was concerned, it was a year much the same as any other. Changes in her staff were nothing to make a song about and if old Ben was failing, well that was no new thing either.

1864 moved along with unhurrying pace, opening new horizons to Esme at her school in Cheltenham, giving her confidence and determination. Dancing, fashion, learning to be a good hostess and one day no doubt a good wife; those things had seemed all she could look for in life and as long as she could remember she'd been but second best. Now she found there was more, there was the challenge of learning, applying her brain to things that mattered. That her new life was due to Beth she hardly spared time to remember; one day she might look back and be grateful but in that first year there was too much else to fill her thoughts.

It was in the spring of that year too that Beth sat for her portrait. Not as Isabella had, hour after hour while first she was sketched and then brought to life in oils. Beth was a product of the times, her restless nature far better suited to the speed of a photograph, so interested in the huge camera that she was hard pushed to compose herself even for the few minutes required of her. Always when Henry looked at that picture, the half laugh teasing him from the library wall, he wished colour could have done justice to her loveliness. The shadowy sepia but hinted at the life in her shining green eyes, the hair might have been no more startling than the brown of his own, for only those who knew her would remember it, its deep auburn that in sunlight could sparkle with a red-gold as light as the twins'.

So the Court settled into a new routine. Victoria and Nicholas thrived, cared for by a doting Jenny. Phoebe would run straight to the nursery as soon as she was home from school, Beth would play with them on the floor completely forgetting the dignity of Beth Copeland and romping with an abandon befitting the Beth Machin that James had watched on the summit of Chazey Hill so many years before. To be sure, under the smartly dressed exterior there was little difference and none knew that better than Henry.

On the rare occasions Henry heard from Amelia (always Henry, never Henry and Beth) she spoke with pride of the brisk trade in the shop, the lessons James gave and recently the church where he'd been appointed organist. There was much that she kept to herself, like the cockroaches on the brick floor of the scullery, a little room at the back of the kitchen lit only by candles, the way the cakes sank when the fire wouldn't draw or burnt when the wind was from the east and it roared away too fast, how she chopped her finger trying to split the wood for the range, or put a coloured antimacassar into the copper by mistake and ruined James's shirts, the way the lace was getting worn on her petticoats and how she hated sewing on the new. So many things were best kept to herself.

It was a hot day in July, with a threat of thunder, the clouds gathering just as they had each afternoon lately. From the kitchen she was indulging in a quiet spell of reading her *Ladies' Journal* as she listened for the shop door bell. James was at King Alfred's where he'd been made assistant piano teacher; only the younger pupils were entrusted to him but it was a start and, as much as the teaching, he enjoyed the company, sometimes staying for tea at the end of the afternoon with Doctor Pilfrey and his little wife who still kept a motherly eye on him.

As the shop door opened and set the bell swinging Amelia put her magazine on the kitchen table and went along the passage that even on a summer's day was dark. Most of the sales were small, a fiddle string, a plectrum for a mandoline, a piece of sheet music. This was no exception; she found an A string for her customer's violin, took his money and was writing the sale in the book kept behind the counter when her second customer appeared even before the first had left. It looked like being a busy afternoon. She shut the drawer where they kept the box for the day's taking and turned with her polite 'shop smile'.

If he only knew the times she'd imagined this, just to look up and see him. The smile faded, her voice seemed to have deserted her.

'Millie.' The door closed behind the satisfied youth, leaving the bell jangling. In those first seconds, caught off her guard, he must have seen what she'd tried to hide – but suddenly it didn't matter. As if from nowhere he was here, only the counter between them, then he took both her outstretched hands in his. Only seconds, yet time enough for all that had to be said in the silence. Then reason took the upper hand.

'Nothing's wrong is it, Edward? You haven't come to tell me something's wrong?'

'No. We get your letters – but letters can't give us a real picture. Is James in?'

She shook her head. 'No. He's been given a teaching post – you remember I told you. Thursday is his afternoon for lessons.'

'Ah. You didn't say which day. Does he leave you here on your own?' Even though that's how he wanted her to be, he didn't like to think she was at the mercy of anyone who might come in.

155

'Yes.' She made a great effort to take command of the situation. 'It's usually very quiet; we don't expect trouble in Newbridge. Why didn't Lucy come with you? I must show you round. See, this is the room I told you of where James gives piano lessons. Is it what you expected?'

Together they stood in the doorway leading to the little room but he didn't seem able to take his eyes off her.

'Amelia . . .'

'Don't, Edward.' Her chin lifted an inch. 'Come through to the kitchen. Let me show you where we live.' She walked ahead of him down the passage. 'It's rather dark. Watch for the two steps – just here.'

How tiny the kitchen suddenly appeared, dominated by the range on which she seemed to spend half her life either coaxing it to burn, raking its ashes, moving dampers to persuade the oven to do what she wanted, or brushing it with a stiff brush and black lead. Today in the sultry heat, even with the window pulled right up, the fire made the room unbearably hot.

Edward looked uncomfortably warm in his clerical garb. Only his stiff white 'dog collar' relieved the black vest, frockcoat, gaiters. No wonder coming into this airless room beads of perspiration broke on his forehead.

'We'll go into the teaching room. The fire makes it too warm here today, but it's cosy in the winter evenings. Really we're very comfortable here. Tell them at home, Edward. Make them realize James is doing well. Mind the steps,' she reminded him again as they went back to the passage.

'No one knows I've come, Millie. I was out visiting and – well, there was the station, Newbridge and you hardly more than an hour away.'

There was no sound in the little teaching room as he turned her to face him. 'Just an afternoon – is it so much?'

'Don't Edward. Please, please, don't make it harder. All these months I've tried to make a new life. I've been busy, I've – '

'And has it worked?'

She raised her eyes to his. 'You know it hasn't.'

He held her close in his arms but even then he didn't kiss her. He never had. Until that moment he'd never touched her.

'What are we to do?' He moved his cheek against her head.

'Not this!' She pulled away. 'Not this, Edward. Lucy is my sister, my dear sister. What sort of a monster am I that I can do this to her?'

The bell jangled loudly as the shop door opened and closed again.

'A customer.' She smoothed her hair. 'Am I tidy?'

'You're beautiful.'

It must have been by habit and instinct that she found the new block of resin her customer wanted for his bow, but even then she forgot to book the sale and still clutched the money in her hand as she came back to Edward.

'Edward.' She sat on James's chair by the side of the piano, her eyes level with his as he sat on the stool in front of the keyboard. 'I knew, of course I knew what was happening to us. Did you think I really came here just for James's sake? I couldn't bear to go on as we were and I thought – even Papa thought – if I went away things would be better for you and Lucy.'

'Your father? You mean he knows?'

'He made it clear in that veiled way he has that I was taking the place that was hers. I doubt if he had the slightest appreciation – or interest – of how we felt, what it meant – you, me or Lucy either.'

His poor Amelia; life had made her bitter. What had become of the sweet happy child she'd been when he first remembered her?

'Can you stay and see James? He usually gets home soon after four.' Again she made an attempt at brother-sister conversation.

157

'My train leaves at twenty to four. I have such a short time.'

For a while they sat silently, a foot apart, but when he reached out his hand she put hers into it (a hand showing signs that she did more than a half share of the work at No 11 Chain Street). The contact somehow helped them. Gradually their hearts settled down to a steady beat, they told each other little incidents of their day-to-day living, they relaxed, they even laughed – in short, they both discovered that deep down they were what they'd always been.

Just after half past three he took out his watch to check the time. Her grip on his other hand tightened, the minutes were running out. That the bell should clang at that moment seemed to them both a cruel stroke of fate, and even worse that the lady customer wanted a copy of a ballad that had to be hunted for. As Amelia took the folders of sheet music from the shelves the seconds raced by. Without a goodbye he'd have to leave her. He was already coming out of the little teaching room.

'I have to come to town again next Thursday, Miss Copeland, so I'll look in then and see whether it's arrived.'

'We're certainly expecting it before then.' She play-acted every bit as well as he. 'I'm sorry it wasn't ready, Vicar.'

With a bow of the head and a mischievous half-wink from behind the customer's back he turned to the door. Amelia wanted to laugh aloud. Dear, dear Edward, nothing had changed him. And joy! He was coming again.

A loud clap of thunder told her the storm had broken. James would be home soon; today he wouldn't stay for tea with the Pilfreys, he knew she hated storms. Yet rather than pull the blinds in an attempt to shut it out, this time as the lady left bearing her sheet music Amelia went to the doorstep, sniffing the change in the air as the first heavy drops of rain fell.

'In for it today,' Mr Ayles from the haberdasher's next door called to her as he raised his blind before the rain got at it. 'You're not like the wife, she's under the stairs already!'

'I was just watching for my brother,' she smiled. And listening for the whistle of the three forty as it puffs its way out of the station, she thought, for from Chain Street an alley known as Union Way cut through to Station Square and on a still day the trains could be heard quite clearly. There it was now; she could hear it before it was lost in another roll of thunder. He'd be in the carriage, jolting and rocking on his way back to Wilhampton as the rain splashed on the carriage window. Wildly extravagant were her silent farewells. She was alive as she hadn't been for months. Next Thursday he would come again.

Just as she pushed thoughts of Lucy to the back of her mind so when James came home, wet and irritable, she made no mention of their visitor. Theirs? Oh no, hers, only hers.

When King Alfred's closed for the summer break they knew they couldn't see each other. But as soon as Michaelmas term started their Thursdays came alive again, those short hours the focal point of their week.

If James had been less wrapped up in himself he might have wondered more at her new-found brightness. Even the foggy autumn days didn't depress her; she was the Millie he'd been used to all their childhood. It must be that she was happy living with him. He'd known he could make her forget the miserable patch their father had inflicted on them.

The last Thursday in November Edward arrived as usual, his train a few minutes late in the fog and Amelia peering through the glass of the shop door waiting for him to emerge from Union Way. Today the cold was biting. He wasn't overdressed even in his heavy coat with its shoulder cape. In the shop, where there was no heating, she protected her chapped hands with woollen mittens, only the tips of her fingers uncovered.

Soon, though, the warmth of the little kitchen enveloped

159

them. The two armchairs were pulled close to the range, the kettle belched steam; here surely was contentment. On such an afternoon no one would come shopping, the noise of the horse-drawn trams rattling past the door, the muffin man's bell and the cry of the fishmonger, these things that usually gave a background of sound, all of them were muffled.

'That kettle's too heavy, let me lift it.' His hand touched hers as she reached to take the large iron kettle from the top of the range. In her other hand she held the teapot – then suddenly she didn't! She must have put it on the table, they must have left the kettle singing on the fire. Neither had meant it to happen but it had and in that first kiss everything else was forgotten.

'Dear God in heaven,' there was no blasphemy in his voice, 'how can this be wrong?' He framed her face with his hands and looked at her. She felt he looked into her.

'No, it's right Edward, it's all the right there is. But we can't have it. That's what's wrong, cruelly wrong.'

'I should have known. Until there was you I didn't dream it could be like this, Mill.'

She leant against him. Then her reason, or perhaps her conscience, stabbed her. 'I must make the tea.'

'No,' He sat down, pulling her to his knee. 'We have so little time together.'

'Edward, it's no use. If we take what isn't ours it can't bring us happiness. If we didn't know right from wrong then it mightn't destroy us, but we do. What kind of faith have we if we think holy vows can be put to one side to give us what we want?'

He was silent. Had she said too much? What right had she to preach to him? 'Edward, my dear precious Edward. How can we love each other and not hurt her? If we could then that's all I'd ask, but marriage can't be like that. She's your wife and you have Edwin, your own son.'

'I've no marriage, no real wife nor son either.'

'Is that what she thinks too or is it because your heart isn't hers?'

'Millie, it's been like this since . . . well, since she found she was expecting Edwin.'

Was it wicked that she was filled with such joy? She sat up straight, taking both his hands in hers. 'So it's the same for us both, and I've lain in my bed at night thinking you were finding some sort of consolation for what we can't have.'

'I want you so much, only you, always you. Not just to take you to my bed, that's but a part of it. I want you to share my days, to put humour back in life again. I want us to talk together of the things that bother us so that worries aren't so mighty after all –'

She took up the list: '. . . to pour your tea at breakfast, to cook your favourite *nouvelle* pudding –'

'You remember that! Fancy that you should remember –'

'I remember everything of the weeks I spent at the Vicarage, how patient you were when I thought I'd been ill-used. It's funny, isn't it, Edward? Papa and Beth, I don't feel like I used to about them. Yet I don't see why, for nothing's changed. James is still bitter, even towards the babies because of whose they are. If I mention them I can tell from his expression. It seems to have eaten into his soul. I suppose because I had other things – well, you – it didn't hurt me so much. Poor James. He used to be so kindly but he's harder, he always sees the bad in everything.' She leant back against him, lulled to silence by the warmth and by an awareness of the rightness of where she was.

For all their customers that afternoon they might as well have closed the shop. No one disturbed them, only the loudly ticking clock on the wall and the occasional crackle of the fire as the coal slipped. She asked him about his parishioners she'd come to know, he told her of his day-to-day calls, who'd died, who'd married. What he didn't

161

need to tell her was how much of his time was spent in helping these people who were such a part of his life. No mention was made of Lucy or what part she played in his work. Amelia couldn't ask, yet surely if Lucy had shared these things he wouldn't have needed to talk to her as he did?

At half past three he had to go. The fog had thickened; they could hardly see the brick wall across the narrow yard from the kitchen window, and dusk had fallen early.

'Next week, Millie. Thursday will soon be here again.'

She nodded, then pushing away all thoughts of Lucy or anyone else, she raised her face, her arms around him. 'I don't know what'll happen, Edward, but if we have no more than this I'll be happy. Just to be together when we can and talk – it's so much more than I thought possible, just to know we care . . .'

He didn't answer. He was probably more realistic than she. Those hours each week might be a gift now, but for how long could either of them be satisfied with that?

They went along the dark passageway to the shop. He pulled the door open, setting the bell jangling and breaking the silence of this strangely eerie early dusk, and she watched him put on his flat wide-brimmed hat, like a Puritan Father, she'd always thought. Then he was gone, the door closed behind him, leaving her alone to peer after him through the glass door as the darkening fog swallowed him up.

Back in the kitchen she lifted the top of the range and added a shovel of coal. Then she curled up in the chair where only a few minutes before they'd sat together. If she had no more than this, she'd said, she'd have everything, but dreaming by the fire she saw a much fuller life, a life with purpose because they shared it, she even saw children. To grow old together . . . Suddenly the emptiness of her Thursdays mocked her.

James arrived a few minutes later, one look at him telling her he was cold and sorry for himself.

162

'I expected at least you'd have tea ready. Sitting here all the afternoon reading, you've no idea what it's like out. Not fit for a man to be abroad in. I tell you I was glad to get home safely. There has been some sort of skirmish across in the alley. I could hear voices so I stepped down to find out what had happened, but there was such a crowd I couldn't see. Some poor devil lying there in the centre of the mob. Newbridge is safe people say. Dammit nowhere is safe.'

'Was he hurt? Who was he?'

'How would I know? I tell you I didn't see him properly. Someone in the crowd said he was a preacher. Isn't that tea ready yet?'

Phoebe jumped down from the Victoria and ran up the steps to the front door. Not often did she arrive home from school to find visitors but today as Algy had drawn past the uncurtained drawing-room window she'd seen Aunt Lucy and, even stranger, her father too. She hurried across the hall towards the drawing-room but Beth's voice halted her.

'Up here, Phoebe. Edwin's here too in the nursery.'

'Are they here for tea, Beth? And Beth, Papa's home as well.'

'Yes. He and Aunt Lucy have a little business to attend to. Come and help Jenny with nursery tea; Edwin will like that.' Once the children were taken care of she could go back downstairs and find what Henry's reaction was to the story Lucy had already told her while they'd waited for him to arrive.

It seemed that all last night Edward hadn't come home. Far from thinking some dreadful fate had come to him, Lucy had watched the hours tick away becoming more and more certain of where he was.

In the drawing-room she talked to her father. 'It's weeks ago, back in the summer, I met Doctor Craig one Thursday

163

afternoon. He enquired after James and Amelia and said he expected I was looking forward to Edward getting home to give me the news. I was very clever, didn't show any surprise. "Indeed I am," I said. "When did you meet him, he didn't say he'd seen you?" "No, he didn't notice me. I was meeting the train as he bought his ticket." I waited for him to come home expecting to hear all about them even though I guessed it wasn't James he'd gone to see. I wasn't blind you know. Perhaps you weren't either. When he didn't mention it I started watching. Each week he went, always coming home just in time for supper and with never a word. So I knew last night he'd be with her.'

'You should have told me before what was going on, child. Do you think I'd stand by and see you treated like it?'

'Dear Papa.'

'And where is he now?'

'It's as I said. He went to Newbridge, as I thought. They say the scourge of garotting is over but it seems not in Newbridge.'

'Footpads?'

'What happened we don't know. James came this morning – Papa, you'd hardly know him with his bristly black whiskers – he says they're looking after Edward in Chain Street. He had been attacked on his way back to the station. Perhaps it was no more than just retribution.' How hard she sounded.

Beth had already heard the tale for she'd been at home when Lucy and Edwin had arrived. Within minutes of their coming the sound of wheels on the gravel path had announced that Henry was home, for as they'd passed the works Lucy had told Arnold, her coachman, to stop and take in the note she'd already written. It had told her father nothing, only stating that she needed to talk to him urgently, and could he come home immediately.

'Is he seriously hurt?'

'His assailant gave his head a mighty blow, probably

164

with a neddy; but nothing that won't mend. No doubt he's uncomfortable, his pockets had been emptied, his watch gone and the ring I gave him. I dare say it's an omen.'

'Lucy, I thought things were well again with you and Edward. Your home always seems a peaceable place.'

She shrugged. 'And so it is, Papa; never do I quarrel with him. Even about his visits to Millie I've said nothing, but I cannot ignore it now. How can I? If he'd only be content to share our house, make a home for Edwin, I'd have no complaint. He has his work, and he can never accuse me of neglecting his home.'

Henry looked at her speculatively. 'That's an empty life, child, for both of you.'

'Men! The only thing that's empty is his bed.'

Henry's frown showed his disapproval. That Lucy could speak so coarsely displeased him.

Now, the children settled with Jenny, Beth rejoined them.

'I'll not stay, Papa,' Lucy was saying. 'How can I go on there, run his house, see his parishioners take him to be a respectable God-fearing man? It's a lie, I tell you. I'll make a fresh home for Edwin, one that's not built on deceit.'

'Your home is here, you know that. How the young swine can do this to you, to you and the boy too. You're to come home, you hear me?'

'Himself' had spoken. Arrogant, a dictator in his own home, only those who really knew him would hear the underlying kindness, and Lucy was one of those; the kindness was her undoing. Her pasty face crumpled and her crying was noisy. In Beth's childhood if any of them had behaved like that her mother would have said: 'Enough of that blubbing!' For blubbing was what it was; her mouth was hanging open and a trickle of saliva oozed from her bottom lip. Henry moved towards her, then stopped, at a loss.

'Beth won't want me here,' Lucy bellowed. 'It's her place now, not mine.' She didn't want to be comforted.

'Don't talk rubbish.' Beth took hold of the situation, speaking sharply. 'Stop that crying and listen, Lucy. This is nothing new to you, you say, and you'd accepted it before. You didn't want him yourself remember. You know you have a home here, of course you have, but for mercy's sake be sure. Don't let pride stand in your way. Perhaps he was on his way home yesterday wanting you, only turning to Amelia because you spurn him. If you love him, then, Lucy, forgive and start again; you'll be the richer for it.'

'You don't want me here. I knew you didn't.' They hardly understood what she said, her words were so drowned by the uncontrolled howling.

'That's not true. If you can't live as his wife, come home and let him be free to make a life of his own.'

'Dammit, Beth, you speak as if you condone this business.'

'Henry, who are we to judge? Edward's a good man – and Amelia, this can't make her happy. Surely you can see that?'

'I don't know what I see, what I think. Lucy, my dear child, don't cry so. Here.' He put an arm around her plump shoulders and took a freshly laundered handkerchief from his pocket. 'Clean your face. Is her room aired? Have we somewhere for the boy to sleep?'

'I like him with me,' Lucy gulped.

'I'll sort something out. Lucy and I can do it together. Now, blow your nose, Lucy; come, pull yourself together, do.'

In truth Beth could have wept with her, for Lucy's world had crashed around her. His fault? Her fault? Did it matter whose? She could have wept for her, for Edward and even – at this distance – for Amelia too. Not for a moment would she let Lucy guess at her thoughts. Brisk efficiency would do her more good than sympathy – that and the glass of brandy that almost took her breath away but helped her to find the courage she lacked before. Together

166

they took warm bedding from the still-room then Beth sent for Rachel to take it to the kitchen to make sure it was aired and have the beds made and hot bricks put in.

Far better to have kept Lucy away from the children and the servants, Beth considered, but despite her white face and reddened eyelids, so swollen that they opened to barely more than slits, she took no pains to hide herself; one could almost believe she wore her tearstains with pride. She insisted on supervising the making up of Edwin's bed, the preparation of his bath in front of the fire now lighted in her old room, and then on her own she bathed him and put him to bed. Jenny always attended the twins, but Lucy would share Edwin with no one. Only he seemed not to notice any difference in her appearance, and while playing with him she almost forgot her troubles and was her usual self.

So it was over, the pretence she'd made of being his wife. The nights she used to lie awake in Edwin's room at the Vicarage, not expecting he'd force himself on her if she refused but hating even the thought of what she knew he wanted. That was when she'd started asking Amelia to stay, relieved to feel she was free, for long after she'd gone to her bed she knew they'd be downstairs talking; that was when Amelia had been so upset about James going and about Beth, and more than likely too that was when in trying to comfort her Edward had discovered his own desires were for her and no longer for his wife.

'We knew didn't we?' Silently she said to the little boy standing before her as she towelled him dry. 'We knew he didn't want us.' Not want his own son – her vision misted as she looked at his little body, for today she was in no mood to acknowledge that whatever Edward had wanted wouldn't have altered her attitude – Edwin was hers. Now she gathered him in her arms, holding him against her warm plumpness. Her mind held nothing but love for him, so dear, to be protected from all life's hurts, to be cared for as daily he grew more precious.

Downstairs in the kitchen there was speculation. Something was very wrong. 'Never seen Miss Lucy so upset, even when her poor mother was taken she bore it bravely. Can something be amiss with the boy I wonder?' Even Mrs Murphy joined in the guessing game.

Arnold had already been sent home to the Vicarage as soon as it had been decided that Lucy should stay, or perhaps he could have thrown some light on it. But there again, Mrs Murphy would probably not have allowed gossip from one house to the other and she'd certainly have seen that all her staff toed the straight line she laid down for them.

Lucy stayed in her room that first evening and after Edwin's bath had been carried away she undressed, put on a nightgown that Beth had worn when she was pregnant (for she could certainly not wear Beth's usual ones with any comfort) and climbed into the bed she'd slept in for so much of her life.

Home! 'This is your home,' they'd both said. So it was. No one could take it away from her; it was hers and Edwin's too. She listened to the sounds she'd grown up with; a step on the marble-floored hall, overhead in the maids' room someone shutting a drawer, Phoebe plodding her way up to bed just as they all had as children, her 'Goodnight, Papa' and his 'God bless you' the same as she'd said it herself thousands of times. She ought to have knelt to say her prayers; Papa had always insisted on it, just as he'd insisted one should take off one's dressing-gown first. He seemed to think the more uncomfortable one was the more likely one was of pleasing one's Maker. She wriggled deeper into the feather mattress. No, she'd not say prayers. She was sorry to displease her father (not that he'd know) but she couldn't pray to that God Edward seemed on such good terms with. If He approved of Edward and his philandering she wasn't going to bare her soul to Him. How sore her eyelids were. The tears had gone now though. In their place was a sort of numbed peace.

Home! She could free Beth to go to the works as much as she liked or do whatever she wanted. Then there were the twins, dear little souls, there in the nursery more often than not with Jenny looking after them. A happy place the nursery, Lucy always liked to go there and now Edwin would share it. She wasn't quite strong enough yet to think of the kitchen at the Vicarage, so she concentrated on all she loved at the Court. Tomorrow she'd have a talk with Beth, tell her that now she was home she was quite willing to run the house again.

That Beth didn't fall so willingly into her plans she wasn't to know until the morning. For the present she was sure Beth would be . . .

Lucy slept.

Whether or not those below stairs wondered about Lucy's sudden arrival, they were to learn nothing from Henry's manner as they met for prayers as usual at seven in the morning.

'And may the Lord help us to do His work this day,' he finished today just as every other day. Beth half opened her eyes as she joined in the chorus of 'Amens'. To look at him, who would guess at the wakeful night he'd spent? She shut her eyes again; he mustn't see her peeping.

As he nodded his head in dismissal the family moved towards the breakfast room and Mrs Murphy led the servants back downstairs to the kitchen.

'Algy, I'd like the trap at the door at ten minutes to eight please, and this morning I shall need you to take me to Wilhampton.'

'So early, Henry?' Beth waited to speak only until they were out of earshot.

'I shall catch the train for Newbridge just before nine. Do you mean to accompany me, Lucy? By now he'll have had time to see sense.'

'Papa I cannot live with him again . . .'

169

Phoebe's gaze went from one to the other; Esme looked miserably at the tablecloth, not understanding what it was all about but uncomfortably aware of the tension and knowing that Edward was the cause of it.

'Just eat your breakfast, my dear,' Henry spoke kindly to Lucy. The fault couldn't be hers. 'No need for you to make the journey. Leave things to me.'

'Papa – '

'Enough now.'

Lucy had never been able to argue with her father. Eat her breakfast, he'd said. The steaming porridge smelt good; she dug her spoon into the sugar and sprinkled it lavishly, then made a well in the middle and filled it with yellow creamy milk. Food was soothing. The image of Edward being brought home and instructed on his husbandly duties became less real. Here she was safe. Papa had said, 'This is your home.' The sweet oatmeal slipped smoothly down her throat. She even managed a smile at her sisters across the table.

James looked up as the shop bell jangled, then seemed to freeze as he stood.

'Father! We weren't expect – '

'Is he here? Edward? Has he left you or is he still here?'

'He's here. But Father he's been hurt. Look, sir, the doctor says he must have quiet. Lucy told you about the attack . . .' He was playing for time, time to take command of a situation that he felt was none of his making. It wasn't fair that his father should look at him like that, eyes as cold and cutting as he remembered! It wasn't his fault that Edward and Millie had let this happen. As if he hadn't problems enough without their bringing more on him!

'Papa.' Amelia appeared in the doorway leading from the living quarters, and at the same second the bell jangled again letting James escape to a customer with the eagerness of a fish slipping the hook and making back up the stream.

Without a word she and Henry moved down the passage that led to the kitchen, shutting the door and cutting off their words from James and customer alike.

'Millie, I've come to take you home.' He sounded so positive, his statement was an order, or so she heard it. The child she'd been would have obeyed, perhaps resented his authority but not questioned it.

'No Papa, my home is with Edward.' There! She'd said it! She forced herself to look her father in the eyes. 'I love him, Papa. He loves me.'

'Millie you can't do this. Edward has a wife – your own sister. That you could do it to anyone, let alone your sister! I blame him. He calls himself a man of God yet breaks his holy vows as if they mean nothing.'

'No, Papa. It wasn't like that. She doesn't want him. I love him. Truly I want nothing but to be his wife.'

'He has a wife.'

'If he can't marry me I shall live with him.'

She knew that had hit home but Henry's only sign of emotion was the tic working in his cheek.

'How long has this been going on? Let me see him, let me make him understand where his responsibilities lie. A wife and a child! And what are you saying? You'll be his mistress? Have you forgotten your mother? What would she say, she you professed to love and model yourself on?'

'Mama would understand,' Millie's calm had gone but not her courage. Suddenly she could say so much that had been bottled up inside her all this time; once started she couldn't stop the words that tumbled out. 'She'd know whose fault it's all been. Nothing was right at home after Beth came. That's where the evil came from. Until then Lucy was happy, we were all happy. Now look at us. Poor James sent away. Nothing's the same any more. You ask what Mama would say?'

James must have got rid of his customer. They realized he was standing behind Henry in the kitchen.

'Mill, don't cry.' He came towards her, for a moment

171

taking his own courage from her outburst. 'She's right, everything she says is true. Beth brought the rot into the home.' It must have been the sight of Henry, so out of place in this tiny kitchen, that made him so brave. Never before had he spoken out against his father; his heart was banging against his ribs and he knew the corners of his mouth were twitching with a will of their own.

Henry's only answer was to dismiss him with a curt nod of his head towards the door. James's championship of Millie had been shortlived, his courage burnt itself out. He was ashamed at his relief in leaving them.

'Beth doesn't come into this.' Henry's hand was gentle as he laid it on Millie's shoulder. 'Child, you can't have thought what you're doing. Lucy and Edward made vows of faith. To come between them is to ask for the wrath of God. My dear, the pain of loving him and making the sacrifice is nothing compared with what must lie ahead if you follow the path of wickedness.'

'You don't understand. She doesn't keep her vows either. She's no wife to him.'

Something of his old arrogance returned. 'Is that for you to decide? Is it your affair what happens between a man and his wife?'

From upstairs Edward could hear voices but not words. James crept up to his room to see if he was awake.

'Do you hear who it is, Edward?' he hissed, opening the door only a few inches to save the daylight disturbing their patient.

'No. Trouble?' His eyes closed. All Edward's throbbing head asked for was darkness and silence.

'It's Father. Laying the law down to Mill, got her in tears. I told him – ' Whatever he imagined he'd told his domineering parent Edward wasn't to hear of it. By the side of the bed a walking stick had been left so that he could bang the floor if he needed anything. Headache or no, he banged with all his might.

'Ah,' Henry heard it, 'that must be Edward. Good. Let

172

me talk to him. If he doesn't know where his duty lies let me tell him.'

'Papa, please, Edward is ill. You've no idea how they hammered him. Please, don't worry Edward.'

'Millie, I shall take you home. Either we tell Edward or you come away without. For my part I have to see him, he's Lucy's husband. Do you expect that I'll allow him to forsake her without raising a hand to help her? Your own sister? Has the devil eaten into your very soul?'

She seemed to slump, her shoulders drooped, her fight was gone; her reddened eyelids stung and try as she did to find control her breath caught in her throat as she still choked on an occasional sob.

It was the sight of her in the semi-darkness of his bedroom that did more to restore Edward than any amount of kindness could. 'Mill, it's to be all right. Don't cry any more, darling.'

In all his visits to Newbridge they'd never planned a future together; they'd dreamed of it, longed for it, but never intended to take their happiness this way. Yet now they both knew there was no way back.

'I've come from Lucy,' Henry greeted him; 'she and your son are at the Court. I am taking Amelia home with me and when you are fit no doubt you'll return to your family.'

'No, sir. Lucy and I have no marriage, Millie and I belong together. This is too big to fight.'

'Too big? Or is it that you're not big enough?' He was frightened for them. What happiness could there be, taken this way? 'Don't do it, my son. You know better than most of us the sin of breaking holy vows. For your own selfish happiness are you asking Millie to risk the damnation of hell fire? You're young, the pair of you, life is ahead of you. Start again, you and Lucy, make a proper marriage of it, if it hasn't been one, have more children. Do what you know to be right – ' Henry the arrogant wasn't used to pleading, neither was he used to being

173

spoken to as Millie now did. Her courage of downstairs was nothing compared with that which she now found with Edward at her side – or was it partly fear that even now her father's persuasions could do what his anger hadn't?

'Why should you stand in judgement? What was it killed Mama but constantly bearing your children? Is that no sin? And then you bring Beth –'

'Enough! I've told you, Beth is my affair, nothing to do with this. You're no more than a child, you can't understand. Come home, Mill, put all this behind you . . .'

'Papa, I cannot. Please, don't look at me like that.' For in Henry's eyes she read a hurt she had no power to heal, things had been said that nothing could wipe out.

Without another word he left them, going down the narrow twisting stairways and through the shop without so much as a glance at James, or a thought of him either. His Millie had gone where he couldn't reach her. She was such a child still (hadn't she proved that by showing how little she understood of his relationship with Isabella?) and he'd failed her.

CHAPTER SEVEN

'Come what may, there's nought to do but accept,' Mrs Murphy had said at the start of that year, but who would have guessed that before it was over Lucy would be home again and that husband of hers gone off with – no, that could never be true! As if Amelia would do such a wicked thing. It must be just gossip. Algy had heard it from Arnold. They were saying at the Vicarage that James had called and Carrie the parlourmaid had unashamedly listened outside the morning-room door.

Tight-lipped Mrs Murphy heard the tale from Algy who told them what he'd gleaned while he waited for Lucy to collect a box of things she and Edwin would need from the Vicarage.

'Seems Mr James was as shocked as she was herself. Didn't have any idea of what'd been going on, he told her.'

'Eat up your supper and we'll have a little less talking, if you please. We'll just wait for time to tell us the truth of it – if Mr James hadn't known then you'll find it's no more than a misunderstanding. A lovers' tiff I dare say and then these wicked brutes struck him down. Once he's better he'll be home and until then of course Miss Lucy will stay here.'

'If that's it, then why do you think she didn't go with the master to Newbridge this morning?' They all knew Algy had taken Henry to Wilhampton for the train and Rachel wasn't going to sit quietly and have Mrs Murphy speak to him like that. 'You'd think because they're her precious family they couldn't kick over the traces same as the next one,' she thought to herself. 'When I carried their supper in he wasn't looking any too sweet, I can tell you. Just a "Thank you, we'll serve ourselves, you may go".

Quite hoity too from the missus and not a bat of an eyelid from him or Mrs Wentworth either.'

'What were you expecting then, m'gal?' Old Ben was like Mrs Murphy, he didn't like the way these young people passed on their opinions about their betters.

'Well anyway,' Jenny interrupted, 'Edwin is a dear little fellow and I hope they stay awhile. Miss Lucy's been in the nursery most of the day – and I'll tell you one thing, whatever the truth of it all may be she's not too put down by it. Been playing with my babies; they just love her. Got a real way with her she has.'

'Ay, always did have; all the babes have loved her. A born little mother she always was.' Mrs Murphy's good humour was coming back.

'Came out to m' kitchen garden she did too,' Ben reported. 'Like old times it was to have her. Even as a wee lass she used to keep me company; allus liked to see the veggies coming along. Suit me fine to have her home – still, likely it's no more'n a visit like you say, Mrs Murphy.'

Indeed, despite the upheaval in her life, Lucy had enjoyed her day. The only jarring note had been the interview she'd had with her father when he'd arrived back from Newbridge. She'd known what the outcome of his visit would be but she didn't want to discuss it; better to put the whole miserable affair behind her. Here she was in her old place again, well almost. Granted Beth seemed determined to hang on to the reins but that didn't really matter. She'd have plenty to busy herself with in the nursery and once they'd all got used to her being home she'd be able to go down to the kitchen just as she used to do. She'd enjoyed the kitchen at the Vicarage: cooking smells, the sound of the kettle lid rattling as it boiled on the range, it had been the hub of the house and she'd loved it because she'd tried to make it a copy of that at the Court. If Lucy thought of a kitchen it was the one she'd known all her life, with Mrs Murphy enveloped in a large white overall performing her culinary miracles at the wooden table. She'd give them a few days to get used to her being here, let the gossip die down, then she'd settle comfortably into her old familiar rut. Familiar, yet better, for now she had Edwin to make life complete.

Even to Beth, Henry said little about his visit to Chain Street. To be honest when he'd set out he'd not doubted he'd bring Amelia home like a chastened child. Over the last year or two she'd been difficult, unsettled, all too ready to believe herself in love. But this was beyond his understanding. He could see how it came about, but that had no influence on his feelings. Edward was a married man and even though Amelia had no vows of her own to break her sin was as great as his in letting it come about.

He felt he should have handled it better yet he didn't know how. So even to Beth he said little; he hadn't the courage to re-live his hour at the shop.

A child he thought Amelia, and yet Beth was no older. With that perception he'd known right from the start she recognized that his hurt was too deep and too new for any words to help him. That night as he knelt so long on the hard floor by the bedside she longed to comfort him but she knew he had to find his own strength. Her shorter prayers said, she was already in bed, but from the warmth of the deep feathers she threw in yet another plea to her Maker: 'It has to be You, only You can help him. I can't get to the root. You do see that, don't You? I wish I could do something but I don't see what. Please, please bring him comfort. I know he's so dreadfully torn by it all and it doesn't seem fair, does it? It's none of it his fault. If Amelia loves Edward like I do him what else can she do? And truly Lucy isn't too put out. Please don't let Lucy be sad — but after all she didn't seem to want him. Let her find compensations.' Then her glance went back to that straight-backed figure. 'Please, please don't let Henry suffer, my darling Henry . . .'

* * *

On the face of it the worst seemed to be over. Lucy was back in a rut that ran straight and smooth. The physical needs of her life were taken care of in a way that gave her conscious pleasure. It was a long time since she'd had to suffer what she considered the nastiness of sex, although until she'd safely conceived Edwin she'd accepted it without complaint; even after she'd withdrawn to the nursery the shadow had been there as long as she'd stayed at the Vicarage. Now there was no such threat. She was free to enjoy the functions of a body that was all her own. And enjoy it she did, indulging herself to excess in all the good things sent from Mrs Murphy's kitchen. Food had always been a comfort and a delight to Lucy; now she gave way to what had every appearance of greed. If disappointment of marriage had anything to do with it, it would have taken a cleverer person than her to suspect it. She dug her white teeth happily into her favourite treacle pudding, let out the lacing of her stays as the months went by and only occasionally let herself give way to self-pity that she was mistress of nothing. Always there was Edwin, and those other two dear little souls soon followed her around as happily as he did. Beth appeared not to be jealous that she spent so much of her time with the twins; she seemed hardly to notice.

Brief letters came from Amelia to Henry, brief replies went back. Stark facts were told to him. She and Edward were moving away from the shop and taking a house near the infirmary where Edward spent much of his time. She told him no details but presumably Edward was caring for the spiritual welfare of the sick and dying and she, no doubt, was still caring for the physical welfare of James who'd become used to having a woman in the house.

From Wilhampton though, where Edward had been replaced by an elderly cleric whose wife had an ear for scandal, before long word was passed to the Bishop that the Reverend Wentworth had not only left his wife and child when he disappeared so suddenly, but had set up house with another woman.

These things take time. When Amelia's letter finally told of Edward's unfrocking Edwin was five years old and Lucy so far removed from the vicar's wife of days gone by that she was scarcely interested.

James's letters were fuller, more colourful, addressed always to her. It was one afternoon in the summer of 1867 that one such letter came, no just any afternoon but a special one for it was Beth's twenty-sixth birthday. It had been at Henry's bidding that the family had gathered, but they all seemed glad enough to come. At least on the surface she had been accepted. The children were outside amusing themselves on the lawn, from Penelope (Margaret and William's eldest), the oldest at nearly ten, to Hal and Edith's little Betsy, a crawling one-year-old. The 'look-alikes' as their cousins called the twins were, as always, the centre of attraction. Perhaps it was the novelty of there being two of them, or perhaps it was the zest they'd inherited from Beth; whatever the reason, they all felt the magnetism of the young brace of red-heads, from Margaret's three, Penelope, Richard and Archie, Hal's young Henry who at five was already Copeland through and through, Edwin their constant devotee, right down to baby Betsy. In truth it was probably triggered by Nick's jolly nature but Victoria rode along on his reflected glory.

''scuse me, Miss Lucy, I brought this for you. Just been handed in by post.'

'A letter for me, oh lovely. Thank you, Rachel,' Lucy beamed. 'From James, how nice.' Of course she knew very well of the rift between James and Henry but she always behaved as if it didn't exist. It was her way of coping with anything that made her uncomfortable. Today, though, with the family there she could read her letter without that unpleasant feeling of divided loyalties, today he was just Jamie, the brother who ran a business in another town.

'Oh, listen, I'm so glad,' she spoke as she read; 'he's

found a housekeeper to care for him. A single person –
elderly I dare say but he doesn't mention her age. Harriet
Shutler. I've really been worried about him. It's not right
for a man to have to shift for himself.'

'I wonder you didn't offer your services.' Esme's teasing
voice didn't quite hide the sarcasm.

'I have Edwin to consider. That's no place for a child.
You may laugh, Esme, but indeed it has worried me to
think of him alone now that Amelia has forsaken him.
Really it was too bad of her to leave Newbridge – selfish.'

They looked at her affectionately; she said not a word
of how badly she'd been used, only James. No one voiced
their thoughts but Beth cut a larger than normal slice of
plum cake and held the dish to her, and they all watched
approvingly as she bit into it.

Silently she read on as she munched. Then: 'He says
how good it is to have his meals cooked for him again and
to take a freshly laundered shirt from his closet – and so I
should hope. Poor Jamie, it's time he took a wife, someone
to really care for him.'

Esme opened her mouth, thought better of it and closed
it again. At nineteen she had lost much of her gaucheness,
and in its place was emerging a woman of distinction.
Esme never would be pretty by any stretch of fond
imagination, but now her tall figure was held erect, her
long narrow feet planted with confidence; as she'd overcome her own feeling of inferiority so she'd outgrown the
'plague of boils', as she remembered those unsightly swell-
ings that had all too often throbbed on her chin. There
had been much she'd had to overcome, not least her
reliance on Naomi. It was more than a year now since
Naomi had married and six months since she'd set out for
South Africa where her young husband's family had a fruit
plantation. None of them knew how much that final
parting had meant to Esme, for one thing she'd certainly
learnt had been to keep her own counsel. Watching her
now Beth's mind went to the lovely Naomi, for even

180

though the two girls hadn't actually lived together for a long time, holiday periods had always found them just as close. Life goes on though. Esme had been offered a post at a school in London to start with the new term.

Beth let her glance travel round the room. There was Edith, just as serene with her smooth dark hair and peaceful expression, quite matronly now although hardly any older than she was herself. And Lucy, oh matronly indeed, but comfortable, an ample bosom to mop one's tears on as the children all found. Esme, yes she was pleased with Esme, she even felt entitled to some of the credit. Hal, 'a chip off the old block', she remembered Mrs Murphy used to say and indeed he was; Margaret, tall, angular, seeming to dominate the feeble Willie – yet did she? Then Phoebe, dear solid little Phoebe – solid still but not so little, developing young and at twelve half child and half woman, carrying her suddenly acquired bosom as if it didn't quite belong to her and was something of an embarrassment. Beth suspected she would have preferred to be in the garden with the children yet she seemed to belong neither with them nor with the adults. She sat up straight and tried to assume the bearing of her elders. Then Henry . . . Beth's eyes moved on only to find he'd been watching her, looking as though he'd been reading her thoughts. He recognized that she smiled even though her lips didn't move and his steel-blue eyes passed their message back. The voices were only a background. She knew this was one of those special moments; she'd remember it perhaps years later. 'My twenty-sixth birthday,' she'd think and know again the warmth of that moment.

James had first met Harriet at King Alfred's where she'd been visiting with Charlotte, an elderly cousin of Doctor Pilfrey's, not as a guest but as a paid companion. A year or two older than himself he imagined (in fact nearly four years, but with Harriet it was difficult to guess her age), a capable, positive woman. She certainly didn't awaken his sympathy for her status but rather his admiration. He even envied the old lady Harriet's attentions as he went back to his solitary home, but it probably would have stopped at that if the visit had run its course according to plan. As it was, after she'd been at the school for only ten days Charlotte Pilfrey had a stroke and died. Harriet was without a home – and James without a housekeeper. That he'd never had one was neither here nor there. Since Millie had left him for Edward he'd found fending for himself irksome and now that they'd been chased out of Newbridge by scandal his loneliness was intolerable.

If Harriet had any misgivings about the unconventionality of the arrangement she didn't heed them. For James she worked with all her strength, and she had plenty. She polished so that the furniture gleamed, she cooked meals such as he'd not eaten since his days at the Court, she laundered his clothes and starched his shirtfronts and cuffs, she learnt just the way he liked his tea and how many minutes to boil his eggs. In short her days were spent in assuring his comfort and, if in the darkness of her own room she dreamed her own dreams, well, she wasn't the first housekeeper to do that. She'd never expected to fall in love; she'd gone through her youth with never a heart's flutter, yet here she was at thirty with her mind behaving with a will of its own. His beautiful hands – she'd never so much as touched them yet in those dreams she held them to her cheek, felt their warmth; and his eyes, so dark and sad, or so she imagined, there in the stillness of the night they smiled at her. She went a step further and imagined he was here by her side, but at that she floundered. There had never been a man in her life, even her father had died when she'd been quite a child. She wasn't ignorant but her imagination baulked at what she didn't understand, and in any case she wasn't sure what part sex played in her feelings. James was on her mind every waking minute, and if he'd come to her room wanting her there

182

would have been nothing she would have refused him; for his happiness nothing could be too much.

Lucy was relieved to know he was cared for but how far from the truth were the pictures she built in her mind – an older woman, a sort of Mrs Murphy! By the time winter came James too was feeling the pull of this shared relationship. How good it was to come home, perhaps from choir practice on a cold Tuesday evening, to find a warm kitchen, the smell of a hot supper waiting, to pull a chair towards the fire and have someone sitting across the hearth. She was easy to be with, she never disturbed the evening with a lot of silly chatter. He found himself watching her as she read or sewed. A handsome woman, a strong face with good bones and a firm chin; on anyone else that large mole on her cheek with a clump of fluff growing from it would have offended him, but not on Harriet. Her nails were good, almond shaped with very white half-moons, her hair pinned back in a neat coil was heavy and thick. Broad shoulders, a long waist, her body upright and firm. Yes, a handsome woman. She'd been with him for six months when looking at her one winter evening he was shaken by a desire to possess her. She turned the page in her book, unaware. Ridiculous, he told himself, don't be a fool; she's not even young, not from your sort of background. Her room was next to his, yet he didn't consider that he might flatter her into giving him what he wanted. He got up to go out of the room feeling his sudden turn of thoughts must transmit itself to her, but she didn't raise her eyes from the book, at least not until the door had closed behind him and then she listened to hear where he was going. A moment later she heard the piano from his 'teaching room'; music had ever been James's way of hiding from himself.

The mood lasted, there was no doubt in his mind. When he finally asked her to marry him he was determined to will her to agree; if he'd known the wild beating of her heart, the sudden joy that surged through her, he would

183

have been amazed. After all, here he was suggesting that she should do the same job but instead of getting ten pounds a year for doing it she'd get the doubtful privilege of sharing his name. And he? With all his might he willed her to promise to wed him. With her he'd be safe (even to himself he didn't acknowledge that was what he wanted): to make love to her would be to be cradled in security. A thrill of excitement tingled through him as her hands reached out to his and as she opened her mouth to speak she felt his lips on hers. Her strong arms were round him and together they sank to one armchair, James holding his face to her bosom and feeling her fingers in his hair. She was frightened by the unfamiliar stirrings in her. This was a James she'd not known before, indeed it was a James new to himself. The burning passion he'd once had for Beth seemed as nothing at that moment.

They were married quietly, only the Pilfreys there to witness the ceremony at St Michael's in Newbridge. Even Amelia wasn't told until afterwards, some instinct warning James that she might make objections. He knew she'd been troubled at leaving him, he knew she'd been glad to hear that he'd taken a housekeeper; but a wife was a different matter. Conscience would prompt her to believe he was clutching at the stable comfort he'd lacked since she'd left him and he wasn't, he told himself, of course he wasn't.

Harriet knew little about the ways of married life and by no standards was she a sensual woman. She loved James dearly, gladly she moved to his room and to his bed and if, as he made love to her, his mounting passion brought no similar response from her, she found a strange fulfilment in serving him. So when he moved towards her and she knew what was to follow, she gave herself to him with the same vigour with which she did everything else. Nothing softly feminine in Harriet, she gripped him with a strength quite equal to his own, and her movements carried him to a climax that if she never shared at least was her reward. If she imagined that babies were to be the out-

184

come, then she was mistaken. The months went by; six months, a year, two years, three. In the early days she would have accepted, even welcomed, his children, but the more time passed the more they both realized her barren state suited them. He was all the family she needed and he gladly accepted her undivided attention. If sometimes his mind went back to his first love, well that was his affair. Somehow the lovely girl that Beth had been (he liked to imagine the years had changed her) would never fit into No 11 Chain Street, and his memories took on a quality of unreality. Good, steady, tough Harry, she was the truth he could depend on. But give of herself as she might she could never wholly possess James.

Beth went through a second pregnancy with the same ease that she had the first and when the twins were six years old Charles was born. There was nothing of his mother in the new baby. It was as if she'd put her stamp so firmly on the 'lookalikes' there was nothing left for the next.

And then there was another difference. Right from the moment of his arrival in the world Charles was socially acceptable. When the twins had been born no notes of congratulation had been received, no flowers sent to bedeck Beth's bedroom. That Henry Copeland could have stooped to marry his one-time groom's sister had still rankled. Time could do one of two things — confirm the view that he'd blundered and would live to regret it, or smooth away the rough edges of his social lapse. In Beth's case it had done the latter.

Nicholas and Victoria had been about six months old when Edith had invited Beth to call with them one afternoon. To be honest Beth could think of far better ways of spending an afternoon than having Algy drive them to Wilhampton, the twins' basket bumping precariously on the seat opposite her and Victoria protesting at her sleep being disturbed. So much of the county's semi-acceptance of Beth stemmed from that visit though, for Edith had seen to it that Beth had been introduced to Mrs Chowne, the most charitable of their local upper crust, who had completely fallen under the spell of the look-alikes. Word spread. Before long Mrs Ridley called at Merton Court, then Mrs Hatcher. The ice was broken, thanks partly to Edie, certainly partly to the spell the babies seemed to cast on all who met them, but not without some credit to Beth herself.

Over the intervening years, by Henry's side, she'd visited the Chownes, the Hatchers, she'd even been accepted at the dining-table by the Ridleys at Brimley Grange. Perhaps the tongues still wagged when the ladies of the county were alone but Beth was lovely enough to arouse resentment that had nothing to do with her lack of breeding.

When Charles was born he was accepted, visited, brought gifts, he was indeed one of the Copeland flock. The twins' appearance was a constant reminder of their mother even if their charm outweighed the fact. Charles, right from the start, showed all signs that like Hal and young Henry he was Copeland through and through.

As a baby he gave no cause for concern and that he was good Beth took for granted. Why shouldn't he be? He had no reason for complaint the way her life had been organized around him.

'The twins never made me feel so captive and with them there were two hungry mouths to feed,' she grumbled to Lucy as she watched Henry and the trap disappear down the drive.

'A mother's place is at home, Beth. And in any case, I'll be bound the moment he's had mid-day feed you'll be chasing off.'

'Chasing is about it! No sooner do I get there than I have to turn around and come back. There's time for nothing. I've a mind to take him with me, get him used to the smell and sound of the place while he's young, eh!' She chuckled at the thought. 'Fed into him with his mother's milk.'

'What a girl you are!' But Lucy said it kindly enough, not for a moment taking the suggestion seriously. After all this time she should have known Beth better! That same day Charles made his first appearance at the foundry, aged eight weeks and one day.

Perhaps Beth was right and the background hammering of metal, the sound of it hissing as it cooled, coming to him so early made these things necessary to him.

She had an office of her own now. She'd learnt to keep the order books, the account books were no longer a mystery and she could deal with the paying of the men. In that room Charles and his wicker basket became accepted over the next few months. He was a contented baby but there's not one born who's perfect. There were days when he was fretful, when Beth would shoot the bolt on the door and unbutton her bodice. This was better than being at home.

'Now my lad, you take that and just stop your nasty noise. There now, isn't that better?' as his mouth closed around her. Silence now except for the frantic sucking. She'd settle herself comfortably at her desk, pick up her pen and get back to what she'd been doing. In a few minutes, the edge taken off his appetite, he'd hold his head back and gaze at her, cooing, dribbling, taking the occasional suck just to let her know he still needed her. Really it proved quite a satisfactory arrangement – not the best thing for his training perhaps to have food constantly on tap, but it made for a quiet life and suited them both. She had said the twins had never made her feel so captive, but when the twins had been born she was still feeling her way at the foundry, she'd not dug herself into such a sure niche.

Beth was one of those on whom progress is built. Not for her ten or twelve months of nursing a baby. He was six months old when one morning, instead of putting him into his basket and carrying him with all the paraphernalia of his daily needs to the brougham (for out of respect for him she let Algy drive them in the most comfortable carriage), she handed him to Jenny.

'He's yours for the day Jenny. I'll tell you about his dinner.'

'Mine! But you'll be home for his dinner? You never mean you're staying out all day?'

'Yes, he's your very own. I've written down just how to make him some gruel – I tried it yesterday and he managed to take enough. Use a tiny spoon and give him a cuddle after he's done. You like a cuddle, don't you, my pretty?' From his grin he seemed to agree with all she said. 'Had it from a spoon, didn't you? You were a good boy . . .' His response was a wide open mouth and an enormous beam. 'Oh Charles, you are a love. Isn't he a love, Jenny?'

'That he is. But 'pon my word m'am, what'll I do if he won't take the spoon? Mighty small he is and I've nowt for him to turn to.'

'And I'll have too much!' Then to the baby again: 'You and I will be pleased to see each other at teatime. I'll come home in good time, Jenny.'

A poor kind of mother, was Lucy's opinion. Well, perhaps she was right but Henry wouldn't have agreed. His lovely Beth, she'd given him three fine children with hardly the bat of an eyelid; and more, much more, she gave him herself, her mind eager, soaking up all she could learn with an enthusiasm that equalled his own.

At the foundry there wasn't a man whose name she didn't remember, and Henry was wise enough to realize the firm never lost by the time they 'wasted' talking to her. She knew of each increase in their families, listened to their problems and tried to console their griefs.

'Better occupied if she stayed home and cared for her children,' some of their wives' opinions were much the same as Lucy's. But if they thought her lacking in affection towards those three children she'd produced so effortlessly

188

and seemed happy to hand to other people to be cared for, they were wrong.

Only Henry truly recognized the two sides of Beth; the one they saw at the foundry, friendly, keen, receptive, always looking for progress, a sharp eye to business; the other just as eager, warm, needing to love as much as she needed to be loved. Romping with the children in the garden – only last week he'd seen her bowling a hoop with the twins and Edwin just as she once had with Phoebe, enjoying the fun as much as they were and not caring for Lucy's look of disapproval. Or abandoning herself to love-making. Beth did everything with all that she was; nothing less could satisfy her.

And in those next years there was much to give her satisfaction. The firm was expanding. Nothing new in that, it had been a constant progression since its first inception, but to Beth it was new and exciting. The introduction of sewerage systems, and the development of existing ones, opened fresh fields to many a foundry and Copelands had always been quick to see scope for future business. This time Beth was sufficiently involved that she was caught in the tide. To her diameter of a pipe became as interesting as this year's model of hat.

'Life is vastly exciting!' she said to Henry as she watched him roll away a diagram they'd been examining. As usual after their seven o'clock supper they were in the library.

He turned towards her, smiling indulgently at what sounded like childish exuberance. Then his expression changed. He seemed to be looking at her afresh. How lovely she was, a picture in that lilac gown – had he seen it before?

'Indeed it is, vastly. And you, my Bethie, you're the most exciting thing about it. You're looking very pretty this evening.'

'It's the gown. Do you like it, Henry?' She twirled for his approval. 'I ordered it in Cheltenham when I went in last Wednesday. It came this morning. I couldn't wait to wear it.'

Margaret would have disapproved of such vanity and Lucy considered it extravagant to wear such a creation simply to have supper at home. But Beth had so many years behind her when she'd had to make do with what she could stitch from other people's hand-me-downs, even though she loved clothes more than any of them.

Henry smiled at her fondly. He had remarkable perception.

'You look beautiful.' His eyes said far more than that, they seemed to devour her. Like a magnet she drew him to her.

Yet as he held his hand towards her it was she who moved, covering the distance between them without a word, her arms around him and her mouth raised to his. The years had done much to mould Beth, she'd grown in confidence and knowledge. Her love for Henry was as simple and trusting now as when she'd been a girl, yet even that had developed, grown with her.

Charles was a gentle child, thoughtful, even-tempered and yet without the spirit that went with Nick's good humour. His eyes were the same light blue as Henry's, his hair very fair – but then, Henry's light brown was probably the adult version of just that shade. Perhaps he bore no resemblance to Beth but in him she found great joy, but not in the personal care she gave him, for as Lucy privately considered, Beth was a poor sort of mother. She loved her children, no doubt of that, but the care of them was left to Jenny or to Lucy herself and, to be honest, even if she thought Beth sadly lacking in maternal love she wanted it no other way.

As Charles developed from a baby to a toddler and from a toddler to a particularly satisfactory little boy, to him Henry stood head and shoulders above everyone. The twins had each other; of course they loved their parents, if they ever stopped to think about it, and Lucy and Jenny too, but Charles was far more aware of the adult world he inhabited and of that world the supreme being was his father. That there was an age difference more than twice the average mattered not a bit; after all to a young child all grown-ups are old. Between Henry and his youngest son was an unspoken bond which took him back thiry years or more to the days when he and Hal had first discovered that same empathy.

As time went on James wrote less often to Lucy, she'd been a willing outlet for his woes in the days he'd had no one else. It's likely that he didn't realize how many months drifted by between his letters and when he did write he told her very little. She would have liked to have visited him, and met Harriet, but he didn't suggest it and in any case one thing Lucy hated was a bad atmosphere and she didn't want to stir up unpleasantness at the Court. She did miss his letters though. There were so few people who wrote to her. Naomi did sometimes and occasionally Esme too, but never Amelia. She supposed she shouldn't expect her to but second-hand news wasn't the same thing at all.

There were days, particularly as time went on, when Lucy's spirits were low. An hour or two downstairs with Mrs Murphy, or perhaps helping Ben out there in the walled kitchen garden, would be soothing but no real cure. She'd been thankful enough to come home, imagining herself still the girl she'd once been; but of course it couldn't be true, she was a woman. The home belonged to her father and Beth and to their family; she and Edwin didn't quite fit into the pattern. On her worst days she even believed she and Edwin spoilt things for the others. Sensitive to her moods, and perhaps sometimes thinking on the same lines himself, as he got older he would seek her company. 'Mother and I are going to the village . . .,' he'd tell the twins, or 'to help Ben', or 'shopping in Wilhampton'. What they did wasn't important; what was important to her was that he sought her out, wanted her to feel especially his.

For the most part though at the Court they were good years, and at the works too. The country was riding high and industry booming. England led the world; more coal was brought out of the mines, more pig iron produced, more slate quarried. No one knew at the beginning of the seventies that soon the bubble would burst. England led the way but already America and Germany were in the field to compete and before long to overtake. Soon they were to look back on those good old days, but in the meantime they were complacent in their increasing prosperity.

That industry was booming had its effect on trade in the music shop. Many a factory worker found himself with enough in his pocket for an occasional visit to the theatre, to come away humming the latest ballad, making a note to see if Copeland's had a copy of the music. It had long been one of the gentler accomplishments to play the piano but now even the poorer homes were looked on as unfurnished if the parlour was without one, its top a table for the most prized knick-knacks, while a banjo was easy to carry even on a picnic. Only the more serious learnt to play the violin but at most gatherings at least one person would arrive carrying his wooden fiddle case under his arm. So it couldn't be lack of trade that upset the even tenor of things at the shop in Chain Street. Harriet wasn't sure what it was, nor yet when it had begun. There was something in James's attitude that kept a barrier between them. He seemed guarded, irritable without cause and, try as she might, the practical, hardworking Harriet couldn't see why. Certainly he'd found security, yet from its safety he looked on life with resentment. Here he was, a young man still, and trapped. The shop, the church, the school, a wife who – who what? He'd pull his thoughts to a halt with a sense of guilt that he could criticize her for the very things he'd wanted. Was it her fault if to her a warm breeze meant no more than 'a good day for drying', or Beethoven's Waldstein Sonata no more than 'a nice tune'? He was ashamed, blamed himself that these things jarred on him increasingly; he knew he was edgy and that she was puzzled. To try to lighten his mood she'd bake his favourite pudding, he'd hide himself in the teaching room pretending to be busy while she made jam on the kitchen range. They didn't quarrel but they seldom came close.

He tried to forget his frustrations by making love and tired though she often was, she dutifully and always actively played her part until he was satisfied. Afterwards they never talked, going their separate ways to sleep, Harriet weary from a long day's work, James temporarily at peace. Strange how it was in those minutes before sleep he'd cough, hardly knowing he did it. A nervous habit perhaps, a hard, dry cough coming when he was still breathless. Always it happened and she found herself waiting for it, blaming those beastly cheroots he'd taken to smoking.

For three years Esme taught in London. There was much she loved and much she hated of life in the city. Never before had she seen the extremes of wealth and poverty, either in Wilhampton, Cheltenham or Oxford and that was as far as her experience went. These things troubled her and her consciousness of the squalor always just around the corner would so often mar her pleasure in the rest. She found there were others like herself not content to take second place in a man's world, like herself yet often with more fight than she'd needed, for Beth had seen the way she should go and smoothed her path. Times had changed, were changing still, but women had to battle. Esme saw a day when it wouldn't be like that, when to be born female would no longer be limiting. Even now, fight though she might and no matter how able she was, a woman could never reach the top; that place was reserved.

At the school where she taught she had to defer to a senior she detested, one Simon Rake. If she could have respected his work she might better have tolerated his sarcasm, his unspoken implication that a woman's rightful place was making a home and only those not desirable to the male had to do anything else.

If Simon Rake had been a different character it could well have meant that Esme's own life mightn't have taken the course it did. Always an awkward child, she'd had no natural easy relationship with the opposite sex. Her father, stern and aloof, had demanded her respect but it was mixed with fear and she'd never come close to him. Hal and James hadn't bothered about her and she'd been more comfortable without them. Her school had been a female world, at college what few girls there were had never been unchaperoned and even though there were ways around such restrictions if one were pressed, Esme had never received so much as a hint of an invitation. Then Simon Rake, by his very tone, made it clear that he found her unattractive, scorned her. She hated him for that, for his assumption that she was waiting for some man to beckon – and that of course included him – for his sour breath that made her turn her head away in distaste, for the tobacco stains on his fingers. And he dared to condescend to her!

Esme had never lacked staying power and she needed the experience, so for three years she worked under Simon. Her dislike of him coloured her views of life in general and of the male sector in particular. In her own family she'd seen little to make her regard them with favour. There was Edward, and the way he'd treated Lucy; James who appeared indifferent to Harriet, or so she'd considered on the one surprise visit she'd paid them (for unlike Lucy Esme didn't let her actions be influenced by her father's opinion): then there was her own children (not that Esme had anything against Beth but that didn't alter her original childish feelings that it had been a disgusting way for him

194

to behave); and even Algy, who they'd all thought had Jenny for a sweetheart, had turned to Rachel because she was more comely. Esme mistrusted men and had no intention of letting herself be hoodwinked by any of them.

She stayed the course as long as she needed and when she read in *The Times* that an assistant teacher was wanted at Bigbury House, a girls' school near the Kent coast, she applied, ready to turn her back on London and feeling all the better equipped for life after three years in the capital. Whether or not she was, Beth might have found out had she seen her more often. Ten years before Beth had realized the root of her problems, and she probably would have again. But Esme seldom went home and from Highgate she moved straight to Bigbury.

Then began the period when she came nearest to happiness and contentment. From the moment she took Mrs Shadbolt's soft hand in hers she knew they'd be friends. To be deputy to a friend, and a woman at that, was just what she'd dreamed of. Beyond her dreams was the closeness that so soon developed between her and Martha Shadbolt, the owner of Bigbury House. There were other teachers on the staff (it was a school with about sixty pupils), but the head and her deputy soon became a team.

She'd been there nearly three months when Martha spoke to her about Christmas. 'Most of the staff go away Esme, the school's closed of course. If you'd prefer to stay here you mustn't feel you're expected to go. I shall be here.'

'But won't you have friends coming – or relatives?'

'I've no family and, to be honest, Bigbury has taken too much of my time for friends.'

'You stay alone?'

'I've been alone for some time.'

Esme was torn with pity. She supposed Martha had lost her husband and tried to fill her life with the school. 'I'd like it if we spent Christmas together.' Her large firm hand reached out to Martha's almost without her realizing what she did until she felt the returning pressure on her fingers.

Later she remembered it; lying in bed she recalled the unexpected stirring of excitement. It was as if both of them in that contact had seen an end to loneliness. Had she been lonely though? Until then she hadn't recognized it but now the past was grey and empty, the future full of hope.

It was over Christmas that Martha told her about her marriage, the disillusionment of the eighteen-year-old girl when, with only a few months of married life behind her, she'd realized that her husband was well on the way to becoming an alcoholic. For two more years they'd been together, occasionally Richard vowing to stop drinking, only once more to turn his spite on her. Bit by bit Esme built up a picture of Martha's fear and repugnance, her final relief (and shame that she felt it) when he'd left her. Much later he'd been put in a madhouse where he'd lived in a world of his own hallucinations until he'd died just over a year ago. Looking back at his wildness she still couldn't be sure how responsible he'd been right from the start.

The winter break saw the barriers quite down between the two women. Only to Esme had Martha ever spoken of Richard; to all the others she'd been a widow for many years. Esme had a friend, someone for her to protect, someone who needed all the natural affection that welled up in her.

When the next summer break came and Beth wrote saying they were looking forward to seeing her at the Court, the answer came back: 'We have a lot to do here and, in truth, this has become my home. Perhaps I may spend a weekend at the Court but to be honest it's a joy to be here with no classes and no students.'

Gladly Beth accepted, it was so good to find Esme contented.

* * *

There were very few things Esme feared, but thunder was one of them. Not that she'd own to being frightened but what else could make her mouth so dry and her insides churn? All evening the sky had seemed low and the air sticky, no movement in the leaves. It was the end of July and so far there had been no storm. Tonight though, surely it was coming. Clad in her long white cotton nightgown, unbuttoned to the waist on such a warm night, she opened her bedroom window wide. Lightning! A jagged flash of fork lightning cut the sky in two, then thunder that rattled the window. Like a frightened horse her eyes flew wide open and her body shook. No rain, if only it would rain. She closed her eyes tight and reached to pull down the blind, then closed the curtains to shut out the night. Again – like an explosion. Upstairs someone was closing a window, one of the maids was perhaps frightened too. The thought was a comfort. She stood in the middle of her room, trembling, her dry throat closed. The next flash lighted the room even through the covered windows, the crash so close she thought the house must tumble – although she was in no state to think at all as she flung open her door and rushed bare foot to the landing. Martha's door opened too, the light from her room behind pouring on to the floor. Her fine fluffy hair was loose and hanging only just below her shoulders, not like Esme's pulled back into a single pigtail, her kind face and gentle eyes showed her concern. A little woman, older than Esme by nearly ten years, she had kept something of the purity of a child. She held both her hands to the tall, trembling girl and silently drew her in and shut the door.

'I didn't know it upset you. I've always loved a storm, the air's so clear after. Esme. Esme dearest, nothing can hurt you . . .' As Esme sat on the edge of the bed she was ashamed of the fear she couldn't overcome, her hands gripped the counterpane and she tried to stop shaking. When Martha's arms drew her close she turned her head against her and as the next clap of thunder came involuntarily she clung to her.

Minutes passed, gradually the seconds lengthened between the lighting and the thunder, the rumbling came from a distance.

They both knew the storm had nearly played itself out but neither expected that Esme would go back yet to her room across the landing. They'd both been upset and by more than the storm.

Martha turned down the gas and pulled open the curtains, then threw up the bottom window. The night smelt pure and clean; even the earth was different. Far in the distance the storm went on its way bringing relief to the parched ground.

'It's beautiful,' Esme's whisper barely broke the silence. She took Martha's hand in hers and held it to her cheek, a cheek suddenly wet with tears.

'Tears? Dearest, tell me . . .'

'I don't know . . . I've never felt like it . . . I don't understand. So happy, so right, so — ' she floundered for words.

'So loved.'

Esme nodded: '. . . and full of love.'

'Stay here with me, my bed's huge. Just in case the storm comes back.' They both knew it wouldn't, but they needed the pretence.

That night they lay close in each other's arms, content just to be together. It was a step further in the friendship that had grown to mean so much, had developed into love. By the time school started again the room that had been Martha's was shared as a normal thing, just as their thoughts were shared, their good days and their bad.

Martha had had two years of marriage, a few weeks when she'd had a glimpse of what it was to be loved, then a dread of Richard's drunken advances until finally the act of love-making had become repulsive. But then there had been no understanding, now there was. And Esme, with an inborn suspicion of men, was at last a whole and complete person.

CHAPTER EIGHT

The lid of the kettle bobbed up and down as the water boiled. However much longer would he keep her waiting?

'Come along, James, do,' Harriet called up the stairs. 'Every other man in the street's been in the shop an hour or more. Aren't you ever getting up?'

No answer, but she could hear he was moving about, she could hear the early-morning cough she blamed on the cheroots he smoked. It looked as though today he would be in one of his difficult moods.

Trade at the music shop had grown brisk, yet a good day's takings seldom put him into a good humour. Ghosts of a much more comfortable lifestyle took the gilt off any small success at the shop. Not so with Harriet, she had no such reminders; she cooked, cleaned, and as often as not it was she who hurried up the passage in answer to the jangle of the bell. She might know nothing about music but she'd made it her business to learn how to fit a new set of strings or what was kept in each of the folders of sheet music, just as it had become her job to keep the shelves clean – and the floor too – and polish the window. Not always did James leave her to attend to the customers; there were days when he still enjoyed the contact, when to count the day's takings gave him pleasure, but they had become rarer and certainly not because trade was less.

'Come along, come along . . .' silently she grumbled.

At last she heard his step and knew without even looking up that, late though he was, his toilet would have been carried out to the last detail. To be well groomed was second nature to him.

'At last!' She planted a plate of haddock on the table.

'Not fit to eat by now I should think. I'll make a fresh pot of tea.'

'Don't nag me Harry, not this morning, there's a good girl.' James knew to be a good girl pleased Harriet as to be a good woman never could. 'Just the tea, that's all I want.'

Something in the way he slumped at the table touched her, her anger evaporated and he felt her strong capable hand on his shoulder. Then the shop bell clanged.

'I'll see to it, you drink your tea. Try and eat your fish dear, you'll feel better with something inside you.'

His only answer was to shut his eyes, elbows on the table, head resting in his hands. Her moment of tenderness went as quickly as it had come. Today was going to be one of those days! He'd sit and brood by the fire in his teaching room; if she spoke she'd be lucky to get an answer. Poor Harriet, she tried so hard. The more she did, the more he let her do. He needed her for his very existence yet sometimes it was as if he blamed her for that need.

When the customer left she went back to the kitchen. The untouched haddock was still on his plate, his elbows were still on the table but now he cradled his teacup in his hands, while a cheroot dangled from the corner of his mouth. His eyes were closed and one could hardly say he was smoking, for all the while a small, dry, bark of a cough tried to escape from his throat.

'Those filthy smokes, they'll be the death of you!'

Her voice surprised him, made him catch his breath. In a second the cup was put down, he'd turned from the table and let the cheroot drop to the floor as he coughed and choked.

'God dammit, woman – ' was all he could gasp. She picked up the offending cigar and threw it on to the fire, then keeping her eyes averted as if she couldn't bear to see what he had become she took the haddock to the back-yard. Next door's cat would think it was his birthday!

'Here, use this.' She passed him a handkerchief from the

pile on the dresser, ironed that morning while he was still in bed. Then, kettle in hand she made for the scullery.

His cough changed. Something about the sound stopped her in her track and made her put the kettle back on the range. Helplessly she stood over him, his hand reached out and grabbed her skirt. For once they looked at each other with all the irritations forgotten. Fear can cut through superficial barriers, and in that moment he knew that his troubles were her troubles, his dread, hers; the only strength he could find would come from her, but this time he didn't resent it, this was too big for petty bitterness. Neither of them said a word as they accepted each other in a way they never had before; it only took a second yet they moved forward a great stride.

He held his handkerchief towards her, it was full of blood. She took her own from the pocket of her overall and gently wiped the trickle of red from the corner of his mouth.

That was the beginning of a new era for them. Still it was she who did the work, he who let her, but now there was a difference, a purpose. She plied him with food and now that he had her sympathy he let himself be cosseted. Milk, eggs, good meat, nothing but the best for James and if more for him meant less for her that was the way they both needed it to be. He gave up his school work, his pupils at home, even the church. They would live on what Harriet could make from the shop.

Each night both hot bricks were put his side of the bed. Harriet let all her maternal instinct find the outlet nature had deprived, and James took to it as naturally as he had to the love his own mother had lavished on him. On the nights when he wanted more than maternal comfort her fear that he should overstrain himself was so obvious that it usually killed his desire.

Christmas was coming, another Christmas when ghosts

of the past made him morose. It was at Harriet's suggestion that he wrote to Amelia; with no church to worry about what was there to keep them in Newbridge for the festival?

In the years Amelia and Edward had lived at Longview Cottage on the edge of the village of Chilworthy they'd found a happiness so complete that to look back was to look at another life. The people of Wilhampton had been fast to turn against him and he'd buried the hurt in working at the infirmary and the workhouse in Newbridge. All his time had been given to caring for those poor souls; habit dies hard and although the setting had been different in Wilhampton, what he'd done had been in the name of his church, yet in Newbridge he had soon found himself just as involved with the destitute, the homeless, the children who worked when they should have been learning so that a few extra shillings could be brought into the family purse (and as often as not poured out of it again while they were left to wait at the door of the public house). Newbridge, Wilhampton – people were much the same, and so they were when gossip spread. He was living with a woman not his wife. Who was he to preach at them? When he was unfrocked they were quick to condemn; it was as if they hated him for the help he'd tried to give. 'Ah, and he acts like 'e was sent from 'eaven above. Do without that sort. Let 'im put his own house in order. Living a life of sin and come visiting 'ere like 'e was Saint Peter 'isself.'

So they had left Newbridge and moved to where no one knew anything of their past. They were Mr and Mrs Wentworth, and so indeed they truly thought themselves. Edward had a mission, the same one that he'd always had, but now he had no pulpit. What he did have was peace, a timelessness given by the house that had stood since that other great queen, Elizabeth, had reigned, a house that would still be standing when the country had accepted the reforms he dreamed of. There was only one way for him to make his voice heard and that was the written word.

His mind was full of stories of what he'd seen, and books became his means of bearing the torch.

As the years went by he became known as a novelist and if he was a reformer too it was by suggestion. He and Amelia had no ambitions for luxury but as money allowed they gradually made their home comfortable; water was brought inside, drains laid and gas piped in for lighting and cooking. Only one thing marred their lives over those years, Amelia seemed unable to give them a child. Three pregnancies, three miscarriages; perhaps it was their punishment for snatching what wasn't theirs. It wasn't until a week or two after James and Harriet had discovered the truth about his cough that at last Amelia was safely delivered of a child, a daughter, Isabella.

Word went out to the family, letters of congratulations were sent, but still between Amelia and the Court the barrier was too high to scale. If Lucy could have found happiness with someone else things might have been different, but there was no chance of that; Lucy was comfortable as she was. Such formal letters passed between Amelia and Henry. Knowing Lucy was there how could she write freely, how could she make him realize her life had taught her to understand as she hadn't been able to in those days when Beth had shattered their security? So brief notes were sent and all of them tied with ribbon and kept at the back of her drawer.

Isabella had been born in September, and now two days before Christmas James was coming. James whom she'd not seen for three years, James who meant more to her than anyone – except Edward and Isabella but they didn't count, she told herself, they were a part of her.

The sight of him shocked her. They'd said nothing of his health, and she'd expected to find him unchanged. That other time when she'd arrived in Newbridge and he'd greeted her with self-assurance and a bristly moustache was nothing compared with the alteration this time. His hair was greying, although he was only in his mid-thirties, but it was far more than that. The bones of his face were so pronounced, his nose looked too large, there were dark shadows under his eyes yet his cheekbones were two bright patches. And his hands, so white and thin, the veins standing out. She resolved he'd go home in a better state!

'I dare say he's glad to have finished teaching for a week or two,' she said to Harriet. The two women were together in the little sitting-room where the men had been excluded while Millie attended to the baby. 'Did he have any trouble finding someone to play at church for him?'

'He's given it up, Millie, and the teaching. He's not been well. Don't tell him I said anything, he didn't want me to. Pretend you don't know.'

'Harriet, how could I not know? I've not seen him for three years remember. I can't believe what's happened to him.'

'He needs rest, good food and rest. The smoke and fog in town aggravates his chest.'

'The country will be good for him.' She sounded brighter than she felt and found herself listening for that low bark just as Harriet did. It was almost as if it was the only way he could force the air from his lungs.

Perhaps the country air did help, that and sharing the festival with Millie. No brick wall outside the kitchen window here; from Millie's kitchen you could see for miles. James had a feeling of well-being he'd almost forgotton. No miracle cure for a diseased lung, but an uplift to his spirit and during the first few days he'd let his mind look no further than the two weeks of their stay.

When he sat at the piano playing the Christmas music it was as it used to be, Millie behind him, her hand on his shoulder; and when they sat around the table laden with Christmas fare it was better than they'd ever known even in those far off days they both remembered with more nostalgia than accuracy, for this time the festival belonged just to them. No falling in with rules laid down by someone else, and as if to put the final jewel in their crown of happiness the baby Bella lay in her basket balanced on two dining chairs, gazing at her newly discovered fingers and crowing at her cleverness.

How quickly the days melted away. On the 5th of January the sun came up brightly, casting its first brilliant rays across the breakfast table.

'To look at that sky who'd believe it can't be spring for months? What about a walk this morning?' Listening to James, Harriet imagined the mornings before them back at Newbridge, how he'd lie late in bed then sit morose and brooding in his one-time teaching room. He'd cough, he'd worry, he'd become ever more depressed. As if his thoughts had followed hers he went on: 'It's what we need, to see the sky, to breathe God's pure air. God, how I hate that place.'

'Then leave it, James.' Edward had seen a good deal of suffering. He didn't like to admit what he suspected he saw in James. 'Not because you hate it, man, but because there's more to life. Get away from the smoke, from the factories belching out their filthy smoke — what your father's place must be doing to Wilhampton!'

'Ah, and much he'll care! It'll be lining his pockets. Why should he worry about the poor devils who breathe nothing but the foul fumes?'

'No getting away from the name is there?' Harriet had a sneaking pride in the family connection even though they didn't know her. 'In Newbridge every drain and manhole has Henry Copeland and Sons embossed on it.'

'Have you not noticed our own drain here? Papa has found his way into our own home for all the miles between us.' But there was a difference; Amelia could say it with a laugh; in some inexplicable way she welcomed his intrusion into her happiness.

Not so James: 'He started out to make tools. I suppose there's better profit in this.'

'Times are changing and he always looked to the future.

I dare say Hal's keen to branch out too. With the present state of agriculture Harknell's must be struggling.'

'Something Copeland's will never do. Dear God, just to think of that place, the hot metal, sweating men, noise, smell – '

'Come, it's too fair a morning to waste.' Harriet hadn't lived all these years with James without being able to recognize the danger signs in his expression. Even when he was fit his moods had been a thing to dread.

'You two go for a walk, make the most of the sunshine. Do you think you might find some early snowdrops? It would be lovely to have some for the window-ledge.'

'Can't we all go?'

'No, we won't come. I'll do some baking and it's coming up to Twelfth Night, time the holly and ivy came down and the tree too. When you get home it'll be done and we shall be ready for spring, so don't forget the snowdrops!'

'Wrap Bella up well and we'll take her if you like,' James suggested unexpectedly.

'What a good uncle he is!' Millie dropped a kiss on his head as she passed behind his chair to pick up the baby. 'Breakfast time, my pretty, then you're going walkies.' The conversation at breakfast had set her thinking, thoughts that weren't new to her. With Lucy in residence there was no way she could go to the Court, but she wished James could feel less bitter. James was ill. Papa didn't even know. It wasn't right but how could she interfere? She took longer than she should with Isabella's breakfast, letting her thoughts wander – memories, dreams, but none of them tinged with the hatred and jealousy she'd once known; her own life was too happy to have room for either.

At last the walkers set off and piece by piece Edward started to take down the greenery that had decked the rooms. He carried it all to the bottom of the garden and burnt it, then unclipped the candles and silver baubles from the tree while Millie went to put the bedrooms in order.

'Millie, where did you put the box for the tree decorations?'

'Up here, in the cupboard. I'll be down soon, I'll bring it.'

'Don't worry. I'll come up.'

Such a small thing. Who could have guessed at the consequences?'

They'd been out for about an hour, the snowdrops picked and the baby asleep. On such a day it was a joy to be in the fresh air and they would probably have gone further if James hadn't trodden on an uneven piece of ground and stumbled. He didn't hurt himself but the unexpected intake of breath started him coughing. They were on the edge of a copse and she stood by helpless as, holding on to a low branch, there was nothing he could do but let the paroxysm take its course. It was the first time for weeks it had happened like this as he held his handkerchief in his hand they were both frightened. Today though there was no tell-tale stain of blood and gradually the battle was won and he leant weakly against the tree wiping the perspiration from his face.

'Let's rest for a few minutes. Can you walk to that low wall?'

He could walk it seemed, but not yet talk.

Sitting side by side on the uncomfortably rough stones she stole a sideways glance at him. He's been so much better, but now suddenly that gaunt, tight look was back, his eyes shut, his mouth partly open, as if it helped him to find enough air. To listen to his breathing was worse here than at home, here where they'd felt the promise of spring, and the only other sound came from the birds in the copse behind them.

'I can't go on, Harry – that place. I dread going back to it. I can't do it, I can't . . .' Like a child he turned to her and she opened her arms and cradled his head against her firm bosom. Such a matronly figure for a woman who'd proved barren.

'James, there love, you don't have to. You don't have to do any of it, dear heart. I'll look after you. There, there,' she cooed, rocking him gently. She dreaded that he'd cry, it wouldn't be the first time and tears weren't far away; that might start him coughing again. 'Listen to me, James, we'll sell the shop, do as Edward suggested. It's a good enough business, it'll sell. We'll come down this way, perhaps even further, nearer to the sea. You have enough money to keep us if we're careful and we'll manage beautifully. If we don't, do you imagine I'm above working? What about if I ran a lodging house? I could. There, darling James, you're breathing better again, it's all over.'

'Dear sweet Jesus, I'm no use. Harry, it's not how I wanted it. I didn't mean it to be like this. I've no strength though, I can't fight.'

'Just be still, just lie quiet. Harry's got you.'

If she was secretly appalled at what had happened to him she hid it from him. She was wife, mother and nurse rolled into one and he clung to her as his only safety.

Isabella was sleeping soundly. For a long time they sat, even after he recovered enough to straighten up, blow his nose and turn his eyes to the distant horizon.

'That's what we'll do, Harry. We'll get rid of the shop and all of it. We'll go to the sea. If we take a cottage we can manage on what Mama left me and what we make on the shop. We don't want lodgers in the house.' He was holding her hand and for a moment he held it to his lips. 'Dear Harry – you know that don't you?'

'Oh come along, you don't need to tell me – nor me to tell you either. Time for all that's long gone. Here, let me wrap your scarf across you better. We've sat too long, the ground's cold to the feet. It's not spring yet. Do you think you can manage the walk home now?'

'Yes, we'll take it slowly. Better get back; Mill will be ready with the dinner.'

208

After a while she stopped to point out the distant hills, really because another wall presented itself and seemed too good a resting point to ignore.

'Harry, I'm going to write to Albert Pilfrey, tell him I can't come back. He'll not be surprised, he's no fool.'

'A good idea. Then we only have to get rid of the shop.'

After a minute he blurted out: 'If I were to stay here – I hate suggesting it but ... but ... I just don't think I can face it. There's no air there. If only I can be where there's air ...'

'Stay here, James, they'd love to have you. In no time I'll see to ridding us of our ties in Newbridge. You could start looking for a place for us to live: Amelia and Edward would help.'

They walked on towards home, keen to get back now and tell the others. They were about half a mile from the cottage, where the road bent towards the village, then branched off up the slope. That was when they first noticed the pillar of smoke, suddenly blackening the blue winter sky.

'Can that be a garden fire? It's in the direction of Longview!'

'Perhaps Edward's burning the tree.'

'But look at it Harry. That's no ordinary garden fire.'

Even as they looked, the smoke billowed higher on the windless day. They hurried, round the bend so that even though the cottage wasn't in view they knew exactly where it stood on the far side of the hill – and stood alone. There was no doubt.

From the village the smoke had already been seen and now the silence was shattered by the ringing of the brass fire bell. They stood to one side in the lane so that the horses could pass, pulling the fire machine with its tender of water and long ladder.

'Wait here with Bella. Let me run on. You stay down here with her,' for the hill got steeper as they rounded the bend and she could go quicker alone.

'No. No, I'm coming.'

She could have run faster without a pram to push and without his hand on her shoulder, but speed could have made no difference.

As Edward reached to unclip the candles from the high branches of the Christmas tree he must have dislodged it in its tub without realizing. He went upstairs to collect the box for the decorations from the bedroom cupboard and even then all would have been well if he'd come straight down again, but today Amelia was in a reminiscent mood and he found her sitting on the edge of the bed, her bundle of family letters on her lap as she reread. Some of them she'd had for years. In the beginning, when she'd gone to live with Edward, she'd read only Henry's condemnation of what she'd allowed to happen and she'd smarted under his words; yet now, perhaps because her own spirit had grown and even in the few months she'd had Isabella she'd learnt to love as a parent, she could read deeper, could recognize that he'd been saddened and puzzled that his family could treat each other so. If she'd only been able to go home then, to talk to him (and to Beth too, for one thing time had proved was that she'd misjudged what she hadn't understood) things could have been so different.

Edward didn't hurry back to the sitting-room below. Together they re-read the yellowing pages and with him her sadness was overcome. Whatever she'd lost had been so much her own fault, for it had started before he'd come into the picture. But he had his own memories; the man he'd been in the first few months of his marriage to Lucy, his son, the love he'd had for his work in the parish – all had faded like a dream and yet it must have gone into the making of what he was now. The minutes ticked away and the letters were tied again in their ribbon.

'Regrets, Amelia? Would you have had it any different?'

He turned her face to his, holding her gently under the chin.

'Us, you mean? Oh, Edward, don't be silly. How could we have done anything different? All my regrets are that we none of us knew how to see things any way but our own. It's so sad, such a waste. We lose our families and they lose us too, just for some nasty feeling of self-righteousness. I had it when Papa married Beth – yet they seem to truly care for each other and who was I to think I knew best? They – at any rate Papa – had it because he believed we wronged Lucy, yet would it not have wronged her more to force her to stay in a married life she hated, and didn't she break her vows even before you did?'

'She had to do what she did – to have given herself without love would have been a greater sin. But I couldn't see that at the time. For all that, now I just thank God; it's what brought us to what we have.'

'And I too, you know that. It's sad though that so much had to be tainted by unnecessary bitterness.'

'Have you left something on the gas – has a saucepan boiled dry?' He sniffed.

'No, nothing's on yet. But it ought to be, they'll be home soon. Edward, I do wish we could help Jamie, he's so poorly.'

'Darling, I worry for him; I've seen it too often. Amelia, sweetheart, to me he looks more than poorly.'

'Oh Edward, do you think it too – what I think?'

He put his arm round her. 'Amelia, you were talking of home. When you write to your father I think you should tell him what we suspect, he has a right to know. We aren't the only ones to regret the barrier the years have made, I dare say.'

'There must be something that can be done for him though –'

'Listen! What's that?'

They listened. Something crackling, a muffled roar.

'Downstairs – it smells like burning!' He opened the

door as he spoke, leading to the small landing and the narrow stairs with a door straight on to the sitting-room. 'Stay here.' He ran down the stairs. 'Don't come down until I tell you.'

She was on the landing watching as he opened the door into the sitting-room. A draught was just what the fire wanted, already it was lapping angrily on the wood but once the door was open thick smoke rushed up the stairs.

'Edward!' She screamed his name, 'Edward, come back.'

Choking, he came. 'Look. Here too. Smoke – between the floor-boards', for only the boards divided the bedroom from the sitting-room. 'Into the other room. We'll drop from the window.'

If he'd had the foresight to shut the door to the sitting-room before rushing back up the stairs, or even to have shut the spare bedroom door before opening the window and letting in a current of air to fan the flames, even then they might have got out safely.

A thatch-and-timber cottage takes only minutes to turn into a blazing inferno. By the time the smoke was seen from the village, and someone had run to fetch the crew who manned the fire engine (one from the butcher's, one from the blacksmith's and the third from where he was sitting atop a cottage mending the thatch) and they'd fetched the horses from the paddock and harnessed them, the flames were through the ground floor.

The window was open and Edward turned to help Amelia from the smoke-filled room when in horror they saw what had happened. The tongues of flame that were now licking through the floor of the second bedroom had reached out to the hem of her skirt where there was nothing to hold them back. A wide skirt of inflammable material was just what they wanted. They seemed to explode into a column of fire as he grabbed at her and threw her on to the bed to roll the counterpane round her. Leaping and crackling the flames touched the sheets, the mattress, then Edward's coat.

Neither of them heard the clanging of the fire bell. The roar around them would have swallowed it up even if they'd still been conscious. When James and Harriet came to the top of the hill they were met with a sight that would haunt them all their days. The inside of the cottage was ablaze, then as the first flames crept through the thatch the upper rooms collapsed. There was nothing anyone could do but let it burn – and pray with all their might that Edward and Amelia had got out before it was too late.

They called and called, even when reason told them it was useless. Perhaps they'd gone to the village, perhaps they'd decided to go walking after all. Perhaps . . . perhaps . . . But in their hearts they knew.

Little Isabella opened her mouth wide and screamed. It was her dinner-time.

Lucy stood at the window watching the drizzling January dusk. Yesterday had been like spring, now today it might have been November. She lit the gas and was about to close the heavy velvet curtains when she heard the sound of wheels on the gravel driveway. It was early for her father to be home and in any case it didn't sound like the trap; she pushed the lace curtain to one side and peeped out, instinctively smoothing her skirt as flat as she could as if that would get rid of the bulk she knew prevented her ever looking well-dressed. On an afternooon like this who would come calling? Her puzzled frown deepened as a man climbed down from the carriage then turned back to help a woman and baby. No, it couldn't be – all these years – older, but surely it was him. Rooted to her peeping post she watched as he said something to the driver (he must have told him to wait, so they're not staying, she decided), then before the visitors had had time to reach the top of the steps she'd hurried to the hall and flung the front door wide for them.

'Why, it's James, Jamie, I can't believe it,' she held her

arms wide and suddenly he was a boy again, and she was the same one he'd always turned to. How often she'd listened to his tales of woe when, home from boarding school, he'd been expected to visit the works, or when after their mother had died he'd thought himself (and often rightly) the scapegoat when Henry's personal unhappiness had made him hit out at those around him.

Then she turned and over the baby's head touched Harriet's cheek with her lips. 'And you're Harriet, Jamie's wife. My dear, it's more than time he brought you. But why didn't you tell us there was a baby? No one told us.' By no one she meant Edward and Amelia but she wouldn't bring herself to say so.

'Lucy, there's been the most dreadful tragedy. It's Mill, Lucy. She's gone,' James blurted.

'Gone. Left him?'

'No, no. Both of them. Yesterday . . . killed . . . burnt . . . so horrible . . . dreadful . . .!' It was hardly possible to make any sense of his words and Harriet took up the story while he flopped into the carved wooden chair that had stood in the hall as long as he could remember.

'Come into the warm. Except for the children upstairs, I'm the only one here but Papa will be home soon.' Lucy led the way into the drawing-room.

It didn't change, that was his first impression. Then he noticed the different carpet, a tall mahogany cabinet that hadn't been there before and a backgammon table in the corner. The piano, his piano, still stood where it always had; he wondered who played it now. The tall silk front so familiar under his touch, it might have been only yesterday. He sat on the revolving stool taking no part in the conversation. Harriet seemed to have the whole thing in hand. From above the fireplace that girlish face looked down on him and he wasn't prepared for the rush of guilt. He'd failed her. How sad she would have been at what had happened to her family, for right or wrong, she would

214

have kept faith with Henry and above all she would have wanted them to keep faith with each other. Now with Mill gone all that business with Beth seemed nothing.

The sweetened milk and water they'd tried to force into Isabella during the past twenty-four hours hadn't been to her liking. Most of the night (and what an endless night it had been!) she'd screamed while Harry had carried her up and down the bedroom of the Vicarage where they'd been given hospitality. At last she'd taken some of the unfamiliar liquid and collapsed into sleep, but the long journey to Wilhampton had been a nightmare, her hunger and fright in those arms so unused to their task had sent her into a frenzy. Only in the cab had she been overcome by the steady clip-clop of the hooves and collapsed again. Now she slept in Harriet's arms.

How ought I to feel? Lucy asked herself as she listened to the tale. Edward and Millie, what they did to me, to Edwin – but what a price to pay! And this little mite, their love child, born of their sin. Is it right that I feel like this towards the living proof of the suffering I've had to bear? But poor wee darling, poor sweet little innocent . . . As if she had a secret way of reading her aunt's thoughts the baby chose that minute to open her eyes. She looked at Harriet and prepared to let out a wail, but then Lucy moved towards her and the little head turned, raised itself, and the mouth opened even wider exposing a fine set of gums and a tongue that trembled as her smile broke.

'Oh, you darling, you poor darling little angel.' Lucy reached out for her, the other two forgotten at the feel of the helpless bundle turning to her for help. 'Come to Lucy, there's my pretty one. My, but you're a little Millie aren't you, that's the way, what a lovely smile . . . ,' she cooed. Even James got up from the piano stool and joined them as Isabella cooed and dribbled to show her approval of this newfound, fat, comfortable aunt.

They were still standing there when the drawing-room door opened and Henry came in. Being on his own he'd taken the trap straight to the coach-house so no one had heard him arrive.

At fifty-one he'd looked young for his years, at sixty-three he still did, but James had always thought of him as he remembered, never imagining any changes time might bring. Just as slim, just as straight, his brown hair had lost its depth of colour now and his side-whiskers were grey; two deep lines had etched themselves down his face at the corners of his mouth – but his eyes were as clear, their steely blue as penetrating as ever and now they were fixed on James hardly able to believe what they saw.

Heaven above, what had the boy done to himself? The last time Henry had seen him had been the day after Lucy came home and then Millie and Edward were chiefly on his mind. It was a visit he preferred to forget and James had played no part in it, only his silent expression showing his defiance. Now though, seeing him back here, Henry's only instinct was to protect him, for something was very wrong.

'James, my dear boy.' While his right hand was held out his left rested on James's shoulder.

Perhaps it was the portrait of Isabella that was influencing James. 'Papa,' the childish name sounded incongruous on the lips of a grown man. 'Papa, it's Mill. We've brought her baby home.'

'Millie? What's wrong with Millie? She's not ill?' The old tone again. Tell me and I'll take control, it said. 'Well? Speak up, boy, where is Millie? Is she here?'

'Papa,' Lucy spoke softly, 'Millie and Edward have been killed. There's only little Isabella to come home to us.'

'Millie! Dear God – how?'

They told him, Harriet who'd not so much as been presented to him doing most of the explaining. As he listened his expression told them nothing, his face was a mask. And when he'd heard it all, without looking at the child, he said: 'You did right to bring her. Her place is here.'

Beth and Phoebe had gone down to Cheltenham. It seemed Beth had felt yesterday's promise of spring too and had decided they should order clothes for the warmer days ahead. The milliner in Cheltenham was the cleverest in town and, with thoughts of the new front-tilted straw creations she knew would flatter her curls, she intended to spend an hour at her salon. Today, of all days, she wasn't at home and wouldn't be back until supper time, today when he needed her.

'You've been a long time bringing Harriet to visit us, James. A pity you had to wait for such an occasion.' Then to this daughter-in-law he felt had a maturity far beyond James's: 'You're welcome here, even though we've been kept waiting so long.'

'If we'd known we were welcome we might have come sooner.' She met his look fearlessly.

'Lucy, see that James's room is made ready. Now that you're here you're to stay of course.'

Whether or not James wanted to stay Harriet didn't know, here where he professed to have been so unhappy. Either way he needed the rest, anything was better than travelling on in the damp cold of the evening. So she accepted the invitation before he had a chance to do otherwise.

'Beth won't be home yet. Dismiss your carriage, James, and Lucy you see the rooms are attended to.'

James's dark eyes smouldered. Do this, do that – then, just as he'd known he would, Henry left them, retreating without another word and closing the library door on them.

When Beth came home that was the first room she went to, for that's where she expected to find him. She carried a hat box containing quite the prettiest fur hat she'd ever seen, tilted to one side on her forehead, her hair curled high behind, she knew it suited and flattered her. Leaving Phoebe to go the drawing-room she hurried straight across the hall to the library.

'We're home, we've had a splendid day. Just you wait until I show – why Henry! Henry, what is it?'

He'd been sitting at his desk, his head in his hands, hardly aware of his surroundings. What they thought of him for leaving them like that he didn't consider, he'd had just to get away. James, hardly more than a boy in his father's mind, yet he looked an old man. And Millie, little Millie. He saw her as a toddler, remembered how she used to follow Bella, looking to her as the centre of her universe, a child so like Bella too, then as she'd grown up the prettiest in the county or so he'd thought. The way she used to watch him, a smile always ready if he'd given a hint of encouragement and such a perplexed expression in those soft brown eyes if his mood had been dark. Had he driven her away, caring for nothing but his own miserable feelings? No, no of course that wasn't true. He'd cared for all of them – but had the child understood? All these years she'd been gone but nothing could fill the gap. He should have told her – but how could he while she lived with Lucy's husband, Edwin's father? Now he'd never to able to tell her. That dear little girl who'd tried to be a model of his Bella, gone, gone in agony. A hell-fire, and hadn't he threatened her that what she was doing could only lead to damnation? Blindly he tried to pray that his spirit would find her, but all he could see was the hurt in her huge dark eyes. Out there was her baby, the only thing left of Millie, brought here to be cared for. Would poor Millie want that even or did her hurt go too deep? But she shouldn't have done it, she must have realized he could never condone what she did . . .

'. . . what is it?' Beth had come; he raised his head. 'Henry, aren't you well?' No wonder she asked for she'd never seen him look like it.

Beth had come. His mouth opened to speak but instead hard, dry sobs shook him. The hat box was dropped without a thought as she gathered him into her arms, not speaking, just holding him until gradually he told her.

218

'Poor, poor Amelia – and Edward too. And the baby? Isabella?'

'They brought her to us. Lucy has her. James and Harriet are here.'

'How has Lucy taken it?'

He'd not thought of her and for the first time he considered what he'd seen. 'She always loves babies,' he answered.

'Perhaps this one will heal her wounds. It's time they healed.'

'Too late, Bethie.' His voice broke. 'Too late. My poor Millie.' The tears came at last. 'Is that God's justice? To burn. Can you think of it, Beth, her flesh to burn, her hair . . .'

'It's over, darling one. No more pain for her now. And they were together.'

'All this time and we let things drift. I should have talked to her, made her realize that love doesn't stop. I should have said all that . . .' It wasn't easy to understand his words. With the flood of tears all his fight for control had gone.

'Henry, dear heart, hush, stop tormenting yourself and be still a minute. How can she read your heart while you carry on so?' Cradling him in her arms still as she sat on the wooden arm of his revolving chair, she stooped and laid her cheek against his unusually ruffled hair. So they stayed for a long time and gradually he grew quieter.

'Open your heart and let her in dearest, just as you learnt to do with your Bella. Bella has known how you've grieved over them all these years, she's known it as surely as you have yourself; now Millie knows. Open your heart, Henry, and listen to her own message, for don't you think she's grieved too? Now you have little Isabella, we all have her, to love for herself – and you'll love her for Millie and for your own Bella.'

How unlike Henry to shiver so. If only James and his

wife weren't there they could stay in the library, needn't go to the table for supper, but tonight that wouldn't do.

'I'll put some more coal on the fire. Come and sit here for a while and get warm.'

He did as she said and from her place on the stool at his feet she looked at him, conscious of his years as she'd never been before. She took his cold hand and held it to her cheek.

It was a large family that assembled for supper. A thousand times James had pictured the panelled dining-room, the oval table with its white damask cloth and the heavy silver cutlery. All of it just as he remembered, and yet less real than the memories that had kept him company. His father was the same, older no doubt, but not mellowed; but he alone was unchanged. At the foot of the table Beth, who'd haunted his memory, might be a stranger. Her hair was as red, her figure as slender, but there was an assurance that surely the little sewing maid he'd known could never have had. And Lucy! Heavens could she be only two years older than him? Her stout figure added to the feeling of comfort she'd always given him, but now her chin had trebled and the bustle that so flattered Beth did nothing but emphasize the fact that her waist had long since been lost. Facing him across the table Harriet looked utterly out of place. Anyone would have been out of place in that seat though, anyone but . . . His vision misted and he took a spoonful of hot soup, swallowing it with the lump that tightened his throat. The others at the table quietly eating were strangers to him, and, he was sure, missing nothing of the conversation or the atmosphere.

Edwin at thirteen was tall for his age, as fair as his father but not a bit like either of his parents. A slim lad, his eyes such a dark blue and with long dark lashes unusual with hair so blond. In other circumstances James might have been more interested and might have recalled his own youth and recognized a kindred spirit with this boy. Today, though, he'd shaken hands and hardly heard Edwin's softly spoken greeting. Then there was Beth's brood. The twins, just twelve and still alike, hair as red as hers even though a lighter shade, and eyes just the same green. In fact they still differed in character, just as Beth had recognized right from the start, but James couldn't know about that. The youngest at the table was Charles, five years their junior, not particularly like anyone except for his light blue eyes. He looked up at that moment, wondering about this 'uncle' he'd heard so little of; their glances met and James found that even the eyes were his own; the colour might be inherited but not the expression.

'Phoebe must have heard the gong. Go and see where she is, Nick; her soup will be cold.'

'Right you are, sir. I'll get her.'

All Nicholas did was at top speed. Already his own soup was half gone and now they heard him leaping up the stairs two at a time. No matter how Phoebe might be dawdling she'd not stand up against him. In fact he met her coming out of her room and for all the cold sponging she'd given her eyes her recent tears were evident.

'Papa's on the warpath, you're late. Oh, I say, Phoebe, I didn't know you even remembered her; you were only a kid weren't you when she went off?'

'I remember her, of course I do. Don't let's talk about it, Nick. Is it all right downstairs?' She dreaded other people's emotions. Phoebe had always liked life to be uncomplicated and this evening she'd not been prepared to be so upset. It wasn't just for Millie; in her secret heart, well hidden by its solid body, she'd looked on Millie and Edward as romantic and even now she found it comforting that they'd departed this life together. It was when she'd gone into the nursery and peeped at the sleeping baby she'd been thrown off balance. So tiny and helpless, its mother and father snatched from it. She'd gently touched its hand, the tiny fingers curled like petals waiting to unfurl.

Nick preceded her into the dining-room where she was about to apologize for being late when Henry's voice cut in with: 'Is that the way to behave, Nick? Just hold the door for Phoebe. I should think so too.'

Nicholas stood back, making an exaggerated bow to Phoebe as she passed him, then closed the door after her. 'Sorry, sir.' In Nicholas there was no fears such as James had known.

Tomorrow he'd go. Even winter at the shop was better than this. The old man hadn't changed a bit sitting there like God in judgement while the family bowed to his every wish. Divine Right of Fathers. Well, thank God he and Harry had no children. Fancy young Phoebe being so upset; her eyelids looked quite red and swollen as she kept them lowered, silently saying a quick Grace.

Then: 'I'm sorry I was so long, Beth – Papa,' she said.

'Drink your soup before it gets cold, my dear,' Henry answered.

The meal wasn't an easy one and for once Beth found herself helpless. She dug in her mind for something to say to break the silence, but what? Tell us about Newbridge – hardly. If they'd wanted to they would have long ago. Millie – no, no one could sit around the table talking of Millie, too painful. Just to think of it, poor, poor Millie. She and Edward had had a rough path but it had led them to happiness; there was no doubt of that – it had been evident in each of her few letters even from what she'd left unsaid. And now, with little Isabella, her world must have been complete. Then why? Where was the God who could take it all from her? What sin had she committed in loving? Beth had been so far away that she hadn't even noticed the silence had been broken. Lucy had been able to say things that Beth couldn't and she and Harriet were talking of Newbridge. Nothing personal. Beth noticed that Harriet kept the conversation general, talking of the town, the church, the school, but not the shop, not their own lives.

'Shall we go to the drawing-room?' Beth's voice dropped into a lull (Newbridge had worn itself out and Lucy was hunting for another safe subject). 'I think it's time you children went upstairs. Say your goodnights.'

To be honest Victoria was glad to go. The room had been full of tensions. Mother had sat so straight and looked uncomfortable, casting a worried glance every now and then at Papa who'd looked strange, almost ill. Phoebe must have been crying. Aunt Lucy was doing her best, so was Aunt Harriet. Uncle James made her feel ill at ease too, and each time he barked that hard cough Papa frowned. Yes, she'd be glad to get away.

'Say your goodnights here,' Beth repeated. 'We shan't go to the library this evening.'

They did as they were bid, the three of them so different. Even tonight's atmosphere didn't take away Nick's twinkle. He kissed Beth and then, his arm still around her shoulder, nodded to each in turn. 'Aunt Lucy, Aunt Harriet, Phoebe, Uncle James, goodnight. And goodnight, sir.'

'Goodnight my boy. God bless you.'

Charles kissed Beth, and followed Nick's example as he listed the others, but only after going to Henry's side and planting a kiss on his forehead.

'Goodnight Charles, my son. God bless you.'

'And you, Papa.'

Victoria stopped at the door to say: 'You'll come up won't you, mother?'

'But of course,' Beth nodded.

'That's all right then.' She was reassured; at least one thing was normal. Holding the door open, she stood still. 'Listen, the baby's crying. Should we do something? Is Jenny there or is she having supper?'

'I'll go.' Lucy was on her feet., 'Leave her to me.'

'Are you and James staying in here, Henry, or shall we

all go to the fireside? Why don't you carry your port in there, it's warmer.'

James was on his feet, the last thing he wanted was a tête-à-tête with his father. Usually after supper Beth and Henry went to the library, her favourite room, just as it was his. Lucy and Phoebe enjoyed a game of backgammon while Edwin played the piano. Tonight James seemed to have stepped back in time; the brass was gleaming just as brightly on the hearth, and he could almost see a young Millie taking a book to choose the reading; but it was Beth pulling the hanging chain under the gas brackets so that the room flooded with light.

'Shall we have some music or would you rather not? Does it stop us talking?' Lucy came back to join them determined that James's homecoming must bridge the years; they must make sure he'd come again. Tonight couldn't be happy – how could it when they'd lost Millie? (She wouldn't bring herself to think of Edward, for the Edward she'd known had been gone so many years.) But at least it must be an evening when they'd share their loss and help each other. Really sometimes Beth forgot herself. After all these years wouldn't you think she'd have learnt better? Fancy sitting on that footstool at Papa's feet leaning against him like that. Had she no dignity? Was that cough of James's a nervous habit? she wondered. She wished he'd cover his mouth. Edwin took chill so easily.

'I'd rather not play tonight,' James said. 'Do you keep the piano tuned?'

'Why of course we do. The twins both learn, really Victoria begins to play quite nicely, and Edwin has a real talent,' Phoebe answered.

'Then perhaps Edwin will play for us,' Harriet suggested. 'You may change your mind later, James.'

Music at least made the lack of conversation less obvious and within the first few bars it was evident that for his years Edwin was an accomplished pianist. James had thought of 'his' piano, picturing it unused, the lid closed, a shrine to the past. How wrong he'd been. At least he'd imagined he would have been missed for his music, but Edwin hadn't learnt to play like this in a year or two, so even that comforting thought had been false. Other than the piano his bark was the only sound.

'How long have you had that cough?' Henry frowned. 'Are you taking anything?'

'It's nothing.'

'My dear boy you should have seen a doctor. You don't look well at all – that wretched place isn't fit to live in if you're not well. You stay here until you're recovered.'

'I tell you it's nothing.' James sounded aggressive.

'We're very comfortable at the shop,' Harriet flashed. 'It may not be large but it's warmer than these great houses' (at least in the kitchen, she added silently) 'and we're well fed. James is much better now.'

Ah! The ice was breaking. Beth was thankful for that. Anything must be better than the cold formality where they all trod with such care. She'd not known how she'd react to seeing James; if she'd feel guilt for her part, for her cowardice in not being honest with him, hatred for what he'd tried to do to her and to Henry, tenderness for the lonely boy he'd been. Strangely she felt nothing.

Lucy lent over Edwin's shoulder and whispered something. Like Victoria he wasn't sorry to get away, he'd found it an uneasy evening. So he followed the pattern of the younger children, the only difference being that his kiss was for Lucy, then thankfully he escaped.

'He plays well, don't you think?' Beth said when he'd gone.

It was James who answered. 'Very. So you've not been deprived of music.'

'Won't you make some for us now, James?' Lucy held a hand out to him. 'To come home and not even run your fingers over the keyboard, why this has always been your piano. The children used to call it Uncle James's piano.'

'Really?' His mouth was twitching but he made no effort

225

to control it. Harriet prayed silently that he wasn't going to make a scene, Beth lowered her glance not wanting to look at him, and Henry thought: Dammit, whatever's happened to the boy? I can't let him go back to that squalid place – but Beth? Would she want him here? And, God forgive me, would I? Watching them together ... Lucy went round to the back of the chesterfield and bent over James's shoulder, rubbing her cheek against his. 'Dear James. You don't know what it means to us all that you're home. And Millie, she must know and rejoice.'

He did try then to keep back the sob that caught in his throat, not just because of Millie but because of everyone, even his mother looking down from her gilt frame. (Strange how a portrait that had been no more than a piece of background furniture suddenly became symbolic.) He coughed, only a low cough – he had breath for nothing more – he gasped, he coughed again. Harriet knew, she'd heard it all too often; she saw him grope for his handkerchief and hold it. At home he would have lent forward and given himself up the paroxysm, but here he wanted to get away. He stood up holding the mantelpiece; he must hide from all those eyes. It was too late though. His whole body was given to the fight for breath as he choked, retched, and finally flopped back on to the chesterfield, his handkerchief over his mouth.

'Thank God, thank God,' Harriet said silently as he grew quiet; 'no blood, thank God,' Perhaps he really was getting better. His rest with Millie had done him good. Better? But how dreadful he looked after an attack. Now he was beyond caring that they watched him, his eyes were closed and his mouth opened with each breath.

'He needs proper attention.' That voice, how he hated it!

'He has proper attention.' Harriet was splendid. James felt removed from the scene, they spoke as if he wasn't there, but he marvelled at her. To use that tone of authority to his father! He should have brought her here long ago.

226

'He lacks no attention, nor care. What he lacks is sunshine. We're only going to Newbridge to put our affairs in order, then we're going abroad, south to the sun.' Never had a decision been made so quickly. Dorset they'd said, but not now, not with Millie gone. No, they'd go south, perhaps to Italy. If only it were warmer and the air not full of smoke and fog he'd be better.

'Yes, he must be taken out of this winter.' Henry made no secret of how serious he considered James's condition and she was thankful even while she deplored his lack of tact.

'Should he not have something now, to ease his chest after that? Some warm milk perhaps?' Beth forgot how difficult conversation had been. The sight of James put all that into the background.

'Yes, I give him warm milk with two eggs beaten in it and a drop of brandy. That soothes him.'

He gave no sign that he heard what they said; in fact they supposed he was asleep but he wasn't. He was too weary to be bothered with any of them. Even Lucy's warmth that had so nearly brought him to tears wouldn't have touched him now.

He drank the milk when it came and when Harriet suggested she should help him to bed he went, one hand on the banister and one on her shoulder. At home he didn't behave like this; she was sure he was capable of walking alone, of getting himself between the warmed sheets. It was as if he were playing a part – and she too, as she went back to re-join the family.

'In that state it's out of the question for him to go back to Newbridge. That cough could develop into something far more serious. You're to stay here until the shop is sold.'

'That cough, as you call it, is no ordinary cough. We've had proof of that.'

'What's the young fool been thinking of? Staying in that wretched hovel, how does he hope to be cured?'

'Many people live in worse, many of your own workers, I dare say.'

'What?' He glared at her. What had his workers to do with it?

'I say the men who work for you. I don't expect you've any idea how they live. I doubt if they have the comfort we make for ourselves in Chain Street.'

'They have nothing to do with the case in point –'

'And you're wrong, Harriet.' Beth held a hand on Henry's knee. 'The houses Henry has built for his men are good; they have drains and closets, and the children all go to their own school for four hours of each day. I don't know what James has led you to believe.' She felt the pressure of Henry's hand on hers and was glad he was warm again. He looked better; strangely this business with James had helped him, put the fight back again.

'The staff houses don't come into it. I can't think why you bring them into it, Harriet. Now this is what you must do –'

No Henry, don't put it like that, Beth prayed silently. Can't you see, my darling, she'll do the complete opposite? She must. So would I in her place.

'Harriet,' she interrupted him, 'to help James we simply have to decide while he's not here what's best for him. He'll only get stubborn and this is no time for that.' Then she smiled, instinctively wanting to help this woman she felt had a spirit something like her own. 'Time enough when you bring him home with roses in his cheeks again.'

'Yes, you're right, I know you are. It's just that James has been proud of standing on his own feet, and I've been proud of it. We can't do anything until we sell the shop and I don't want to leave him here without me – he depends on me more than he realizes and – well, I'd be lost.'

'Then, my dear, leave me to tie up the business side of it. Let me send you abroad –'

'No, no, I can't do that. Don't you see? It would destroy all he's worked for.'

'I'll talk to him. Why should he object to a wedding present, even at this stage? Hal had a house, the others all had handsome amounts. Does he want to be different?'

He didn't. Put like that he accepted without hesitation; put a different way he might have taken a little longer. Two days later he and Harriet left by train for Dover where they boarded a boat to France and started on their long journey south.

A brief letter of explanation had been sent to Albert Pilfrey, and the keys of the shop handed over to Henry with a letter of authority for him to deal with their affairs. James had no wish to go inside No 11 Chain Street again and he severed his links with Newbridge without a backward glance or a moment's regret for the elderly couple who'd been his friends. He even felt bright as he stood on deck on the cold, calm January morning setting out on the next stage of life's exciting highway – and not a week before he had looked no further than Longview Cottage.

CHAPTER NINE

It couldn't last of course, for April was only in its second week, but something must be done to welcome the cloudless sky and gentle warmth in the breeze. Another ten days and Archie, young Henry, Nicky and Edwin would have gone back to boarding school, while Victoria and Charles would again be taken each morning to Wilhampton. There, at the Vicarage where Edwin had been born, they were taught by the present incumbent of St Agnes's, one Reverend Grimforth, an austere and scholarly cleric well suited to his name and better fitted to teaching than to the welfare of the parish that had meant so much to Edward.

On this particular morning family prayers were barely over and Mrs Murphy and her helpers on their way down the stairs to the kitchen to attend to serving breakfast when a loud knocking came on the front door.

'It's all right,' Nick called out. 'I'll open it. You go on down.' He pulled back the bolt and the family watched expectantly, for this was hardly the hour to come visiting.

'Henry! Is something up?' he greeted his cousin.

'Only the sun. Good morning, Aunt Beth, Grandpa, everyone.' He looked as fresh as the morning. At fifteen he was a tall boy, his light brown hair not straight yet only hinting at a wave, his light blue eyes as striking as Henry's – and Hal's too. 'On a day like this we should go somewhere. What do you say to a hamper of food and the top of Chazey Hill. Am I too early for you, Aunt Beth, do you mind?'

'Mind? Why, you're like a breath of fresh air, Henry, and just as welcome. Can you eat a second breakfast?'

'To be truthful it would be the first. I'm afraid I left a note on the hall table saying where I was going and disappeared before anyone was so much as downstairs — well, any family I mean.'

'You excused yourself from prayers?' Henry's tone spoke his disapproval.

'Oh, Henry, he was nearer his God under the clear sky than in a dark hall,' Beth defended.

'Perhaps — but I doubt his thoughts were as humbled as in listening to the Word.'

Young Henry was about to take up the point but thought better of it. 'May I take breakfast with you?' he asked instead.

Nick giggled.'You should do penance by going without, isn't that the right way? An empty belly in place of sackcloth and ashes.'

'Hush, that's enough,' Phoebe whispered. 'I'll run down and tell them we have one extra.'

'I wrote a note and put it through the door at Aunt Margaret's before I came here. Richard will be wild when he thinks of us, and there he'll be totting up his columns of figures,' for Richard was seventeen and his school days behind him. He'd gone into a firm of accountants where he was being articled and on a day like this freedom must beckon to him.

'You'd better make the most of it too, young fellah-me-lad. This time next year you'll be off to the sweated labour,' Nick chuckled.

'Oh well, that's different.' The younger Henry turned to the elder; 'You know, Grandpa, I really am looking forward to finishing at Rugby and getting to the works.'

'Good fellow.' What a satisfactory boy this one of Hal's was, always interested, even as a child, but then Hal had been the same. Young Nicholas had his mind full of other things — a satisfactory boy for all that. Then Henry's glance fell on his youngest. It was wrong to have a favourite amongst one's children, he tried to overcome it, but he had no power to prevent this special affinity with Charles. 'Now, enough talking at the table from you young people. Concentrate on your breakfast. And you, Phoebe, are you going on this spree?'

'I was just considering it, Papa. If Penelope's to be there, yes, I think I shall.'

So the party increased and from a walk to the top of Chazey Hill it developed into a full-blooded outing in the wagonette, complete with cricket bat, butterfly nets, as much food as Phoebe and Mrs Murphy could cram into a large hamper, a stone jar of ginger ale and even fishing rods; for if they weren't walking they might go anywhere and even though they didn't fish the river near home during the breeding season there were good trout to be taken in Whitefriars Lake on the far side of the hill.

It wasn't until the wagonette had left, with Edwin holding the reins, that Henry went to the foundry. On occasions he still left the house by eight o'clock, but by no means every morning. Hal always went in early; it was he who now watched the day-to-day running of the workshops. Each department had its foreman, the man who made sure no one was late, no one slacked, and no one let anything pass that was not up to standard. Those foremen were responsible to Hal, who in turn took direction from Henry. And into that pattern Beth had woven herself like a bright thread that touched at every level. Those houses she'd told Harriet about with such pride had been due to her – not that Copeland's was alone in building for its staff, many a factory did it. Until she sowed the seeds Henry had never considered it. Although he was a fair employer and was never short of workers, he hadn't looked into how or where they lived. Beth had known a different sort of life though; she remembered only too well the overcrowding, the outside closet, the mornings when the fire wouldn't draw and the long wait for warm food and water. Even more than that she thought of how she'd wanted the chance to learn, of her few hours each day at school (and she'd been luckier than so many) and of how most of her knowledge had been gleaned the hard way

232

with no one to help. At heart she was as keen a reformer as Edward has been, and better able to see the results of her schemes. Henry had bought a meadow on the outskirts of Wilhampton, they'd drawn up the plans themselves and the builders had been put to work. Henry Street came first (the name was Beth's choice and nothing would dissuade her), a long terrace of houses on each side of the rough hoggin track; then two years later alongside it had come Foundry Lane. Beth had left her mark, for without her it's unlikely if any of this would have happened, and certainly Peter Hawkins wouldn't have been hired to teach the children in that brickbuilt schoolhouse at the far end of Henry Street.

Beth still loved the works, the noise and activity. Even the sweating bodies of the men never revolted her as they had James. It was a fine thing to sweat in one's labour, to do one's job with all the energy and force one could muster; it was the only way she knew. Whether in loving, working, playing, laughing or weeping Beth gave all that she was.

She was in her bedroom, the contents of a large drawer emptied on to the bed so that she could sort it. This afternoon she had in mind to visit Mary Giles, the young wife of a pattern-maker from the works; poor girl she'd been brought to bed with her first child, stillborn. She worried Beth; disappointment, loss, distress – all those things she expected, but Mary had become distant from everyone. Poor Johnny, her young husband, was powerless to help her, just as they all were. It was probably silly to imagine she could do what he couldn't, but she had to try. Something different to wear might encourage her to get up from her bed. Perhaps this pale coffee lace blouse would cheer her. It was unworn, still wrapped in tissue; surely any girl must love it. She held it in front of her thinking how pretty it was. The gift must be something she wanted herself though, nothing less would do.

'Beth, may I come in?' Lucy tapped on the door. 'I was

just going to bath Bella but Jenny's already done it and got her in her chair for breakfast.'

'You two! We'll have to see if we can't find another baby from somewhere.'

Lucy looked at her sharply. 'You're not – '

'I wasn't thinking of me. It's time Phoebe had a husband, Lucy, but she goes nowhere to meet anyone.'

'She's happy at home. You'll never turn Phoebe into a socialite. I think she's very like me – in more than looks.'

'If she is, then she'll need babies to care for and a husband is a necessary condition of getting them.'

'More's the pity!'

'Fiddlesticks! I dare say husbands are like eggs, mostly good but some addled. There's one I'm feeling pity for just now and that's Johnny Giles, you know, Lucy, the tall pattern-maker with a blond beard, handsome young giant of a man. His wife just lost her baby you remember.'

'And pity for her too. To suffer all that and have nothing at the end of it.'

'Somehow we have to get her back on the tracks again. She's hardly more than a child, she'll have more babies.'

'You're not taking her that pretty blouse are you? Why Beth, it's new.' Beth was carefully folding it back in its wrapping. 'It would suit you so well.'

'I couldn't give her a hand-me-down. Don't you see I want her to feel new and fresh again herself?'

There were times when Lucy just couldn't understand Beth. Surely amongst all her clothes (and heavens above, she had enough!) there must be things that would please Mary Giles without giving away that exquisite and completely unsuitable lace creation.

While the two women replaced the remaining articles in the drawer and carried it back to the huge walnut wardrobe the wagonette called at Margaret's to collect Penny and Archie, then on to the house on the High Street so that Henry's ten-year-old sister Betsy could join the party. Nine people made a fuller load than the wagonette was designed for though they weren't all full-sized people. Only Edwin, behind the reins, had a place to himself, the others packed in as best they could with Charles sitting on the food hamper. The discomfort only added to the fun and on such a day even Phoebe, a staid twenty-one-year-old, felt no older than little Betsy.

At the lakeside they knew just the place they intended to make their picnic spot, the short turf reaching to the water's edge and the woods behind them on the slope of Chazey Hill. While the girls spread the rug on the ground and prepared 'basecamp' as they called it, Charles and Archie went in search of wood to build a fire, Nick and Henry started to sort the rods and lines and Edwin unharnessed the horse and took him to the shade to tether him. The day stretched before them long and free.

It was an hour or so later and Victoria, Betsy and the boys had all wandered off on their own amusements leaving the grown-ups, as they called Phoebe and Penny.

'Phoebe.' Penny lay flat on her back stretching her arms behind her and holding her face towards the sun. 'Do you sometimes feel — almost frightened — no, perhaps not quite that, but — yes, what else, frightened? When you're young like the children you're so sure of everything ahead of you falling into the right pattern. But I'm eighteen — and you're twenty-one. When will it start?'

'But surely Penny you've been to so many parties and balls over the winter months. Why Aunt Margaret always seems full of talk of the whirl of your engagements.'

'It's ever so dull, Phoebe. I go the Hatchers' parties at Wilton End and the Balls are there and the Crisps and the Chownes. Then I go to the Chownes' at Matchams Hall and who do I find but the Hatchers and the Balls and the Crisps! And so on. It's not life, it's not adventure. When I was younger I used to think you were silly because you never wanted to be part of it, but, Phoebe, it's not one jot exciting. After the first party the others are all the same.

The only jolly part is having pretty clothes, but what's the point in that when there's no one . . .'

'Oh, Penny.' Phoebe laughed affectionately, 'there's plenty of time.'

'And what about you? Don't you want to meet someone madly exciting, perhaps a handsome captain in the Hussars or an explorer from darkest Africa. Don't you want – '

'No, I don't want a captain in the Hussars who'll go away and be a soldier while I stay at home, and certainly not an explorer to get lost in darkest Africa,' the solid Phoebe chuckled. 'But, yes, I want a husband to care for, a family to share with him. I don't know Penny, I suppose we have to wait and see what life brings to us.'

'But don't you see, that's how people get left behind, that's what worries me. Like Esme, she must know by now she'll never find her Sir Galahad. Fancy spending all one's life teaching nasty little girls things they care nothing for.'

'I'm sure Esme doesn't see it like that.'

'You know what I think, Phoebe?' Penelope sat up and turned to the aunt hardly older than herself. She looked so serious. An attractive girl, Phoebe thought looking at her, her face was long and lean but the bone structure good, her eyes very dark blue; the freckles across the bridge of her nose were pronounced today in the sunshine, freckles that went with the sandy colour of her thick glossy hair. Surely life would never pass her by?

'You tell me.'

'I think you're too content. That could be dangerous, don't you see, lull you into letting time go by and before you know it you'll be another like Aunt Lucy?'

'Lucy's happier now than she ever was with Edward I dare say. I was too young to be told or to understand at the time, but I could feel she was at odds with herself.'

'That was real romance though, Edward and Aunt Millie. They gave up everything just for each other.' She sighed.

'What a shame they couldn't have found their happiness without upsetting everything and hurting other people. There must have been someone else Millie could have fallen in love with if she'd looked.'

'There wasn't though; that's what's frightening. All the balls one can go to, all the suitable bachelors one can meet, none of it counts for anything when true love comes. Don't you see, that's what scares me? Perhaps it never will and there's nothing one can do.'

'Funny girl you are to worry so. You'll find before long you'll look back and laugh at your fears,' the solid Phoebe reassured her. 'Now then, where have the others got to? It's time we lit the sticks. A lovely pile of cones they've left us. We'll get the water boiling in no time.'

The fun of the picnic took over and eighteen-year-old Penny forgot her fear of being left on the shelf, as her mother referred to Esme's single state. Kneeling on the short turf she screwed some paper into twists and made a pyramid of sticks around it while Phoebe went in search of the rest of the party.

Too content? Life slipping by? If they thought that of her then she was glad. The way her thoughts and longings had turned these last few months had been her own secret and she was relieved to think she'd kept it so well. Always she'd believed that one day she'd meet someone, fall in love, marry, have a home of her own, a family; just as Penny said, when you're young you never doubt. She'd met so few eligible young men, none of them a bit like she'd expected fate to guide her to. Then last autumn walking in Matlock Woods collecting beech leaves for the house and blackberries for the kitchen all that had altered. So handsome was he that a more experienced head than Phoebe's would have been turned, his fair hair and beard looking wirey and full of life, seeming to show his strength just as clearly as the muscles on his bare arms. In October sunshine he'd stripped off his sackcoat and hung it on a branch with his neckcloth, opened the buttons of his shirt

237

and rolled up his sleeves. At first he'd not seen Phoebe so engrossed had be been in sawing the fallen tree into logs, and what had made her stay she'd never know, for it was out of character for her.

'Warm work on such a day.' He'd spoken as if they already knew each other, wiping his handkerchief across his face and round his bare neck as he straightened up.

She'd cleared her throat, hoping her voice wouldn't betray her excitement as she'd answered. 'You'll have a warm winter for your labours. It's making fine logs.'

'Ah. There's another down through yonder; the gales at the weekend took them both. You've been having a fruitful afternoon too I see.' He'd indicated her bunch of copper beech and on her arm a basket well full of brambles for Mrs Murphy's jelly. The sun through the trees; the gold on his hair, his open shirt displaying the fair matting on his chest – she'd never seen such a man. And he? She was no beauty certainly but there was something about her that attracted him. Could it have been the honest blue eyes, the 'no nonsense' way she moved, the unexpectedly small pretty hands, or could it perhaps have something to do with her being Henry Copeland's daughter? A little of each perhaps. She'd only stayed a few minutes but the next day, despite it being Sunday and not a day to gather brambles, she'd come again just by chance, of course, for she wouldn't have admitted even to herself that she'd hoped he'd be there. That afternoon she'd gathered no fruit and he'd sawn very little wood. The next Saturday the sun had still shone, a good day for blackberrying. It wasn't until the following week that he told her about his wife.

Now, walking round the edge of the lake to where she could see Nick and Victoria fishing, she thought about him and about Millie who should have found someone else to love. Life wasn't like that, she knew that now. But she'd not do what Millie had done, she'd be sure they were never more than companions and if he wanted friendship from her what harm could that do his wife? She tried not to listen to what he'd told her of his marriage or, at any rate, not to let herself be tempted by it. If he was miserable and unloved surely it harmed no one to let him talk about it, to let him feel there was someone who cared about his happiness? She'd always liked to wander in the woods on her own just as she'd played on her own as a child, so no one gave a thought to her solitary walks.

She waved at the others as she neared them, watching Nick's patience as Vicky concentrated on casting her feather on the clear water. He signalled that the others were on the wooded hill so after more sign language had told them that it was time to eat she continued her search. Charles and Betsy came with their nets and jar of butterflies; Henry, Archie and Edwin, feeling themselves the men of the party, emerged deep in serious discussion on the merits of the new narrower cricket bat. Rounding them all up Phoebe herded them back to basecamp where a blackened container of water was already steaming (they could well have done without a warm drink on such a lovely day, especially with that large jar of ginger ale to get rid of, but tea-making was all part of the fun) and as she followed them, half hearing their chatter she knew she'd grown beyond it and yet had nothing in its place. The talk with Penny had upset her more than she'd admit, although already the younger girl seemed to have forgotten all about it.

If Beth had hoped to find Mary Giles in a happier frame of mind she was disappointed. It was nearly a month since she'd lost the baby and this was the fourth time Beth had visited her.

When there was no response to her knock she opened the unbolted door and called up the stairs: 'Mary, it's me, Beth Copeland. May I come in?' Purposely she said 'in', not 'up', setting the mood; she implied she expected to find Mary downstairs again.

'I'm up here, Mrs Copeland.'

'Why, Mary,' Beth's energy and good humour seemed to send the girl further under the untidy bedcovers, 'I was expecting you to be downstairs. How can you lie there on a day like this? It's not good for you, you'll get weak if you lie abed so long.'

'I've no strength. And what is there to get up for?'

'Get up and you'll find out. For certain there's nothing to lie there for.'

Mary glowered at a point somewhere above Beth's head. Just because she was married to Henry Copeland, did that give her the right to come giving her orders?

'You must be tired of yourself – and Mary you'll get worse. Now, just let me help you. I'll go downstairs and put some pans of water to heat, then I'll bring the tub up and we'll fill it here. I'll help you Mary, make you sweet and fresh again.'

'You know I can't bath yet.'

'Of course you can, water won't hurt you. But at least let me bring the water and you can wash. When did you last do that beyond your hands and face? Let's make you pretty, Mary. I'll do you hair, eh? What do you say?'

'Why should you do that for me? You of all people?' Mary's lip trembled. 'No one else bothers.'

'I don't like pretty things to be wasted and you're a pretty thing. I'm going down to light the gas and put the pans on. I've brought you a little present, you can look at it while I'm downstairs. Shan't be a jiffy.'

It was good to get down to the brick-floored scullery – not that that looked very wholesome but at least the air was purer than in the bedroom where the girl lay, day after day, unattended. What a prospect for a man to come home to. Fancy having to climb into that stale bed each night! Beth took off her flat straw hat, rolled up her sleeves and got ready for the attack. When she heard the sound of

240

Mary crying she knew she was making some headway. She'd wait a minute or two then go up to her. Tears would help, they'd melt the ice round her heart. Poor, poor child. Beth sat on the wooden kitchen chair trying to imagine what she must be suffering. What if it had happened to her, would she have taken it like this? But then it couldn't ever be like this for her. Henry would never let her suffer it alone. Wasn't it Johnny's loss too? Then why couldn't they help each other?

She went back up the stairs, her brisk manner gone now as she took Mary in her arms. The smell of stale bedding, dried sweat and blood was nauseating but in her compassion she hardly noticed. And when the flood of weeping was finally over Mary gave herself over to the capable hands that washed her, changed her sheets and her nightgown, then put powder on her hair and brushed it. At the end of an hour, the windows flung wide open and some rose water shaken around, Beth was satisfied.

'Tomorrow I shall send Brigit over — she helps at the Court. I'll put your washing in the copper ready and she'll see to it for you, and she'll tidy the house. Then the day after that I'll come again and it'll be time you were up.'

'It's not just the baby, Mrs Copeland. It's all of it . . . he doesn't want me . . . doesn't see me. My mother warned me, she said when I married him I was nailing my own cross, it was only a passing thing with him. We never talk; I don't know anything about the things he fills his head with, always he's got his nose in some book. I never did understand much from books. I don't ask a lot, honest I don't, only that he comes home wanting to be with me, to walk out together, to make the house nice. He never notices if I get it all bright and shiny, just takes up his book and if I want to talk 'bout ordinary things he looks so irritable. I don't know what to do.' Her face had crumpled like a child's and as she talked she cried again, helpless tears. 'Only in bed he wants me, in the dark and with never a word. Like I was a thing, not a person, just

241

put there for him to . . .' She didn't know the words to use and her voice was lost in a snort.

'That's important too, Mary. All the talking in the world and all the books too can't be enough without that.'

'It's all I have. He knows I've no learning. But he just takes it, without knowing me, don't you see? Like when I pass him his dinner and he doesn't look up from his paper, just takes the plate and eats – like I'm a thing, just a thing.'

'Here, wash your face in cold water, or you won't be a pretty thing. And now just you listen to me, Mary Giles. He married you didn't he and you had no learning then? And where are you different now? Are you as jolly as you used to be? Do you show him you're pleased to see him when he gets home? Are you as warm in his arms? Or is it you who thinks of yourself as a "thing" as you call it?'

'You make it sound so easy, but it's not, honest it's not. I've nailed my cross like my mother said. How can I look pleased when he come home? I don't feel pleased. I dread him coming for the sour look on his face. I don't want him lying there heavy on top of me again, taking his pleasure. He did it just the same when I was weary with carrying the babe and look what happened. If he'd left me alone I might have had my baby, but now I got nothing . . .'

'That's poppycock. It does you no harm nor a baby either. Mary, why don't you ask your mother to stay with you? Where does she live?'

'In the better land, she died last September.' Then with a spark of spirit: 'He didn't care when I lost her. Said he was sorry but he didn't care. Just ate his supper as if it was nothing.'

'Perhaps he doesn't know how to show kindness. Some men are frightened of it. You know Mary they can be great children in some ways.' She rolled down her sleeves and buttoned her cuffs. 'You didn't say – did you like the blouse?

'Oh Mrs Copeland, I never said a word! Whatever must you be thinking of me! It's the most elegant thing I've ever

242

had, truly it's beautiful. I'll be frightened to wear it, it's fit for a princess.

'Then, Mary, when you do wear it you'll look like a princess. Now I must go. I said I'd ride home from the works with Henry. Downstairs there's a game pie Mrs Murphy made; it'll eat well hot or cold. Don't forget, the day after tomorrow you and that bed are going to part company – and, Mary, just look at that clear sky won't you, isn't it calling to you? The forget-me-nots are a carpet of blue and on my way I heard my first cuckoo.'

The afternoon had brought better results than her previous visits but even so she wasn't happy about Mary, or Johnny either. As she went up the wooden stairs to Henry's office she caught a glimpse of the young man and felt a fleeting sympathy for Mary who at eighteen had been swept off her feet by the handsome creature he was, his broad shoulders and strong arms, the blond hair and close beard; then her sympathy turned to him, for how empty his life must be with poor young Mary.

'Ah, Bethie, here you are.' Henry looked up from his desk, holding his arm to her. 'Here, come and see this. I've been giving some more thought to that new press. I wasn't happy about the height of the levers.'

'How can you make them lower? It would be much less tiring to use. Show me, Henry.'

'See, I've lowered the whole thing and done away with the trough underneath. We'll have the levers at the sides – one each side. Then the juice gets forced out of the fruit into this gulley in front instead and is funnelled off.'

She came to his side, her arm around his shoulder, and bent over the drawing. Her thoughts were only half on the cider press, the other half on herself and Henry and all they shared. Over his bent head she looked out of the window and remembered what she'd said to Mary only a few minutes before. A clear sky, spring again with all its promise; at home the children would be back from their picnic and here with the background symphony of hammers, metal wheels trundling over stone ground, the occasional voices or even whistles of the men as they worked – all of it so precious to both of them. Silently she said: I truly do thank You, and I do appreciate. Was it wicked to want time to stand still, to be frightened of a future that would change what she had? She rested her cheek against Henry's head.

He turned and looked at her quizzically, eyebrows raised and a teasing smile on his face: 'And to what do I owe that may I ask? Or is it by way of approving the innovations to the press?'

She shook her head, shrugged her shoulders, momentarily lost for the right words.

'Beth . . .?'

'It's everything. You, home, the children, the workshops, the cuckoo I heard this afternoon – but really it's you, us – even the press.'

He said nothing, but then she'd said it all. So he held her hand to his cheek for a moment then stood up.

'Home. Let's go home. Hal will be here for an hour or two yet. There's something I want to talk to you about.'

'About the foundry?'

'No, nothing to do with the foundry. Let me get my hat and we'll talk as we ride home.'

At any time what she was to hear would have delighted her; today was more than just any time; it held all the promise of spring and hope.

It was Richard Hatcher who'd mentioned only that morning to Henry that he was selling the house that at one time had belonged to his parents at Chalcombe. 'I've always liked the place – grew up there, happy days they were,' he'd said, 'but since the parents have gone year after year it stands empty. We go down occasionally, have a break there, but it's no wonder Madge has her mind set on Weymouth. Chalcombe has nothing to offer the ladies. I wonder you don't do the same thing, Henry, find somewhere you could go away to out of sight of the works, somewhere for the women and children to summer. Good train services these days. It's the vogue with the ladies, bless 'em,' he'd laughed indulgently. 'They fancy the idea of strolling along the promenade. Well, most of them . . .' he'd ended lamely, picturing Beth and her enthusiasm for the foundry.

'I'd not considered it . . . but, yes, the children would enjoy it. Do Lucy good to get away too. In Weymouth you say you're buying?'

'Ah, that's where Madge wants to go. Freddie Chowne has a place there. Lovely town he tells me, band concerts by the sea, a safe sandy shore. None of that at Chalcombe. When I was a lad it was a nice enough little spot, no industry at all, but it's a good natural harbour and over these last years some feller's built up quite a fishing fleet there. No place for the ladies nowadays. Some ways I'll be sorry to let it go, but I can understand Madge. Just look at the time, man! I've got my living to earn and so have you, else there'll be no house by the sea,' and he'd been off.

So as Henry drove the trap towards Wilhampton he told Beth what he had in mind; he'd been looking forward to seeing the pleasure on her face.

'Well? What do you say, Bethie? We were happy in Weymouth weren't we?' he added remembering their honeymoon. 'It would do the children good, the water is safe, plenty of bathing machines. Well?'

He was surprised when she didn't answer immediately, and even more surprised by what she finally said.

'I've heard about it too from Kathleen Chowne, Henry, the fashion parades of the ladies while their husbands are at home earning their bread. Of course we we happy there, it wasn't like that for us. No, Weymouth's not for me! Madge has talked of Chalcombe, "The only thing in its favour," she's said, "is that it's near enough so that we don't have to stay long." They go just for one night once in a while.'

245

'You don't want a house by the seaside?' He couldn't hide his disappointment; he'd been so sure of her delight.

'Not at Weymouth. But Henry, let's go and see Richard's house at Chalcombe. We could go there so much more often, both of us I mean, even for weekends. All very fine saying the sands are lovely for bathing. The children can swim over stones as easily as over sand – and if they can't then it's high time they learnt. I certainly can, and I don't need a bathing machine.'

That evening at supper they told the family what they had in mind.

'Chalcombe! But, Papa, Madge says there's no one there but fisher-folk. They even bring their catch in and attend to it' (Lucy jibbed at such an expression as 'gut it') 'by the waterside. A holiday house somewhere would be lovely for the children – '

'And for all of us, Lucy,' Phoebe chimed in. 'Wouldn't it be wise just to look at Weymouth first, Papa? After all Mrs Hatcher knows both places.'

He looked down the table. His answer was addressed to Beth as she let her glance travel from one to the other, then back to him. His word was the law they all accepted; silently she begged him.

'We shall have a look at Chalcombe, eh, Bethie?'

Beth said nothing, but she smiled at him, a gentle smile that seemed to exclude the others. Was that why Lucy's mouth set in that hard line, or was it merely what she'd heard of Chalcombe?

After that they wasted no time. The key was borrowed from Richard and by Friday morning Henry and Beth were being rocked and bumped as the train sped southward.

'Careful, Beth, you'll get a smut in your eye. Keep your head in.' Henry held his hand towards her to steady her back to her seat in the swaying train. They had the compartment to themselves, the blue plush of the first-class seats quite wasted on Beth who had one hand planted firmly on her hat as she leant out and peered ahead along the track.

'Look, Henry, look! The sea! Can you see it? See the boats out there, all the coloured sails!'

Then the track ran parallel to the shore. She knew Chalcombe must be close, it was time they arrived; but so far there was no sign of approaching habitation. The whistle screeched and immediately they were plunged into darkness. She drew her head in with a start and fumbled with the window strap.

'Let me do that. Keep your eyes shut.' Henry took the strap from her and wrenched it to close the window. 'All right? It's just a tunnel. It'll be light in a minute,' she heard him say as if to reassure her.

'A tunnel! Henry, isn't this fun!' Sometimes she seemed no more than a child even after all the years they'd shared. Her hands reached to touch him, he felt her arms around his neck as they stood isolated in the smokey darkness, her body leaning against his, her lips almost on his as she whispered: 'How far under the ground are we, I wonder? Deep down in the earth, no one but us . . .' There was laughter teasing her voice, but he silenced her just as she'd meant him to. Daylight was creeping back.

'Bethie, my Bethie, what's to do with you . . .?'

'You're doing nicely,' just as they raced over a point on the line and were both thrown back to their seats, her hat knocked over her eyes.

The train was slowing down, the tunnel had taken them from the shore to what must be Chalcombe Halt. She straightened her hat and pinned it securely as he reached for his hat and cane. No porter came to open their door, first class or not. Henry climbed out and held his hand to her.

'I don't see a cabby outside.' Indeed he saw no sign of life except for two men loading into the train wooden boxes of what proclaimed themselves to be fish.

'It can't be far. Come on, Henry, it's shanks's pony for

us!' Even this was a novelty, adding to the excitement. At home they never walked together. Even to church on Sunday mornings they went in the trap. She slipped her hand through his arm. There was no need to tell him how enchanted she was with all she saw. A cluster of houses built early in the century, a dozen or so among them far older, roofed in thatch, then a row much newer, red brick and obviously added since the days that Richard Hatcher had been a boy there. In the porch of one of these an elderly man was sitting and Henry enquired of him where they might find Penrhyn House.

'Mr Hatcher's place that'll be? 'tiz empty you'll find. Not often 'e visits these parts nowadays. Straight on down Fore Street, you'll zee it, there at the back o' the green. Can't miss it. Big place it iz.'

Fore Street prided itself that it was the village centre. There was a village store, its windows packed with goods on the inside, stickers on the outside proclaiming cocoa was the way to a good night's sleep, porridge the healthy start to the day and enquiring of the passer-by whether he'd had his daily dose of a certain brand of fruit salts. Next door to the grocer was the chandlery, then a few cottages before they came to the butcher's shop so small it could take only one customer at a time but following the usual tradition of pride of window space being given to the pig's head, jaws wide open to hold a lemon; next came a coal yard, a boatbuilder's yard, another general shop with less concern for one's healthy diet, for here the sign in the window invited one inside to inspect the new arrival of linen, the poster hanging next to a side of bacon. A cottage gate bore a sign that here they'd find Mistress Josephine Walker who was skilled in dressmaking and on the corner of the next alleyway was the cobbler.

So they walked the length of Fore Street towards the green. Beth's eyes missed nothing.

By Chalcombe standards Penrhyn House was indeed large, although it had no more than six foot of garden in

248

the front and backed straight on to the shingle. Built in the reign of George III, it must have stood alone long before the row of fishermen's cottages had been built between it and the harbour wall. Now it looked vaguely out of place set between the sea and the green where today the fishing nets were stretched out for repair.

Henry looked about him doubtfully. 'Now we're here we'll see the house, but Bethie I can't see this being a suitable place, my dear. If you don't want Weymouth we could always go on from here to Torquay, it's not far.'

'Just smell the air, Henry. What is it? The sea?' Her eyes shone as she linked her arm through his.

'Fish, I'd say.'

'Yes, I suppose it could be. Torquay my eye! This is a proper place, it works for its keep!'

Penrhyn House showed itself to be a solid family residence, brought up to date by Richard Hatcher's parents, one small bedroom being turned into a bathroom with a gas water heater, and with gas lighting. Whether it had five bedrooms or six didn't bother Beth; she made up her mind as soon as she saw the view from the large bay window of the drawing-room. The red cliffs, the huge expanse of sea, the harbour where even now the boats that had come in at high water were being unloaded.

'Oh Henry, isn't this –'

He held up a hand to silence her. His head raised he was obviously listening. Yes, voices upstairs. He turned back into the hall just as two women came down the stairs, one of them fashionably dressed (not what one would expect in Chalcombe, but then he reminded himself the same could be said of Beth), olive skinned and eyes so dark they were almost black; the other was patently local, clad in a dark grey dress and white apron, her hair pulled tightly into a knot on top of her head, her cheeks weathered rather than sunburned.

''Af'noon, zur,' the aproned one greeted him, 'and how

249

did you come to get in? The master's not here, if you're come calling . . .'

'I'm a friend of Mr Hatcher. I understood from him the house was unoccupied. I have the key.'

'Well now, jus' you fancy that, zur. The very minute I come across to show Mrs Trafford over. For sale the house is, to be sure. Perhaps he told you that did he, zur?'

'That's why we're here,' Beth joined them. 'We're buying the house. Do you have a key too?'

'Oh aye, I keep the place clean and aired, al'ays have. Mrs Trafford here, she's the one who be taking the house. Jus' been waiting for Mr Hatcher to be ready to sell, she has.'

Black eyes and green eyes locked in a wordless tug-of-war, then Beth stood back from the foot of the stairs to let them pass. 'We'll go upstairs, Henry. We ought to look at all the rooms.' She ignored the woman's remark and led the way quite expecting that when they came back down the others would have gone. Not so.

'Mrs Trafford she's gone, but I thought it right to stay – zee to it the door gets locked safely. If you see Mr Hatcher he'll want to know that I'm keeping a good eye to things for him. Mrs Ogbourne's my name, Emily Ogbourne.'

'Good of you to wait, Mrs Ogbourne. I'll tell him it's in good hands,' Henry promised her.

'Y' zee, zur. 'twould be only right and proper Mrs Trafford takes the place. 'Tiz her man, our Mr Ellis Trafford, who owns all the boats you see out yonder. Not a fish comes from the sea around these parts but it's taken by him. Hardly a man in Chalcombe don't work for him and his fishing one way and another. Lives in that cottage on the cliffside, you'll see it when you go outside, jus' above the harbour. But she hankers after this place, and I don't doubt but he'll get it for her.' She chuckled as she added: 'Not been wed that long they haven't. If she wants it, 'tiz my bet he'll see she gets it. Pretty little lassie. Ah, he

250

may like his old cottage well enough, but you mark my words, he'll give her what she wants.'

And that last sentence was the undoing of Eugene Trafford's hopes. If she want it, he'll see she gets it, indeed! Henry had watched Beth as she'd gone from room to room, had seen her expression as she'd looked out of the windows. He was no more sensitive than most, but in those few minutes he'd been aware perhaps for the first time that one thing Beth had never had was a home of her own, a place where she hadn't to tread in someone else's footsteps. A new carpet here, different curtains there, oh yes, she'd made a few changes at the Court, but for all that it was the family home, it always had been.

He put his arm around her shoulders. 'We'll catch the afternoon train back to Wilhampton, but first we'll find something to eat. Is there an inn in the village, Mrs Ogbourne?' Nothing in his voice to hint at his silent resolve. Penrhyn House was to belong to Beth; not to him, not to the family – and certainly not to some fisherman!

'Jus' along by the harbour, the "Lobster Pot" tiz called. Never tasted sweeter fish than ol' Arthur Arkwright'll give 'ee. Look now!' as they came out into the spring sunshine, 'over there on the green, 'long with ol' Jo Binns, that's our Mr Trafford, him who's buying the house.'

Beth looked to where she pointed. Even at this distance she knew one thing, this was a man who'd fight for what he wanted. She felt Henry's hand on her elbow as they came down the steps to the narrow front garden and then out to the cobblestone path. As if he felt her gaze on him Ellis turned towards her. It wasn't Henry he looked at, of that she was sure; under his scrutiny she lowered her eyes, a rare thing for Beth. But what she'd seen was imprinted on her memory. A tall man, well built, dark beard, curly hair, broad shoulders, sleeves rolled up to the elbows showing his strong arms browned by sun and wind. Only for seconds did she look at him, but in that time her imagination ran away with her unbidden, in that moment she was aware of the strength of those shoulders, she pictured him stripped to the waist as he unfurled the sails, his whole being radiating health and vitality. She pulled her thoughts into check; no wonder she lowered her gaze!

Henry hardly spared him a glance, and at that point not a thought either.

Back in Wilhampton he sent Beth home without him in the station cab, determined that he would be first in the field and Beth should get her house. He went straight to see Richard Hatcher, a self-made man with a successful clothes factory and a reputation for extracting every last farthing. Such is the way if a business is to prosper. Henry was no fool, Copeland & Sons was evidence of that. Today he wasn't prepared to haggle; Beth wanted Penrhyn House and she should have it.

'There's some fisherman who'll be approaching you – I'll pay what I have to. I want that house. Give me your word you won't let me be out-bid.'

'Trafford's not a man to be trifled with, Henry. Hasn't been wed to that French wife of his above a while. He'll not lose out in her eyes; he'll top you you may be sure.'

Richard was apparently determined to sell to the highest bidder, friendship played no part.

'If you want to play it that way, man, I'm not short of a pound. That house is for Beth. I want your word.'

The bidding and out-bidding was unknown to Beth. All he told her was that he was hopeful of their acquiring the property. It was at the beginning of June that she arrived one day at the foundry to find him seated behind his desk, a large parchment envelope in front of him and wearing an expression she couldn't quite read.

'Come in, Bethie. Close the door.' He stood up and held a hand towards her.

'What is it?' It was obvious he had something important to say.

In answer he passed her the envelope. She took out the sheaf of papers, frowning over the legal phrasing. 'Penrhyn House' 'in the Parish of Chalcombe,' this she could understand.

'You've got it? It's yours, Henry?' Her cheeks were two bright patches of pink. All these weeks she'd tried not to let herself remember the place, tried to build a defence against disappointment.

'No, Bethie. Read it – it's not mine – it's yours, your own.'

Never for a moment had she expected this, her own! Had he seen how much she'd wanted it? Yes, and cared enough to do it this way. Until that moment she'd never acknowledged even to herself what she'd never had at Merton Court.

'Henry.' So unlike Beth, her eyes were full of tears as she turned towards him, laying the envelope back on the desk. 'Henry . . .' Then wordlessly she was in his arms, leaning against him; it was one of the moments they'd hold for ever.

The next week the foundry saw little of her. She ordered furniture, drapery, even china and glass. Everything new, everything her own. Where did she get her energy? he marvelled. The days didn't seem long enough for all she wanted to cram into them, yet none of it tired her. At the end, in bed she'd lead him into love-making, always such a necessary and joyous part of their lives and now, in those days of early summer, heightened by the excitement that made her adrenalin flow. He marvelled at her, he responded to her, he adored her – and something else. If Beth was energetic and tireless, Henry's nervous vigour was brought about by more than love or even desire; behind it there was fear.

Through those weeks while Henry had negotiated for Penrhyn House Beth had made her regular visits to Mary Giles. It seemed the girl was putting her loss behind her. Each time Beth arrived she found the little house clean,

Mary quiet and pale but unfailingly dressed in the elegant lace blouse. 'Then you'll feel like a princess,' Beth had told her. Well, she gave no sign of that, she gave no sign of any kind of emotion. But time is the greatest healer; there'd be other babies.

So Beth was as unprepared as anyone when Henry came home with the news. Mary Giles had been found dead – and worse, it was Johnny himself who'd found her when he'd gone home that day for his dinner. The stench of gas had met him as he'd opened the front door; life had long since left the form he'd stumbled into as he'd rushed choking into the kitchen.

'I should have seen. Henry, why didn't I see? She seemed better. But I should have realized. Nothing really interested her. How's poor Johnny?'

'Impossible to say, poor boy.'

'I should have seen . . .'

Phoebe listened to them. She felt they must all be able to read her mind. Mary gone! He's free! Mary, poor, poor Mary, to do that, to so hate living that she'd do that . . . He's free! How could she have been so miserable? Surely she'd had everything to live for once upon a time? Only my age, Phoebe reminded herself. Just think, we were children at the same time, played the same games, learnt the same rhymes. Here I am, the future suddenly so wonderful. He's free. She's gone, wiped out. Please God take her soul, give her peace. Free! He loves me. Now there's nothing to keep us apart.

If she'd looked at her surroundings and then pictured his humble cottage in Henry Street she might have realized just how much still stood between them. Such elation filled her heart, then in its place shame that sickened her. Forgive me, forgive my greedy, selfish heart. Give her peace, make her happy in what she's found now. Let me make up to him all he must have suffered.

The others were moving to the dining-room for supper. Phoebe followed.

* * *

254

That was in June, only days after Henry had given Beth the deeds of Penrhyn House.

It was late that same night, and Beth was lying by Henry's side, his deep even breathing telling her that he'd long since drifted into sleep. Always it was like that. Half an hour ago they'd moved together to a climax of love that had left her wide eyed and at peace, while it had carried him to sleep. She curled close to him, her arm around him, happy in the thoughts that chased each other through her brain. A Georgian house, wide views of sea and cliffs, a smell unfamiliar to her nostrils – sea? seaweed? fish? – a village green where nets were spread, the shade of the curtains she'd chosen that day, the round walnut dining-table so different from the long mahogany one downstairs, the voices of the fisherfolk calling to each other, their vowels broad and their dialect almost unintelligible, Henry, her beloved Henry, the look in his eyes as he'd handed her that envelope the other day, the sound of his voice just now as he'd whispered her name over and over: 'Bethie, my Bethie . . .'

Then, bringing her to a sharp halt, driving away all the contentment that was carrying her towards sleep, Mary Giles. How dared she do it? A girl with all her life before her, so frightened to face up to suffering that she'd destroy the wonderful gift of life! How dared she! Why couldn't she have listened to the birds as they sang their spring-time chorus, walked in the woods and seen the bluebells? Whatever happened, whatever sorrow life brought, surely one must always see the promise, the reassurance?

It seems so plain – but is that because I've never been tested? She rubbed her cheek against Henry's shoulder. I've been so lucky. Involuntarily she shivered and shut her eyes tight as if to ward off what she wouldn't face. Think of the good things. Who are you to condemn poor Mary? She didn't have her husband's love, not properly, not like you have. Pull yourself together, Beth Copeland, for the devil that taunted her wouldn't be crushed. You're being emotional and silly. Henry doesn't alter. Feel how warm he is. She wrapped her leg across him. No he doesn't alter, he's not getting old. A ghost of a smile showed something of her normal spirit was reviving. Old indeed. Fitter than many of the youngsters I'll be bound. But even so she wasn't free of the fear that had nudged her. 'Henry – are you asleep, Henry?' she ran her fingers through his hair.

'Umph?'

'I can't sleep.' He felt her foot moving on his leg, her hand on his thigh. 'Henry, hold me close. Poor Johnny – and poor Mary – what went wrong for them? They could have had more babies. If they'd only shared . . .'

Henry was awake now. He recognized she was frightened although he didn't understand fully why.

'Beth, what is it dearest?'

She didn't answer him, indeed she didn't know what disturbed her. It was as if something drove her on to prove that she had nothing to fear. Fitter than many a youngster, she'd told herself and as if to prove it she had roused him from sleep.

Esme was coming home for the weekend, a rare thing during term time. The school holiday wasn't due to begin for more than a month. All that anyone expected to hear from her was her regular fortnightly letter, written on Sunday, delivered on Tuesday. This weekend Beth had promised herself that she and Henry would go to Chalcombe for their first visit, sending Mrs Murphy and Jenny on ahead. A visit from Esme would make that impossible. Of course they were all anxious to see her, Beth probably more so than any of them. She secretly prided herself that much of Esme's self-confidence stemmed from her guidance; always she took pleasure in the girl's company, felt they could understand each other.

Then, with the house putting its best foot forward to feed a guest (for such Esme seemed nowadays) it was no time to remove Mrs Murphy from the kitchen. Downstairs the Court was still under her control. Certainly no one else was allowed to do more for the dining-table than prepare the vegetables and wash the pots and dishes. These days, though, there was an assistant housekeeper, Alice Jenkins, and in truth she was quite capable of running the house. Once Esme's visit was over Beth intended to send Jenny and Daisy to Penrhyn House for the summer, then either Mrs Murphy or Mrs Jenkins could visit when the family were to be there. First though, there was this weekend, seen at that time to be no more than two pleasant days of Esme's company and a week's delay in that first trip to Chalcombe.

On the surface that's all it was but, had Esme not chosen that time to come, had the Sunday not followed the course it did, so much might have turned out differently.

CHAPTER TEN

Although it was nowhere near dark when they took their places for supper on that Saturday evening, the rain beating a steady tattoo against the window gave them a closed-in feeling, uniting them around the damask-covered table. Charles had been allowed to take his place with the others, so altogether there were seven. The amount of serving dishes carried to the sideboard told them this was no ordinary meal, Beth had ordered something special to turn Esme's visit into a celebration.

The baron of beef was carved, plates passed, serving dishes handed round, then once Matthews and Daisy had left them, heads were bowed and six voices added to Henry's to say 'Amen' to the grace he recited. Then, and only then, were tongues loosened.

'I'd forgotten how well you eat here. My word, I'll be fit for nothing but sleep after this,' Esme laughed.

'Is the food poor at Bigbury House, dear?' Lucy looked with concern at her sister; the girl was no more than a bag of bones. At her age she should have more flesh on her. A few weeks of Mrs Murphy's puddings that's what she needed.

'Oh yes, we have quite enough. Our main meal is at mid-day. We take it with the pupils, then in the evening Martha and I usually do something for ourselves. We enjoy it.' There was pride in her voice. They'd never known her to talk of friends; she'd always been a loner, the odd one out once Naomi had married.

Lucy smiled at her. 'You get on well with the principal? What a difference it must make.' Esme had never made a secret of her contempt for Simon Rake.

'Martha is splendid. We're very close.'

Henry screwed up his eyes and looked at her. Why should she sound so defiant, as if she expected them to object to this Mrs Shadbolt?

'That's nice, dear,' Lucy spoke reassuringly. 'Sad for her to be widowed so young. She's had the school some years I believe you said.'

Again Esme's tone defied their criticism: 'Yes she has, but she's not a widow. She left him, she had to, he treated her disgustingly.'

'My dear, the poor soul . . .' Men! Weren't they all alike? Lucy's thought swept Edward's treatment of her into the same category. 'Was he truly unkind, or did he – ?'

'I think, Lucy, we've gone far enough,' Henry checked her, to the disappointment of Vicky and Charles who were just getting interested.

Esme told them more about the school, the countryside in Sussex where she and Martha loved to walk, about an outing she'd taken a party of pupils on . . . Phoebe listened, thinking back to the conversation she and Penny had had when they'd picnicked on that early spring day. No mention of any young men, not so much as a veiled hint. Yet Esme appeared content with her place 'on the shelf'. She'd always been the clever one – 'not like me,' she admitted – then let her thoughts stray down the path so familiar to them. The rain had hardly stopped all the week, so she'd had no chance of walking to her meeting place with Johnny, not that he would have been there. She'd heard that he'd had family to the cottage, even relatives of Mary's. How dreadful it must have been for him. She'd wanted to write, had made two attempts but each time had thrown them away. How could she write in sympathy? Yet her heart was torn with pity.

That evening the family all stayed together in the drawing-room, there was still a feeling of occasion. Vicky played the piano (a poor performance compared with dear Edwin's, Lucy considered, but nice that the child tried)

259

and Charles sat so quietly with his pack of cards playing patience, hoping he'd not be noticed. Of course his scheme failed; soon he was banished to bed and not long afterwards Vicky followed. Beth sensed that Henry was getting restless. He'd sat with the family as long as he wanted. When she saw him take out his pocket watch and look at it Lucy was prompted to say: 'Indeed, how the evening has flown. I'm in the habit of early nights these days. Papa and Beth are usually in the library you know. I've become a real early bird.'

'An early bird is up with the dawn, Lucy,' Esme laughed. 'I doubt you're that.'

'Oh, you! You're too clever for me. You know well enough what I mean. I'm putting my sewing away and going up. Goodnight, Papa, goodnight everyone.'

'God bless you.' Henry's reply amid their goodnights.

Phoebe too had had enough; she wanted the privacy of her own room to be able to give rein to her secret thoughts. Soon she followed, and after Henry's 'I've one or two things to see to in the library', Esme and Beth found themselves alone.

'This is nice.' Esme pushed a cushion into the small of her back and looked at Beth affectionately. 'Now tell me all about your new house, and Chalcombe. What's the village like?'

'Esme, it's like a dream. Not a holiday place; you mustn't expect a promenade or shelters from the elements or a bandstand. It's real. It earns its keep. You'll see for yourself when you come in the holidays.'

'I'm not coming – this is why I'm here this weekend. Martha and I are renting a cottage near Windermere. We're going there for the whole time the school is closed.'

'That's a long time to spend together. You must find each other very easy company.'

Esme was silent for a moment, biting the corner of her mouth, seeming to size Beth up as if she were undecided whether to say more. Then: 'Do you remember what I used to be like, Beth, all spots and self-consciousness? You helped me more than you'll ever know. Be yourself, you said, find out what you are and be yourself.'

'And have you done that?' Beth spoke quietly. Suddenly knowing what she was going to hear and preparing herself so that she'd not fail Esme. 'Has it brought you happiness?'

'Such happiness, Beth. Swear to me you'll never betray my confidence, not even to Papa, especially not to Papa. He'd not understand, he'd be hurt, even ashamed. I couldn't stand that. I'm not ashamed, I'm proud.'

'Tell me, Esme. Is it Martha?'

Esme nodded, forcing herself to meet Beth's eyes, her chin high. 'I love her as truly as any woman can love. I want no one but her. Can you understand that? They'd all say that I should have my eye open for a man — Beth, please understand.' She reached and took Beth's hand. 'Together we're complete, it's the right way for us both.'

'Then, Esme, I'm truly glad for you both. To share one's life is precious. Just to see you tells me you're doing what is right for you. Bigbury House has made a new woman of you.'

'The money I had from Mama is going into the school. It's not a great deal, but Martha is making me an equal partner. It's so good, Beth, to look ahead and see the way, to know we'll be together . . .'

Later, in the privacy of her room, Esme undressed then took the pins from her coiled hair and brushed it ready for its plait. She was glad she'd talked to Beth. There had been something unreal about her homecoming this time, almost as if she'd played a part. But not now, now she felt honest again. 'Be yourself.' Well, and so she was. Eagerly and without another glance at her reflection she twisted her long, thin hair into its nightly plait, pulled on her white nightgown and taking paper and pencil climbed into bed. 'My darling Martha,' she wrote.

261

Much later, from where Beth lay with her curtains undrawn, she could see the glow from the light still burning in Esme's room.

By next morning the rain had gone, the world was fresh and sparkling. And we could have been at Chalcombe . . ., Beth thought as she pinned her hat ready for church. Through the long and toneless sermon (for Oswald Bacon, the pallid young cleric of St James's never spoke for less than half an hour and never sent one home with any clear idea of his message) her thoughts wandered. She peeped sideways at Esme remembering her nocturnal confession. She imagined Henry's shocked anger if he were to guess.

Next to her Henry sat rigidly still, his gaze fixed on the pasty priest but his mind as far away as hers. Damn it, man, it can't be anything serious. Never been ill in my life. It if happens again perhaps I'll have a word with old Doctor Bailey. Deaf as a post though – what could he do about it? Probably nothing. When it happened yesterday it had been hours after a meal; couldn't have been indigestion. Had just reached to open a drawer – and the memory of the agony that had gripped him filled his mind. Won't mention it to Beth, might frighten her. Dammit, it frightened me. Rubbish, pull yourself together, man, it's probably not going to happen again. You're fit, of course you're fit, always have been. Mustn't worry Beth. Oh dear Lord, let me stay fit and strong. She's such a girl yet. Don't let me get old before my time. Grant us long years together . . . Where, this morning, was the man who didn't ask but tried to accept?

As if he knew his father's mind was elsewhere, Charles fingered the marbles in his pocket; one alley, large clear glass with blue and yellow stripes, and was it four or five small ones? The rattle broke into Henry's reverie, brought a frown to his face and a restraining hand to his young son's knee.

At last it was over, the closing hymn sung and the congregation filing out into the sunshine.

'Look, Henry,' Beth tugged his sleeve, 'just ahead, by the gate. There's Johnny Giles. Poor Johnny, I dare say he couldn't face their own church this morning.'

'He's by himself. You go on to the trap. I'll catch him and have a word.'

'Henry, if he's alone at home shouldn't we give him dinner? He must be so low.'

'Indeed he must. Wait by the gate the rest of you. I'll fetch him to walk home with you.'

There was nothing in the sight of Henry, as he hurried after his young pattern-maker, to suggest his health gave him cause for worry.

So Johnny paid his first visit to Merton Court. To his credit, as the array of dishes was set out on the sideboard he held his muscles in control so that no tell-tale rumble of emptiness could hint at what the smell of the roast leg of pork did to him.

'This is indeed good of you, Mrs Copeland.' Phoebe was proud of the way he spoke to Beth, courteous but confident. A man from the works he might be but no ordinary workman. 'I have an afternoon of letter writing ahead of me, and I shall face it with a better heart after your kindness.'

Hal had spoken to his father in glowing terms of Johnny. He'd come to them a year or two before as a pattern-maker but according to Hal he had a good working knowledge of metal and a driving ambition to learn. As the meal progressed Henry was tempted to talk to him of the works, the steel they brought in now from foundries further north, replacing so much that had been made with cast iron.

Phoebe listened to them, proud of Johnny, sure her father must realize what an asset he was.

The dishes from the first course were carried out, fresh brought in: a damson pudding, a bowl of steaming custard, a claret jelly turned from a three-tier mould on to a plate where it stood, a transparent, wobbling delight. This was the way to live! Surely fate must have given him this opportunity, one not to be missed.

'What you were saying about the linkage, sir, what stress would be needed of the steel?'

To talk shop at the table was unheard of at the Court. Even when Hal had lived at home he and Henry had kept their discussions for the library. It was an unspoken rule of many years but today Henry encouraged Johnny. A promising young man as Hal had said, and, in any case, they had little else in common.

'What time can we go, Esme?' Charles whispered across the table to his step-sister, 'as soon as we've finished, can we?'

'Attend to your food if you please, my son,' Henry admonished. 'No talking at the table.'

'Sorry, sir.' There was nothing cowed in Charles, his apology was made cheerfully enough and his eyebrows, raised in Esme's direction, gave him the silent answering nod he needed. She had promised to come walking with him and he had put his butterfly net in the bush near the side door ready to collect on their way out. If they didn't get away quickly Lucy and the bassinet would be ready for their daily stroll, and that would mean no going through the meadows – and no butterfly net either, for Lucy wouldn't let him take it on a Sunday.

So when Beth suggested: 'Why don't you walk part of the way with Johnny?' he thought of Matlock Woods with hope. The bassinet couldn't be wheeled there. Phoebe thought of it with hope too.

But it wasn't to be.

The others didn't notice. Only Beth was looking Henry's way as they stood up from the table. He seemed to catch his breath, then grip the back of the chair unable to breathe. It happened so suddenly; for a second he stood rigidly still, paralysed by the pain that this time seemed to squeeze the life out of him, sending sharp knives through his chest, down his shoulders and arms. Involuntarily he cried out as, still clinging to the chair, his legs gave way under him and he sank to his knees. Beth had seen it happening, the others had all been turning away from the table. It was she who was first at his side, on her knees too, her arms around him.

'Let me help,' Johnny was strong. 'Let me help him to the couch.'

'No, get cushions, let him be still. Esme,' Beth turned thankfully to her for already Lucy was wringing her hands, and promising to be no use whatsoever. 'Send Matthews for Doctor Bailey. Tell him to find him and bring him.'

'. . . passing . . . in . . . minute,' Henry tried to speak.

'Hush, don't talk, darling. Let's lie you on these.'

Charles and Vicky must have stripped the drawing-room of cushions. Now Henry found himself being lifted on to them. With the movement the pain exploded, his breathing was shallow and quick, beads of sweat stood on his forehead.

'Go outside all of you, he needs air. Open the window wide, Johnny.' She eased her arm around Henry's shoulder, then laid his head on her lap as she sat with him on the floor. With his head raised he seemed to breathe more easily.

'Better . . . passing . . .,' and this time his voice was stronger. Oh, thank God, thank God, her heart cried, then, don't let him be ill, please, please. Do what you like to me, but not to Henry.

The others all went outside, probably to wait in the hall within call.

'The doctor will soon be here. You'll be better then.'

'Moving . . . chair. That . . . did . . .,' then, his eyes shut, screwed up as if to ward off the pain, 'Oh Bethie, Beth . . .'

There was a change. Not the fast, shallow panting of a few minutes before. Now each gulp of air had to be fought for, he didn't seem to know how. Each breath expelled was a moan so feeble it was hardly audible.

'Henry, oh God, don't let it be happening. Make him

well ...,' her words tumbled out, her cheeks were wet. 'Henry, Henry, hear me,' she whispered urgently, bending close over him, 'look at me.' If only he'd open his eyes she wouldn't feel he was slipping beyond her reach.

Seconds. Minutes. He seemed quieter, his eyes were open now.

Thank God. Oh you fool, Beth, don't cry. What's the use of crying like an idiot?

He raised his hand. For a second before it dropped he touched her wet cheek. 'Bethie ... no tears ... my ... Bethie.'

Beth never cried yet now shock, fear, frustration, at her own helplessness, all these thing combined; she wept, gently moving her cheek against his forehead. 'My love, my love.' She was so full of emotion, endearments, like tears, were their only expression. 'My blessed, beloved, precious love.'

His face moved against hers, did he hear the feeble moan as he breathed? Another change, quick gasping breaths, each like the whimper of a terrified soul. She took his hand, it was as if in his fierce grip he put all his strength, warding off the torment of his body. Whimpers grew to groans. His head thrashed from side to side, his eyes stared wildly yet seemed to see nothing and she felt his nails digging into the palms of her hands.

'No, no, don't let it happen, no, no . . .' But suddenly he was still. His head flopped back on her supporting arm, his nails no longer cut her hand. She was rooted to the spot, too frightened to move, as at the same moment the door opened and Esme ushered Doctor Bailey in.

The remaining hours of the day must have ticked away. Beth seemed to be standing in the wings as the scene of a play unfolded. With vague surprise she saw that Hal was there, then Margaret and William. Voices; whispers; instructions; arrangements; the clang of the front door bell; footsteps on the marble floor of the hall, something being brought in, then footsteps again, slowly this time, bearing a load, from the dining-room. This time fear sent her from the wings on to the stage, she almost stood outside watching herself. Four men appeared, carefully easing their burden towards the front door. Despite the bright sunshine outside the house was in semi-darkness with all the blinds lowered except in the library where she'd hidden herself away. From the doorway of the drawing-room she could vaguely see Lucy mopping her eyes with a man's-size handkerchief.

'Where are you going?' Beth's voice was loud, sharp, in the silent house.

Hal followed the bearers from the dining-room. Now he came across to her and put an arm around her shoulder. 'Come away, Beth, you shouldn't watch. It's better Mr Huntley takes him, better for the children.'

'No! No! Carry him upstairs. Let him lie in his own room.'

'Beth, my way is wiser.'

'Don't you hear me? I say he's to lie here.'

The undertaker's men looked to Hal for instructions.

'Upstairs I say.' She heard the unfamiliar screech in her voice and hated them, even hated Hal, for doing this to her.

'If you change your mind, sir,' the bearer said, 'just let us have word. I'll send someone this evening to arrange the body.'

Beth turned back into the library and closed the door.

'Seems there's to be all of them here for their supper,' Mrs Murphy said. 'Nothing like a bit of good food to put the heart back. Mind you cut up enough cabbage, young Emmie,' to the scullery maid, 'and go out and get extra peas. Children won't be there for supper; they'll be kept upstairs along with Jenny . . .' She had to keep busy, keep her mind on the only way she knew to help — feeding the family. Oh dear, oh lawks, never thought to see this day! That I didn't, never a better man lived than the poor dear Master; ate 'is dinner up right as rain — proper upset me it has. 'Here, young Emmie, don't stand there gawping, girl,' no need to snap like that but she couldn't help herself. 'Get along with those veg.'

'Right you are, Mrs Murphy,' Emmie cut into the cabbage. She'd only been with them a few weeks; today's excitement was no more to her than a peep up the area steps to watch the visitors arriving.

'They'll expect one of my puddings, a nice steamed raspberry with a suet crust.' Can just see him now. To go like that! Like a candle snuffed out. Just hark at my innards rolling round, and if I've got the gripes is it any wonder? Forty years I've known him, nothing'll ever be the same here. She blew her nose, then reached for her big white overall.

Someone was coming down the stairs, a heavy tread.

'Miss Lucy, dear, what a day! Never thought we'd see it.' She wiped her reddened eyes in her handkerchief then plunged her hands into the flour.

'Nor I, Mrs Murphy. I thought I'd just make sure you were expecting everyone for supper, they're sure to stay. Beth seems to have locked herself away.' She was quiet for a moment, following a new train of thought. 'There'll be changes, there must be. I dare say Hal and Edith will come here now — not that Hal would see me put on the street, oh no, he'd never put his sister out.'

'And her?' Nodding her head upwards as she scooped out more flour. 'What'll she do I wonder?'

'Dear knows. Papa may have left her the use of the house. After all there are the children too.'

'I heard Mr Huntley and his men come.' Mrs Murphy sniffed again. '. . . can't believe he's gone. Better man never lived than your poor dear father.'

Lucy's tears overflowed again.

'There now, Miss Lucy duckie, just you have a good cry.' She wiped the flour off her hands. 'Just you come away into my sitting-room, let me make you a nice cup of tea. Do us both good.' This time it was the corner of the white overall that wiped her eyes and polished her nose.

The family seemed to have taken over. Upstairs Vicky and Charles stayed with Jenny. No one suggested they should come down for tea or supper, they seemed to have been forgotten in the commotion. They knew what had happened but they'd had no experience of death. Only time would teach them the reality of being without Henry. Vicky was twelve; she looked ahead and was frightened by the void; Charles was seven, he looked no further than the present and even in these few hours he'd already missed his father. Hal had sent a cablegram to the boys' school asking that Edwin and Nicky should be sent home immediately. Only when they arrived would they be told.

Just as the children instinctively stayed in the nursery, so Beth hid herself in the library. He seemed nearer there; she sat at his desk, she rested her hands where his had rested, she touched his pen, his inkwell. Yet all she did had a dreamlike quality. She couldn't look to the future.

The door bell clanged. Steps on the stairs, then overhead. Later the tread of the men coming down, Hal's voice and finally the front door closing.

In her own home she found herself creeping into the hall, then up the stairs, looking back to make sure no one was watching, then softly opening the door of her room, their room, and slipping inside. In the middle of the bed he lay, dressed now in a long white shroud, his hands crossed on his chest, his ankles tied together. Like a statue, his complexion ashen and yet there was about him a look of peace. She sat on the edge of the bed, his side, she leant down and rested her face against his cold cheek. 'I try not to ask, I try to accept,' he'd told her. But this? How could she accept this? Downstairs she heard the gong ring out. Supper time. They'd all be there, his family, grieving for the man they knew, firm, arrogant, honest, all-powerful.

'Henry,' she spoke to him. Surely somewhere he must hear her, her Henry, gentle, loving. Only she had understood his loneliness, his need to love and share. 'Henry, stay with me, without you I'm – oh Henry, Henry . . .'

With the passing minutes from somewhere a new calm came to her, or was it that she was numb? She heard voices downstairs, the family were leaving. Time must have lost all meaning for her, she had no idea she'd been upstairs so long. As they all congregated in the hall they saw her coming down the stairs, her face pale, but apart from that showing no sign of emotion. Grief had played havoc with the others; Lucy's face was swollen and blotchy, Margaret's long nose red, Esme was tearless but somehow had acquired that old look of uncertainty, red blobs on her neck and the hand she held out to Beth sticky with perspiration. Beth looked around the little group. Copelands. All part of Henry, all with their own memories. She was outside it all. The man they mourned wasn't her Henry. She gripped the corners of her mouth hard between her teeth.

She'd given no thought to Johnny since dinner, whether he'd stayed or gone home while they waited for the doctor, and neither did she remember him over the next few days. It was Hal who made all the arrangements, wrote to Naomi and to James, had the signs made to nail on the gates of the foundry the following Thursday, its black edges catching the eyes of many a passer-by.

At the Court letters arrived. As if by magic, news spread in hours. A dozen times Phoebe read hers from Johnny, his sympathy her only comfort in a sad world. She'd seen that he'd also written to Beth, but then so had many of the men, some in a scrawl barely legible, words mis-spelt and the message put together with far more effort than most of the letters that came to the house. They felt able to write to Beth; they knew she would care nothing for their mistakes, she would read the sorrow that came from their hearts.

'Such a kind letter from Mrs Ridley, Beth,' Lucy said the day before Henry's funeral. 'You'll have heard too of course.'

'No.'

'Well now, fancy. Just me — and they said they'd seen Hal. And from Wilton End too, their sympathies to me. And I thought you'd made such friends with them all. Still, I've known them all my life, they know how dear Papa was to me, indeed to all his family.'

'Of course they'll write to Beth,' Phoebe scowled.

'Yes, perhaps they will. Here, Beth, you may read it. Such a kind letter.'

Easier to take it than argue. Beth let her glance scan the lines of the page. It was as if they mourned the death of a stranger, the words 'your dear father', 'our dear friend for long years', 'an example all his children must be glad to follow' meant nothing to her. What had this to do with Henry, her Henry? She was lost, frightened. Without him what was she? As if to defy them she raised her chin as she passed the letter back.

But Phoebe was wrong. No word came to Beth. In losing Henry she had lost more than a husband.

They gathered in the dining-room, Hal leading the way and drawing out the chair at the head of the table for Mr Edgewick while Beth went automatically to the one at the foot. The solicitor cleared his throat, undid the hard case he'd laid before him, took his handkerchief from his cuff, cleared his throat again, wiped his nose, returned his handkerchief to his cuff. Then: 'This is indeed a sad occasion, Mrs Copeland.'

She acknowledged his remark with a slight inclination of her head.

Again he cleared his throat, fiddled with this cuff.

Get on, man, get on. Hal wanted nothing more than to get the afternoon over. Until they all knew exactly where they stood it was impossible to plan ahead. The responsibility of Beth and her youngsters would rest with him. No doubt his father would have left provision but he'd have to see she invested wisely. Did she appreciate how much it would cost to run the Court if he agreed to her staying on there? Perhaps he'd have no choice, perhaps his father had left it to her for her lifetime –

'. . . to each of the servants at Merton Court at the time of my death, except for Florence Murphy to whom I bequeath a sum of fifty pounds in gratitude for her years of loyal service.

'To each of my children living at the time of my death I give a sum of two thousand pounds provided that if any child of mine to whom an interest in residue is given by my Will or any Codicil dies in my lifetime and leaves a child or children the interest of such deceased child shall not lapse but shall be taken by his or her child or children.

'I give all my property of whatsoever kind and wheresoever situate subject to payment of my debts, funeral and testamentary expenses and the legacies bequeathed by this my Will or any Codicil hereto to my beloved wife Elizabeth.'

'If my said wife dies in my lifetime . . .'

The voice read on, it seemed to have no end, but now it was just so many legal words, it meant nothing. No wonder the poor man had fidgeted with his cuffs, cleared his throat and wiped his nose; no wonder he'd had trouble in finding his voice. As he finally folded his papers he waited, not knowing what he expected. Young Hal had worked man and man with his father for years. Well, he'd tried, he'd spoken to Henry. No use though. James might not have wanted to come into the business, but in time he hoped Nicholas might – then there was Charles. He knew

Beth would be fair to Hal, he'd never lose by her treatment. His faith in her had been complete, his mind made up.

The papers put away, Mr Edgewick muttered something about not detaining them, time the enemy and, dear me, yes, later than he'd realized, not quite looking at anyone and not expecting an answer.

Edith's colour was unusually high. To treat Hal like it! 'Each of my children' as if he were no more than James or the offspring of that sewing maid! She looked across the table at him. Not a sign of what he must be feeling. Anger? Hurt? Disappointment? Shock? Just as if they'd heard what they'd anticipated he stood up and extended a hand to the solicitor.

'It was good of you to come, sir. We know you're a busy man.'

The little man took his hand but didn't manage to meet his glance; then he turned towards Beth. 'Mrs Copeland,' at least here he had nothing to fear; she must be well pleased with herself, 'if you want help or advice, we served your late husband for many years and trust we may have the same pleasure for you.'

She inclined her head. Later she'd think about it all, what was expected of her, her commitments. Whatever she'd imagined would come out of this day (and recently she'd done very little intelligent thinking) she'd never considered that all Henry's responsibilities could become hers. She wanted Mr Edgewick gone, all of them gone, except Hal. She must talk to Hal.

She rang the bell for Matthews. She was aware she'd taken control of the siituation, the others hovered, seven pairs of eyes on her.

'Matthews, see Mr Edgewick to his carriage please and then have tea sent to the drawing-room.' Did she imagine a new wariness as they watched her. 'Hal, while Lucy pours the tea, come with me to the library, will you? I'd be grateful if we could talk a few minutes.'

'Talk! Indeed we must talk.'

She led the way across the hall. She and Hal had worked together for so long, and she'd always found him fair and kind. How happy she'd been at the foundry, finding a niche in that life that meant so much to Henry. She was on dangerous ground. She wouldn't let herself remember, couldn't bear to think of the emptiness without him. As if for reassurance she sat in his chair, behind his desk.

'You understand what this means, Beth? Father obviously had great faith in your judgement.'

'Nothing can ever fill the gap, Hal, but I've always been interested and you, well, you and Henry worked almost as one after all these years.'

'Me? Oh no, Beth. I've split my time over these last eighteen months since Ede's father died, but from now on Harknell's will be my future.'

'But Hal, you've seen the foundry grow, you – '

His calm broke. 'I've seen the foundry grow, ah, almost from nothing I've seen it and I've seen you grow too. Father built the business and he built you too. Well, now we shall see!' So unlike the normal Hal always even tempered and kind. Now his eyes frightened her. 'Dear God, how you must have wormed your way into his mind with your pretty ways. Honest and just he was, as fair as ever a man lived. He picked you up, put you on a pinnacle and expected us all to do the same. Well, now it's over! You've got what you were after and I wish you joy of it, but don't – '

'If he were here you'd not speak to me like that. Hal, must it be like this? Today we're both overwrought . . .'

His answer was no more than a look, and it hit her like a blow that in all these years when she'd thought of him as a friend deep down he must have hated her.

One last attempt. 'You're wrong. If you think that, you're wrong. But I'm not explaining myself, not to any of you. What was between Henry and me belongs to us, to us and our children.'

'So it would seem.'

'Tell Lucy I shan't be joining you for tea. You'd better go back to the others.' She wanted him gone, the charade over.

'I'll collect Edith and leave. Tomorrow I shall have to go into the works; I have a few personal things to fetch away.'

'You're really doing this? To all you worked for, all he worked for?'

'Oh come Beth, didn't you say yourself your interest is there?'

Without another glance at her he left; a moment or two later she heard voices in the hall, then the front door closed behind him. She'd eaten hardly a thing all the week. Could that be why she felt so sick?

The stillness in the workshops made the place feel strange to her. Today the doors had been closed but the fires still burnt, banked to keep alight until tomorrow.

Despite Phoebe's plea Beth had come by herself. 'Today of all days in any case you shouldn't be alone on the road in the dark, it's not safe. At least let Algy drive you – or better still let me come, or Esme and me both . . .'

Before Esme could add her weight, Beth was half way to the door. 'No. Tonight I want to go on my own, that's why I've waited. The men will have been in and checked the fires and gone again by the time I get there. It's kind of you, both of you – but I must look at things, try and think. I can grapple better by myself.'

'As long as that's why,' for Phoebe had visions of Beth running away to lick her wounds alone. The day must have been a nightmare. 'But take a good lantern. Oh and do be careful, Beth, a woman on her own, it's not right.'

'Poppycock! Whoever heard of robbers on the road between here and Wilhampton, and I know every inch of the way. To please you though, Phoebe, I'll take a stout stick and I wouldn't be afraid to use it!'

No use arguing with Beth, it never had been and today had shown a grim determination in her. Her face was pale; they'd never seen her with such dark smudges under her eyes. Dressed in unrelieved black, her widow's veil hanging to her shoulders there was an unfamiliar dignity about her.

Dusk had given way to darkness by the time she crossed the stone floor of the workshop, her lantern held high. Hundreds, even thousands of times she'd climbed these stairs, turning left along the gallery to the room she made for now. Yet tonight in the empty building even the sound of her step on the wooden stairs was different, the shadows cast by her lamp strange. She wasn't nervous, not of intruders or even of the eerie atmosphere, but only she and her Maker knew how frightened she was of the task before her. With Henry by her side she'd had such confidence; she'd talked of the tools they'd produced, she'd made suggestions (sometimes even good ones), known about the men's wages, the paying of taxes, the ordering of steel. To understand from the wings was a far cry from stepping on to the stage to play the main role. That she'd been a woman in a man's world hadn't mattered, she'd been his woman, almost a part of all he was. And now? She felt herself to be no more capable than young Victoria or any of the children. The children – his children. For them as well as for him she must find a way through the woods. He'd trusted her, hadn't he? He'd expected that she could carry the torch until one day it would be shared by Nicky, yes and Charles too. But was that the truth, the whole truth? He'd not expected to leave her so soon, he'd not expected Hal to desert her.

'There's only me, Henry, there's so much I don't understand. When I used to listen to you and Hal talking of melting points of alloys, of metal fatigue, of heat treatment, chemical reactions – oh dear heaven, the list is endless and I know nothing – did you think I understood? When you talked I felt I did, yet now I can see I was outside it all.' The more she remembered of the discussions

276

she'd heard so often the more ignorant she knew herself to be.

What was that? She listened. She must have imagined it. Hal wouldn't come tonight. As if to reassure herself she reached out to turn up the gaslight that hung above the desk, the brightness making her feel less vulnerable. Not a bit of use sitting here dreaming and worrying. She had to look at the things in his drawer, at the order books, at the – There it was again! A tread on the stair! Her heart was banging, thank heaven she'd brought that stick. The feel of the stout wood in her hand gave her courage. Ought she to throw open the door, confront whoever it was? Yes, that was the brave thing to do. She crept across the room. But supposing he carried no lantern, he'd see her in the light from the room and have the advantage. She'd wait, here behind the door, so that she'd see him first, she'd –

'Mrs Copeland, is that you?'

'Johnny!'

'I saw that someone was in here, wondered if anything was amiss. Than I thought I recognized your trap in the yard.' He blinked in the bright light.

'Thank goodness it's only you.' How stupid, she couldn't stop shaking, even her voice sounded strange to her ears.

'Should you be here at this time of evening? Why don't you let me drive you home?'

So silly to be behaving like this. Sitting gratefully in Henry's chair she held her hands hard flat on the desk top to steady them, her teeth clenched. His voice was kind, full of sympathy, almost harder to bear than having to pit her wits against some unwelcome intruder.

'Come now, Mrs Copeland. Leave all this to his son until you feel more ready.'

'Hal's finished here. He's not coming any more – just to collect a few things tomorrow. He has enough to do at Harknell's.'

277

'Not coming? But surely Copeland's comes first, especially now?'

'In future, Johnny, the works are mine. Henry left things like that.'

He was knocked off balance. This was something he'd never considered. 'If it's a loyal staff you're wanting then rest assured you have it. And – well, I don't want to presume, please don't misunderstand me – but if ever there's anything I can help with, perhaps just to talk to someone about things . . .'

She was being swept along, wanting to clutch at any hand held out to rescue her. 'Is that why you were brought to us, just that very day?'

'A kind of providence you mean? I'd like to think that. Look, don't worry about any of this tonight. Let me drive you home. Tomorrow things will look easier by daylight; they do, you know, I've found that myself. The nights are the hardest.'

She thought of the nights he must have battled through alone, and truly alone as she'd never be. Here in this room so much a part of her blessed Henry he suddenly seemed very close. She shut her eyes and Johnny wondered whether she listened to him at all.

'Yes,' she pulled herself back to reality. 'I'll come back by daylight. But tonight I'll take some of his books home with me.' She took a key from the chain purse she carried hanging around her waist and unlocked the desk drawer, lifting out a neat stack of books. 'I'll look at these at home. You're right, Johnny. It's kind of you to offer to come with me but I brought myself and I can take myself back again. See, Phoebe made me bring a stick – and when I heard someone on the stairs I was ready to use it too!'

'I'll not hear of you driving yourself through those woods at night.'

'Fiddlesticks! I swear I'm capable of fending for myself.'

'I don't doubt you are, but do you think Mr Copeland would have you abroad at this hour on your own? Now you see I'm right, you know he wouldn't permit it. For him you'll let me escort you.'

Kindness was so hard to bear. She stood up, straightened her shoulders and picked up the books. 'Then Johnny I'm grateful to you. But first we'll stop at Henry Street and collect your sleeping things. If you come to Merton Court at this hour you must stay the night.'

He needed no persuading.

Victoria couldn't sleep. Everything was wrong. Papa had gone and the knowledge that she'd never see him again kept hitting her no matter how she tried to direct her thoughts. Last week he'd been with them, solid and sure, as much a part of life as the food they ate, the warmth of a comfortable bed, the God that somewhere was watching over them. All these things one accepted without question. Now he wasn't part of it any more and with his going she felt that nothing was truly safe. Mother, Nicky, Charles, home, Aunt Lucy, how could one be sure of anything? Even Mother? She'd always been so full of fun but since Papa had gone she hadn't smiled once. She looked stern, pale, a worried line had cut its way between her clearly marked eyebrows. It seemed nothing was certain. Even God? If He was so kind why had He done this beastly thing, taken Papa and with him all the happiness from the home? Aunt Lucy was jumpy and quiet. At any other time if Vicky had been miserable Aunt Lucy would have been ready to listen but these last few days even she'd been different. Charles wasn't like himself; he'd cried because a wing had come off his peacock butterfly, he'd cried when Jenny had sent him from the teatable to wash his hands; yet Charles never cried and at least once a week Jenny had to send him away to wash. And Nicky, home from school but somehow apart from her; perhaps it was because of Nicky she was loneliest of all. Because Papa wasn't there he was trying to make himself a man, separate from

Charles and her. When he'd gone away to school it hadn't altered anything for them any more than it would next term when she went off to Bigbury House with Aunt Esme. They might not always be together but that hadn't mattered; they'd known that deep down they were close. Yet now he'd been home for three days and she was as lonely as before he came. What good did it do anyone taking Papa away? It wasn't as if he'd been old or ill like Mr Tomkins at the dairy. When he'd died she'd heard Mrs Murphy telling Aunt Lucy it was 'a blessing, poor soul', but how could it be a blessing to steal Papa away? In his misery Charles hated a God who took away the father he loved, Vicky hated Him too but for more than that. Lying awake she was lonely, frightened, yet she didn't understand what frightened her. Today all the family had been here, the children kept upstairs after the service until that solicitor had gone. Perhaps it was always like this when there was a funeral. Her mouth was dry, her tummy churned as she remembered; from upstairs she'd watched as they'd left, kissing Aunt Lucy, whispering, Mother nowhere to be seen. Then after it was dark all alone she'd gone off in the trap, to the works, Aunt Lucy had said looking tight lipped. So it had been Aunt Lucy who had looked in to see they were safely in bed. Even that was different. Vicky hated change.

When she heard the sound of the trap on the gravel driveway she crept to the window. She might call to her mother and ask her to come up. Again she was disappointed, for Johnny Giles was there. She climbed back into bed. Charles was lucky, he was young enough to cry and not be called a baby. Victoria felt under her pillow for her hanky and blew her nose.

It was much later when she heard footsteps on the stairs, they were coming to bed. Then a man's voice. Johnny Giles! Sleeping here at the Court! Like so much over the last few days, nothing was normal and comfortable any more. Then the house was quiet. What was that? Again she crept from bed and looked out of the window. Her mother was awake still, reaching to pull her window open further; so she couldn't sleep either. Vicky lay down again, wondering about her mother alone in that big bed. Until tonight she'd slept on the couch in Papa's dressing-room. How must she feel now, one pillow smooth, one side cold and empty?

Beth didn't hear the footsteps in the corridor. The first she knew that anyone was there was the rattle of the door handle. Like a shot she was sitting upright, not knowing what she expected. It was the second time tonight her thoughts had been interrupted by an intruder.

'You're awake, Mother, I heard you.' It was only a whisper.

'Vicky, what is it? What's the matter?'

'Shall we be awake together? I thought perhaps we could.'

The twins were both tall for their age and seeing her in this light (hardly light at all for there was cloud in front of the moon), it struck Beth that she was hardly a child any longer. She held out a hand.

'This won't do, sweetling. Did something disturb you?'

'I've not been to sleep. Can we be awake together?'

'In you hop,' Beth moved over. 'We'll see if we can't be asleep together. Why it's more than midnight already.'

Two red heads side by side. In her own room Vicky had tossed and turned; here, even though to be in this bed was as strange as everything else that had shaken her world, yet in Beth was security. Almost as soon as her head rested on the pillow she slept and, for the first night for nearly a week, so too did Beth.

Across the corridor someone else lay awake. Thoughts chased round and round in Johnny's mind. Copeland's with no man at the helm; Phoebe, soft, warm, generous, she might be young but there was nothing of an empty-headed child in Phoebe. As if by contrast, and with a rare pang of conscience, he remembered the pale, pretty girl who'd been his wife, as small as a child and with no more passion or understanding. He thanked whatever providence had brought him to the Court last Sunday and recognized with gratitude that because Henry had introduced him into their home his being here would be acceptable to the family. And Beth? In the darkness he smiled confidently. He'd been worried, thinking that with Hal Copeland in charge things might prove difficult. Today had dealt him the trump card. In the morning he and Beth Copeland would, no doubt, drive to Wilhampton together. The start of a new era!

And so it was. But he'd not taken into account that Beth had a mind of her own. If Henry put the responsibility of running the business on her shoulders, then the burden was hers. So the next morning Algy drove Johnny to the foundry when he took the children to the Vicarage for their lessons and Beth shut herself away in the library. Today Hal was coming to collect his things; today she must take a grip on the future.

CHAPTER ELEVEN

It was a month or so later that Phoebe suggested: 'Surely, Beth, Johnny could help you? You could see that Papa thought very well of him – it's almost as if he was sent to us – that very day . . .' she hated to talk about it, 'like a sign.'

'He's not had the experience, Phoebe.'

'You could help him to get it.'

'He's a pattern-maker.'

'He won't always be. And anyway – Beth, can't you see? Haven't you guessed? No, I suppose you've had more to think about. One day Johnny and I will be married. Not yet, not so soon after Papa . . . I wish I could have told him.' Then defiantly: 'Why do you suppose I come so often to Wilhampton, and do you think I always walk on my own in the evening?'

'You meet Johnny Giles? Well, even so, you've known him no time at all. He's a handsome young giant, enough to bowl any young girl off her feet, but Phoebe,' she took Phoebe's hand, 'it's all been a shock to you, and all that dreadful business with poor Mary, that must have thrown him too. It'll pass, things will settle down again for you. Truly you must not meet him alone – poor Lucy would be mortified for you,' but she somehow failed to sound as shocked as she intended. 'You've hardly had a chance to know him, Phoebe.'

'You're wrong. I do know him, I've known him for months, for a year nearly and I've loved him from the beginning and so he loves me too.'

'Did Mary know?'

'No, I swear she didn't. Long before I met him he had no marriage.'

'Neither did she, poor child. Your life, your background, it's been so different from his.'

'I could give him a proper marriage, that's what's important. You were happy with Papa and I've learnt since I got older that lots of people said your marriage was wrong.'

'We knew it wasn't.'

'There you are then! Johnny and I feel that too.'

Beth didn't answer. How could Phoebe understand what it had been like for Henry and her? She turned away and walked to the window looking out on to the long evening shadows falling across the garden.

'Give him a chance, Beth. Please.'

'Phoebe, Copeland's can't afford chances. Hal is intent on ruining us, he's made no secret of it. Copeland's will thrive, that I swear, but business and sentiment don't make good bed-fellows. We need all the trade we can find, we need to expand. If Hal wants a fight he shall have it.'

'And Johnny?'

'Umph?' For a moment Beth had forgotten this latest problem.

'I'll see what I can do. But don't rush anything. Before you think of marriage let us all know him better.' And that was as far as she'd go.

The sky was heavy, the air still. Even the birds in Matlock Woods had been silent as Beth had driven her own trap towards Wilhampton. Today was important, no longer could she put off doing something about Johnny; not just for Phoebe's sake or Johnny's either, but for her own.

As she walked through the great open ground-floor workshops the heat pressed in on her; steam from the cooling metal, the acrid stench of sweating bodies, how many years she'd been coming here, always excited by the sight and sound of it. Yet now the joy had gone, the adventure and challenge had become no more than a threat, a sick fear that she might fail. Each day she came here; even on Sunday afternoons she ignored Lucy's half audible tut-tutting and mutterings that she couldn't think what the world was coming to, Sunday was given as a day of rest. She sat at Henry's desk. Amongst his surroundings she sought desperately to find his spirit, to be guided in the way he wanted her to go. She vowed that she'd make Hal rue the day he'd walked out on his father's business; she'd bring him down. Hatred was rare to Beth. What she despised she ignored, or so it had always been, but her anger against Hal was almost tangible that he could do this to anything so dear to Henry.

This morning, instead of making for the stairs, she crossed the floor of the workshop and went into the adjoining room where Johnny worked.

'Johnny, I'd like to talk to you later. Will you come up at, let's say, half past ten?'

'I'll come before if you like.' He stood up. 'I can easily leave this and come straight away if you've something to discuss.'

Had he known her better he would have read the warning spark in those green eyes. 'Half past ten, please,' and she turned and left him. Something to discuss indeed! And if I had, I'd not look to him for guidance! Silently the truth nudged at her; she had no one else. With determination she stamped on the thought, her head high as she mounted the stairs.

So much had changed for everyone at the Court over the last weeks, she knew. The fact that Johnny frequently came home with her to supper was but one thing extra. Phoebe gazed at him with open adulation. Vicky tried to pretend he wasn't there; both she and Charles from training and habit took no part in the conversation but they still managed to convey in their silence their objection to his behaviour. Papa had never discussed the foundry at the meal table, never said to their mother: 'In my opinion we should do . . .' this or that; 'If the strength of the metal is there, the finish is of little importance with spare parts. We could turn out more blades, more discs, shares, any of these things for the same manpower if we told the men to cut the time they waste on details of finish . . .,' or 'If you ask me I'd say . . .' Lucy concentrated on her meal, mentally blaming Beth for carrying the workshops to the home; Phoebe wished dear Papa were here – how impressed he would be, how happy for the union that would bring Johnny into the family!

And Beth? How did she react? On his first visit, even his second, she took comfort from his interest, even though she didn't follow his advice. Last night, though, had come as the final straw. After the meal she'd gone to the library as she usually did, intending to think over what the day had brought, plan her course for the next.

A tap on the door. The children must be coming to say goodnight she'd thought.

'Come in. Bedtime already?' She looked up as the door opened.

'It's not the children, it's me. I thought, Mrs Copeland – Beth – if we spent half an hour together now we might sort how we can expedite that order from Meredith & Bryant. I couldn't help seeing it on your desk when I brought you those samples this morning. A large order, a test for us, I shouldn't wonder.'

'Johnny, go back and keep Phoebe company. You're here as her guest, not mine.'

'She's always said how you and her father used to work together after supper. A good idea. A quiet half hour is worth twice as long at the foundry. I've given some thought to the order, my advice would be – ' She would have interrupted him sooner but she had felt impelled to listen, hardly believing her ears.

'If I want your advice, Johnny, I'll send for you in working hours. Now if you'll excuse me I have things to do. I wish you goodnight.' He hadn't argued.

No doubt this morning he had expected it was that same

286

advice she was seeking. At half past ten he came. It took but a few minutes to tell him what she had in mind and he listened, without interrupting. With something like defiance she faced him across the desk. She knew it wasn't what he or Phoebe had expected. 'He's to be family,' only last night Phoebe had pleaded yet again. 'And you treat him as if he's no more than any other worker.'

'Poppycock! How many times in these last weeks have you had him here for supper? Do I bring any other worker home?'

'That's not what I mean. Do you intend to run the foundry on your own? Johnny's right, Beth, it's a man's place. Papa could see he wasn't like the others.'

A personable young man, ambitious, with a working knowledge of the trade and, unless she was mistaken, an urge to see more of life than Wilhampton could offer. If after six months of what she had in store for him he still wanted to marry Phoebe she'd make no objection.

'But surely now of all times you have better use for me here,' he said when he heard Beth's plan. 'I can keep an eye on the men for you (a woman can be mis-used; they'll think they're on an easy wicket with no master). It's for your sake I'm saying this Mrs Copeland – Beth.'

'Johnny, this business isn't going to suffer because of Mr Hal's disloyalty. We've never had a man out on the road seeking our work, but I'm taking no chances with the foundry for the sake of false pride. You'll be doing your part by bringing in the orders.'

It wasn't what he'd planned but in the short term the idea did have an appeal. The railway network was good, he would sometimes do his journeys in a day, but more often he'd stay overnight in an inn. That must be better than fending for himself in Henry Street – and a few days' absence from Phoebe would ensure a warm welcome when he returned.

Together he and Beth worked out his itinerary, listing his calls. He jotted down names, he appeared to be giving his full attention to what they did, but in truth his mind was busy with something else. He'd recognized Beth's determination right from the start but, never the most sensitive of men, he'd blundered on with his 'In my view we should' or 'If you ask for my opinion'. Stubborn, had he thought? Pigheaded would be nearer the truth! What prospect could he have, even married to Phoebe? A few months ago she'd been the governor's daughter. Now what was she but an orphan living in her stepmother's house – albeit with a £2,000 nest egg?

He nodded his head in agreement with Beth's suggestions, he listed which day he was to go to Oxford, which to Northampton, to Reading and Swindon. She had every reason to believe the interview had gone off well, he seemed satisfied. Phoebe would be pleased.

For the first time since Henry's death she left the foundry by four o'clock. This mists of fear were clearing. She couldn't see into the future, she was still too numbed to want to look despite all the energy she'd put into these last weeks, but today she had taken a step forward.

The threatened storm hadn't come, the clouds had thinned, she felt a slight stirring of breeze. She breathed deeply of the heady scent of summer as the steady clip-clop of the pony carried her homeward. The oppression of the day was lifting, yet at the thought of Merton Court, Lucy tight-lipped, Phoebe with thought of nothing but Johnny, her spirits sank. Only a few more days and the boys would be home from school, but how different the holiday would be this year. She remembered other summers, the friends who'd visited – families of 'her' friends, or so she'd foolishly believed – the laughter on the tennis court, the competitions on the croquet lawn behind the stables. As if in answer to her thoughts came a sudden flash of inspiration.

'I know what I'll do. I'll take the children down to Chalcombe. Jenny can look after things there. They can spend the holiday at Penrhyn House. Oh Henry, Henry, it was to have been so different . . .'

Beth had left the foundry by four o'clock; it was still not quite five, nowhere near the end of the working day. Where, then, was Johnny going? He'd scrubbed his hands at the pump in the yard, combed his hair and even, in a last attempt at making himself presentable, polished the toes of his boots against the back of his trouser legs. Then, without a word to anyone, he went out from the sweltering workshops into the afternoon air. Down the road, past the end of Foundry Lane and Henry Street, through the Market Place, along London road past the hospital into Station Road. He seemed to be heading towards the other side of the railway, beyond the brewery and towards – but why should he go there? Up the steps of Harknell's strode Johnny and a minute later a lad from the packing shed (with oil on his fingers and pimples on his chin) directed him to Hal's office.

The following Monday saw him on his way northwards to Shrewsbury and, too, it saw Jenny and Daisy head in the opposite direction to open up Penrhyn House.

'Look Mother, the sea! Can you see the boats?' She heard Nicky's voice as an echo of her own. If she shut her eyes, let her body be swayed by the rhythm of the rocking train, let her hands rest on the plush seat, she could almost believe he was here.

'Put your head in,' she said, again hearing his warning voice, 'you'll get a smut in your eye.' Then darkness, the tunnel. Henry, I'm so lonely for you. She bit her lips in the acrid darkness, frightened of the way her mouth trembled at the corners.

The twins had their noses pressed to the window waiting for daylight to appear again, Charles sat opposite her, quiet, obedient and always a little way out of her reach. They emerged from the blackness, all three children now watching expectantly as they realized the train was slowing down.

Jenny was waiting on the platform and Beth jumped down from the carriage with as much eagerness as any of them; the smile she turned to Jenny a clear sign of the sudden lightening of her spirits.

'And what do you think of it here? Isn't it the most perfect place you've ever been to?'

'Well, m'am, I've not been to that many – Wilhampton, Newbridge, Tilmarsh o'course – but yes, yes, it's a pretty enough spot.'

For weeks Beth had met with rebuffs, slights enough to make her life a battle even without the ache of loneliness. Small wonder that as the little party strode off from the station she trod with determination. Chalcombe had been a happy place, Henry had wanted her to come here. The family, the jealousy and bickering had no place at Penrhyn House.

An elderly man was mending a wooden chair in his front porch, his waterproof over-trousers proclaiming him to be a fisherman. Beth's face beamed at him, her first spontaneous smile for so long. He took his clay pipe from his mouth then lifted his tall bowler hat.

''af'noon to 'ee. You'll be headin' for Penrhyn House.' News travelled fast in Chalcombe it seemed.

'I've brought the children to stay.' The smile still stayed as they passed down Fore Street.

He watched them go, then put down his hammer and went in to report to his wife that 'that young widow-woman and her chillun have come. Dare say it's a good thing she took the house instead of the Skipper. Them youngsters deserve a treat losing their Pa like they did.' Indeed there was little the village hadn't gleaned for in the ten days Jenny had been here she'd paid enough visits to the two general shops to stock up the store cupboard. She'd been to the post office to buy a stamp for her letter to Mrs Murphy, more than once she'd been to the quay to buy fish straight from the boats and wherever she went people had time for a word or two. What one didn't hear another did, information was pooled, passed on; Beth's welcome owed much to Jenny.

The house was waiting for them, much of the furniture taken over from Richard Hatcher, but the various pieces Beth had ordered and had sent down all set in place. She opened the huge walnut wardrobe and surveyed her clothes, all sent ahead by train and unpacked by Jenny ready for her arrival. Outdoor garments in one cupboard, dresses in the other. On the dressing-table were her brush and comb, her silver-backed mirror, her ringstand and toilet water. Nothing here of Henry's. How strange it felt, no sign of him anywhere. At the Court his brushes still stood with hers, by his side of the bed was the table with the Bible that each morning he used to carry down to the waiting assembly. It wasn't the trappings of living that held a person close though, that was something she'd already learnt in these weeks without him.

The tide was low. For the first time she saw that beyond the shingle was sand, not golden as she remembered from Bournemouth or Weymouth, a rusty sand. Already the children were outside; she could hear their voices, a new note of excitement. Wilhampton, the foundry, the Court and stiff-lipped Lucy were another world. For two days she could push it all from her mind. Such a short while ago she'd not have believed that she could escape from the foundry with this relief, it had been woven into her life. Woven because it was Henry, he'd made her a part of all he was. How different now he'd gone.

Throwing the window wide she leant out to watch the children. There! Hadn't she known this was the right place for them. Already they seemed to have found friends; instead of just her three outside there were six and the twins had wasted no time in shedding their shoes and socks (in Vicky's case her white stockings and she had tucked the hem of her dress into the elastic of her bloomers

291

in a way that would have set Lucy tut-tutting in shame). They were with a girl and a boy somewhere about their own age, while Charles, still fully dressed, was with a slightly-built olive-skinned lad so tidy in appearance that he looked out of place by the water's edge.

A knock at her door and Jenny appeared.

'Did I put your things away right, Mrs Copeland? Is there anything you need doing?' It was no more than an excuse, she'd looked forward to Beth coming.

'Everything's lovely, Jenny. Tell me, who are the children with?'

'Let me take a look,' Jenny was ready to show her superior knowledge. 'Well now, the little fellow with Master Charles, he's called Franck – French he is, talks much the same as you and me, mind, a bit more careful of his words like but easy enough to understand. His Ma, she's married to Mr Trafford, him who has all the fishing boats. Fancies herself does that one; not my place to say so, but looks at me real hoity she does.'

'I remember her. And the other two?'

'Well, the little girl, somewhere about eleven I think someone said she'd be, but grown up for her years. They call her Liza – dare say she's Elizabeth same as you are yourself m'am – her father is this same Mr Trafford. And the other one (his hair always puts in me in mind of straw, colour bleached clean out of it and looks like it never sees a comb), he's Ted Stebbings. You'll mind you came by his Pa's place, the boat builders' yard back along the shore.'

'My word, Jenny, you sound like a local already.'

'Well, ma'am, folk like a chat and it's me that fetches the shopping in. You'll soon get into the way of it here.' Her face puckered into a worried frown. 'But a weekend doesn't give you long. A real holiday that's what you could do with.'

'I'm going to enjoy it anyway, Jenny,' Beth said with resolve. 'I've made up my mind. And I'll come as often as I can while the children are here.' Yet even as she spoke

292

the words seemed to mock her. She raised her chin. 'And how are you and Daisy getting on? I've not seen her yet.'

'Oh m'am, we're real settled in. I see to the house and Daisy does the cooking, not that there's been a lot.' In ten days great strides had been made, they'd neither of them had the freedom of a house before.

Children waste no time with preliminaries, they plunge straight into the things that matter. So it was that very first evening Ted, Nicky and Charles went fishing from the beach. Ted managing to produce the necessary rods and lines. It seemed Franck wasn't interested in angling but he looked content enough with his own company. Liza and Vicky went walking up the cliff path and from the look of them found plenty to talk about. The rigid hours kept at the Court had no place here. Beth sent word to Daisy that they'd eat a cold supper when daylight was fading and the children came in.

Good to see them having such fun, she told herself not once but repeatedly, trying all the time to believe that some of the pleasure was hers. Her evening was long, spent alone. From the window she watched the boats unloading in the fading light, she saw the fisher girls sorting the catch. Then lamps were lit on the quay. Men were calling to each other; she didn't understand what they were doing, nor yet what they shouted. In truth the dialect was so broad that even if she'd known the way the fishing trade worked she'd still have been unable to recognize their cries.

No talking at the meal table had been a life-long rule, so at supper they answered her questions, told her something of their new friends, but there was none of the excited chatter she'd heard outside. Only later when they'd gone upstairs to bed did it start again. They ought to be asleep but why spoil their fun? She heard footsteps as they padded into each other's rooms, shrieks of laughter from Nick, even Charles's voice regaling them with the story of the crab he'd unhooked. By the time silence fell it was quite dark.

Upstairs in her own room she didn't light the gas. Instead she pulled the curtains right back and in the dimness let her eyes get attuned. By instinct and touch she unhooked, unlaced, unpinned and generally made ready for the night. Again she went to the window. Outside the air was still, the only sound was the rhythm of the sea, the gentle splash of each wave, the shifting shingle as the water rolled back.

Even so late it was hot, sticky. She rested her head against the cool glass, clenching her teeth against the sudden wave of – what? Loneliness, longing, frustration, desire . . . all these things.

Alone she climbed into the large bed, the bed she'd ordered for two to share; how different she'd expected her nights to be. She lay on her back, stretched out straight, her eyes shut as she listened to the waves, willing herself to sleep.

Henry, it's you I want. You understand, you know what it's like to be alone. She thought of the love they'd shared, his need as great as hers. He'd understand. His hands, tender, firm . . . Eyes still closed she imagined it was his touch she felt. Henry, stay with me, close to me, close to me. The seconds ticked to minutes. He was close, she knew again every movement, almost heard as she had a thousand times: 'Now, Bethie, now – '. She bit hard on the sheet to stifle her cry. Every nerve in her responded. For all her lonely, wakeful nights at the Court she'd never found him this way. Now tonight for that first wonderful second all heaven was hers; then as her body quietened so came a blackness darker than she'd ever known.

She rolled across to the other side of the bed, his side, the sheets fresh and cool; she buried her head into the pillow that should have been his and wept as she hadn't in all these weeks.

* * *

'A visitor for you Mrs Copeland, m'am. It's Miss Stebbings come to see you.' Then in a whisper: 'You'll remember, 'tis her father that builds the boats.'

'Bring her in, Jenny, and then will you ask Daisy to send us up some tea.'

All morning the children had been out playing and Beth, determined to enjoy every hour of her visit, had put on stout shoes and climbed the cliff path. Wherever she'd looked her gaze had met with such beauty; the sea, the clear sky, the screeching gulls hovering or swooping over the fishing boats, then inland the rolling hills as far as the eye could see. Not another soul on the cliffs. If only she could paint, write poetry or music, find a way of holding all she saw and sharing it.

'Why can't it be enough, just to see all this for myself?' She turned slowly, her eyes taking in the scene: 'All of it so lovely, yet empty. And if it's empty the fault's mine, it must be . . . Pull yourself together, Beth Copeland, God's given you this wonderful day, a home here amongst all this, children who seem happy (how easily they adjust; even Charles rushed off this morning keen as mustard), then be grateful. Accept. Isn't that what you have to do? Be grateful, feast your eyes and absorb all this . . .' That had been this morning. After they'd eaten their dinner the children rushed off again and Beth, whether from habit or as an escape from a solitary afternoon, was sitting at the bureau jotting down notes of things she had to do when she got back to the foundry. So a local hand of friendship brought a smile of pleasure to her face as she turned to greet her visitor.

'Mrs Copeland, I'm Cecily Stebbings. Young Ted out there with your children, he's my brother.'

'Oh yes, they told me. You look after your father and Ted. How kind of you to come to see me.'

Cecily must have been more than double Ted's age but even so she was a good deal younger than Beth, in years if not in outlook. A plain girl, her figure matronly, solid, her broad hands hardened by work, her brown hair lustreless and worn in a bun on top of her head, over which was pinned a flattish brown hat, trimmed only with a band of the same shade and anchored securely enough to defeat any gale the Channel might throw at it.

'I was glad you got the house.' It seemed she was as short on social graces as she was on beauty! 'That French woman, Eugene Trafford, she was set on it you know. Made his life hell I'll be bound when she didn't get what she wanted.' She sniffed. 'By and by you're sure to meet her – unless she flies the coop first that is.'

'I met Mrs Trafford briefly. We both viewed the house at the same time.'

'He should never have married her. Still, like I say, she'll be off one of these days, Chalcombe's not for her sort. And what about you? Won't you find things dull here?' Cecily was a far cry from those callers at the Court who'd seen fit to cut Beth from their visiting lists.

'I've brought the children down for their summer holiday. Jenny looks after them and they'll have a better time here than at home at present. They'll make friends in the village I'm sure; already they play with your brother and the Traffords.'

'That lad, he's not a Trafford. He belongs to the French woman. The only Trafford is Liza, she's from Ellis's first marriage. His wife died when the baby came; just a girl she was herself. He should have taken another wife, someone who'd care for the little mite. Not that our m'lady does that. Herself, that's all she cares for. The little girl needs a woman. Looks like a water gypsy. I do what I can, well I can't do a lot now that he's got a wife.' Another sniff. 'Used to though. And for him too. Known him all my life, you understand. There's nothing I'd not do for Ellis.'

Beth began to understand the story behind her visitor. 'Nothing she wouldn't do', but it seemed she'd not been asked.

296

'Here comes tea.' She heard Jenny's step. 'I'm so glad to have some company.'

'Ah! children aren't enough, are they? I've had the children to care for. Eldest of five I was, all at home when Mother passed away. Just Ted left now; he was the afterthought. Like I say, children can't be enough – you'll find out soon enough. Sad to lose your husband so suddenly. Mrs Ogbourne told me what a nice gentleman he was.'

'Milk and sugar?' Beth changed the subject. She'd rather talk of the French woman and Ellis Trafford's mistaken marriage than of Henry with this stranger.

'Both please. Those boys, they shouldn't be kicking that football out there on the quay. Do you see them?' Cecily had come with good intentions of using her best drawing-room behaviour, but this Mrs Copeland wasn't nearly as forbidding as she'd expected and a glimpse of the children playing out on the quay was enough to send her to rap on the window, even though they were far too distant to hear.

'There now! It's in the water and the tide's running at a pace too! Oh my dear Lord, oh you silly boy you, he's jumped for it. It's your boy. Oh, my dear Lord. Quick.' She was already out of the door and hurrying across the hall. 'We must get help. Tide's rushing out . . .'

As Beth followed she saw through the window that Charles and Ted were still on the outer harbour wall. It must be Nicky!

In the shelter of the harbour the water rose and fell with the tides; even when the white horses pranced on the open sea it was calm here. The narrow entry was the danger area; when the tide fell the water rushed through the gap, a swimmer would have no hope nor yet could he pull himself up the high wall.

Beth's mind was a jumble of emotion. Fear, anger at herself that she hadn't known and thought to warn them, an earnest plea that Nicky would swim clear of the current, all these things crowded in on her. If Victoria saw what had happened she'd go in after him, even Charles might, for they swam; but not well enough for that. As she ran Beth was unfastening her skirt and bustle; water in that would pull her down.

Nicky had fallen on the far side of the harbour into the deep water of the open sea. From the quayside they couldn't see him. Cecily was plump, her legs fatter and her breath shorter. Soon Beth had outdistanced her and was running along the outer harbour towards Ted and Charles.

'Can you see him? Get down Charles!' All in one breath, for Charles was climbing the wall to see over the edge.

'Ah. Steady now, no need to panic.' Ted's slow West Country voice meant to calm her but instead it urged her into a final spurt. 'Boat's gettin' 'un.' The boy pointed. 'Mr Trafford, he was on his way to check the lobster pots – or goo'ness knows how we'd 'a fared.'

Nicky, pushing the ball in front of him, was swimming steadily with the tide away from the harbour towards the advancing boat.

In minutes they were on the beach, Beth still unfastened, half laced and with hands that seemed incapable suddenly of obeying her.

'Silly boy.' Cecily was the first to greet them as they jumped into the shallow water of the shore. 'Might have been drowned. Current's enough to sweep you away. I'll tan young Ted's behind, that I will, taking a ball out there.'

'It was me, it wasn't Ted.' Nick was a sorry sight, but clutching his football firmly for all that. 'I didn't realize.' Then to Ellis: 'I'll not forget what you told me, sir – and I'd love to come with you to the pots. I'll only be five minutes changing, honestly – 'and he was gone, seeming unaware of the fright he'd given everyone.

'Mr Trafford – I'm Nicky's mother, Beth Copeland. I'm so thankful you were there. He didn't know about the current. I ought to have thought. I ought to have warned him.' She could hear her voice was unsteady and was

298

ashamed that now Nicky was safe she was trembling so that she still hadn't managed to do up the fasteners she'd torn open. So silly, the danger was over now; at the time she'd been ready to plunge in without a thought, yet now she felt, 'I'm like some silly flibbertigibbet.'

'I've talked to him.'

'Needs his behind tanned.' Cecily put in. 'That would see he remembered.'

'He's a brave lad,' was Ellis's opinion, 'and a good swimmer too. I've said I'll take him back to check the lobster pots, but I'll send him home in one piece, I promise.'

'It's good of you, thank you.'

It had happened before, when she'd seen him on the Green. His eyes met hers, but this time she didn't lower her gaze. In a flash she knew he saw her for what she was, saw beyond the sudden reaction that had left her shaken and wordless. And it worked both ways. She looked at him – dark curly hair, dark eyes, close-cropped beard, a man of strength and courage – but she saw more. 'Made his life hell when he didn't get Penrhyn House' hadn't Cecily said? Involuntarily Beth's lips twitched into a smile. Oh no, she'd only met Eugene for a minute, but one thing she knew for certain. Ellis Trafford wasn't one to be upset by a discontented wife; married or single he was his own man.

Cecily's visit had been brief, she didn't come back to the house from the beach. The last Beth saw of her was as Ellis and Nick rowed out towards the pots and Cecily had turned to Ted with: 'Just as soon as they get back, home you come. I'll have tea ready. Perhaps Ellis might drop back with you.' Then to Beth: 'Like home to him our house is. I like to keep an eye. She doesn't know how to care for a man nor for a girl either.'

The next day Beth took the train home. Lucy had always looked on her as a poor sort of mother and perhaps she was. Even so, watching the children turn happily back to

Jenny she felt strangely empty. There was nothing new in it, it was the way she'd brought them up; they'd never clung to her nor she to them. But then she'd had Henry.

As the train carried her back she resolutely turned her thoughts to tomorrow and its challenges.

The weeks of summer passed, holidays ended, the boys went back to Rugby (at least Nicky and Edwin did) and Vicky to Bigbury House. Penrhyn House was closed. Johnny spent at least four days of every week away bringing orders from their old customers but very little else.

'I spent my day with Edith,' Lucy said, one evening in November. 'Such a joy to be in their happy home. Hal's doing splendidly at Harknell's, well, we shouldn't say Harknell's now, it's Harknell & Copeland's. There's a new building planned, fine new workshops, with his bit of money from Papa I dare say. Edith says he's quite set that all he and Papa did won't be squandered. He's made up his mind to carry on there what they did together.'

'What rubbish you do talk, Lucy. It's a different trade and always has been at Harknell's. He should have stayed where he was if what he and Henry did meant so much to him. But I'm glad he didn't. I can do without someone whose loyalty I can't rely on. The men I have are good, loyal to me as they were to Henry. If Hal wants a fight I'll give him one. You may tell them that when next you visit their happy home!'

Brave words, but hiding a heavy heart.

Like many another industrial town Wilhampton was developing fast. Two years ago the Royal Victoria Hospital had opened in London Road; Henry had supplied the ironmongery, just as the year before that, when a new Town Hall had replaced the old, 'Henry Copeland & Sons' had been stamped on every drain in the place. Now had come Beth's first local challenge – and that was the point; because it was local it was of vital importance to her. Henry would have been given the work, she mustn't let him down. The railway company was to build houses for its workers on the far side of town and new engine sheds in sidings near the station. She'd put in a tender for the work and whilst it wouldn't be a huge order she felt it a test she mustn't fail.

The day after Lucy's visit to Edith's 'happy home' Beth waited in her office for the arrival of Sydney Harrison from the railway company. She heard voices as someone brought him up the stairs. Instinctively she moved to look in the mirror that hung on the wall, her hand touching her hair. What sort of a man he might be she had no idea but of one thing she was certain; no man was blind to a pretty woman and Beth was no fool. She knew nature had treated her well and she gave it every assistance.

It seemed he was no different from any other. He saw her smiling greeting as something she'd saved especially for him; as she offered him a glass of port to restore him after his journey from London he accepted readily, letting his fingers touch hers as he took the glass, feeling a stirring in his pulses that had nothing to do with the price of ironmongery. My word, but she was a beauty and no mistake! Dressed in unrelieved black with that vivid hair she'd make most women pale into insignificance. He'd been told the governor had died and his widow had turned the son out; he'd expected some elderly harridan.

'You've read my figures, Mr Harrison, and now you've come to see me. May I understand from that you find my quotation agreeable?'

'Your quotation is indeed interesting but may I say, Mrs Copeland, to visit you here is my pleasure whether or not I am able to place the contract with you?'

Her smile gave him no hint that she found him pompous, and rather foolish; fortyish, his over-tight waistcoat straining at the buttons over his rounded stomach, his hair balding but combed from a very low parting to disguise the fact, his full lips not quite together and in some indefinable way his attitude silently conveying he was bestowing his favour on her by his presence.

'I'm sure if I am given the order we shall have many such meetings. Indeed I'm glad you didn't find the trip tedious,' she encouraged him.

Tedious or not it was worth it to be met by anyone so delightful. Recently widowed too! Certainly she'd made him welcome – getting lonely probably. He raised his glass to his lips, studying her closely as he sipped the port.

'There's more to this contract than the houses and engine shed in Wilhampton. At least there could be more. Whether the rest comes to you depends.'

'How much more? And depends on what? Is my price not right? I've cut it very low; this order is important to me, Mr Harrison.'

'And I want to give it to you, dear lady, that I promise you. There are to be houses in Newbridge, workshops at Tarnford; the line will shortly be extended further; there is a great deal of work for the right company. Ah yes, a great deal of work – staff need housing, engine sheds and workshops needs ironmongery. I like to think that company could be Copeland's.'

'It will be Copeland's. We can do it, our work is second to none, you'd not regret it.'

How earnest she looked, he'd enjoy giving her the contract. There'd be more visits here too, hadn't she hinted at it herself?

'I'll be frank. Your figures are no lower than I've had from elsewhere – I'll mention no names.'

'I see.' She frowned over the papers before her, mentally doing her sums. 'Mr Harrison, give me the contract and I'll reduce my price by two per cent. I can go no lower. That cuts me to the bone. No lower at all.'

'Let me take you to the Railway Hotel for your dinner. We'll celebrate.'

'Then the work is ours?'

'Dear lady, how can I refuse when you look at me like

that?' His fat little stomach puffed itself out, Beth tried not to look.

'You'd refuse fast enough if I priced too high,' she laughed. 'Yes, I'll come to dinner with you. I declare I'm quite ravenous.' It must have been relief that made her hungry but she was wise enough not to say so as she put her papers in the drawer and locked her desk. She took her hat from the cupboard, black astrakhan of a style as becoming as ever, pinned it on to her bright, upswept hair, draped her matching cape around her shoulders, picked up her muff and was ready.

'Charming, charming,' he muttered, so sure that in the early months of finding herself with no man she must melt at his words. But then he didn't know Beth.

Dinner over, the details of the contract agreed, Sydney Harrison took his departure, leaving Beth with the certain knowledge that today Copeland's had reason to be proud of her.

She must share her news with someone. From the workshops came the metallic sound of hammering, the smell of molten metal. It drew her down to walk among the men who served her so well.

'There's a deal of work coming our way – from the railway company,' she shouted above the clamour to a group of elderly men who'd been with Henry for years.

Will Jennings answered for them all when he shouted back: 'Splendid m'am, that's what we like to hear. You'll see, we'll not let 'ee down.'

The following week Sydney Harrison saw fit to call again. It seemed he anticipated being in the area frequently and, it seemed too, that the contract once placed with Copeland's he assumed the right to claim Beth's time whenever he saw fit. She wanted the railway trade, both now and in the future, but his visits found her constantly on her guard, sheltering behind a constraint alien to her nature.

In a month he visited the foundry five times, three of

them completely without reason. As Algy drove her trap homeward on a wintry evening in December she looked back to the day the contract had been signed. Copeland's would have been proud of her, she'd believed.

No, they wouldn't not now, Henry wouldn't be proud. He would have been given the work because he deserved it. He was the best man in the business. I'm nothing! I use the only tool I have – and I'm ashamed. Horrid little slug, trying to paw me with his nasty fat hands and I smile sweetly because I want his work. Oh Henry, I try, truly I try. I just don't know enough. Did you believe I did? Did you think I understood the things you and Hal used to talk about? I try to read. I take your text books from your case; the more I read the less I seem to understand. I'm so muddled – so I flatter that hateful little slug, just to get orders! She remembered Sydney Harrison's parting remark: 'I'll be in Wilhampton for a few days next time, perhaps we'll take supper together, eh my dear?' and his clammy hand reaching out to take hers. Ugh! If it weren't so repulsive it would be funny. She shugged her shoulders pulling her cape tight around her as if to throw off the memory.

Suddenly, so clearly that she wondered why she'd never seen it before, she knew exactly what she had to do.

CHAPTER TWELVE

Henry and Hal had talked a language she didn't understand – but there were plenty more who did. How long ago was it since Hal had come straight from school into the business, the basis of his knowledge learned and ready for his father to train?

There were men who'd been through university, men who could outwit Hal, she'd be bound. Her lips twitched into a smile as she imagined Copeland's managed by just such a man.

The idea of a manager came to her unbidden (conceived of Sydney Harrison's clammy hands) and being Beth she lost no time. That same evening she penned a letter to *The Times* with her advertisement but, there again, being Beth, she kept her own counsel.

It was to be a day for decisions. Johnny came to supper and during the meal Phoebe said: 'Beth, it'll be 1877 soon, a new year. Surely by now you'll agree to Johnny and me being married?'

'Hush, Phoebe,' Lucy whispered. 'It's for Johnny to make such a suggestion. Here at the meal table too!'

Beth laughed. 'Meal table or no, this is as good a time as any.' Indeed Phoebe had sensed that this evening her mood was right. 'Yes, another year. So, when do you want the wedding to be? There will be arrangements and you'll have to decide on a home.'

Secretly Johnny had imagined they'd live at Merton Court; he'd be the man of the house. It seemed Beth thought otherwise.

'What about Easter?' she suggested.

'But Beth, that's so far away.'

'Well, dear,' Lucy put in, 'it can't be in Lent and earlier than that gives no time at all – it's so soon after Papa . . .'

'I shan't miss Papa any less at Easter or Whit either. He'd be so pleased about it.'

'Now what do you think of this?' Beth beamed at her. 'I hear that Wilton House is for sale, in Eldon Avenue. You remember it; grey stone, only built about two years ago, very smart and modern, it even had its own bathroom. Quite a showpiece it was thought to be. What would you say to my giving it to you for a wedding present?'

Quite a lot apparently. Everyone talked at once. For the first time for months the Copelands were looking ahead and liking what they saw.

'Papa put Hal into his home for his wedding gift. How different things were then,' Lucy mused, but if she meant to cast a shadow she failed.

'I remember,' Phoebe was so happy this evening she spoke without thought, 'we were bridesmaids, Esme, Naomi and me. I'd never had a gown so pretty.'

Beth remembered, too, the hours of stitching, the hot summer, the evenings by the river, the girl she'd been.

'You'll have one prettier by far for your own wedding.' No one would have guessed her thoughts. 'What about the beginning of February, would you both be happy with that? Would that give us time?'

'I only want a quiet wedding. I never did like parties, you know I didn't.'

Again Lucy spoke. 'In any case, who but the family is likely to come? Here we are but a fortnight from Christmas and not a single invitation for the children – well Edwin has some cards, he'll be going to Chowne's for supper and a dance and to Brimley Hall too – but nothing for the younger ones.'

Beth met her look squarely; she knew just what Lucy was saying in her veiled way. Then instinct guided her to answer as she did. It takes but seconds for pictures to flash into a mind, at any rate a mind like hers. Christmas at the

Court, Henry with her: Christmas at the Court without him. The children running on the beach, Nicky in a boat with Ellis pulling on the oars as they rowed to the lobster pots, Nicky learning to unfurl the sail as they faced the open sea . . .

'It's as well they haven't invitations, they'd have to refuse them. I shall take all the children to Penrhyn House for Christmas'; then, relenting at the sight of Lucy's face, 'there's plenty of room, Lucy, we can all go.'

'Oh dear, oh dear, Christmas away from the Court, dear, dear what a pass it's all coming to,' Of course, though, even at home it couldn't be the same this year. Dear Papa gone, Hal certainly wouldn't visit and probably not Margaret either. 'The children and dear little Bella, they bring the joy of the festival. If you're taking the children there's nothing for Edwin and me to stay here for.'

'And you, Phoebe?'

'I shall ask Hal if I can stay there. It's not that I don't want to come . . . you do understand, Beth?'

'Of course I understand, goose.' Hal was only roads away from Johnny.

A day of decisions indeed. Before she wrote her letter to *The Times* she had one more thing to do; if Penrhyn House was to be warm and ready for the family it was time to send Jenny and Daisy on ahead.

Downstairs Jenny and Mrs Murphy were in the old housekeeper's sitting-room, Flo Murphy's favourite way of spending the evening. Not with anyone else would she put her aching feet on a stool, even undo the tight buttoning at her waist.

'. . . get m' first layer of icing done tomorrow,' she was saying. 'The children reckon to see the cake getting dressed up when they get home for their holidays. What sort of a Christmas it'll be — '

A knock on her door cut her words short and Rachel's head appeared.

'What is it now? Who's wanting me at this time of an evening?'

'Not you, Mrs Murphy. It's Jenny the missus wants, up in the library.'

'I'll pop up straight away.' Jenny stood up to follow her.

'Not like that you won't, my girl. Just you smooth your hair and take off that pinny. Let her see you're tidy 'long of me in the evening. As if she's got anything to say that couldn't wait till morning. This hour after supper's our one bit of rest. That looks better – and Jen, when she's done with you, you might look back, I'll sit here and wait,' which was her way of saying 'Come and tell me what she wants.'

So she waited, little guessing at the conversation upstairs.

'Well Jenny? What is it? I thought you'd be pleased. The children will be there and you enjoyed it there in the summer.'

'It's not that Mrs Copeland, m'am. 'course I'll do as you want. Me and Daisy got on fine there. But – well, it's just that Christmas . . . Christmas seems different. Only jus' now Mrs Murphy was saying that tomorrow she'd get the first icing on the cake, have it on before Miss Vicky gets home on Wednesday. All for nought if we're not to be here.'

'Jenny,' she could say to her what she couldn't to any of the family, 'I dare say I'm running away but – I don't want Christmas here.'

'Oh m'am, what must you think o' me?' Jenny chewed her lip, weighing up how to find the words she wanted. 'It's hard for everyone m'am; not like it is for you, I don't mean that, but – oh lordie me, I'm not saying it like I wanted.'

'Go on Jenny, tell me.'

'Well m'am, Mrs Murphy, she's been right upset by the master going, she don't say much but I can tell. Christmas won't be easy for her either. She's tried so hard to put a

308

bit o' heart into things; her mincemeat's ready, the puddings hanging up, the cake done bar the icing, all that. Now seems you ain't goin' to be here.' Jenny's grammar was falling to pieces in her anxiety. 'And y'see m'am, she'd only got me to talk to, proper talk. She'll tell me when 'er legs get puffed and that – not a word to anyone else, they just think she's got out o' bed the wrong side. I know 'ow 'ard it is for 'er some days. I'll be that worried for 'er left with no one – '

'Jenny, I think it's time we made a few changes. Penrhyn House needs someone there all the time, someone to make a family home of it. I suggest you and Mrs Murphy go down there, Daisy can come when the family do at Christmas. Tell Mrs Murphy to pack up her puddings and cake, eh?'

'Oh m'am, 'twould be that good for her. The sea air is a real cure, folk say. Why, even 'er legs might get the benefit!'

'Tomorrow get packed up. She'll have to leave her icing until she gets there,' Beth laughed.

'Jus' one thing m'am. I wouldn't want her thinking you and me . . . we've been sorting it all out. When I go down wouldn't it be a good idea if I say you'd sent just for me to save 'er climbing the stairs at the end of 'er day?'

Beth nodded. What a dear Jenny was. Servant or no, in all these years she'd had no better friend.

'And then, jus' one thing more. I'll tell Mrs M that she's to run Penrhyn House, make a home of it like she does here, that's why you want 'er there. I'll be there to help, do as she says.'

Beth wondered whether Jenny was a natural diplomat or whether experience had taught her the way to a peaceful life. Either way, she must have handled Mrs Murphy satisfactorily for four days later, her best hat securely pinned and her Sunday coat worn on a Friday, she was undoubtedly in control of the party that set out for Chalcombe. Algy travelled with them, handling the boxes, hampers and a large trunk.

When he returned the next day he sensed a new freedom at the Court. 'Downstairs' breathed a sigh of relief and set about preparing for its own festivities. What if Mrs Jenkins' cakes didn't rise so high, nor her pastry crumble so lightly? That was a small price to pay.

Dressed for her journey Beth turned this way and that, surveying herself in the long mirror in her bedroom. All these months she'd worn her widow's weeds for Henry yet it was now, as she fastened the final clasp of her apricot gown, that he seemed closest. She looked like herself. She could almost hear his voice: 'Bethie, my Beth again.' She slipped the long rope of pearls over her head, instinctively held herself straighter, taller. Apricot hat, musquash cape and muff and she was ready.

Except for her they'd all travelled down on the 19th of December. In the days between then and Christmas Eve, when she joined them, they'd brought life to Penrhyn House as they couldn't to Merton Court where Henry's spirit still dominated.

And more than that, Lucy had made a friend. Even when Edward had deserted her she'd never had to cook or care for a family, yet she believed it was true when she told Beth: 'Such a nice person Cecily Stebbings is and she and I have so much in common, we knew it from the first moment. She's had a hard life too; they all depended on her you know. We seemed to understand each other, recognized it as soon as we met.' Beth remembered Cecily and felt she ought to have expected it.

Certainly having a friend had put new life into Lucy. In the few days she'd known her Cecily had apparently unburdened herself, no doubt over a pot of tea and a wedge of cake. Repeatedly the conversation turned her way.

'It's the boatman's fault you know, men can be so blind. Still, he's learnt his lesson this time no doubt. Kindness itself she is to Liza – that's Liza outside on the wall with Vicky.'

'Yes, I know Liza. Ellis Trafford's daughter.'

'Ever since she was a mite Cecily's been like a mother to her. Goes to the house, bakes little extras – at least, she used to until that French woman came.'

'I suppose he can marry whom he wants. Glory be, Lucy, if he'd wanted a woman to bake his buns and sew on his buttons he'd take a housekeeper.'

'No better than she ought to be. The village was full of gossip about her, no shame in her, carrying on with him so blatantly, so Cecily tells me. Then with no warning they're wed and,' she looked around the empty room and spoke in a whisper, 'that not as soon as they should have been. On the way with his child she was, but she had a fall – an accident on purpose was what some folk said – broke no bones but lost the child. Well formed it was and I know that's the truth for Cecily was with her, waiting for the doctor, but she had to look after her herself. And that but two months after the wedding.'

'How sad for them.'

'Sad indeed! Do the devil's work and you pay the devil's dues.'

'I take it Cecily doesn't get on with Mrs Trafford?'

'I should think not! But', she chuckled, 'neither it appears does Mr Trafford. Even now, at Christmas mark you, she's off with friends, taken her son with her. The boy's about ten. She's been married before, or so word goes, but Cecily has her doubts.'

Beth only half listened, more impressed by Lucy's new interest than in the gossip itself.

'She'll pack her bags for good one of these days, then Cecily will be ready. He'll have the sense to see it this time. She'll make a proper wife for him, look after his home and his child.' She glowed with pride for the wonders of her new friend. 'You should just see the way she cares for her father's place and she's as good as brought young Ted up. Remarkable what we have in common.'

'This is a lovely place for the children.' Beth changed the

311

subject. 'Fancy Boxing morning and there they are on the seashore. They don't seem to mind the cold.' 'The children' never included Edwin. He spent hours in his room reading – Merton Court or Penrhyn House it made no difference.

'Are you sure you won't change your mind and take tea with us all at the Stebbings'? My, but aren't we lucky to find ourselves with an invitation out after just these few days?'

'The children played with Ted all the summer holiday.'

'Oh yes, the children – but this is a family party. Cecily always has people in on Boxing Day. I told her we could only come if it was something quiet, we'd not feel festive so soon after losing dear Papa – '

'What rubbish you do talk! The children deserve all the fun they can get. But no, I won't come. I've things to do and, to be honest, I want to put on my boots and stride up that cliff, get some fresh air in my lungs.'

Lucy didn't answer but she must have heard for when she arrived at Cecily's – and this time even Edwin had been winkled out of his shell so all four children were with her – she said: 'Beth didn't let me persuade her. She's off back tomorrow, you know, and she seems to have promised herself a breath of air this afternoon, talks of walking over the cliffs while the light lasts.'

Perhaps Ellis heard what she said from where he stood by the window talking to Tom Stebbings; perhaps in any case he'd only called in not meaning to stay – after all, an afternoon of games with the children was hardly his line; or, there again, perhaps, like Beth, he looked at the light blue of the winter sky and felt the pull of the fresh air. If Cecily had harboured other hopes she was disappointed.

Beth climbed the steep path from Chalcombe over the headland and down the far slope, then on along the cliff's edge, up again, then down through a patch of undergrowth and bracken and on up the next slope. At the top she stopped, out of breath and, she realized, a long way from home in the gathering gloom. Time was against her, she ought to turn back but instead she sat on the damp mossy ground clasping her knees and gazing out towards the fading horizon. How still the sea looked from this height. Not a breath of wind stirred the surface. Like her own life the day seemed to be held in limbo. The sun was going down like a ball of fire over the hills behind her but tomorrow it would rise again. She didn't analyse her thoughts but deep in her was a sense of hope. What lay ahead she had no idea, she wasn't even ready to find out, but this afternoon she had a new confidence that day would come again.

She scrambled to her feet, keen now to start the homeward journey. Down the first slope, through the bracken; by now the light was going fast and she stepped out more quickly. She ought to have watched what she did, she'd noticed on the way out how many holes and burrows there were; the grassy clifftop must have housed scores of rabbits and badgers. In a second it happened, her foot slipped into a rabbit hole as she hurried and she was thrown flat on her face.

Dragging herself up she put her foot to the ground involuntarily letting out a yelp of pain. If she'd broken the bone surely she wouldn't have been able to move her foot, she told herself. Heavens though, how it hurt! She shut her eyes, took a deep breath and forced herself to move forward. The pain shot up her leg, she clenched her teeth. Somehow she had to get home. On this steep hill the easiest way was on all fours, and that's how she was crawling slowly forward when Ellis appeared on the brow above her.

'Wait. You shouldn't move,' he shouted coming towards her.

'Fine thing to say! I didn't intend staying here all night. It's just my ankle, I caught it in a rabbit hole.'

'Sit down, let me see.'

She sat, obediently holding her leg towards him. Already the ankle was swelling and the top of her foot puffed.

313

'Can you move it!'

'Of course I can, you saw me.' She was ashamed of her tone but really what else did he deserve? He spoke to her as if she were some careless child!

'I mean your toes. Can you wriggle your toes?'

'Yes.'

He looked around as if sizing up where they were. 'Well, there's nothing else for it, you must be carried. Stand up, then I'll lift you.'

'Rubbish! How do you think I'd have managed if you'd not come?'

'With extreme difficulty and a lot of pain,' but this time there was a laugh lurking behind his words. 'Do as I say. Stand up. That's a nasty sprain.'

She would have given a good deal to be able to put her foot to the ground and find it would take her weight, the pain easing; but there was no hope of that. She turned from where she sat back to the crawling position, then she knelt up, clenching her teeth ready for the next move. He leant down to help her and she was ashamed of the tears that filled her eyes as the pain shot through her.

'This won't be comfortable for you. I'm sorry, but I'll have to hump you. Up we go,' and there she was, thrown across his shoulder, her bustle pointing skywards, her hat pushed to the back of her head and only held on at all by its pins, while he gripped her around her knees.

So up the hill he went. At the top he stopped, breathing deeply.

'I could stand down while you rest. Would that help?' Her unceremonious mode of travel had left her chastened.

'No, I've got a good grip of you, best stay aloft.' His voice was deep, the broad vowels of the West Country not as pronounced as in those she heard shouting on the quay but enough to set him apart from those she'd become used to. Suddenly he laughed. 'We meet in unexpected circumstances, Mrs Copeland. The last time I saw you you'd been tearing off your clothes to jump into the water.'

'And again you'd come to our rescue, I've seen you since then. I was in Chalcombe the following week for a day or so, and I watched you take Nicky in your fishing boat. He's told me how you've been teaching him to use the sails.'

'Ah, in the *Helping Hand*. Yes, so I did. He's a grand boy that son of yours. I could make a real seaman of him.'

She didn't answer. Hanging over his shoulder may have had something to do with it – given her a new view of the world. Nicky a seaman! An unlikely future for him but one thing she did know, and in that moment accepted it for the first time; never once had Henry been able to look to the time when young Nicholas would willingly enter the business with him. Hal's Henry, yes, Charles probably – but Nicky, never. Some of her recently born hope and confidence in that tomorrow deserted her. The future was bleak and the battle lonely.

Down the final slope they went, both lost in thoughts and he needing all his breath to carry a load that got heavier as they went.

His house stood in the shadow of the cliff up a narrow lane that led from the harbour. It was too dark by now for her to see it clearly; a stark grey building three storeys high, a door leading directly on to the street and with sheds attached, housing for nets, lobster pot and pony trap. Only later did Nicky tell her that the pony grazed in the meadow behind Fore Street.

'Take off your stocking,' Ellis ordered as he lowered her carefully into a chair and lit the oil lamp. 'I'll fetch water and a bandage.'

'I'm nearly home now, you don't need to worry. I can manage now that we're on the flat.'

'You are a singularly pigheaded lady. Can't think why I bother with you,' but there was definite laughter in his voice this time, even though she had an uncomfortable feeling it must be 'at' her and not 'with' her. 'Take your stocking off, there's a good girl, and that hat too.'

315

She craned her neck to see in the mirror of the sideboard. Oh glory be! Did you ever see such a sight? Her hair falling in loose curly strands, her hat balancing on nothing! Impossible to keep her dignity and even as she looked the face in the mirror broke into a giggle. His reflection laughed with her, hers with him. Then he turned away to the scullery to fetch cold water.

Left alone the pain in her ankle was almost forgotten, and the hammering of her heart had nothing to do with her fall. So much of life merges in memory; periods of happiness, periods of worry or sadness; but out of these are moments that shine bright and clear no matter what befalls. Such had been that brief exchange, something that would stay with her for ever like the song of the blackbird on that still evening so long ago when Henry had told her he loved her, like that awareness that had held her (and Henry too, she'd known) that afternoon at the foundry the day she'd heard the first cuckoo. Only last spring, only months away . . .

She rolled her stocking down and took it off as he came back with the bowl of water and a bandage.

'This'll take the smile off your face I fear. I'm sorry but cold water will do it good.' His hands were infinitely gentle as he took her foot and drew it steadily into the water.

'Oooh!' It was almost a whistle as she sat bolt upright in the chair.

'Quickest way to put it right. In a minute I'll strap it up, just hold it there first.'

'Quick is what it must be. I go back to Wilhampton in the morning.'

'You'll do no such thing.'

'Indeed I shall. I have a foundry to run.'

'You'll be no use to a foundry with a foot like this.' Gently he dried it. 'This is going to be tight but I want you to leave it on until the doctor does it for you again tomorrow.'

'Yes, all right.' She didn't say that the doctor she had in

316

mind was in Wilhampton, but no ankle was going to keep her here. 'Is Liza at the Stebbings' party? I thought you'd be there.'

'Tea parties aren't my idea of fun, nor yours I take it? I saw your family were all there.'

'They invited me, it was kind of Cecily. I spend so much of my time indoors. You've no idea how good it was to put on my boots and climb that hill, to get away from everyone.'

'Haven't I? I think I have. I do it myself, but my therapy is to get out to sea, even in a row boat. You can look back at the land, see all your problems in perspective. To be alone is a necessary part of life.'

'Of yours perhaps. Not really of mine. To share is life's greatest blessing; it was like that for me.'

He'd been pouring two glasses of port wine, now he passed one to her. 'Drink that, it'll do you good. If that's how your life was then you were lucky, or is it that we get back what we put in? Perhaps that's it. Some of us don't deserve as much as others.'

'Yes, I was lucky.'

'I saw you the day you first came to see the house. Would that have been your husband with you?'

'Yes.' What made her talk to him as she did she didn't know; it was as if some power outside herself led her. 'Yes, that was Henry. I used to work for him when I was a girl. I was the sewing maid in his house. Whatever I am today is because of Henry. He was everything to me, husband, lover, family, teacher, friend ...' Blindly she talked, not caring that the tears that had welled so suddenly brimmed over.

'To love anyone like that, to be loved by them, even if you lose them, surely you must be luckier than most? So many of us don't feel the sorrow only because we've never known the joy.'

She put down her glass and fumbled in the pocket in the lining of her cape to find her handkerchief.

'I'm sorry, I don't usually behave like this.' She blew her

nose in a valiant attempt to find her composure. 'I've never talked like that to a soul . . .'

'Then I'm honoured that you said it to me. Drink up your port and I'll carry you home – give the village something to chatter about.' The twinkle was back again. Instinctively he'd known she'd wanted it that way.

Five minutes later he lowered her to the couch of her own sitting-room and to his parting shot of: 'You're to let the doctor strap it again tomorrow,' she smiled and promised that she would.

Word spread fast in Chalcombe. By morning there were few who hadn't heard of how the widow from Penrhyn House had been carried home. The tale varied from a broken leg at one end of the scale to a 'tot too much Christmas jollop' at the other. Likewise word spread when at nine o'clock that same morning Bill Squires, the carrier, was summoned to the house and the lady in question was seen to emerge bearing heavily on two sticks, her children gathered round to wave her on her way. And that's how it was that as her train steamed and juddered to a halt at the platform Ellis hurried through the entrance.

'What in the name of all the saints do you think you're doing?'

'Mr Trafford, good morning.' The pain in her foot told her he'd been right but she had no intention of letting him have a hint of that.

'If you're not the most pigheaded woman! Here, let me hand that grip aboard. Now the sticks . . .,' and gently, despite his language, he helped her into the carriage. 'Are you being met?'

'I shall manage. There are porters at Wilhampton and I'll take a cab.'

He wasn't satisfied. 'You're to be met. This foundry you're so keen to get to, has it a telephone? Give me the number.'

'Wilhampton 23,' she told him. 'And Mr Trafford – thank you for bothering,' (her green eyes couldn't quite behave themselves, he meant to be angry but she wasn't fooled), 'even for being cross with me. I do have to be there today, it's especially important.' The whistle blew. 'I'll explain next time.'

He was back on the platform. 'When will that be?'

'At the weekend. Saturday.'

'Only if that ankle is better.'

'I promise. If not then sometime next week. As soon as I can.' She pulled herself up using the open window to hang on to. The train was getting up steam, any second it would jolt into life. She wanted to say something, anything, she didn't even know what.

'I'll take young Nick out, Mrs Copeland.' It was he who spoke first.

'Beth – and thank you, Ellis.' The train lunged forward, its engine hissing ferociously. It's doubtful if he heard what she'd said.

He was as good as his word. At Wilhampton she found Johnny waiting on the platform.

'You shouldn't have come back, you ought to rest that ankle. There's nothing I couldn't have handled for you.' His tone was solicitous. Surely if she were laid up for a while he must get his chance.

'Today I have an engagement; someone is calling I particularly want to see myself.'

'Health should come first.'

'Time enough for health later.'

Once in the foundry the stairs proved a problem. 'I could do with Ellis to hump me up here.' Despite the pain she inwardly chuckled at the memory as, using the rail, a stick and all her will power she gradually made her way up. Today was indeed important. It would have taken more than a sprained ankle to keep her away.

There had been various answers to the notice she'd put in *The Times* (a notice that had apparently gone unread by Johnny and by Hal too, for no word had filtered into

319

the family). Of them all one stood out far above the rest, a Scotsman by the name of Stewart Lovejoy.

'A university man,' Beth smiled to herself. 'Ha! that'll give Hal a run for his money.'

In her mind was a picture based on the bare facts she knew and had embroidered with a good deal of imagination. The result was a man in his thirties, large, untidy, sandy haired with a bristling beard, wearing swirling kilt. Somehow this figure had grown to become her salvation; once he was at Copeland's her anxieties would melt away.

So when she called 'Come in' in answer to Stewart Lovejoy's knock, she was unprepared. The age must be the same – 35 his letter had said – but this dark, thick-set, clean-shaven man was so different from the one she'd conjured up in her imagination that her heart sank. She held out her hand to him but didn't attempt the painful business of standing.

'Mr Lovejoy, you're prompt to the minute.'

He took her hand and his firm grasp restored some of her hope.

The interview started. He told her of his experience, of his ambitions; no doubt he had plenty of both.

Finally she asked: 'And why do you want this post, Mr Lovejoy? You seem impressed with Daycombe & Ladbrook's. You say you've been there ten years.'

'Mr Ladbrook is hardly older than I am myself. We agree over the way we operate – but I need to hold the reins. I'll be frank with you', and she recognized that would always be his policy; yes, she liked him more as the minutes went by, 'if I'm to come here we must be honest from the start. I'd heard your late husband talked of in the trade, always with respect. I heard of his sudden death and word was that you were carrying on. Naturally when I read your notice in *The Times* I wrote. With due respect, madam, I felt that here I would have a clear field.'

'For six months I've steered us through quite rough waters and we're not sunk by any means.' He didn't take his eyes off her as she spoke. My word, but his was the direct approach! Yes, a good man, straightforward, no cunning about him. 'You don't mince your words, I'll say that in your favour. Well Mr Lovejoy, if you want the post it's yours. I believe my husband would approve of my appointing you. I'd not expected to need anyone, I feel I'm failing him – but I'm out of my depth. There! Now I've said it!' And surprised herself too in speaking so freely to this stranger.

'Och! But you've done a splendid job holding things together all these months. How can you expect to fill Mr Copeland's place – he was a man of great ability, of years of experience. It may be hard for you to accept someone else here, but it's an insult to his memory to believe he can be done without and the loss make no difference.'

An insult to his memory. That was a new angle.

'I think you speak your mind too freely, with no understanding.'

'Och no, madam. Sometimes a body can stand too close, be too involved, can't see the whole picture. If you want your husband's work to thrive then someone who knows the trade as he did must do the job. That's all I'm saying. Whether or not you think you and I can pull together, that's not my place to say.'

'And I've already said it. I like a man to speak his mind, I expect to do the same myself.' This stranger running Copeland's, making the decisions. But it's the only way. Henry, am I doing right? I must be, tell me, show me I am . . . She ran her fingers along the smooth edge of his desk top, her glance moved to his inkwell, his hat stand, his cabinet of books. Stewart was talking but she hardly heard him, she hardly dared breathe. Henry was near, her spirit reached out to his, his to hers bringing a new peace. In the way that a lonely mind works she was sure he was telling her Stewart was that salvation she sought.

* * *

Phoebe was in such a state of excitement these days that even a manager brought from outside and installed over Johnny's head had no real power to cast her down. That Beth could do such a thing angered her on Johnny's account, disappointed her too because she'd always looked on Beth as wise as well as kind and this showed her in a new light. Briefly she'd felt a flash of resentment but only briefly. Life was brim full of hope and promise, she had no room for anything else.

On the 15th January 1877 Stewart took up his post and on the 10th February Phoebe was to be married. Mrs Johnny Giles. With such pride she prepared to set up home in Wilton House. There was plenty for the family to talk about in those first weeks of the new year.

'Oh dear, oh dear,' Lucy muttered to herself, 'that some stranger can be put in charge and there's poor dear Hal struggling to keep things going at that other place. Oh dear, dear, all Papa did handed over to a stranger. University man indeed! Papa never was, nor Hal either, and they did well enough.' Then happier thoughts would take over. 'A trip with Phoebe to buy linen. Fancy that! Asking me and not Beth. Blood's thicker than water when it comes to it — and no wonder, treating dear Johnny in that over-handed way. I'll mention our outing at supper, make sure she knows we can do without her advice!' But at supper she was disappointed. It seemed Beth had gone to Chalcombe.

They were much too wrapped up in preparations for the wedding to wonder at how often her place at the table was empty. In any case during these last months she'd so often stayed late at the foundry that they were used to eating without her.

'If it weren't for me poor little Charles would be quite neglected,' and this time Lucy wasn't far from the truth.

It never entered their heads to wonder what Beth did on her frequent visits to Chalcombe. They might well have been surprised if they could have seen her being lifted over the shallow water and lowered into the rowing boat, or standing on the deck of the *Helping Hand*, an oilskin coat over her bustled gown and a sou'wester keeping the wild wintry spray from her red hair. They had no more idea of what her days in Chalcombe were than they had of the workings of her troubled mind. The moment of peace she'd found had given way time and again to uneasiness, memories of Henry and Hal working always in unity, thoughts of someone else, clever, capable, taking up the cudgels to destroy Hal. No wonder she turned so willingly to that other life, something that had no tie with the past and no connection with the future.

Phoebe's wedding day came. Hal gave her away and on the surface the family presented a united front. The crowd congregated outside St James's to watch the bride and groom lead their party out, did not hear the whisper of Edith's: 'Lucy told me the widow's clothes had been put aside, but today, wouldn't you think she'd show more respect?' nodding her head in the direction of Beth in a peacock blue gown and coat. Today Margaret was in deep purple, Edith in light grey, Lucy in black and white. 'Six months and not a day more,' Lucy said, 'it's shameful!' And some of the villagers – to say nothing of Mrs Murphy who'd been brought back to the Court to supervise the wedding breakfast – thought the same.

'. . . to have and to hold from this day forward until death us do part.' The familiar words echoed in Beth's mind as they came out into the winter morning. Death – part? No, never that. What would he feel today to see this charade of friendship? See? Oh yes, surely he could see. Hadn't she known as she'd listened to the vows that he was with her. From that eternity where he waited for 'his Beth' he could read her heart, hers, Hal's . . . 'Oh Henry you didn't mean it to be like this. I've done what I believe to be right. How happy Phoebe looks, and so she should; he's a fine young man for all his pushy ways. With Stewart to guide him he'll grow to be as clever as he thinks he is.'

The children had all come home for the wedding, and Esme too. Penelope followed the bride and groom; being bridesmaid to Phoebe was something she hadn't anticipated, since Phoebe had seemed to be so settled on the shelf until romance took her by surprise. Vicky followed side by side with Hal's Betty. Oh yes, a united front to be sure, and Copelands every one of them. By Henry's side Beth had had a place. Now she was outside the magic circle of the clan. Even Johnny, answering some smiling remark of Hal's, seemed already to be one of them.

It was the same at the Court. Every leaf was in the huge dining-table, the hum of conversation proof that they enjoyed being together. She let her mind wander but William, on her left, had no idea of it as she appeared to listen to his kindly voice regailing her with a description of the pagoda he planned to have built when the weather improved. On her right sat Nicky, still of an age to be 'seen and not heard' at the table. He understood his mother better than most and his own thoughts had a similar habit of wandering.

Practical, solid, unadventurous though Phoebe had always been, yet her going left a great blank. She had been Beth's friend for so long, the only one of them all (no, that wasn't fair, Beth reminded herself, Esme's letters never altered) who hadn't changed towards her since Henry had gone.

Small wonder that in those weeks she so often escaped to Chalcombe where Mrs Murphy and Jenny had returned the day after the wedding. Even to herself she didn't admit that it was more than the sea and a home that was truly her own that called to her. Sometimes she took Charles with her but at that time of year and on his own the shore held little appeal. He clung to the cosy atmosphere of the nursery with Lucy and little Isabella. Poor Charles, not one of them really understood what it had done to his life to have lost Henry and the stability he'd taken for granted in his home.

In the unspoken language that's often plainer than any words, Beth knew Ellis was attracted to her, knew he watched the house for a sign that she was there, a light in the drawing-room or an upstairs window open. Like a drowning man reaching for the raft she turned to him. The slug-like Sydney Harrison would willingly have given her all the attention she craved had he been given an opportunity but since Stewart Lovejoy had been at the foundry she had managed to avoid him. The young manager always treated him cordially but that wouldn't have lessened the slight he would have suffered had he been able to see Beth's eagerness as she hurried along the quayside at the sight of Ellis.

Cecily missed nothing. Neither apparently did Eugene.

'Good day to you, Mrs Copeland.' Beth was standing by the harbour wall and turned at the sound of her name.

'Mrs Trafford, I didn't hear you come.'

'Your thoughts were on something else. I expect you were looking for my 'oosband.' Her English was good; only the silent aitch and the long 'oo' set her apart.

'I beg your pardon? Why should I be doing that?'

'Ah!' There was no humour in her laugh. 'Why indeed! I am not blind and I 'ave seen it all before. 'E plays a pretty game. If you've a mind to be bedded you must find 'ees appetite to your liking.' So it was more than silent aitches that showed the language wasn't her own; her choice of words was surely cruder than she intended. Even so the message was clear.

'You've no right to talk like that – about me or him either.'

'If you are so upset by the chattering I wonder you chase after a man who is 'oosband. 'Oosband and father too and little use as either, but a 'oosband 'e is.'

'You're quite wrong in what you're suggesting. He is a friend, mine and my children's too, he – '

'Ha! Friend! You take the 'ouse I meant to 'ave, you try to take the 'oosband I 'ave. I spit on you.' But fortunately

325

she didn't. With a flounce she turned and left Beth standing.

The boats were out. Beth supposed Ellis must be at sea and Eugene's 'looking for my 'oosband' to mean watching for the *Helping Hand*. It must have been some minutes later, so deep in thought had she been that she'd notice neither time nor cold as she'd gazed unseeingly at the fading horizon, that she recognized his step, Eugene's accusations flooding back as she turned to him.

'I've just met Eugene. What did she say to you?' He shot the words at her with an angry glower.

'Forget it, Ellis, she just misunderstood. People gossip with so little cause. I put Eugene in a wretched position and I'm sorry. Sorry because it means I can't come on the boat with you. I shouldn't be out here now alone with you before their prying eyes.'

'I'd not expected prying eyes to concern you, nor gossiping tongues either.'

She shrugged her shoulders. 'I'm not bothered a jot, not for myself. I don't give a fig what they say. While they're talking about me they're giving someone else a rest.'

He was smiling now, his dark eyes twinkling, his anger evaporated. There spoke the Beth he knew!

'But I've no business putting her in a position where – '

'Dammit, don't pretend I have to spell out the relationship between Eugene and me. I'm not trying to seem a misused husband. The whole thing was a bad move, from her point as well as mine. I'll tell you . . . Here at Chalcombe a Breton trawler had sheltered. I'd met the skipper.' He smiled to himself as he talked, remembering his French friend. 'It's a long story how it came about but I went back to Brittany with him. Only there a week, my French is limited, mostly their English non-existent, but I met Eugene. She spoke good English, she was beautiful. It was summer, she knew the rules of the game as well as I did. Even when she followed me back here we both knew it for what it was. It was unfortunate, careless, selfish on my part, call it what you will. Things had already changed and it was over even before she told me she was expecting my child. A son it would have been. She lost it soon after the wedding.'

'So,' Beth asked herself, 'why shouldn't I take the friendship I can?' but a voice of truth — conscience — whispered: 'Friendship? Is that all you want of him, or he of you?' And yet another voice prompted by fear of the hurt to follow as well as by pride: 'A game? Does he think I know the rules just as she did? A few months of fun. Is that what he wants?' Echoes of Eugene's voice reminded her that there had been others. It was a game he was skilled at.

Footsteps hurried down the lane from his house towards the harbour.

'Here comes Liza.' Beth turned towards the child but her smile of welcome was studiously ignored.

'Mama said I'd find you here,' she said to her father. 'She says I may help you in the shed.'

'Tell Mama I'm not working in the shed. You'd better run along back Liza, I'm going to see Mrs Copeland home.'

'Liza can walk with us.'

'Not this time. Go back Liza — and you can tell her where I am.'

There was something touching about the droop of her narrow shoulders as Liza turned back up the lane.

'Was that necessary, Ellis? She could have come.'

'Liza? She can help me any day. I wish I could say that of you. How's that manager getting along? Surely you ought to be able to come more often, stay longer?'

'Soon I shall. And at Easter the children will be here, Lucy too I expect.' Purposely she spoke lightly.

With Liza gone he took her arm and instead of turning towards the Green and Penrhyn House he led her to the cliff path. Willingly she went. Her evening would be long and solitary and she didn't want to start on it before she

327

had to; at least that was the excuse she made to herself for the sudden lift in her spirits.

Dusk was falling. Back at the house Mrs Murphy's displeasure was apparent in every movement as she prepared the pastry for that night's pie. Such thumping as it was getting ought, according to all the rules, to bring it to the table hard and heavy. Somehow though, being Mrs Murphy, the paste would respond. The black cloud of her mood would have no effect, the offering put before Beth would crumble at the touch of a knife. From the window of the drawing-room, where Jenny had been adding coals to the fire, she'd noticed Beth alone by the harbour wall; later from Beth's bedroom where she'd been putting out her dress for the evening she'd looked again and seen Ellis there too. She said nothing of that to Mrs Murphy; she'd learnt when to keep things to herself. At the last check, though, she'd found the harbour wall deserted as dusk was falling – but that was nigh on two hours ago. If the missus didn't get back soon she'd have to say something. Where could he have taken her? Alb Marsh, the mate on *Annabella* had told her a thing or two about that Mr Trafford and his lady friends, told her with pride almost and certainly in good humour; after all a man was entitled to have a bit of fun. Just so long as the missus doesn't let herself be used. She's not been used to his sort, married all those years to the master. Oh lawks I wish she'd get back, no knowing where he might 'ave took 'er. A sly peep at Mrs Murphy. Won't keep 'er thoughts to 'erself much longer, that she won't. I don't want to be a party to speaking ill of the missus. Oh come on home, Mrs Copeland m'am. Whatever are you at out all these hours? A thump as Mrs Murphy banged a saucepan on the range – another as the front door shut. 'Thank the Lord for that; she's home now!'

'That sounds like the missus back, Mrs Murphy. She must have been paying a call. I'll slip up and help her get changed for supper in a minute.'

328

'You'll slip up now from the sound of it,' she said tartly as the bell clanged.

But when Jenny came down it was to say: 'The missus won't be changing her dress and, Mrs Murphy, there'll be an extra at the table. It seems Mr Trafford is taking supper here.'

'Humph!' was the best Flo Murphy could do from lips so straight and tight, but after a minute or two she said: 'Not changing of an evening indeed. It wouldn't have done for the poor dear master. Sooner Miss Lucy gets down here the better. That one upstairs needs an eye to her. Fancy keeping company with that fisherman.'

Jenny picked up her tray and made believe she hadn't heard.

Tomorrow Beth was going back home. Even her usual short visits were two nights; this time she was running away. 'No, that's not true, not running away – pausing for breath and I can't do that here. I'll go in the afternoon. I'll see him in the morning,' for mornings she could handle. If she were here tomorrow evening he'd come again. She felt she was at the top of a slope, a slight movement and she'd slip out of control, hurtle down too fast and probably get hurt at the bottom. She wasn't ready, she was being driven by instinct not reason. From the safe distance of the Court she'd be able to stand back, take stock, think straight. That was the truth of it; with Ellis near she was lost.

But why? What was the magnetism in him? It wasn't simply that he was good looking, many men were that, then what? 'He's so – so male. All his men know it, they all look up to him. And those eyes; they look as if they scan far horizons, is it those? Or his weather-beaten skin? His gentleness?' All those things must have had something to do with it but mostly it was within herself. 'When I'm with him I'm young, free, I'm myself, I don't toady to convention. I say what I like, do what I like . . .' Ah, now she was coming nearer to the truth, now she knew why

329

she was running away rather than spend another evening with him.

He was a married man yet it was not thoughts of Eugene that troubled her, but of Henry, the Court, the foundry, the children, her other world, the responsibilities that demanded of her something so different from the girl (for girl was what she had felt herself to be) who had run hand-in-hand with him down the grassy slope of the cliff, their laughter spontaneous and only dying when at the bottom he'd stopped and turned towards her, holding her elbows firmly in those strong hands.

'Beth,' how soft his voice had been, 'I'm never free of you.'

'Don't, Ellis. I'm going away tomorrow.'

'Running away? From me?'

'No, not from you.' She rested her hands on his shoulders. 'From myself I think. I feel I'm being pushed. Here I can't think, can't stop myself.'

'Don't think, Beth. Follow your instinct. Isn't that what you've always believed?'

'I don't know what I think any more.'

How strange that when he'd held her in his arms it hadn't been with passion but with tenderness, his lips on her hair.

The evening had been different again. Together they'd eaten, then the table cleared they'd played cards. Any of the children might have spent such an evening. Ah, once it could be like that, the half admission of what was happening was close; but if she stayed another day they must move further.

Then the evening was over, Ellis gone. In her room Beth made ready for bed and turned out the gas. Now only the flickering flames of the fire gave any light. With her hair brushed and curling loose around her shoulders she looked little different from the girl she'd been fifteen years before, seen in the flattering soft glow from the coals. She unbut-

330

toned her nightgown and pulled it off, standing further back from the glass, turning first this way, then that. She'd had three children yet she was as slim and straight as a bride. Her hands moved down her body, then back to her breasts. How could she be the same? The firm, pert roundness of her youth was altered, slim still, 'but used,' she thought, a thousand memories crowding in on her. Turning from the glass she knelt on the rug before the fire. 'A bride did I say? No bride can know, no bride can feel like I do'. Tonight she didn't fight. Time and again in her loneliness wasn't this the way she'd recaptured the unity she'd known with Henry? The glowing coals warmed her naked body. Tonight she didn't cry out to Henry nor yet to Ellis either and later, lying straight and still in her large bed, she hated herself.

Penrhyn House had been Henry's gift to Beth, but having spent Christmas there, knowing that that was where the children would be for Easter and because she had a friend who'd written regularly through the long weeks of winter – 'looking forward to the days of spring when you'll visit again' – Lucy took it for granted she'd be at Chalcombe to enjoy Mrs Murphy's hot cross buns.

As soon as the children arrived home from school she travelled ahead with them, Charles, Isabella and Daisy. Beth was to come down on Maundy Thursday.

At the foundry Steward was proving all she'd hoped, yet the figures showed no improvement despite Johnny travelling far and wide. Everywhere it was the same, he told her. Didn't she read her newspaper? Oh yes, she did. All too well she knew the state of industry in the country. The boom of the 60s was petering out; competition from Germany, France, these days even from America, was fierce. Not so long ago England had been alone in the field, she'd made the most steel, mined the most coal. Her production was still good but others were catching up, the bubble of prosperity had burst, England was making haste too slowly. So for all Stewart's ability it was no easy road.

On that Maundy Thursday Beth decided to call at the works on her way to the station. She wanted to make sure that Stewart knew the custom at Copeland's; on Easter Saturday when the men were paid each had an extra shilling and sixpence. Not that it fell to the manager to pay the men but it was right that he should be told.

She would have had a more carefree Easter if she'd not made the call.

CHAPTER THIRTEEN

'And you? What did you do about it? Och!' With every angry word Stewart's Scottish background became more apparent. 'I suppose you doffed your hat and bid them good-day! No fight, no persuasion, and given no reason for the change. They've traded with this company since it began. I've seen the records. Och man, it occurs to me, and not for the first time, that you're not worth the wage we pay you.'

Beth had stopped to listen.

'Don't you dare take that tone with me!' She had no idea who she'd expected Stewart to be talking to but certainly not Johnny! 'You're forgetting yourself, forgetting your position here. Manager you may be but that doesn't give you the right to put on airs and graces to the family. This is a family business and just you remember it.'

Time for Beth to interrupt.

'Good morning Mr Lovejoy – Johnny. May I know what this is about?'

'Am I to be treated – '

'Hush Johnny. Mr Lovejoy, who is the client? What's amiss?'

'Meredith & Bryant. Giles visited them on Thursday, it seems, and tells me their business is to go elsewhere. Our oldest and largest customers.'

'Where? Why? Johnny, what did Mr Meredith tell you?'

'They've a right to trade where they like. And I'll tell you why. I had no need to ask, it's as plain as the nose on his face. It's bringing in a stranger, an outsider. They stood by you – us – until then. Old Mr Meredith thought highly of your husband, I'm sure of that.'

Beth's eyes flashed. How dare he! 'Where have they put their trade?'

'I can guess. You must have seen what Hal's doing, they must have heard the talk amongst the men. Furnaces are new to Harknell's.'

Stewart exploded. 'New to Harknell's you say. Damn it man, they are certainly not new to Copeland's. Is Harknell's price lower, is delivery faster? You seem to have asked nothing.' He was much too angry to curb his tone out of deference to Beth. 'I'll go and see them myself, try and strike a bargain with them.'

Johnny shuffled the papers he was holding. It wasn't like him to bluster as he did when he said: 'Oh I say, I'd not do that. I'll go again if you want someone to – I tell you it's the idea of someone from outside here – old Mr Meredith has always dealt with a Copeland.'

The door of Stewart's room was open and it was at that moment Beth saw young Henry coming up the wooden stairs. So long since she'd seen him here, he was like a ghost from those happier days. The light brown of his hair, the set of his shoulders, he was a Copeland through and through. Generation after generation the genes were strong – her Henry, Hal, now young Henry.

She moved to the door, something in the boy's attitude telling her that he'd come for a purpose; indeed he'd not been inside the works since Henry's death. 'Come and see me later, Mr Lovejoy, I've a few things to talk to you about and I'm leaving at mid-day. Next week when Easter's behind us I'll go myself and see Mr Meredith.'

'Oh Beth, that's no work for a woman,' Johnny put in. 'Leave it with me, just leave it with me.'

Henry was at the open doorway. Unexpectedly he interrupted. 'Aunt Beth, can you spare me a few minutes? I wouldn't bother you here – but this is important.'

Beth led the way into her office and closed the door.

'What is it, Henry? Is something the matter at home?'

For one wild moment she thought perhaps he'd been sent as a harbinger of goodwill. Last week he'd left school, come into the business with Hal. Could he have persuaded his father to hold out an olive branch?

'No, no, nothing like that. Aunt Beth, I feel quite sick at the whole thing. None of it should have happened ... Father can't have realized in the beginning. I can't believe he meant it to be like this ...'

'For pity's sake, Henry, let me into the secret. Here, sit down. Start at the beginning.'

'I don't know when that was. I dare say it was last year when he stopped coming here; that's when he put the work in hand for the new buildings – he must have known then. Aunt Beth I may not have had any experience but I've heard things, even in these few days since I came from school I've seen enough to make me face Father with it, come out into the open. Copeland's isn't doing well and I can tell you why.'

'Be fair, Henry, it's not just Copeland's. Do you ask me to believe Hal's making an easy fortune at Harknell's? It's the same the country over, wages are high, profits are low. Is that my fault? Is that what you're telling me?'

'Are you satisfied with the orders Johnny brings you?'

'Is anyone ever satisfied? Henry, I've not been beaten, even on my own I wasn't, and by God I never will be. Stewart's a fine man, you know. You can tell Hal that, a fine man with a fine background.' Beth bristled. Henry could see he was telling his tale badly.

'Just hear me. If you knew how I hate what I have to tell you ... But first I must make you see Father's side. To him Copeland's was what he and Grandpa built together. When he felt it had been snatched from him (don't interrupt me, please listen, that's what he did feel) he tried to take what they'd built with him. Not to destroy what Grandpa had done but to carry it on, Copeland and Harknell. "They used to work side by side", he told me last Christmas. "Now they're harnessed".'

'But that's nonsense, Henry. This is Copeland's, this room is where Henry worked, these workshops where the goods were made. This is Henry Copeland & Sons and so it shall be. Nicky is growing up and one day Charles too.' (Her words mocked her, Nicky here!) 'They're his sons just as truly as Hal.'

'Aunt Beth, what I've come to say is this. Have you room for another man here?'

'I don't understand. What are you saying?' Could Hal be regretting what he'd done?

'I've talked to Father, I've told him what I'm doing – and why. It's me, Aunt Beth, I always said I wanted to be here, I used to talk to Grandpa about it when I was just a lad. I've had no experience, I may not be much use to you yet – but I am a Copeland.'

She beamed at him, hating herself for the way her lips trembled with a will of their own, warning her not to trust her voice.

'I could see how things were as soon as I went into the works – Harknell's I mean. It's that rogue Johnny; he's behind it, Aunt Beth. Father is honest, I swear he is. He was angry, hurt, determined to fight you all the way, but Father is never sly. I told him I was coming to you. He showed no surprise. I almost thought – not that's silly, but I was going to say he seemed relieved. "Don't tell your Mother we've had differences, I won't have her worried. What happens here is for us alone, I won't take work into the home." That's all the fight he put up.'

'Henry never did either, let trade here shadow the home, I mean.'

'It's that swine Johnny, for that's what he is, Aunt Beth. All the time he travels for you he's bringing trade to Father. He spreads the word that Copeland's is done, Harknell & Copeland's is where the future lies. And I've no doubt Father pays him well for his pains.'

She didn't say anything. Just as her spirit had flared a moment ago now she felt crushed.

'Aunt Beth,' he reached across the desk and took her hand, 'we'll sort it out, eh? Remember how we had it all planned, when I left school? I always knew I'd be coming here – with Grandpa and Father. This man, Mr Lovejoy, you say he's a fine man, he'll help me to learn won't he? We'll sort it out, eh?'

She shut her eyes but she couldn't hold back the hot tears that crept down her cheeks to be wiped away inelegantly with the backs of her hands.

'It's not the way he meant it to be. Should I have refused, pulled right out and handed it to Hal?'

'No, Aunt Beth, you did right. Anyway do you think he would have taken it – in those circumstances? We're all family, Aunt Beth. Somehow we've lost sight of it these last months, but he knows now that I'm coming here, if you'll have me, and he knows why.'

'Poor Hal.'

'And Johnny?'

'How can I throw him out? He's Phoebe's husband.'

'He's not straight. Father's prepared to offer him something. Johnny's not straight – but Father can handle him.'

'Then I'll wash my hands of him with pleasure. Talk to Hal, tell him Phoebe mustn't be the loser.'

'As if I have to remind him of that. Even now, Aunt Beth, you should know Father better than that. But if you ask me Phoebe's bound to be the loser with that one.' There was no forgiveness in Henry. His father he could understand, even excuse, but Johnny never. Of one thing he was certain, what he'd done was right,

'Henry Copeland, you're in business.' Just as suddenly as Beth had dropped so she bounced back. 'In that cupboard you'll find some glasses and a bottle of Madeira. This deserves a celebration. While you pour the wine I'll fetch Stewart.'

But she didn't go straight to Stewart's room. Johnny heard her quick step coming along the corridor. No doubt she'd changed her mind about him making another call on

Meredith & Bryant. Confident now, he stood up as she threw open his door.

'I think, Johnny, you'd better go to Harknell's, see Hal. Not for the first time either. This time, though, don't come back.'

Johnny swallowed. 'You'd do that to Phoebe? Beth, you can't do that.'

'Hal's expecting you. I wouldn't hurt Phoebe. She'll hear none of this from me.'

The bluster was back now, he had nothing to lose. 'I wouldn't have stayed here anyway. What future could I have with you and that blue-eyed Scotsman? Copeland's you say – not a Copeland amongst you, nor will there be. That lad of yours won't settle and even young Charles –'

'Get out, Johnny.' The very sight of him rubbed salt into the wound. How blind she must have been all these months; she'd never suspected, she'd entrusted Phoebe to his care and all the while he'd been hand-in-glove with Hal. Her anger was at herself as much as at him. She turned and left him, stopping at Stewart's room to ask him to come and meet Henry.

Ten minutes later, the bare facts told – Henry was joining Copeland's and Hal had offered Johnny work at Harknell's – three glasses of Madeira were raised as Beth gave them the toast: 'Henry Copeland & Sons, from this day forward.' No right-minded men would willingly exchange this eager bright lad – his own son into the bargain – for Johnny Giles. But Stewart was no fool; he was wise enough to know when to keep his opinion to himself. The toast drunk, he voiced Beth's own thoughts when he said: 'If there's rivalry between the firms I doubt Mr Hal will have the same heart for it with his son here.'

Secretly Henry too hoped that this was the first step towards healing the rift, but from the determination in Beth's expression he deemed it wiser not to say so.

'My! How the morning's flown. I've a train to catch if I'm to get to the seaside.' Beth stood up. 'I'd scribbled a few notes of the things I wanted to tell you, Stewart. I'll give you the paper, you'll understand I'm sure. I'll be back on Tuesday, then on Wednesday I shall go to see Mr Meredith.'

She'd get to the bottom of the story Johnny had been spreading. To keep the truth from Phoebe was one thing, to keep it from the trade quite another! Meredith & Bryant's custom must be regained, and in her mind she was remembering other, smaller accounts that had been lost in the months of Johnny's jaunts. Women or no, with Henry under Stewart's wing, she'd go travelling.

She resolved that her few days in Chalcombe mustn't be spoilt by Lucy knowing what had happened. She could imagine the tight-lipped disapproval: 'Poor dear Hal, now his son taken from him,' or 'Surely Phoebe's husband's place is in her father's business.' It wasn't that her words would have the power to hurt – they were too predictable – but they'd certainly sour the weekend and she was determined that nothing must do that. Silence wasn't enough to put it from her own mind though. A good honest fight she could accept, but not this! To think how she'd been hoodwinked all these months, and worse, to think that, professing love for Phoebe, he might all the while have been playing a double role. Was he honest about anything? Was Phoebe being used as a rung on the ladder he meant to climb? The whole thing sickened her. Only young Henry, idealistic, seeing black and white clearly, gave her hope. Over the Easter festival she wanted to forget, but like a threatening black cloud it was there.

On Saturday afternoon she was in time to sail with Ellis and all the children – with Abe acting as mate – on the *Helping Hand*. No fish were trawled; it was an opportunity for Nicky to handle the sails, or that was the reason Ellis gave for the trip, and eagerly Beth agreed to come along to 'see how he fares'.

So the days passed, Sunday afternoon's hailstorm

ruining many a new hat but giving way to clear skies, a red sunset that promised well for tomorrow's holiday.

'Everyone goes, Mother,' Nicky told her at supper that evening. 'We have to take our dinner; it lasts all day.'

'Beth, you can't let them go off to a place like that, they're but children.' Lucy's words fell on deaf ears. 'Really what I say counts for nothing!' She was thankful to hear Edwin muttering something to the effect that mad dogs couldn't drag him there, so she took what comfort she could from that and from another helping of Mrs Murphy's cinnamon sponge.

'It's about four miles to St Mary's Bay. Charles can walk it, can't you Charles?' Vicky was as keen as her twin it seemed. 'Liza says she always goes – with Tom I suppose and Franck. We can, please Mother, say we can?'

'Beth, such a rabble there'll be there,' Lucy tried again. 'It was bad enough at home on St James's Day but these fisherfolk are rough and wild, they'll take too much ale most likely.'

Easter Monday the fair came to St Mary's Bay and not just an ordinary fair it seemed. There would be a dancing bear, a fortune teller, a boxing contest, all the usual things, but as well as those there would be a greasy pole to walk and this time over the sea, and pillow fighting with the contestants balancing on a plank between two boats. All that and rowing races, stalls with shellfish, stalls with humbugs ... no wonder almost to a man Chalcombe looked forward to the annual outing. Thinking of it as she listened to the children, Beth's eyes were as bright as theirs.

'St James's Day is a poor thing these last few years, Lucy.' So she must have heard the warning voice. 'Since Wilhampton has grown so busy people don't look forward to it like they used to. It used to be splendid . . .' When she was a child? When she went there with Henry? She remembered both, thoughts of Henry led her back to the foundry, to Johnny. Resolutely she turned away, back to St Mary's Bay.

340

'I'll come too, I love fairs – the bustle, the noise, the smell, yes, that's what we'll do, we'll tell Mrs Murphy to pack us up our dinner and we'll all walk there. We'll try our luck at everything!'

'Even the greasy pole, Mother?' Nick teased.

'Ah! Well, perhaps I'll leave you to uphold the honour of the Copelands there, m'lad.'

'Honour of the Copelands indeed. More like a lot of gypsies behaving so,' but this time Lucy didn't voice her thoughts. 'The day may well not be fine,' was all she said.

That red-headed strolling player who'd turned Jane Machin's head some thirty five summers ago must have been behind Beth's love of the fairground. The next morning she set off with all the enthusiasm of the children (the twins and Charles, but nothing would change Edwin's mind; he preferred a day with his books and the piano). Ted Stebbings and Liza were waiting for them at the end of the cliff path.

'Where's Franck? Isn't he coming?'

'He's not allowed to come. He wanted to but Mama said he couldn't.'

'Yet she let you? That was jolly mean, mean to Franck,' Charles frowned. 'Perhaps you oughtn't to come, Liza. Was he very down about it?'

'I had to come anyway. I told him I'd stay at home too – he cried and Franck's never a cry baby – but she said I had to come.'

'Didn't your father have anything to say about it?' Beth couldn't help asking.

'He wasn't there,' was the only answer she got.

The party toiled up the hill, Beth and Liza with Charles, the others in front.

'Come on, Charles,' Liza took his hand, 'hold on to me, I'll give you a helping hand.'

'A helping hand – like the boat,' Charles chuckled.

'Yes. That's why Father called it that, 'cos that's what I am, his helping hand.' She spoke with pride and a touch of defiance too. ' "She" isn't, Mama I mean. It's me who helps him with the nets and I can check the ropes and know all the different sorts of fish they catch. She doesn't.'

'Does Franck?' Charles enquired.

'No, Franck'll never make a seaman. Anyway Mama wouldn't want him to, I can tell.'

There were people ahead of them and people behind. It seemed most of the population of Chalcombe (at least the younger ones) journeyed this way to St Mary's Bay on Easter Monday. The fishing boats were all tied up in harbour. So where had Ellis gone so early? Beth told herself she wasn't interested; strange then how often the question came to mind.

It was years since she'd been to a fair and never had she been the one with money in her purse! The more she spent the more she enjoyed it. They watched the humbugs being pulled and twisted, then cut into chunks; they paid their penny to turn the handle of the hurdy-gurdy; Nick joined the line waiting for the greasy pole and, like the others, he stripped off all but his combinations knowing the ducking he had in store. There were plenty of bushes on the grassy cliffs around the bay and a dry pair was waiting in the bundle with his dinner! The sun shone, the hurdy-gurdy churned out its music that is hardly music at all. Only Charles, smaller and younger than the others, seemed uncertain.

'Isn't this fun, Charles?' Beth squeezed his hand encouragingly. 'I've always loved fairs.'

'Did Papa ever go to a fair?'

'Oh, my word, yes. At Tilmarsh he always used to go when he was a young man, before I even knew him he went. And he took me too. Great fairs we used to have there, but not any more. Everyone used to go – like they do here. But nowadays it's like Aunt Lucy says, men drink too much ale and there's not much real jesting. Oh yes, Papa would have thought this a very fine fair.'

Charles nodded, seeming satisfied. He'd seen Aunt

Lucy's expression last night at supper, he'd been unsure. Now he could enjoy himself.

'Ahoy there!' Ellis was coming towards them.

'Father! You didn't tell me you were coming. I would have waited and come with you. You can share my dinner. Aunt Cecily did it for me and I've got enough for a fishing fleet, she said.'

'Then I'm glad I've come.' He ruffled her dark curls affectionately enough, but his eyes were on Beth. 'Let me see what money I can spare,' he said to the children. 'There's half a crown, sixpence each for you. Off you go and enjoy yourselves. Mrs Copeland and I will carry the food and you join us for dinner at the top of the cliff.'

It wasn't what Beth had expected of the day but willingly she turned her back on the frolics, more willingly than she liked to admit.

They climbed the narrow and sometimes overgrown path and at the top found a grassy patch backed by brambles and sheltered from the wind. What made her tell him about Johnny and young Henry she didn't know. Perhaps it had something to do with their isolated retreat, the fair far below, Chalcombe miles away and Wilhampton in another world. She'd wanted to forget it, to make a carefree oasis of the day. He knew the foundry had come to her from her husband but, until that day, he knew no more.

'I'd say you're well rid of him, Beth, and he'll have met his match in Hal.'

'And Phoebe? She believes he's a walking miracle.'

'Then don't grudge her her illusions. I dare say theirs isn't the first marriage to start that way. She'll come to terms, as she has to. Let her keep her dreams as long as she can.'

'You sound bitter, perhaps you've reason. I know different. I never lost my illusions – because they were based on the truth. When I was first married I thought Henry almost a god, and I never had cause to change my view. I lost my

343

awe of him but . . .,' she paused, then mentally shaking herself and forcing new spirit into her voice: 'life goes on and we have to do what we can with it. So you think I should just wash my hands of Johnny and Hal too and be thankful Stewart Lovejoy is at the helm?'

'Ah, that I do and more than that, be glad young Henry's there too. For if your husband still has an eye on things I'll wager he's the happier for it.'

They sat silently, watching the movement of the fair far below and beyond it the open, empty sea. The conversation seemed to be over when she said: 'But could I have acted differently? Right from the start ought I to have bowed out, asked Hal? – but then he was too angry, too hurt.'

'Beth, you did what you had to do. Your husband put his trust in you and to bow out, as you call it, would have proved he'd been wrong. It'll work out, give it time. It's my bet that young Henry moving across is the first link in a chain between you. Keep faith with what you feel is honest and right then you must succeed.'

'Honest, right, you say. And here am I planning to carry tales to Mr Meredith and to other customers we've lost.'

'And by God so you should. Hal and Johnny dealt the hand, it's up to you to win the trick.'

She lay back on the mossy grass and closed her eyes; the air was still chilly but the mid-day sun brilliant. For a moment Ellis was forgotten. She felt light, her cares lifted (shared would be nearer the truth, but to Beth it amounted to so nearly the same thing). Only briefly did her eyes stay closed; a touch of his lips on hers and they flew open to see his face only inches from hers.

'Do you ever give a thought to me when you're in that world where I've no part? Do you want me like I want you?'

'Ellis don't, don't.' She sat up. 'You've a wife, a child down there who calls her Mama.'

'Yes I've a child but I've no wife nor ever have had in Eugene as you very well know. Answer me – do you forget me when you get on that train? You haunt my thoughts, I wish to God you didn't. I wish I could love you lightly, love you and leave you like any other woman I've taken.'

'Do I want you? you say, and then in the same breath "any other woman". As if I'm some common whore for your pleasure because you wife shuts her door against you.' Her voice was ice cold, yet there was an unnatural pitch to it. Inside her a thousand butterflies fluttered. 'And I talked to you of my blessed Henry.' Her teeth clenched on the heel of her thumb; all her will power went into holding her chin steady.

'You talk to me of Henry, yes, and I'll tell you why. Because he'd understand how I feel about you. Some whore you say, oh, Beth, Beth, I've never wanted a woman as I want you — I want you in my bed (or out here under the clear sky), I want you waiting on the quay as I sail back into harbour, I want you pouring my tea in the morning. I want to laugh with you, I want mine to be the shoulder you cry on.'

Again she was lying, eyes closed, her sudden tension gone.

'And if I want all that too — still you have a wife.'

'Ay, I have a wife.' He lay back too, taking her hand firmly in his. He felt her fingers cling.

'Just tell me, Beth. Let me hear you say it.'

'Yes, I want all those things. I'm ashamed of my own longings. I don't think I'm like other women, they —'

'That you're not,' he spoke softly, teasing her now. 'I've never known one like you. You and I together, Beth, we could make the bells of heaven ring.'

'It's madness, all of it. Nothing to do with real life, either yours or mine.' He heard the break in her voice and at the same moment saw the children climbing up the path towards them.

'Here, take a swig of this. The others are coming,' unscrewing the stopper from his flask as he spoke.

She poured the fiery liquid into her mouth, neat rum, enough to make her eyes water as she gulped!

'What's wrong, Mother, aren't you well?' Nicky was the first up the hill.

'Nothing's wrong,' she gasped. 'I felt shivery sitting here. Mr Trafford gave me a gulp from his flask to warm me.' Then to Ellis: 'I've never tasted anything like it. It's sweet, warm, rich . . .'

'Not a drink for the timid ladies. Like stolen fruit, Beth, always the sweetest.'

The children were back. Liza had been right, Cecily had sent far more food than any child could eat; no doubt she'd had Ellis in mind.

In the afternoon there were the water races. Beth could understand now why Ellis had rowed from Chalcombe instead of walking the cliff path like the rest of them. There wasn't a man to compare with him; he pulled off his oiled wool sweater and rolled up his sleeves. His wrists and arms had the strength of steel, his open shirt showed the dark hair on his chest; his broad shoulders, his curly hair and clipped beard, everything about him set him on a different plane from any of the other competitors.

'Give me a talisman.' he asked it of Beth but Liza was quick to push a handkerchief into his hand, her best silk one given her by Cecily for her birthday. 'Thanks, Liza, that should bring me luck. And what about you, Beth, you'll find me something, eh?'

She unpinned her brooch and fastened it to his shirt. The others were already at the water's edge; only Liza stayed with them and as Beth secured the charm she moved closer to her father.

As he pulled away from the shore in the line of starters her voice strained after him: 'Have you got the good luck hanky?' He didn't seem to hear her. Of course he won. It was evident from the initial pull at the oars, he was going to come home first even with neither handkerchief nor brooch.

346

The hours of daylight were still short, it was only early April, so soon after the race they had to start the homeward journey. This time they travelled in style, rowed by Ellis with one pair of sculls and Ted and Nick sitting side by side with one each. What had been said on the cliff top hung close to Beth, close but not near enough to have reality. Later she'd think, she'd remember; she knew the moment would come, but not yet. Tomorrow she'd go away, she had problems enough to face, but for now these too were held at bay as they glided homeward, the only sound the even rhythm of the oars breaking the water.

'. . . didn't I tell you she'd not last?' Cecily's voice could be heard as they came into the hall.

'Hush,' Lucy answered, 'they're home.'

'Indeed we are, and what a day we've had.' Beth spoke as they poured into the drawing-room. Whatever secret the two women had been sharing was swallowed now in the children's excitement.

'Look Aunt Lucy, have you ever seen one like this before? It's called a coconut. I won it. Will it taste like cocoa do you suppose?'

'Charles dear, how clever of you. No I don't believe it does. Perhaps Mrs Murphy knows what you have to do with it.'

'And see, Aunt Lucy, I bought you these ribbons. They were so pretty I thought you'd like them.'

'Vicky, they're lovely. I'll trim the bonnet I'm making Bella with this pretty pink.'

'I didn't get you anything, Aunt Lucy,' Nick put in his spoke, 'but we had humbugs and I've saved you some. It looks sticky but truly it tastes jolly good.'

Lucy beamed at them all, the purpose of Cecily's visit overshadowed. How could she so often feel herself hard done by when the children gave her such affection? 'Bless your hearts. And you've had a happy day? I'm certainly glad to see you're safely home.'

Three voices proceeded to regale her with tales of the

347

day and Cecily, her news so momentous it had to be told, turned to Beth. 'She's gone. Didn't I always say she would? Good riddance to her too. Taken the boy, I will say that for her. To tell the truth I expected one of these days she'd be off and leave him behind. She knows I've always been like a mother to Liza, Franck wouldn't have lacked for care. But no, she's packed their things and gone.'

'Where?'

'How do I know where? Wherever her latest beau is I dare say. Trapped Ellis she did and now I suppose she's taken a fancy elsewhere.' She'd been so enjoying the telling of her tale that only now it seemed she saw it was to Beth that she spoke. Her expression changed, she was wary, guarded. 'Or perhaps he's told you already. Real to-do they had last night it seems – but you'll know all about that.' She gave Beth a smile that was no smile. 'Been with you all day I'm sure. He's a lad for the ladies is my Ellis.' She was little short of coy now. 'Always has been. Doesn't mean anything, never alters the man he really is – been the same all his days – but that one, she made up her mind she'd hook him. Well, much good did it do her.'

For once Beth seemed lost for an answer. 'You'll be late for bed if we don't get on, you children. Ring the bell, Nicky, and we'll tell Jenny we're ready for supper as soon as we've had a wash. We'll none of us change this evening. Will you stay, Cecily?'

'Dear me, no. I just came to have a chat with Lucy, tell her about things. I must get back and see to some supper for mine. Liza will be back in her bed in my attic tonight. Poor Ellis can't leave her alone and the boats will be off on the tide before daybreak.'

Lucy wasn't bothered about Ellis's arrangements; she was too taken aback by what Beth had said. 'Not change! Beth, never have the children come to the table looking like it! Out in the air all day, they look like gypsies. Tut-tut-tut . . .'

'The children and me too.' Beth was pleased enough

with their appearance, evidence of a good day's outing. 'But we're far too hungry to worry about clean dresses.'

Lucy's sniff was her only answer. All the years dear Papa had schooled her and yet Beth was what she always had been – the stable lad's sister! It was no way to rear those dear children; the sooner they were back at school the better. How proud she was of Edwin, so smart with his fair hair brushed, his Eton collar stiff and white. Lucy smoothed her hands over her plump stomach and walked to the front door with Cecily for a last whispered word.

The next morning Beth was catching the early train to Wilhampton.

'By the way, Lucy,' she said as she was about to leave, 'we've had changes at the foundry. Young Henry wants to be at Copeland's and quite right too, and Johnny sees a better future for himself with Hal.'

'It's bringing that stranger in, putting him higher than Johnny. Dear, dear, poor Johnny and he's worked so hard on his travels.' Predictable as ever Lucy gave her opinion. Or was she? For once Beth had cause to wonder as she went on: 'I'm so glad about Henry though. Nonsense to expect the boy to go into Harknell's; Copeland's is where he belongs.'

Once back at the foundry she spent what was left of the day with Henry. She might have none of Stewart's knowledge but she'd had years of experience, and the confidence she'd lost when she'd been alone had returned. Nowadays she played a role she knew and understood and certainly she was able to give the boy a broad-based outline on to which Stewart could build.

The working day was almost over. She'd already sent Henry home and had heard Algy and the trap arrive ready to collect her.

'Mrs Copeland,' Stewart called as he knocked on her door, 'are you still here?'

'Yes, Stewart, I'm just off but come in.'

'There's a caller for you on the telephone – it's from

Chalcombe, someone called Trafford. If you wait I'll pass it on to your instrument.'

Chalcombe! The children – the sea – the fishing boats – a hundred possible accidents crowded her mind. No one would make a telephone call without very good reason. Stewart's thoughts were much the same. He knew nothing of the boats, the high harbour wall, the dozens of possibilities, but he knew only trouble would bring a message this way. He pressed the key and turned the handle, waited until he heard Beth's bell ring, then replaced his ear-piece. Not his business, he told himself, but she might need him; he'd be prepared. So outside her door he listended to the one-sided conversation.

'Ellis, what's happened? Is it the children? . . . Gone? All day? . . . Yes, yes I knew about Eugene, but would she have tried to follow her? . . . No, that's what I thought . . . But Cecily's place is like home to her, why should she? . . . No of course you don't know. I'm sorry, I'm being no help. Ellis, what can I say? I'll come back, that's what I'll do. There's a late train I'm sure . . . Of course (Yes, of course he'd needed to talk to her) I don't know what time, but I'll come straight to your house.'

Liza had gone. No explanation, no hint, Cecily said she'd had breakfast at six o'clock with the rest of them and that was the last she'd seen of her. She hadn't worried when she'd strayed off home, why should she? And in any case Liza always spent hours on her own, sometimes by the boats or in the sheds, sometimes on the rocks; no one ever thought it necessary to keep an eye on her.

'As the morning went on I took it she was off playing somewhere, likely enough with Vicky Copeland. She didn't come in for her dinner. That's when I started to wonder, sent Ted round the village when he told me she'd not shown up at Vicky's. No one had seen her, not all day.' Cecily wasn't easily upset, but as the afternoon had worn on and she'd watched the fishing boats nearing harbour she'd been haunted by pictures of what might have befallen the child. Nothing would keep Liza from the quay as the *Helping Hand* tied up, yet today she wasn't there. So Ellis heard the story. Perhaps his imagination was less fertile than Cecily's, for he hardly listened to her suggestions: 'She might have run off after Franck, fond of Franck she was.' What about that fair she went to yesterday? Can't trust fair people, likely they've taken her, they're moving off today.' Ellis's eyes scanned the cliff face, the rocks. Somewhere she must be lying hurt.

It wasn't until later when he went to her room, driven by some inner voice that despite all his reason told him to listen to Cecily's warnings, that he noticed her pillow lying without a cover. Strange. He opened her drawer a few inches, a cold hand of fear touching him. Her few clothes were gone – and that trinket box that had been her mother's, hadn't that always been her most treasured possession? That was gone too. Helplessly he looked around as if some explanation would present itself. She'd seemed the same as usual; he'd not noticed that anything had upset her. Surely with Eugene going she would feel freer. He needed help, he didn't know where to turn. That was when he rang Beth.

By the time she hurried though the village, passed the Green and Penrhyn House, to the quay and up Middle Lane to his house, it was quite dark. 'Let her be safe, don't let anything have happened to her, let her be home,' she begged. The door was unlocked, the lamp lit.

'Ellis, I'm here,' she called to the empty room, surprised at the appetizing smell of food. No reply. Perhaps he was upstairs; that would be it, she must be home and he'd be upstairs with her in her room. From the hall-way she called again: 'Ellis, is she back?'

A bedroom door opened and Cecily came out.

'You! Haven't you caused trouble enough, upsetting the

poor mite like you have? Now you come here bold as brass at this hour of the evening.'

'Upset her, how could I have upset her? She was with us all day yesterday – '

'Ah, so she was. I thought that other one had no shame the way she set her cap at him but at least she didn't do it in front of the child.'

'I'm not wasting time talking to you. I didn't come all this way to listen to your rubbish. Where's Ellis?'

'Out. There's a party of them, searching the cliffs.' She bit her lip, her anger at Beth nothing compared with her alarm for Liza. 'Taken lamps they have to shine down, see if she's slipped – poor little soul, poor little love. And you come waltzing in here as if you own the place! I heard about the carryings on yesterday, lying on the grass there. Seems half Chalcombe was a witness to it, small wonder she's upset. How much of his day did he give to her? Not much I hear. Eyes and hands too busy with you.'

'Have my children run off thinking I ignored them yesterday? No, of course not.'

'Likely your children don't care for you like she does for him. You're never with them. What sort of a mother do you call yourself?'

Beth turned towards the door, she had no intention of explaining herself to Cecily; if that was the way she saw things what did it matter?

'Why don't you stay away from here!' In normal circumstances Cecily would never had spoken like it, but there was nothing normal about this nightmare of an evening. Liza was as dear as her own brothers and sisters and somewhere she was out there hiding, lost or even hurt. Anxiety loosened her tongue just as it made her voice harsh. 'We don't need your sort in Chalcombe. Now that the French women has gone, why can't you leave us alone? He'd look to me, I've always known it. You with your fancy clothes, your airs and graces and fast ways, I knew what you were even before I heard of your behaviour yesterday. Think yourself no end of a lady – well, we'll see. We don't take to those sort of goings on here, we – '

Beth had gone.

At Penrhyn House the children, Lucy and Mrs Murphy had all retired for the night. She arrived just as Jenny was bolting the door.

'I want a lamp, Jenny. Find me one while I put on some stout boots, then I'm joining the hunt.'

'Then, m'am, I'm coming with you. No time of night for you to be wandering the shore alone.'

The party on the cliff top had moved along in the direction of St Mary's, their lights no more than mere dots in the black distance. The tide was low now. Beth and Jenny walked on the beach, they shone their lamps into the caves, they called. The night was empty.

By the time they returned along the quay their boots were sodden, the hems of their dresses too, the tide was coming up the beach and the rocks were covered. A light still burnt in Ellis's sitting-room. Cecily must be waiting for the search party to get back.

Cecily had said it was because of Beth that Liza had gone, and so it was.

'Take a cloth and wipe these dishes for me, there's a good girl,' she'd said as she'd cleared away the breakfast, 'I can see you'll be here for nights often now she's gone off, so we'll have to work together.'

'I'm not a baby, Aunt Cecily. I'm old enough to make breakfast for Father, to take care of our home.'

'No need for that. You've always a place here, both of you, and he likes to know I look after you. Since you were a babe it's been like that. Now that she's gone you'll see how happy we shall all be.' Thoughtfully she looked at Liza, wondering how far she could go. She didn't want things repeated to Ellis. 'There's only one person can spoil things and that's Mrs Copeland. She's got pretty ways, knows how to butter up a man. She's the one we have to watch out for, make sure she doesn't get the chance to spend her time with your father.'

'He likes her,' it was hardly more than a growl, 'keeps looking at her. Yesterday – it was funny – as if we weren't there sometimes.'

'What had they so important to talk about then, dear? There's a good girl. See how quickly we get done when we do things together. Oh it is nice to have you here. What did they find to say that cut you out then?'

'Nothing, They hardly said anything at all to each other. If they talked it was to us, yet it was just themselves they were thinking about. I could tell.' She mumbled, her words aimed at some point on the floor.

'Poor little soul.' Cecily put her arm around her. 'Men are such fools where a pretty woman is concerned. That Mama you had here, she was bad enough – '

'That wasn't a bit like with Mrs Copeland. I don't think he cared that I was there, Aunt Cecily . . .' Her dark eyes were full of hurt.

Cecily put the last of her plates away and sat down at the kitchen table. 'He doesn't see I'm there either. All he sees is that woman. Think how happy we could be without her . . . Don't tell him what we say.'

Then, taking a broom and duster from the cupboard: 'I'm off upstairs, are you coming?'

'No, I'm going home. He may have left me things to see to. It's my place now, Aunt Cecily; I want to be able to look after him.'

'Yes, love, of course you do. Mark my words, though, he won't notice. Eyes for nothing but that red-headed m'lady.'

Back at home Liza went up to her own room. The house was very quiet with Eugene and Franck gone. Father wouldn't be back until tea-time or later. She sat on the edge of the bed remembering what Cecily had said. Wouldn't notice her, eyes only for Mrs Copeland; yesterday that had certainly been true, no one else had existed for him. She shivered, the morning was cold, the house was cold, the world was cold, empty, lonely. He'd never made her feel cut off before. Often he didn't talk to her; she was happy working silently with him mending a net or sitting by his side in the shack where he did his books. Some fathers were different, she knew, some of them were all hugs and kisses. Hers wasn't like that; she'd never expected it. Mama had told her about Vicky's mother, how he was always watching for her, waiting to take her on his boat or lately go to her house. And now he didn't care about anyone else. She gulped and pulled her hanky from her pocket to blow her nose.

'Didn't even really want my hanky.' She said it aloud. By now she was crying. 'Only took it to please me. It was her talisman that mattered – I hate her, I hate her, I wish she could be killed . . .' But if she were, he'd be sad, he'd still be no nearer, perhaps even further away.

For a long time she sat there, her tears no more now than an occasional gulp. Gradually the idea came to her, she knew what she had to do. Like so many only children she was old for her years, half child and half woman. Instinctively she knew one thing and what she did stemmed from that hysterical thought: 'I wish she'd be killed.' In grief one would hold his love.

She had no bag to pack her things in, the pillow-case was the best she could do. Her few clothes were crammed in and her one or two treasures carefully added. Downstairs she stopped to take a large lump of bread from the earthenware tub in the larder and cut a slab of cheese, then she was ready. The folds of her winter cape were full, it wasn't difficult to carry her bundle hidden out of sight but even so she didn't want to be seen going through the village.

Up Middle Lane and into Commons Road she went, over the top of the hill, leaving Chalcombe and the sea behind her.

CHAPTER FOURTEEN

For a day the talk of the village had been Eugene's departure, but for no longer. By the next morning word of Liza's disappearance spread; Eugene, who'd never found favour in the community, was forgotten.

The short bright spell of weather was over. A dull sky brought cold drizzling rain, but even so parties set off to scour the area. Had she had any money? Could she have taken a train? It seemed unlikely; from the sixpence Ellis had given her at the fair she couldn't have enough left to be any use. Like Vicky, she'd bought ribbons and she'd paid to see the dancing bear. No, she must have walked. In all directions people searched; they looked in hay barns, in cattle sheds, and in the village there wasn't a house where the coal store wasn't checked, even the wells were prodded with long poles.

At the end of the day Beth and Ellis came back to his empty house, neither admitting their hope of finding her safely there before them, neither acknowledging their hollow disappointment at finding no sign of her.

Beth was seeing a new side of Ellis. 'What have I done wrong, Beth? Over and over I think it; somewhere I've let her down. She never seemed unhappy – and God dammit you can't tell me she's chasing after Eugene and Franck. So what have I done? What have I not done?' In twenty-four hours he looked ten years older, haggard with sleeplessness, sick with fear.

'It's not you. Ellis, she worships you – perhaps that's the trouble, she's given her love just to you.'

'Then what's she doing this to me for?'

'She's muddled, she doesn't understand.' A new strength seemed to sustain her. She felt his need, she knew so well what had knocked Liza's world awry. Her heart reached out where it always did in moments when alone she was weak, to Henry. Steady, reassuring, always her rock and her anchor. He guided her now. Just to think of him was to know where he would turn for help, where his trust would be.

Firmly she took Ellis's hands in hers. 'Close your eyes Ellis. Together we'll beg for her to come back. When two or more are gathered . . . Now Ellis.'

His fingers gripped hers, his eyes shut. 'Oh dear God, somehow I've failed her, forgive me, send her back . . .'

Beth heard the break in his voice, she took up the plea: 'Be with her and don't let her come to harm, don't let her be frightened, she's just a child. We should have thought. Bring her back to him.' And silently, only half formed in her mind, but stirring her conscience for all that, was the bargain she was striking with her Maker. She hadn't the courage to find the words for it but her inner voice whispered that if Ellis had this second chance the sacrifice they laid on the altar must be her.

At some point their hands must have loosened their hold, for as she finished speaking she was holding him in her arms. He'd had no sleep since the dawn sailing on Tuesday. It was now nearly midnight Wednesday. Fatigue and hunger, fear and anxiety, all these combined to bring him down as they sank to the couch he turned his head away from her, his voice tight and strained. 'God help her. Give me another chance.'

Cecily must have been in. On the range in the kitchen was a saucepan of soup. Beth brought some to him, just that and bread. He picked up the spoon, then put it down.

'Try and eat. Tomorrow we'll take the trap, go further. You must eat.'

'What about her? Who's feeding her?' He leant back with his eyes closed.

'Well, one thing I know,' here was the old Beth again, the fight was coming back, 'she'll need you to look after her when you finally track her down. Not much use if you're faint from hunger and tiredness. Come on now, take a spoonful, dip some bread in.'

He did as she said, obediently, like a child, hardly seeming aware of what he ate. She rinsed the plate in the scullery and when she came back he was asleep, so deeply asleep that he didn't stir when she raise his feet on to the couch and put a cushion under his head. His coat was hanging on the back door; gently she covered him then left.

The next morning by the time she woke it was after nine o'clock. Breakfast was over. Jenny had taken the law into her own hands and told the family: 'We're not to disturb the missus,' and believing the instructions had come from her they left Beth in peace.

When it came to the question of hunting for Liza, even Lucy's tut-tutting was silenced. That a child could be unhappy enough to run away from home seemed too dreadful to contemplate. No doubt Cecily was right; it was because of her father and Beth. Ought to be ashamed, the pair of them. Nothing in it of course, nothing serious. Beth was showing herself in her true colours and, as for him, as Cecily had said, he'd always been the same. Women were his playthings, he'd pick them up and drop them easy as wink. The little girl, bless her innocent heart, she'd not know about that, she'd misunderstand. She must be found, brought home and cared for. Dear Cecily would look after her. Time enough once she was safe to turn to Beth; and just imagine how Papa had expected them all to respect her. Bah! A no good wanton; likely she always had been.

All four children from Penrhyn House had gone over the cliffs, covering the same ground, but morning bringing new hope, perhaps there was somewhere they'd missed. By the time Beth hurried to Middle Lane she found the shed empty, the trap already gone.

No use walking the same lanes again. She went to the

station. She'd catch the first train that came, no matter which way it was going, she'd get off at the first station and start from there.

Radleigh must have been six or seven miles inland, a group of cottages, a stream with a mill, a church, an inn, a disproportionately large rectory, a huddle of cottages, a saddler, a blacksmith and surprisingly enough a platform where the train hissed itself to a halt. First she enquired at the inn. No, no child had called there, nor at the grocer's. What had made Beth so sure she didn't know, but she'd climbed down from the carriage full of a new hope and, because of it, now the disappointment was all the greater.

'I'm looking for a little girl,' she shouted to the blacksmith above the clamour of his hammering.

''Morning m'am.' He unbent his tall frame and turned to her. 'Looking for what, did ye say?'

'A little girl. About eleven, dark, curly hair. Has she called here?'

'That she hasn't, m'am. You mean she's lost? Where's she from? Round these parts?'

'No, she's from Chalcombe. She disappeared two days ago. Her father's out hunting in the trap – he may come to Radleigh himself – I came by train.'

'Run off of a purpose you're reckoning?'

Beth nodded. 'She took her things. If you see her, if anyone tells you they've seen her, her father has the fishing boats at Chalcombe, Trafford is his name.'

'I'll keep my eyes open for the lassie, but there's nowt to bring her here you know. Try yonder up the road and round the corner in Penny Lane; you'll find Percy Murdock the baker there. Happen she'll have asked for a bite to eat.'

Hope rose again. Beth thanked him and went on, only to draw another blank at Percy Murdock's. It was as she came out of the bake-house that she bumped into a man, his shining leather gaiters, check jacket and tall brown bowler setting him apart from the others she'd spoken to. A landowner no doubt, probably the Squire.

'Mrs Trafford,' his tone brooked no argument, 'your little girl, I believe I have her at the Manor. Came to our door on Tuesday night, soaked from head to foot and covered with mud. I'd have sent her packing back home but she begged me not to. Said you'd gone off somewhere ... some cock and bull story, I couldn't understand half of it. Said she was older than she looked and used to housework — that her Mama never did much.' His tone left Beth in no doubt of what he thought of the Mrs Trafford he supposed her to be. 'So we gave her a place in the kitchen and I'm not so sure she's not better off there than with a mother who uses her —'

'I'm not her mother, I'm a family friend. Her father's crazed with worry, has been searching every hour since he found her gone. Please, where is she? I'll see she gets back to him.'

'You'd best come with me to Joe Soames's smithy. I'll collect the cart and we'll fetch her out.'

Five minutes later she was riding by his side in the governess cart. She'd traced Liza! The force that had driven her was suddenly gone and she felt a strange numbness. What was that bargain she'd made as she'd petitioned for the child's safe return to Ellis? Outside the Manor she waited in the cart, five minutes, ten — then the Squire (for she had no idea of his name) came back, this time with Liza. One look at Beth and her face crumpled. Relief, the man supposed and even Beth hoped that had something to do with it, but she knew all too well that she was the last person Liza had wanted to see.

They were taken to the railway halt and there left. When a train to Chalmouth was due Beth had no idea. There was no sign of one coming. Liza showed no resistance, yet no repentance for the trouble and concern she'd caused either.

'Your father's been half crazed with worry. Whatever made you do such a thing to him? Will you miss your

Mama and Franck so very much?' If only that could be the reason!

'She's not my Mama and I shan't miss her at all.' Her head was turned away, her voice insolent.

'Then what made you do such a cruel thing to him?'

''S' not cruel,' she mumbled, still not looking at Beth. 'Didn't think he'd hardly notice.'

'Oh, Liza, that's not true and you know it very well. You and you father do lots of things together – why what about the jobs you do with him in the sheds? Who would help him?'

'Why don't you?' Her bottom lip stuck out, and the corners of her mouth were not quite steady.

'Why don't I? Well, he's never asked me to. I suppose he didn't know you were tired of helping him.'

''Course I'm not.'

A trail of smoke came into sight; the train was coming. Beth wished she had longer, a six-mile journey gave her no time at all. Luck was with her though, at least the carriage they got into was empty.

'Liza,' she plunged straight in as soon as she'd slammed the door, 'I don't know why you did what you did and you don't need to tell me. But tell him, be honest with him. How would you have felt if he'd gone away, left you without so much as a word?'

Liza was crying now, great shuddering sobs. She wiped the back of her hand across eyes and nose alike.

'Here, have my hanky.'

'Don't want it. He only wants you, only wants your things. "Run away Liza", he says, "I'm going to Mrs Copeland's, go back indoors" – "Go round and see Aunt Cecily" – "Go 'way" – "Go away" – that's what he wanted, me to go 'way.' Her voice had been gruff before, now her sobs seemed to come from the depths. Every instinct in Beth was to take her shaking little body in her arms and Beth always followed her instinct.

'Don't,' Liza struggled, 'don't.'

'Stop it,' Beth shook her. 'We've only got a few minutes, Liza, listen to me.' The shake had done more than the embrace. Another back of hand wipe and two woeful darks eyes turned her way.

'I don't know what you believe about your father and me but whatever it is can't come between you and him. You are his own daughter, a part of him, something different from anyone else whether you're thinking of Eugene, me, Aunt Cecily. I remember when I was a little girl.' (And strangely, now after all these years she believed what she said was true.) 'There's a different relationship between a father and daughter from any other. You can love lots of people – one of these days you'll grow up and get married but it won't alter how you feel for your father, not a scrap. No one else can ever take your place for him, nor his for you. Now blow your nose.'

'He didn't want my hanky,' a solitary tear escaped, 'didn't bring him luck. It was your brooch – '

'Oh what nonsense! You know and I know, it was neither. He won the race because he was the finest man who rowed in it. You should be proud to have him for your father.'

''Course I am.' She took the proffered hanky and blew.

'Now then I want you to think a bit more and I'll tell you a secret.'

'Tell me one?' Liza's spirits must have been reviving. At the thought of being made Beth's confidante she passed the handkerchief back and sat up ready to listen.

'Yes, you, because I know how much you care about him. You see, it's because he is what he is that as I've come to know him I've learnt to love him too. That's a secret, mind, not a word to a living soul – cross your heart.'

'Cross my heart,' she nodded solemnly.

'That doesn't mean I love Nicholas, Victoria or Charles any less than I did though. We don't slice up our affection like a slab of cake, a piece for one and a piece for another. For all sorts of reasons I can't be in Chalcombe very often

– but when I am I want to be with him. Is that greedy? Is it wrong? It's not taking anything from you, Liza – nor from the twins and Charles.'

Liza was quiet, seeming to digest this piece of adult reasoning. When at last she spoke the train was already nearing Chalcombe. 'They wouldn't like it 'cos they'd want you still to love their Papa.'

The carriage was rocking furiously from side to side as they lost speed.

'I'll always love their Papa. Oh, Liza, how can I make you see? One day you'll know, but it's now that matters.'

The little girl stood up and with a pathetic dignity pulled her cape around her shoulders. 'Seems a rum sort of love to me,' her tone held criticism, almost pity. 'I'm glad you shared your secret – and thank you for bringing me home to Father. It was horrid in that big house.' The train clattered to a halt.

Ellis wasn't back when they got to Middle Lane; but Beth didn't wait. She told herself that Liza deserved to have him to herself in the first moments of reunion, but in fact it was more than that. This afternoon she'd said things that she'd not admitted even to herself. 'I've learnt to love him too.' So there it was, spoken, positive, accepted and no longer pushed to the back of her consciousness. 'When I come to Chalcombe I want to be with him.' And so she did. She'd been drawn to the place from that first day, but how would she feel here now if it weren't for Ellis? Then there was something else that drove her away; there was that bargain she'd made as she begged that Liza might be brought safely home. Beth called it faith; Henry might have frowned on it, called it superstition. Either way, Beth had never been one to break a promise.

She'd come from Wilhampton on Tuesday evening, so on the Thursday evening she returned. 'A thousand things to do,' she told Lucy and the children, 'but you stay on, see the rest of your holiday out here.' Only her heart knew what she was running from. Yet when the children went back to school and Lucy, Charles and Isabella returned to the Court, despite Lucy's: 'How our table does suffer. Mrs Murphy's skills wasted down there,' it was more than stubbornness that made Beth reply: 'No use a house at the seaside and no one there to see it's ready when we need it.'

Between Lucy and Cecily letters passed, news came that 'little Liza is making a real home for her father'. Certainly each day Mrs Ogbourne came to prepare the meals and much more beside, but Liza felt needed at last. 'Perhaps we were wrong, perhaps a certain party I won't mention hadn't set her cap at him,' Cecily decided, although her own hopes had faded. Lucy remembered her own views as she'd watched, to say nothing of a hint or two dropped by Mrs Murphy. 'No, not Ellis Trafford. She'd not stay away so long if she were after him,' she concluded. 'It's the flattery of any man, that's what she's after, must have a man to pay court to her. Poor Papa was quite bewitched by her pretty ways. Without him to make a fuss of her she must be feeling the blank and no mistake.'

So April gave way to May and each week Beth spent days travelling in Johnny's tracks, winning back what Copeland's had lost and, she prided herself, gaining new ground too. It was only a temporary thing and she made that clear wherever she went.

'I shall engage a new man,' she told old Mr Meredith, 'but this time I'll be more wary. Before I hand my trust to anyone else I wanted to see you myself, to reassure you that Copeland's is far from declining; indeed, the contrary. My husband never fell behind with a delivery date nor yet could his work have been bettered. I promise you his standards will always be upheld.' Whether it was the proud tilt of her lovely head, the hint of battle in her green eyes or simply that in the olds days they'd always been happy with Copeland's and were glad to re-establish the relationship, whatever the reason the order book grew full. 'Henry Copeland & Sons, from this day forward' they'd toasted on that Maundy Thursday. As summer came it seemed their trust had been justified.

And all these weeks she tried to put Ellis from her mind. She hadn't succeeded but at least her days were full and her life had a purpose as she travelled. Word of what she was doing filtered through to Chalcombe, from Lucy to Cecily, from her to her father, from him to Ellis. It seemed she had no need of him. A proud man, an arrogant one too; even to himself he didn't consider his lifestyle inferior. Granted the Copelands were monied – well, if that's what she wanted . . .

There are limits to how far good resolutions can carry one, there are limits to the loneliness one can bear, especially when the warm sun shines from a clear blue sky. Somewhere the thought of a far horizon was beckoning, the tall chimneys of the foundry belching their foul smoke mocked her. It was the end of May, early evening and Algy was waiting in the yard to take her home. She and Stewart had spent an hour or more talking, always business, always in unison. She smiled at him as she closed the drawer of her desk.

'The evenings are lengthening, Stewart. Have you settled in the town? Have you made friends?'

'I've met a number of people – I'm never a person to need a lot of entertainment, my interests are here in my work. Dull people might think, but it's not. I find it adventure enough.'

She nodded. How lucky she was to have him here. That he misinterpreted the gesture led him to say: 'Yes indeed the evenings are lengthening; they are emptier by far than the days. Mrs Copeland, it's presumptuous of me even to suggest it, but we always find things of interest to talk about – may I invite you to take supper with me at the Royal?'

'Presumptuous!' She laughed, wanting to take the sting out of her refusal, 'it's no such thing. But no, Stewart. From here I'm going straight to the station, I shall be away

365

for a few days. The foundry is safe in your good hands.' The decison had been instantaneous, she'd clutched at it almost in fear, as an escape. She and Stewart worked together in such harmony, only now did she see the danger signs. The danger wasn't that he was going to get hurt, it was of herself she thought. Only she knew the aching loneliness. With each week it grew harder to bear the foundry with young Henry and Stewart, the Court with Lucy and Charles, the nights an empty void of solitude. She knew herself well, she was honest, Stewart wasn't unattractive . . . The 7.15 train from Wilhampton took her on her way to Ellis.

The tide was low when she arrived, the boats at sea. On an impulse, instead of going to Penrhyn House, she went first to Middle Lane. There was always a chance he'd not sailed that day; sometimes Abe took the *Helping Hand* without him.

'Mrs Copeland, Mrs Copeland.' She turned at the sound of Liza's voice and waited as the child ran to catch up with her. 'I've been to Aunt Cecily's. Father's fishing for hours yet so I'm going home to bed now. Would you like to come home with me – I could make us some supper cocoa?'

Something must have taken away Liza's mistrust of her, whether it was their talk on the train or because she'd stayed away so long she couldn't tell.

'That sounds lovely. I missed my supper. Cocoa will be splendid.'

It was more than the warm, sweet drink she welcomed, it was Liza's confidence, the friendly way she passed the cups so that Beth could mix the paste while she heated the milk; it was the acceptance. A far cry from the lost little soul she'd been the last time they'd been together.

'You're happy, Liza?' Beth was never one to beat about the bush. 'You and your father look after each other. Cecily wrote and told Lucy how well you're getting along.'

Liza nodded. 'Oh yes, we are. And I remember the

things you explained, 'bout me being different from anyone else from outside, anyone like you or Mama. I've thought a lot about it.'

'And you know I'm right?'

Again she nodded. 'But I expect he does need a grown-up friend. I play with Clemmy – her Pa's the baker you know – and with Vicky when she's here, so I suppose he needs someone too.'

Beth smiled at her; she was learning fast.

'When I've had my cocoa I have to go to bed. I promised Father I'd be in bed at the proper time and be asleep when he came in.' She picked up their empty cups and together they washed them. Then Beth went to Penrhyn House.

'Oh, Mrs Copeland, m'am, it's that good to see you and so unexpected at this time o' night too.' Jenny's welcome never varied. 'I'll get you something to eat; there's a nice cut of cold beef and I'll – '

'No, Jenny, I'm not hungry. What I want more than anything is some hot water for a bath.'

'Then I'll get the geyser lit. It'll take a while to hot up though, m'am.'

'I know. Don't you wait up, Jenny. Just light the geyser; I'll see to the bath myself. Today I've travelled from Northampton to Oxford, then to Wilhampton, then on down here – I declare I'm full of smuts from the railway.'

'And ready for bed too, I expect. I'll put a light to that gas.'

As she warned though, the geyser took time. It was more than an hour later that Beth lowered herself into the bath tub, the steaming water smelling of the scent she'd so liberally tipped in. She shut her eyes revelling in the tingle of the hot water on her skin. Only now did she let herself face the step she'd taken in coming here. She'd broken her silent and secret promise – but did that matter? Liza had been glad to see her. That hurdle had been removed.

Finally she pulled up the plug and heard the water gushing away down the pipe, she towelled herself vigorously, she brushed her hair. Tomorrow she'd see him! Even now through her bedroom window the lights on the returning boats were clear.

Between the cool sheets she lay, longing for it to be morning. She turned on her left side, a moment later on her right; she pummelled the pillow, lay on her back, she sat up and peered through the window. The lights were much nearer now. Again she lay down. In the morning she'd see him! This way she tossed and that, sleep never any nearer.

Upstairs slept Mrs Murphy and Jenny – and certainly one of them proclaimed the fact, the resonant snores echoing down the steep attic stairway when, much later, Beth opened her door and crept out. Like a thief she tiptoed barefoot down to the hall, then out into the night air, closing the door silently by turning the key in the lock, for a slam would shatter the stillness. Only then did she slip her shoes on. She'd not meant to do this when she'd undressed for bed. Even as she stepped as lightly as she could towards the harbour, she was surprised to find herself where she was. Dawn was already bringing silvery light in the east, the world was held in that moment of wonder before the sun casts its first golden ray.

In the light on the deck of the *Helping Hand* she could see him clearly, watch unseen as the boat was tied up. Her heart was pounding. To come to him at his hour of the night was to show her true feelings; no pretence, no drawing back. Perhaps he'd changed, perhaps he'd forgotten – but she knew he hadn't. He saw her as he followed Abe down the plank on to the harbour but even then he didn't come straight to her. He turned back, obviously giving instructions to Abe about the off-loading.

Then he was by her side. Away from the light his white teeth were all she could see of the smile she knew would be dancing in his dark eyes. 'You took your time.' he said softly. Surely at a moment so precious he couldn't tease. Didn't he know how hard she'd fought against coming?

'I've had things to do.'

'Ah.'

'And you've thought? And here you are.' This time he wasn't teasing.

They moved away from the harbour, not towards Middle Lane but the other way to the path up the bracken-covered cliffside. They came to a place about half way up, an area of grass amongst the gorse and brambles and only now did he turn towards her.

'So, my Beth, you thought and you came back.' He laid his mouth on hers, hardly touching her, feeling her breath warm against him. Beth was lost. She'd hovered at the top of that slippery slope so long, it took no more than that to send her hurtling out of control. Her mouth moved hungrily on his, she pressed against him glorying in the certainty that he wanted her just as she did him.

'Beth,' he buried his face in her hair, in her neck, 'you smell like a country garden. I must stink of that boat.'

She moved her head against his shoulder, felt the strength in his chest, even heard his heart pounding. 'No, you smell of the sea . . .' She'd known well enough which way she was heading but neither of them had anticipated this urgency. The unexpectedness of having her in his arms was driving Ellis, the joy of it driving her. He was unbuttoning the bodice of her dress, her fingers helped, drew his warm hand over her camisole to her naked flesh. Beth had passed the 'point of no return'. Somehow they were on the ground. She'd been hungry for this moment, starved. It wasn't the first time she'd made love under the open sky. Then she'd been a girl, James a callow innocent. With Henry she'd found the bliss of true unity – and with Ellis? 'We could make the bells of heaven ring' hadn't he said? With all the abandon of an untamed animal she gave and she received; the bells of heaven pealed, her head and her heart were alive with their clamour. Afterwards she was left trembling, breathless, shaken by what had consumed her.

'Beth,' he breathed, 'I've never ... it's never ...' He turned to her, his head on her breast, giving up the search for words.

The dawn light was strengthening. She raised her head, saw the picture they made and sat up, knocking him off balance. 'Look at us! Ellis, get dressed, pull your breeches up.'

Her voice revived him. 'And you your skirt down,' he laughed softly, 'but first ...' and leaning towards her he gently touched her lips with his. Suddenly she was full of energy, ravenously hungry and despite having been awake all night she was ready for the day; in fact she was bounding with health.

Back at the house she let herself in quietly. It wasn't quite half past five even now and the steady rhythm of the snores from the attic continued undisturbed.

There is no turning back the clock. When, a week later, Beth returned to Wilhampton she was a different woman from the one who'd take sudden flight to Chalcombe. Perhaps Stewart sensed the change. He didn't again ask her out to supper.

With the summer holidays the children and Lucy arrived and this year Liza spent more time at Penrhyn House. Ted had joined his father in the boat-building yard, Nicky was off to sea at every opportunity, only Charles spent hours alone with his crabbing line or his paintbox. What more natural than that the two girls should want to be together, even sharing Vicky's double bed often enough. Things had worked out so happily with Liza that Beth forgot her side of the bargain.

'That was good. We'll make a cook of you yet!' Ellis put his knife and fork together on his empty plate.

Beth laughed, not in the least offended. 'Fresh, sweet fish straight from the sea. It would take a poorer cook even than me to spoil it.'

Today had marked another stage. They'd spent the afternoon in his shack where she'd learnt how he calculated the men's bonuses. Each member of the crew was paid a wage but on top of this there was a bonus at the end of the month based on the price fetched for the catch from each particular boat. Fourteen shillings a week was a skipper's wage but this could be doubled by the bonus, and so with each member of the crew right down to the lad whose thankless task it was to coil down the dripping fathoms of warp in a confined hole below deck each time the trawl was hauled in. The boy's share was small but he knew the more often a trawl was made the more pence the trip would bring him. It was called 'sailing by shares'. Until today Beth had half understood what it was about, but now the business woman in her was alive to learn about a new industry. She'd watched and listened as he'd explained how he calculated what was due to the crew of *Sweet Abigail*, helped him with that of *Tom Thumb* and from there on she'd been on her own. The afternoon had flown, a new companionship was born between them. Now, with Liza at Penrhyn House for the night Beth had cooked their supper. All too well she could imagine the accusing looks Lucy would have waiting for her, the tut-tuts and the 'good thing for the children they have me'.

No mossy ground for them this evening. Willingly and not for the first time she went with him to his bed. Later, quite unable to tear herself away, and this for the first time, she slept in his arms as the hours of night passed. She woke to find him already up and dressed, downstairs she could hear the rattle of crockery.

By stark light of morning the room looked unfamiliar, shabby, the painted iron bedstead chipped, the windows none too clean. (In fact they were no worse then those at Penrhyn House; the salt and spray soon destroyed even Jenny's ministrations.) At that moment the grandfather clock on the landing chimed and struck the hour. Seven o'clock! In the unexpectedness she felt like a thief caught stealing from a beggar's bowl. At seven o'clock Henry, unchanging always, would round the bend in the stairs, the Bible in his hand – his hand, his dear hand. 'Henry, Henry, what am I doing? What have I done? Why did you leave me? Henry, truly I tried, I even tried to stay away. Yet here I am, someone else in my bed, someone else running the foundry.'

She threw herself out of bed, naked, the sight of her reflection sending her thoughts deeper into the maze which seemed to have no end. To look at herself now didn't rekindle those years with Henry . . . 'If it's to be bedded you want, you'll find his appetite to your liking,' Eugene's voice seemed to taunt. She started to pull on her clothes.

'Here, I've made madam a cup of tea,' Ellis came in. He put it down, coming behind her and pulling her against him. 'If I could hold back the tide –'

'Don't!' She pulled away.

'Beth, what is it? Is it because you stayed? You wish you'd gone last night?'

'It's all of it. It's sordid, gropings in the dark. I'm like some – some – oh like any of the women you've taken and, dear knows, there have been plenty.'

He looked puzzled. 'Why now? You know that's not true. Why do you say it now?'

Blindly she went on dressing, ignoring his question. 'Oh no, not true. Easy for you to say that when you've a wife somewhere.'

'Do you think I've not been trying to trace her? When I do I'll get free of her. Beth you're the only woman I want, could ever want.'

The fight seemed to have gone from her.

'I'll tell you what's the matter. The clock struck seven. Not midnight like it did for Cinderella, but seven. I saw my Henry,' she sat on the edge of the bed, 'so sure, so gentle, wise and kind, my blessed Henry.'

'At seven? Why Beth? Tell me.'

'Each morning as the clock struck he'd come down to

the hall, never a second late, always just the same, to lead the house prayers. We'd all be there, the family, the servants. At seven I was in your bed – '

'Our bed, Beth. The bed where you should spend your nights in my arms. You and I are strong enough to defy the rules because we truly belong together. You know it.'

She shook her head. The maze was leading her in circles; but she reached out and took his hand.

'I can't promise you marriage – one day, please God, but that's for the future – I can't give you fine clothes, carriages, servants, fine houses. You know what I am, you know what I have. All I can give is my love.'

'Isn't love everything?' She smiled but there was no cheer in it. 'I've houses enough now, servants, wealth, responsibilities. What would we want with more?'

'Oh no, Beth. If you come to me, my woman, my partner and, please God, one day my wife, you don't bring the trappings of that other life.' He moved to the door, not looking at her as he spoke. 'The tide's high, I must go.'

'Your woman you say! A woman has a mind, a right to use it. What you want is a possession, a bed-mate.'

Now he looked, his eyes meeting hers unwaveringly. 'Is that what you believe? If so you'd best get back to the Court and the foundry. Those are my terms, Beth. More than I've ever believed it possible to need anyone, I need you. Bed-mate be damned. I've told you before – Be here when I get back, I beg you be here. But it's all or nothing. No more gropings in the dark, as you call what we've had. If you come to me you come openly; we'll show the world what we think of the whispers there will be but make no mistake, I'm not a plaything for when you can take time off from some foundry.'

And he was gone – frightened perhaps of what he'd hear if he waited.

The house was quiet as she let herself in. Lucy often retired to bed early; it was unlikely she'd missed her and certainly the children wouldn't have guessed her room had stayed empty.

'I'll have a word before you go creeping off up there.' Mrs Murphy's voice started her, coming from halfway down the basement stairs.

'I'm creeping nowhere! I've just come in from a walk.'

'A word I want – and not before time. I've held my peace till this for the poor dear Master's sake, but no more – '

'Come in here, Mrs Murphy.' Beth led the way into the drawing-room and closed the door behind them. Any minute Lucy and the children would be down for breakfast.

'Now then? You want to see me about something?' Already she knew what she would hear. Her chin was high, she met Flo Murphy's accusing glare squarely.

'Don't know if you think I'm blind or stupid. Well, let me tell you this, I'm neither, nor ever have been. The Master put you on a pedestal. For his sake I served you, Miss High and Mighty that you al'ays were – '

'How dare you take that tone – '

'Oh, I dare and what's more I'll dare tell you this! I've seen more 'n enough these last months, throwing yourself after that fisherman. How you can do it, cheapen yourself to a man like that after the Master. Not fit to clean his boots! But this is the end o' the road. Where have you been all night? Send his child here so that you can warm his bed for him!'

Beth clutched at a dignity she was far from feeling. 'Mrs Murphy, you've been at the Court a long time but that doesn't give you the right to stand in judgement.'

'Me? 'Tisn't for me to do that my girl. Your day of judgement will come right enough, but in the meantime, think on this – if I can see what I do with my poor mortal eye, what can the poor Master think when he looks at you?'

'I'll hear no more of this. What I do is my own concern, mine and Mr Trafford's.'

'Mr Trafford! Not fit to mention in the same breath as the Master. But it's not my concern, like you say, that it isn't. I wash my hands of you. Before the sun goes down I'll be away. I've known tom-cats behave better!'

Lucy had come in while she was speaking – and probably been listening at the door even before that. Without a word Beth walked past them then, once across the hall, ran up the stairs to her room. She couldn't undo what had been done – undo it? The joy, the love, the freedom, the laughter she and Ellis had shared? – but neither could she see what lay ahead.

Echoes of the old housekeeper's ravings followed her. 'What must the Master feel?' What, Henry? What? She turned the key in the lock of her door, she walked to the bedside, even pushing the rug away so that she knelt on the hard floorboards.

'I try to accept,' he'd said.

'Help me, Henry, point the way to me. I was so lonely, that's how it started, but now it's not just that. I'm alive again, I'm me when I'm with him, just me. I feel young – as if everything's before me. Hear me, Henry, my blessed beloved Henry. When you learnt to be happy with me I never took what was your Bella's. It's the foundry, the Court, the family, the bitterness – help me, make me strong to do what is right.'

For a long time she knelt. Anyone seeing her might have thought she was asleep she was so still. At the thought of the foundry, the family, her brow had been furrowed, she'd chewed her lip. But gradually a stillness came to her, her face showed a new calm, almost a smile. She didn't understand it herself but she felt relieved of her problems. 'Help me,' she'd begged; in life he'd never failed her. Now as she opened her heart to him memories crowded in, the trust and affection between him and Hal, young Henry as a child so keen always to visit the workshops, and now

375

there he was just as they'd planned. Even Mrs Murphy and her years of faithful service. The dear Master she'd called him, and so he was. Thoughts of Mrs Murphy brought other ghosts, a table laden with good food, the family gathered around. His family, all of them, bone of his bone.

A new resolve came to her.

An hour later she was on the train heading northwards. At Wilhampton station she hailed a hansom cab, said something to the driver, then instead of turning right towards the foundry they set off in the other direction, left along Station road, past the brewery, in through the gates of a company that seemed bent on extension, new bricks stretching far back into the yard behind the old.

By the time she'd done all that had to be done the day was well towards over. How right it seemed that after all these months of bitter enmity it was Hal who saw her into her carriage and waved her farewell.

As Wilhampton disappeared and they moved through open countryside she sat back, her eyes closed.

So it was done! Hal hadn't been easy, as stubborn as she'd expected, but at last they'd gone together to see Mr Edgewick. Merton Court was in Hal's charge but would come to Henry when he was twenty-one. That was right and fair, he was the eldest grandson. Copeland's and Harknell's were to merge, the rivalry must truly end. The children would grow up without the bitterness that was driving a wedge between them all. A long way off it might still be but, as Hal had said: 'One of these days Charles will be here with us.' Her children would never be the losers by today's work; a percentage of the profits would go to each of them.

What she'd done in these last few hours must have healed the rift in Henry's family.

She'd signed away his legacy. 'All that I have I leave to

my beloved wife Elizabeth'. The train jolted over the points, she put her hands on the plush seat to steady herself. Oh, but he'd left her more, far more. The love they'd shared she'd hold and cherish for ever, 'in this world and the next' she silently promised, seeing again those light blue eyes smile tenderly at her.

Rain ran down the windows of the carriage. The motion of the train was soothing; she knew a sense of peace. A new hope, a new freedom. Her future was untrammelled. It was as if the mists were lifting, showing the sky clear, the day full of promise.

At Chalcombe she hardly waited for the train to judder to a standstill before she stepped (almost jumped) on to the platform. How the wind buffeted. It hadn't been like this when she'd left Wilhampton. By now the water would be high again, the boats back in harbour. It was no evening to be at sea. She turned out of the station yard, her head bent against the wind and rain as she started down the hill towards the village.

He would be home by now. She'd not stop at Penrhyn House, she'd go straight past and on to Middle Lane – or so she thought. But Jenny saw her and a moment later was down the front steps and running after her.

'Mrs Copeland, m'am, I'm that glad you're back. Such a day we've had,' she shouted against the wind.

'Whatever's the trouble, Jenny?' For trouble there must be for Jenny to be in this state.

'Mrs Murphy, she upped and went, oh m'am today's been just one thing after another . . .'

'Let's go in the house.' Out here in the storm they couldn't talk. Her mind leapt ahead to Ellis, but duty led her into the hallway of Penrhyn House with Jenny. 'Now, tell me.' She closed the front door.

'We'll first, m'am, it was Mrs Murphy. Packed a grip and went, she did, and Miss Lucy and Master Edwin with her. Took what they could get into their boxes – they'll send for their things, Miss Lucy said.'

'Back to the Court?'

'No, m'am, off somewhere together. I tell you it's been a right bad day. Then came Master Charles's fall, off the breakwater he tumbled, gave his knee that deep a gash on the rocks! Got it clean for him and wrapped it up but I never seen a cut bleed like it. He had a few tears, well 'course he did, but he's never one to fuss, bless him. I kept him indoors – but then who'd be out a day like this. They're all upstairs in his room playing ludo or some such.' It seemed the next stage of the saga wasn't so easy to tell. 'Now there's some sort of trouble down in the harbour. From the window you can see the folk gathered in all this weather. The children haven't got ear of it; best they don't, I thought. Mr Stebbings has been rounding up his men. They've hauled the lifeboat out; I saw them running to the boathouse.'

Beth turned into the drawing-room and crossed to the window. Sure enough the fishermen were back but they weren't unloading their catch; the fishergirls had the empty baskets waiting but she could see something was amiss. She craned her neck, looking for Ellis.

A tremor of excitement seemed to run through the group on the quay. Arms were raised pointing, she could imagine their voices.

'There! Didn't I say? There goes the lifeboat now, see m'am, going round the headland.'

It was the first time Beth had seen it, sixteen men pulling at their long oars, the deep-sided boat battling across waves that looked powerful enough to destroy it. One glance and Beth's eyes turned back to the quay. Ellis! Where was Ellis? Sick with fear. Wasn't that the expression? She knew the truth of it. The thumping of her heart was somehow connected with the ache in her shoulders and arms, the empty void in her stomach.

Jenny must have understood something of what she felt. Mrs Murphy had left her in no doubt of the 'goings on' between Beth and her fisherman friend.

'He'll be all right, m'am. Never was a finer seaman than Mr Trafford, the men all say so.'

Beth nodded. 'Is Liza with the children?'

'No m'am. I've not set eyes on her since morning.'

A gap on the quay where the *Helping Hand* should have tied up; a lifeboat tossing on waves such as she'd never seen.

'I'm going to the quay.'

'You can't wait there on your own. I'll come with you.'

'No Jenny. Stay with the children. Give them supper as if nothing's wrong.'

Even so Jenny came as far as the front gate. 'Oh, Lordy, m'am,' she gasped, the wind crushing the words back into her. 'Did you ever see the like of it?'

The rain was harder now, no summer shower this, but lashing, cold and relentless. Beth was gone, half running, half walking towards the group. The lifeboat had disappeared round the headland and she imagined the next bay, the craggy rocks. She'd not wait with the crowd, she'd climb the cliff, look further along the shore.

'It's Father! Something's happened to Father — the lifeboat's gone out.' Liza ran to meet her.

'They'll bring him home safely.' Beth took the child's hand in hers, to give comfort and to find it too. Liza didn't answer. The fear in her dark eyes spoke for her.

Please, please, I beg, please bring him back, Beth implored silently. Could it be less than an hour ago that she'd been in the train, so sure, so confident of the future? Ellis is my future, the only future. Please, please . . . she pleaded.

Matt Clode, the skipper of *Daisy May*, came across to them, resting his large, weathered hand on Liza's shoulder.

'Did you see what happened?' Beth had to raise her voice against the storm.

'Squall come zudden, no warning. Then I saw the *Helping Hand* — floundering she seemed. Wind that strong, couldn't hear a man's voice — ain't nothing now to what it was out there. I saw the *Hand* cut away its topmast, but the rain, like a grey wall 'twaz 'tween uz. Seemed the skipper was in trouble, couldn't hold a course, rudder seemed t've gone. 'Tis them rocks that's the curse. Many a ship's ended on those grey devils.'

'He'll get her home.' Beth's voice defied the elements. Many a ship perhaps, but Ellis never! Please, please not Ellis. Bring him back, let him be safe!

'Come on Liza, we'll look from over the cliff. We can't wait here.' Cut off by the jutting headland they could see nothing. Unloading of the other boats had started. Everyone wanted to work, needed to be occupied; she and Liza couldn't stand idly by simply waiting.

Wordlessly they climbed up the long steep slope, down the first incline, up the next. At any other time the ghost of a cold winter afternoon might have haunted her, a solitary walk and a homeward journey thrown over his shoulder. Today she could think of nothing but the picture of a boat far out on that cruel sea. How could men fight against such power? Yes, they could, they must; she had to cling on to that. The track sloped down again (so many rabbit holes, but today she didn't spare them a thought) then up and across the brow where she'd sat that Boxing afternoon as the sun had slipped away below the hills behind her.

At the top of the cliff she and Liza came to a halt. Instinctively they gripped each other's hands as they took in the scene. She'd not expected to see the *Helping Hand* so near to the shore. Oh dear heaven, they all knew the rocks around that headland and into the bay! The lifeboat was alongside the *Helping Hand* now, that much they could see, that and men far below them trying to reach the safety of the rescue boat. To recognize anyone was impossible through the curtain of rain; the boats were both being tossed, together, apart ... It was the fishing smack they watched, sucked back, thrown against the rocks, sucked back again with every towering wave. Suddenly the little

ketch (for from this height and against such a sea that's
what it appeared to be, small and helpless) seemed to be
thrown right out of the water then hurled back, the fore
and mizzen masts cut away, the sea washing over the deck
and the remaining crew who fought to hold on. She knew
Ellis, knew he'd be the last off. Wordlessly she prayed.
Then again the boat was thrown to the rocks. The sea was
winning the battle, the *Helping Hand* was losing its power
to hold on. The – oh, dear heaven, no, it couldn't be
happening – it keeled over and broke up.

Liza was crying. They stood rooted to the ground, too
far away to hear the tearing of the timbers and yet the
noise of it filled Beth's mind. They were soaked to the skin,
the cold rain squelched in their shoes yet neither of them
seemed aware. The *Helping Hand* was disappearing from
sight, the lifeboat pulling away.

Could it be only this morning she'd woken in his bed?
The guilt, the shame she'd felt seemed to belong to another
life. Shame? She should be proud; she was proud and
grateful that he loved her, that it was her he wanted. But
what now? If . . . No she wouldn't, she couldn't, bring
herself to face that 'if'. Her mind couldn't even start along
that road. She wanted to rush back down that cliff path,
she longed for the joy of seeing him as the lifeboat pulled
into the quieter waters of the harbour. But what if . . . No
. . . All thought stopped.

'Come on, Liza, we must be there first. He'll be needing
us.'

'But supposing . . .,' her words were lost in the wind.
And in any case the lifeboat wouldn't have pulled away if
they hadn't been sure, they would surely have waited,
searched . . .

'He'll be cold, and wet too. We'll take him to Penrhyn.
Jenny will have hot food for him.' She shouted as she half
ran. But supposing . . ., her own heart echoed. She stamped
down her fears, picturing the lifeboat pulling for home,
everyone safely aboard. Ellis would be watching for her.

381

What was it he'd said that morning? 'Be here when I get back. I beg you be here.' She must be there, she must be there. Pulling Liza she ran.

The squall was dying as suddenly as it had blown up. Even the rain was no more than a steady enveloping drizzle as the lifeboat men pulled hard on their oars and the boat turned into the harbour. So many men crowded aboard. But she saw only one.

In minutes the boat was tied up, it's rope lashed around the pillar where the *Helping Hand* had always moored. One by one they clambered up the iron ladder to the quay – then he was there. She pushed Liza forward; she could wait now, her moment would come.

As he stooped to gather the child into his arms he looked over the top of her head at Beth. They'd come a long way since the clock in his hall had chimed seven o'clock this morning. She moved nearer to him, the tears of relief blurring her vision and running unchecked down her cheeks. Suddenly she seemed to be made of cotton wool.

He held out his arm and she came to him, feeling herself taken into his embrace. Liza's arm came around her too as the three of them clung together.